PRAISE FOR
PIECES OF SKY

"Readers may need a big box of Kleenex while reading this emotionally compelling, subtly nuanced tale of revenge, redemption, and romance, but this flawlessly written book is worth every tear."

—**Chicago Tribune**

"In her auspicious debut, Warner kicks off the Blood Rose Trilogy . . . Warner develops [the] romance with well-paced finesse and great character work . . . Warner makes great use of the vivid Old West setting."

—**Publishers Weekly**

"Romance, passion, and thrilling adventure fill the pages of this unforgettable saga that sweeps the reader from England to the old West. Jessy and Brady are truly lovers for the ages!"

—Rosemary Rogers

"*Pieces of Sky* reminds us why New Mexico is called the land of enchantment. A truly original new voice in historical fiction."

—Jodi Thomas

"Generates enough heat to light the old New Mexico sky. A sharp, sweet love story of two opposites, a beautifully observed setting, and *voilà*—a romance you won't soon forget."

—Sara Donati, author of *The Endless Forest*

"From the first page, it's clear why debut author Warner has won several awards. Her western romance is a striking portrait of the territory in all its reality, harshness, and beauty. Like Francine Rivers, Warner creates a novel of the human spirit's ability to conquer emotional and physical obstacles. She conveys her characters perfectly, giving them lives of their own. Readers will be waiting breathlessly for the next book in the Blood Rose Trilogy."

—**Romantic Times**

"A very good book." —**All About Romance**

"It's been a very long time since I read an engaging and sweet historical romance such as *Pieces of Sky* . . . I absolutely loved Kaki Warner's writing."

—**Babbling About Books**

"I loved everything about this book."

—**Roundtable Reviews**

Berkley Sensation titles by Kaki Warner

PIECES OF SKY

OPEN COUNTRY

Open Country

KAKI WARNER

Doubleday Large Print Home Library Edition

BERKLEY SENSATION, NEW YORK

This Large Print Edition, prepared especially for Doubleday Large Print Home Library, contains the complete, unabridged text of the original Publisher's Edition.

THE BERKLEY PUBLISHING GROUP
Published by the Penguin Group
Penguin Group (USA) Inc.
375 Hudson Street, New York, New York 10014, USA
Penguin Group (Canada), 90 Eglinton Avenue East, Suite 700, Toronto, Ontario M4P 2Y3, Canada
(a division of Pearson Penguin Canada Inc.)
Penguin Books Ltd., 80 Strand, London WC2R 0RL, England
Penguin Group Ireland, 25 St. Stephen's Green, Dublin 2, Ireland (a division of Penguin Books Ltd.)
Penguin Group (Australia), 250 Camberwell Road, Camberwell, Victoria 3124, Australia
(a division of Pearson Australia Group Pty. Ltd.)
Penguin Books India Pvt. Ltd., 11 Community Centre, Panchsheel Park, New Delhi—110 017, India
Penguin Group (NZ), 67 Apollo Drive, Rosedale, North Shore 0632, New Zealand
(a division of Pearson New Zealand Ltd.)
Penguin Books (South Africa) (Pty.) Ltd., 24 Sturdee Avenue, Rosebank, Johannesburg 2196, South Africa

Penguin Books Ltd., Registered Offices: 80 Strand, London WC2R 0RL, England

Cover illustration by Alan Ayers.
Cover design by Lesley Worrell.

PRINTED IN THE UNITED STATES OF AMERICA

ISBN 978-1-61664-544-1

To Sara—princess, warrior, friend.
And to Brian, the remarkable young man
she brought into the family.

Acknowledgments

My thanks to:

Sara Straley, for my beautiful website and her patience in *trying* to teach me how it all works.

Carlee and Jason, for their excellent advice on medical and weaponry issues.

Heather and Adeline, for being the inspiration behind Penny . . . more or less.

And with special thanks to Nancy Coffey and Joanna Stampfel-Volpe of Nancy Coffey Literary & Media Representation—to Wendy McCurdy, my discerning editor—and to Kathryn Tumen, my hardworking publicist, all of whom have worked so diligently to make this dream a reality.

Bless you all.

Prologue

Savannah, Georgia, October 1871

"MOLLY? WHAT ARE YOU DOING HERE? HOW did you get in?"

So much for a warm welcome, Molly McFarlane thought, setting down her valise and turning to meet her sister's husband as he came down the staircase of his elegant Savannah home. "The door was open."

"Damn those children." Reaching past her, he shut the door so forcefully the panes in the window beside it rattled, then he stood back and glared at her. "Why are you here?"

"The doctor sent for me." Taking time to

curb her irritation, Molly unpinned her hat and hung it on a hook beside the door before turning to her brother-in-law with what she hoped was a pleasant expression. In truth, she despised Daniel Fletcher, especially after the callous way he had treated the family—most particularly, his two stepchildren—after her father's death a month ago. "How is she?"

Fletcher made a dismissive motion. He seemed distracted and on edge. Not his usual, fastidious self with that unshaven beard and soiled shirt. "Fine, fine. There was no need for you to come all the way from Atlanta."

"The doctor seemed to think there was. Lung fever is quite serious." Hearing the snappish tone in her voice, she reined in her temper. "I'm not here to interfere, Daniel. I've come as her sister, not a nurse. If there's anything I can do to—"

"There isn't," he cut in. "You're not needed."

Molly looked steadily at him, refusing to back down, wondering as she had so many times why her older sister had taken such an unpleasant man as her second husband. Grief over her first husband's death had been part of it, no doubt. And fear of raising a six-year-old daughter and eight-year-old son on her own had added to it. It had taken less than six months for Nellie to realize her mistake.

"May I see her?" she asked.

Being the weak, bullying man he was, Fletcher looked away first, his gaze as shifty as that of a guilty child. "Oh, all right. Stay if you must." Muttering to himself, he went down the hall to his office, slamming the door hard behind him.

Molly wondered how he could bear to go into that room. She had only had the courage to venture through that door once. The walls had been cleaned by then, the reek of gunpowder and blood masked by the cloying scent of funeral flowers and smoke from Fletcher's cigar. But Papa's ghost had lingered. She could feel him still.

"Did you come to save Mama?"

Glancing up, Molly saw her nephew, Charlie, perched on the top step of the stairs. He looked lost and small and too knowing for his eight years. He'd already lost his father and grandfather. Was he to lose his mother now too? "I've come to try," she answered.

"It doesn't matter. He'll get her anyway."

"Who will get her?"

"The monster. He'll get us too." Jumping to his feet, Charlie darted away, his footfalls ending with the thud of an upstairs door.

Frowning, Molly started up the stairs. As she rose above the entrance hall, she looked down through the open parlor door to see the room was a shambles, rugs thrown back, drawers half-open, books scattered about the cluttered floor. Apparently, Fletcher hadn't seen fit to hire a cleaning girl during Nellie's illness. Molly sighed. Well, if nothing else, at least she could clean up the house for her sister.

Outside the master bedroom, she paused for a moment to prepare herself, then knocked. When she heard no response, she gently pushed open the door.

The room beyond was still and dark, the curtains pulled tight over the tall windows. The air was rank with the smell of soiled bedding, illness, and despair. Except for labored breathing, it was silent.

Molly pressed her lips tight against a rush of angry words. How long had her sister been left unattended? When had she last had her bedding changed, or her face washed, or her hair brushed? Had Fletcher simply left her in the dark to suffer alone? “Nellie?” she called.

“Molly? Is that . . . you?” The voice was a weak rasp, followed by a bout of coughing that seemed to rip through her sister’s throat.

Rushing across the room, Molly bent beside the bed, her years of medical training at her father’s side overcoming her disgust with Fletcher and her terror for her sister. “Yes, I’m here,” she said in the calm, soothing voice Papa had taught her.

Nellie looked ghastly, a mere shadow of the lovely woman she had once been. Her skin seemed stretched over her bones and showed an unhealthy pallor except for two bright spots of color high on her cheeks. Her lovely green eyes shone feverishly bright, and her welcoming smile looked more like a grimace.

Recognizing encroaching death when she saw it, Molly sank weakly onto the edge of the mattress. *Dear God,* she cried in silent desperation, *don’t take Nellie from me too.* “Oh, Sister,” she choked out as tears flooded her eyes. “Why didn’t you send for me?”

"Daniel . . . wouldn't . . . let me."

To cover her shock, Molly brushed a lock of lank auburn hair from her sister's hot forehead. "Well, I'm here now, dearest. And I won't leave you."

"You must." Reaching out, Nellie grasped Molly's shoulder and pulled her closer. Her breath stank of the infection in her lungs. Her eyes glittered in her gaunt face—but with desperation, not madness.

"Take my . . . babies," she gasped. "Before it's . . . too late."

Molly struggled to understand. "Take them where?"

"Away . . ."

"From Daniel?"

"He's up to . . . something. Bombs. A new . . . war." Her voice was so weak Molly had to lean close to hear. Every word was a wheezing struggle. "Thinks children . . . took papers. Hurt . . . them." A coughing fit gripped her and Nellie writhed, eyes scrunched tight, fingers clawing at the bedclothes as she struggled to drag air into her flooded lungs. Once the spasm passed, she opened her eyes and Molly saw that desperation had given way to grim determination. "Promise me . . . take them away before . . . too late."

"But, Nellie—"

"Must hide them . . . keep safe." Nellie was panting now, her eyes frantic. "Now. Tonight."

"I c-can't just leave you."

"You must." Tears coursed down Nellie's temples to soak into the filthy bedding. "Keep babies . . . safe. Promise me . . . Sister."

Weeping in despair, Molly nodded. "I promise."

A WEEK LATER, IN A DARKENED ROOM IN JEANerette, Georgia, two hundred miles west of Savannah, Daniel Fletcher peered nervously through the shadows at the man seated in a wheeled chair behind the wide cherrywood desk.

It irritated him that Rustin didn't have the lamps lit. Even if the old man didn't need light, the rest of them did. He looked around, sensing other people in the room. Probably the artillery expert, maybe the Professor.

"Well?" Rustin demanded in his papery voice. "Have you found it?"

"Not yet," Fletcher answered, hoping his voice didn't betray his growing alarm. Why hadn't any of the others spoken? And why hadn't Rustin offered him a chair? He felt like a fool standing there in the dark talking to a disembodied voice.

He had never liked Rustin. Even though the old man was the glue that held them all together, Fletcher thought it hypocritical that after stealing all that gold from the Confederate coffers, Rustin would use it to foment another rebellion a decade later. But this wasn't about breathing new life into the wounded South. It was about money. And power. "I've literally torn the place apart," Fletcher said nervously. "If my wife hid it somewhere before she died, it's gone now."

"Who else could have taken it?"

"No one was in the house but me, my wife, and her children. Occasionally the doctor came by, and near the end, Nellie's sister came, but the book had disappeared long before that."

"Could your father-in-law, Matthew McFarlane, have taken it? He must have known something if he came all the way from Atlanta to confront you about it."

Fletcher felt that quiver of guilt move through his stomach. *Poor, stupid Matthew.* His wife's father had always had an overblown sense of integrity. "He had heard rumors. That's all. He knew nothing about the book when he—when I questioned him."

"And now he's dead." It was a moment before Rustin spoke again. "How old are your children?"

"Stepchildren. Eight and six, I believe."

"Have you questioned them?"

Battling the urge to wipe his clammy palms on his coat, Fletcher glanced around, wondering again why the others hadn't spoken. This was beginning to feel like an inquisition. Turning back to Rustin, he said stiffly, "The children are no longer at the house." *And good riddance.* Always underfoot, poking into things they shouldn't. He was glad to be shut of them.

"Where are they?"

"I—I'm not sure."

Finally a voice erupted from a darkened corner. The Professor's. "Christ, man! They could have taken it and might even now be showing it to the authorities!"

Fletcher could hear whispering in the

shadows, a furtive, hushed sound, like rats skittering behind walls.

"They wouldn't have left on their own," Rustin said. "Who is with them?"

"Their aunt, my wife's sister. Molly McFarlane."

"Why did she take them from your care?"

That dry, choking feeling returned to Fletcher's throat. He coughed to clear it. "I d-don't know."

Anger swirled in the closed room like coils of greasy smoke.

"She must have taken it," a voice accused.

Fletcher shook his head. "How could she have even known about it?"

"Maybe your wife told her."

"You imbecile!" Rustin cut in with such an explosion of vehemence Fletcher flinched. "You idiot!" Leaning forward in his chair and into a pale slant of light penetrating the edge of the drawn drape, Rustin spread his bloated hands on the desktop. His milky eyes seemed to stare into Fletcher, although Fletcher knew that was impossible. "You go find them, you bumbling fool! You find that woman and those children and get that book back! Now!"

"Y-Yes. All right." Fletcher edged toward the exit. As he swung open the door to the blinding brightness of the hallway, Rustin's voice drifted out behind him.

"Send for Hennessey. Just in case."

One

East of El Paso, Texas, November 1871

"THAT OLD MAN LOOKS LIKE A BEAR, DOESN'T he, Aunt Molly?"

Blinking out of her reverie, Molly glanced at her niece, Penny, who was leaning to the side of her aisle seat so she could see down the narrow walkway of the railroad passenger car. "He's so big and hairy."

Following her line of vision, Molly saw that the bearded man slouched on the rear-facing bench at the front was staring at her again.

Pursing her lips, she shifted her gaze to the shoulders of the woman seated ahead of her. Men didn't usually study her so intently—healthy men anyway—and it made her acutely uncomfortable. But Penny was right. He did look a bit like a bear with his great size and all that dark hair, although it could only be from a six-year-old's perspective that he be considered old.

"He isn't scary like the other one," Penny added, sending a shy grin in the man's direction.

Molly gently pulled the curious child back in her seat. "What other one?" she asked, trying to sound unconcerned.

"The ugly one. He was watching us too."

Watching us? Skin prickling, Molly looked around. "When? Here, on the train?"

"By the kitty in the window. 'Member the kitty in the window?" Penny bounced her heels against the front of the bench seat and smiled. "I like kitties."

Molly vaguely recalled a tabby dozing in the display window of a general store in . . . where was that? Omaha? But she hadn't noticed anyone watching them. "Is that the only time you've seen him?"

"He was in the town with the pretty red rocks too. He waved at me, but I didn't wave back."

He followed us to Utah?

"I didn't like him." Reaching up, Penny twisted a curl around her finger as she often did when she was anxious. "He looked like a candle."

"A candle?"

"His face was all melted. He was scary."

Melted? Was he old? Did he have a burn scar? Molly thought of all the faces she'd seen in the last weeks, but none stuck out. She had tried to be vigilant in case Fletcher had come after them, but what if he had sent trackers instead? The thought was so unsettling it was a moment before she could draw in a full breath.

"I had a kitty once, but he went dead." Penny peered up through her flyaway blond hair. "Can I have another one, Aunt Molly? I promise I won't sneeze."

"Perhaps. We'll see."

What if someone had followed them this far? What if he was on the train even now? Nervously Molly glanced at the other passengers then froze when she found the bearded man staring at her again. Suspicion blossomed in her mind.

Several times that morning she had looked up to find his assessing gaze on her. At first, she had thought nothing of it. They sat facing each other, after all. Since the man was apparently too large to fit comfortably into the narrow forward-facing passenger seats, he had taken the bench at the front of the car. It was natural that their gazes might cross occasionally. But after years of being invisible and for the last three weeks trying desperately to attract as little notice as possible, Molly found it disconcerting to be the object of such interest, idle though it might be. Could he be a tracker sent by Fletcher?

The man looked away, but Molly continued to study him.

He wore a thick shearling jacket, so she couldn't see if he wore a gun. But those work-worn hands resting on his knees hinted that he earned his living doing more than just waving a pistol about. And his face, despite the low hat and concealing beard, didn't seem particularly threatening, although that dark stare was a bit unnerving.

Turning her attention to the window, she tried to remember what she knew about him. She had first seen him that morning when the train had stopped in Sierra Blanca to fill the tender with water, and she and the children had gotten out to stretch their legs. He had been supervising the loading of some sort of machinery onto a flat car. The men assisting seemed to know him, as did the conductor, who had stopped to chat with him when he'd passed through the coach earlier. That meant the bearded man had reason to be here other than to track her and the children. It was simply coincidence that they were on the same train. That, and nothing more.

Letting out a breath of relief, she glanced at the children. On her left, wearing his usual scowl and chewing his thumbnail, Charlie stared morosely out at the west Texas landscape bouncing by. On her right, Penny dozed, her thumb stuck in her mouth. It was a habit she had resumed of late and indicated she battled the same troubling fears that Charlie did. That they all did.

Hopefully, soon it would be over and they would be starting a new life in California. She would find employment—either as an assistant to one of her father's medical colleagues, or in a clinic or hospital—and then they could cease this erratic flight. If she only knew what it was they were running from and why, maybe she could find a better way to protect them. But Nellie had been so weak and distraught the night Molly had spirited the children away from Savannah, Molly hadn't questioned her. Now she wished she had.

Feeling the weight of exhaustion pulling her down, Molly tipped her head back against the seat and closed her eyes. How long had they been traveling? Two weeks? Three?

The children had hardly spoken at first. Confused and terrified, they hadn't understood why they'd had to depart in such a hurry or why they'd had to leave their mother behind. Penny still didn't understand, but Charlie did. He had lost so much in his eight years, it made him fearful of what might be taken from him next. Because of it, he trusted no one. Not even her.

When she opened her eyes, Molly's gaze fell on her nephew. She had no experience with children. She didn't know what Penny and Charlie wanted or needed or expected, and her inadequacy terrified her. But she loved them with all her heart and hoped to find a way to reach them and gain their trust. They were all that was left of her family now—probably the only children she would ever have—and she was the only thing that stood between them and Fletcher and whatever threat he posed. She was resolved to protect them at any cost.

Moved by concern for her troubled nephew, Molly reached over to stroke the fall of auburn hair from Charlie's furrowed brow.

He jerked away.

Molly let her hand fall back to her lap. "Charlie," she said, and waited for him to look at her. When he did, she saw fear in his eyes, and more anger than any child should ever carry. "Why are you so angry?"

He stared silently at the back of the bench in front of him, his lips pressed in a tight, thin line.

"I know you're upset about your mother."

His head whipped toward her. "Why didn't you save her? You're supposed to be a nurse. You should have made her better."

"I tried, Charlie. I wanted to help her. More than anything in the world."

He glared at her for a moment more,

then the fight seemed to drain out of him. "It doesn't matter," he said and turned toward the window. "The monster would have gotten her anyway."

The monster again. Molly sighed. How often over the last weeks had she awakened to her nephew's screaming night terrors? "There is no monster, Charlie," she told him as she had so many times. "It's just a bad dream."

Charlie continued to stare out the window, a wall of silence between them.

With a sense of defeat, Molly looked down to see that her hands had curled into tight fists. With effort, she opened them, forcing her fingers to straighten one by one until they lay flat against her thighs. At least she had control over her fingers, she thought wryly, even though everything else in her life seemed to be spinning into chaos.

A distant voice rose. More shouts, then footsteps pounded overhead as someone raced across the roof of the passenger car toward the rear. A moment later, metal squealed on metal so loudly the children covered their ears. The brakes abruptly took hold, throwing the car into such a violent lurch Charlie fell against the window frame and Penny almost tumbled off the seat before Molly caught her.

Suddenly the train began bucking like a wild thing. A woman screamed. Men's voices rose in alarm. The screech of metal grew deafening, and acrid smoke seeped through the rear doors from beneath the back platform where the brakes were.

"What's happening?" Charlie cried, clinging to the armrests as the car rocked and shuddered.

"I don't know," Molly shouted over Penny's wails. "Hold on!"

Another lurch threw Penny out of her arms and onto the floor. Molly reached for her and was almost knocked to her knees when a falling passenger slammed into her shoulder.

"Penny!" Molly shouted, scrabbling for a handhold, terrified the child would be trampled or smothered. But before she could reach her, big hands scooped the shrieking child from the tangle of passengers and thrust her into Molly's arms. A flash of dark brown eyes, then the bearded man stumbled over thrashing bodies and charged into the smoke billowing at the back landing. The car rocked so hard windows broke and valises flew from the overhead racks. The screams and shouts and noise of the squealing brakes was deafening. Then with a crack as loud as a gunshot, something tore loose from the undercarriage at the rear. Feet braced against the seat in front of her, her arms wrapped tightly around the wailing children, Molly looked back out the shattered rear window to see the last three cars of the train topple off the tracks in a thunderous roar of splintering wood. Immediately their car shot forward so violently her head cracked against the backrest, before their coach rammed into the car in front of it, and shuddered to a stop.

Dizzy from the blow to her head, Molly ran trembling hands over the terrified children. "Are you hurt? Are you all right?" Charlie nodded and swiped a sleeve at a small smear of blood on his chin. Penny tearfully held up her arm, showing a scrape on her elbow. "I'll tend that as soon as we get off," Molly assured her, so relieved her voice wobbled. "Hold tight onto my hands." Working their way through the chaos of shaken passengers milling about in the smoke, Molly managed to keep a grip on the children and get them out of the car. By then, men had beaten back the flames where the brakes had caught fire beneath the rear platform, and other men were pawing through the wreckage of the baggage car, looking for survivors. Once she made certain the children were unharmed, Molly settled them at a safe distance from the wreckage, then went back to help where she could.

Most of the injuries were relatively minor—bruises, scrapes, a few broken bones and cuts from flying glass. But three people were missing, and it took an hour for the men digging through the rubble to find them. Both the conductor and a brakeman were dead. The third man was barely alive. The bearded man.

An hour later, after loading the dead, the injured, and the rest of the passengers into the less damaged of the two passengers cars, the train continued on, finally limping into El Paso several hours later.

Luckily, word of the catastrophe had already reached town, and a railroad representative named Harkness, the local physician—a gaunt man with a dark patch over one eye—and several townspeople led by a Reverend Beckworth and his wife, Effie, were waiting at the depot to meet them. While the Beckworths herded the battered passengers to their nearby church, and the undertaker carted off the dead men, the physician, Dr. Murray, had the injured man carried directly to his infirmary on Front Street.

"Not that I can do him any good," Molly overheard him say to the nervous railroad representative. "Poor bastard will probably be dead by nightfall."

"Christ." Harkness wiped a handkerchief over his sweating brow as he studied a column of figures in a small tablet. "This will cost the railroad a goddamn fortune. Two already dead, and another on the way. That's three hundred each in death payments to their families. And I haven't even added up the cost of repairs or what we'll have to settle on the injured. Christ."

After assuring the Beckworths he would come to the church as soon as he had finished with the bearded man at the infirmary, Dr. Murray hurried down the street, leaving Harkness muttering and scratching numbers into his book.

Molly and the children followed the other

passengers to the church. Again, she helped where she could. As she stitched and bandaged, Harkness's words kept circling in her mind. Three hundred. Not much for a life, but enough for a new start. A widow could live a long time on three hundred dollars.

As soon as the doctor came into the church, Molly settled the children in the rectory under Effie Beckworth's watchful eye, and ducked out the back door.

An idea had come to her—a despicable idea—but she was desperate. And if she had to do something despicable to keep the children safe, she gladly would.

Unless she was too late and the bearded man was already dead.

She found Dr. Murray's infirmary easily enough. After slipping through the side door, she paused in the shadowed hallway, listening. Outside, the chaos continued—dogs barking, men shouting, the clang of the fire bell. But inside, all was quiet. She started down the hall, checking doors as she went.

The doctor's living quarters were on one side of the house while the infirmary rooms opened along a long hall heading toward the back. Praying Dr. Murray would remain at the church awhile longer, Molly moved silently toward the medical rooms in the rear.

The familiar odors of unguents and balms and chemical solutions wafted over her, pulling her backward in time. For a moment she thought she heard Papa's voice reassuring a patient then realized it was a groan coming from one of the two rooms at the end of the hall. The door on the right was closed. The one on the left stood open.

She peered inside.

It was deserted and dark, the single window shaded by a thin curtain. A desk faced the door. Two chairs stood before it, their slatted backs at rigid attention as if braced for bad news. Against one wall stood an examination table partially hidden by a privacy screen; against the other, an overflowing bookcase.

Not the room she sought.

She moved to the door across the hall. As she neared, she heard a rhythmic "shushing" sound, which she recognized as labored breathing.

She cracked open the door.

Afternoon sunshine reflected off the glass-fronted cabinet on the east wall, the shelves of which held medical paraphernalia and varying sizes of brown medicine bottles with glass stoppers and white labels. In the corner beside it stood a straight chair next to a spindly wooden stand with a chipped washbowl on top and a basket of soiled towels below. Perpendicular to the back wall and separated by a small cabinet with a lamp were two cots.

One was empty.

In the other lay the man the doctor said was dying—the man who could save her and the children. The bearded man. Her heart pounding so hard she could hear the rush of arterial blood past her ears, Molly approached his bed.

Dr. Murray had done a halfway job of tending the obvious injuries. Bandaged and wrapped, but no stitching, and the patient still wore his trousers and boots. Leaning over the bed, Molly quickly assessed his condition.

He appeared to be unconscious. Beneath the beard, his face was swollen and bruised. A bloody bandage, held in place by wide gauze strips, covered the left side of his head. A deep laceration, she guessed. Or possibly a concussion, if not a fracture of the skull. Gauze strips also swathed his bare chest, tufts of dark hair poking through the stretched cloth. His shallow breathing indicated a rib injury, but the absence of a pink froth on his lips told her his lungs hadn't been punctured. More bandages covered his left forearm. Judging by the distorted shape and the amount of blood that had soaked through the wrappings, he probably had a compound fracture. The hand below it was swollen and discolored. She saw no wedding band or evidence he had worn one recently.

Good. It would only complicate matters if he had a wife somewhere.

The thought shamed her. She pushed it aside, and trying to ignore the smell of blood and sweat and chemical compounds, she bent over him, needing to look into the face of the man she was about to deceive in the vilest way.

Seeing him up close, she realized that without all the hair he might have been handsome, although it was difficult to be certain with all the swelling and bruising. Dark brows, a wide, stern mouth, a strong nose marred by a small lump of scar tissue along the bridge that indicated a long-healed break. His eyes were closed beneath dark lashes spiky with dried blood, but she remembered they were brown.

She felt a shiver of unease. She didn't know if he was aware of her or not . . . if he was staring back at her through those slitted eyes or not. The thought made her heartbeat quicken.

Taking a step back, she let her gaze drift down the long length of his body.

He was bigger than she had thought—dwarfing the cot, his booted feet extending well beyond the low foot rail. The boots were well made, with rounded toes and sloped heels. A horseman's boots. Over denim trousers, he wore a tooled leather belt with a silver buckle. On his right hip, facing forward, hung an empty holster with back-to-back R's burned into it like a brand.

Right-handed. Also good. If he lost his left arm, he could still function.

The absurdity of that caught her unaware, and a sound escaped her throat. Almost a laugh, but not quite. The sound of hysteria. She pressed fingertips to her lips to stifle it. The doctor said he was dying.

What would it matter if he left this world with one arm, or two?

But what if he survives?

The thought bounced through her mind, spinning out other thoughts like stones cast from beneath a racing wheel.

What if he woke up and realized what she'd done? He was a powerful man, strong enough to have lived this long despite his injuries. What if—

No, don't think it!

Furious that she had let her emotions get away from her, Molly pressed a hand against her churning stomach and struggled to bring the panic under control. He was dying. He probably wouldn't last the night. He would never know.

He. He who?

What had the conductor called him? Wilkes? Weller? She had to know. She couldn't do this without at least knowing the poor man's name—who he was, how he lived, where he was going.

With his heavy shoulders and muscular arms, he had the look of a man more accustomed to the plow than a horse. But those weren't a farmer's boots, and a farmer rarely wore a gun on his belt. Maybe he was just another anonymous cowboy. She hoped so. She hoped he was a loner with no home, no family, no one to come around asking questions.

Was he kind? Was he loved? Would he be mourned?

Sickened by the thought of what she was about to do to this innocent man—the same man who had saved Penny from being trampled on the train—Molly swallowed hard against the sudden thickness in her throat. Gently she brushed a lock of blood-crusted hair from his bandaged forehead. He didn't appear much older than she. Early thirties. Too young to die.

Another absurd thought. She had seen enough death to know the young died as easily as the old, and fairness had nothing to do with it. Perhaps she'd lost the capacity for grief. She didn't know. She didn't care. All that was important was that she get enough money to keep her and the children moving west.

Money this man's death would provide.

She rested her palm against his bare shoulder, needing to feel his skin against her own, as if that might ease the guilt that clawed like a beast in her stomach.

He fought hard. She felt it in the tremors of his sturdy body, saw it in the strain of muscles in his neck as he struggled to inhale against the restrictive bandages. His quick, gasping breaths seemed loud in the small room, and hearing them made her throat ache in sympathy. Feeling an unaccountable sadness at the waste of another life, she bent down to whisper into his ear. "Forgive me. There's no other way."

"What are you doing in here?" said a voice from the other side of the room.

Startled, she jerked upright.

Dr. Murray scowled at her from the doorway as he dried his hands on a piece of toweling. Gaunt and middle-aged, he wore a black leather patch over his right eye and had less hair on his head than on his chin, which was mostly gray stubble. He looked irritated. "What do you want?" he demanded, the words slightly slurred, as if he'd been drinking spirits or had just awakened from a deep sleep.

"Do you know . . ." She made a vague gesture toward the patient. "I couldn't tell . . . he's so . . . there's so much swelling. Do you know his name?"

The doctor tossed the cloth into the

basket of soiled towels beneath the washstand then with careful deliberation rolled down his sleeves as he walked toward her. His wrists were slim, his hands narrow and long-fingered with short, trimmed nails. An artist's hands, but cleaner. "Harkness called him Wilkins," he said, stopping beside her. "Hank. Or maybe Henry. I don't remember."

She was relieved Dr. Murray didn't smell of whiskey, but was concerned about his slow movements and slurred speech. Was he ill?

"I remember you from the church," he said, studying her. "You helped."

Molly nodded.

Frowning, he looked around. "Don't you have kids? I don't want any kids running through here, messing with my things."

"They're with Effie—Reverend Beckworth's wife—at the church."

He made a dismissive gesture. "Go back to them. There's nothing to do here." Leaning over the patient, he pushed up one lid then the other.

Molly noted the dark brown pupil of the patient's left eye was marginally larger than that of the right. Was he bleeding in his brain?

"Is it true?" she asked. "He's dying?"

The doctor nodded, a single dip of his head as though he had little energy to waste on extravagant motion. Pulling a stethoscope from his apron pocket, he fitted the earpieces into his ears and held the diaphragm against the patient's chest. "If the head wound doesn't kill him, gangrene in his arm probably will." Motioning her to silence, he tilted his head and listened. After a moment, he removed the earpieces and returned the stethoscope to his pocket.

"You're sure of it?" Molly persisted.

With a huff of impatience, he swung toward her, moving his entire body a quarter circle so he could glare at her with his one eye. It was a sad eye, more gray than blue, with a downward slant that hinted at more than mere weariness. "The man was almost crushed. He shouldn't even be alive. Goddamned railroads." His good eye narrowed in speculation. "What's it to you? Who are you?"

Molly hesitated, knowing the lie she was about to tell would damn her forever.

Could she do it? Should she? Would it even be legal?

Doubt swirled through her mind. Her stomach knotted and acid burned hot in her throat. She took a step back, then thought of the children and stopped.

She had no choice. She had to have that money.

God forgive me, she prayed silently. Then hiking her chin, she looked Murray in the eye. “I’m Molly McFarlane,” she said. “Henry and I were to be married.”

Two

"IT'S NOT RIGHT," EFFIE ANNOUNCED. "YOU must do something."

Reverend Thaddeus Beckworth set aside his worn Bible, removed his spectacles, and pinched the bridge of his nose between his thumb and forefinger. Ever since his wife had settled into her rocker across from his, he had been aware of her growing agitation. She had made certain he was aware. A few sighs, then energetic rocking that grew steadily more vigorous until her heels bounced off the floor with enough force to send her prized collection of Chinese porcelain songbirds dancing atop the fireplace mantle.

It was a game they played—how long could she maneuver for his attention without actually asking for it, versus how long could he hold out before putting aside whatever he was doing and capitulating. It was a game without malice, founded on his desire to avoid conflict and her need to seek it. If there was one thing Effie Beckworth thrived on, it was a good, rousing crisis.

And today had been rife with crises. Injured passengers milling about, children to mother, mouths to feed. Now all the stranded travelers had been moved from the church into rooms at the hotel, the children were back with their mother, and Effie had nothing to do but bedevil him. Bless her heart.

Smiling fondly at the woman who had been his helpmate for thirty-two years and who, despite her meddling ways, had a kind and giving heart, Thaddeus said, "Certainly, my dear. Do what about what?"

"About Molly McFarlane and those poor little tykes." Her heels thumped on the floor as the rocker came to a stop. "You must talk to the railroad people, Mr. Beckworth. To that solicitor, Mr. Harkness, before it's too late."

Ah. Yet another crisis. "And what shall I talk to him about, my dear?"

"The man in the infirmary." Leaning forward, his wife lowered her voice to gossip level. "He's dying. And I think the railroad should pay him, don't you?"

"For dying?"

"Exactly." She sat back, looking pleased that he understood. "If they pay the other dead men, they should pay him too. Don't you agree?"

"But he's not yet dead, Effie."

"He soon will be. Harkness said so himself. And what will happen to those babies then?" She paused to dab at her eyes with a lacy handkerchief she'd pulled from who-knows-where. Then thrusting sentiment aside, she hiked her chins and puffed out her nicely rounded chest. "You must talk to them, Mr. Beckworth. Show them the error of their ways. It's the Christian thing to do."

Preaching to the preacher. With a sigh, Thaddeus replaced his spectacles and opened the Bible. "Of course, dear. I shall speak to Mr. Harkness tomorrow."

"Or I could, I suppose," she offered thoughtfully. "I am more familiar with the particulars, after all. Perhaps he's still at the hotel directing passengers."

"Yes, well . . . perhaps . . ."

Her smile was grace itself. "As always, Mr. Beckworth, you know best."

"Do I? I'm never sure." And he still had no idea what she was talking about.

ON THE SECOND FLOOR OF THE EMPIRE HOTEL in the two-room suite the railroad had assigned to them, Molly stared out at the moonlit face of El Capitan, the tallest peak in the Guadalupe Range north of El Paso. It was an uninspired view, notable only in that it was best viewed at night, if at all, and it was so different from the country she had left behind. No long-limbed oaks or fragrant magnolias here, only scrub and cactus with a few cottonwoods along a creek. This wasn't a sheltering country. Not that it mattered. She wouldn't be here long. By this time tomorrow, she would either be moving west with the children or behind bars.

Nothing was going right. Harkness was dragging his heels on her claim, she was almost out of money, and Charlie's nightmares were getting worse. Maybe she should have told Effie Beckworth the truth instead of lying about a fiancé. Or left the children in her care and tried to draw the follower off their trail. She could run faster alone.

But run where? And just what was so important to Fletcher that he would send trackers after them? If she knew what he wanted, she would wrap it in a bow and hand it to him. This endless flight was taking its toll on all of them.

Motion drew her gaze. Across from the hotel, a man in a wide-brimmed hat and dark coat came out of the saloon doorway. He stood for a moment, glancing down the street in one direction then the other, as if looking for someone. Then hitching his trousers, he stepped off the boardwalk and started toward the hotel.

Molly drew back then realized that with the room dark, he couldn't see her.

Halfway across, he stopped and removed his hat. Light from the hotel windows revealed that he wasn't old, nor did he appear to be disfigured, so he wasn't the man Penny had seen in Omaha and later in Utah. Maybe he was someone new. Fletcher had enough money to send a hundred trackers after her and the children.

A woman came into view. She spoke to the man, then he took her elbow and escorted her back across the street, where they disappeared into Mrs. Haversham's Restaurant and Tea Room. When they didn't emerge after several minutes, Molly allowed herself to relax, although she kept watch at the window, just in case.

Always on guard, never at rest. How much longer could she keep this up? She couldn't run forever. But she could never go back home either.

Had he put flowers on Sister's grave? Did he suspect why Molly had spirited his stepchildren away in the middle of the night? He must. Daniel Fletcher wasn't a stupid man. That she had eluded him this long was a miracle in itself. And now their very lives rested on a stranger's death. The thought sickened her.

"What's wrong?"

Startled, she turned to see Charlie in the doorway that led into the bedroom. As always, she felt a jolt that seemed to compress her lungs. It was like looking into her sister's face—those same auburn curls and wide green eyes, that same frightened, anxious expression that always cut so deeply into her heart. It was like a reproach from the grave.

I'm trying, Nellie. But I don't know what to do.

She was out of ideas. Out of strength. Out of money. If the railroad didn't reimburse her for the cost of this room and their meals while the tracks were being repaired, they would be out on the street. Where was she to find words of hope for this lost child when she was so weary and frightened herself?

She forced a smile. "Nothing's wrong."

"Then why are you crying?"

Lifting a hand to her cheek, Molly was surprised to feel dampness. She thought she had lost the capacity for tears long ago.

"Is it the monster?" Charlie blurted out. "Has he found us?"

"There is no monster, Charlie."

"There is too! I saw him!" His eyes darted around the room. "You can't stop him. No one can. He'll kill us just like—" His words stopped abruptly.

"Who, Charlie?" she pressed. "Who is this monster and whom did he kill?"

Before Charlie could answer, six-year-old Penny appeared at his shoulder, her blond hair a tousled mop, her brown eyes bleary with sleep. "Don't shout, Charlie. You know Mama doesn't like it when you shout."

Her brother rounded on her, his face twisted in anguish. "Mama's dead, you big baby. So is Grandpa. And I can shout if I want!" With a sob, he ran back into the bedroom.

"I'm not a baby," Penny yelled after him. "You are!" When she got no response, she turned to Molly. "I'm gonna tell. He'll get a spanking for sure." Looking pleased at that prospect, she stuck her thumb into her mouth and stared solemnly at Molly as if waiting for . . . what?

Trapped in despair, Molly stared back, wishing she had someone to tattle to, someone who would soothe all her worries and make everything right again.

"THAT WRETCHED MAN! HE WON'T DO IT."

Thaddeus looked up from his half-finished sermon, surprised to see it was dark already. Effie stood in the doorway of his study, feet braced, fists on hips, ready to do battle. Hopefully, not with him. "Who won't do what, my dear?"

"Mr. Harkness. I just talked to him at the hotel. The scoundrel won't pay her."

Molly McFarlane—the woman with the children. Thaddeus set aside his pen, relieved he wasn't the cause of his wife's ire. It was regrettable they had never had children of their own—it would have provided additional targets for Effie's energetic attention.

She swept in, a calico whirlwind of maternal purpose, and flung herself into one of the doily-laden chairs fronting his desk. "It defies belief, Mr. Beckworth. Simply because they're not yet married, Mr. Harkness says the railroad isn't obliged to pay her a widow's portion. The very idea."

Thaddeus marveled at her reasoning. "They may have a point, my dear, insomuch as she's neither wife nor widow and the man in question isn't dead."

"He soon will be, and then what will become of her and the children?" She pressed her hanky to the heaving bosom he so admired. "We must act now. If we wait until he dies, it will be too late. No, no. You know what you must do."

"I do?"

"Of course you do." Lifting her topmost chin, she gave him a smile that would make any God-fearing man sweat. "You must marry them as soon as possible. Tonight. Then when he dies, the railroad will have to pay her the settlement."

Thaddeus regarded his wife with a growing sense of alarm.

"Don't give me that look, sir. It's the only sensible solution."

"But Effie, the man couldn't participate in his own vows. I don't think it would even be legal."

"No matter," she said, waving aside ethics as easily as shooing a fly. "Who's to question it? The railroad?" That smile again. "And risk being accused of cheating a widow and her fatherless children out of their fair portion? I think not."

Frightening, that's what she was. It occurred to Thaddeus that if his wife had been allowed command, the War of the Rebellion wouldn't have lasted a month.

"We must do this, Mr. Beckworth. For the children."

"The children?"

"Those poor dears. It quite breaks my heart."

Thaddeus sighed, accepting the inevitable.

Reading that as assent, she shot to her feet. "I shall fetch them now."

"Now?"

"He's quite ill. We haven't much time. Hurry along."

AN HOUR LATER, IN THE INFIRMARY IN THE BACK of Dr.Murray's house, Thaddeus reluctantly presided over the quiet ceremony that united Molly McFarlane and Henry Wilkins in holy matrimony.

The bride wore a faded brown dress, a blue shawl loaned to her by Effie, and a stricken expression. The groom wore fresh bandages and a rumpled, too-small infirmary nightshirt. Thankfully the children were not witness to this charade, and remained asleep at the hotel in the care of the church's choir director. Effie and Dr. Murray stood solemn witness at the foot of the bed.

The exchange of vows took less than five minutes.

Not exactly an exchange insomuch as the groom was in a stupor and unable to speak, but the ritual seemed to please Effie, and for that, Thaddeus was grateful. He'd learned long ago his happiness was heavily dependent upon hers.

Dr. Murray showed little interest in the proceedings. The glazed look in his eye gave rise to the suspicion that the good doctor might be sampling his own medications, but Thaddeus made no comment. The man was a tangle of troubled emotions the reverend had long struggled to unravel. Maybe after this railroad mess was over, he'd try again, but for now he let it go.

Train wrecks and hasty marriages. What a troubling day.

OVERNIGHT THE WEATHER TURNED FROM MILD to bitterly cold, and by the time Molly got the children up, dressed, and over to the Beckworths', they were shivering too much to complain about being left there while Molly went to the infirmary.

"A blue norther," Effie told them, as if that explained the forty-degree drop in temperature overnight with no sign of a storm and barely a cloud in the sky. "But don't fret," she added with a jiggling laugh. "By the end of week we'll be sweating like pigs in a slaughter line and complaining of the heat."

Molly couldn't wait.

Leaving the children happily spooning up oatmeal with molasses in Effie's warm kitchen, Molly braved bone-chilling gusts and icy footing to make her way to the infirmary. When she finally reached the doctor's house, she was so numb with cold she couldn't tell if her nose was running or not. She wiped it anyway. After hanging her coat on a peg by the door, she moved quickly down the hall to the sickroom in the back.

Was he dead? Alive? Alive, awake, and anxious to meet his bride?

Faintly queasy at the thought of what she might find, she paused outside the door to prepare herself, then stepped inside.

Henry lay as she had left him, the rasp of his breathing telling her he was alive. Relief surged through her, loosening that tight knot of guilt that had kept her awake most of the night. Then she noted how cold the room was and how violently he shuddered beneath the single thin blanket. Alarmed, she yanked the covers off the empty cot and threw them over his shivering body. What was Dr. Murray thinking to leave Henry so exposed to the chill? Growing more furious by the moment, Molly tended to nursing chores Dr. Murray should have taken care of hours ago. Had he just left the patient to die?

The patient. Henry Wilkins. Her husband. God help her.

Ignoring a flutter of . . . something . . . guilt, anger, maybe hunger . . . she changed Henry's bandages, listened to his heart and lungs with Papa's old stethoscope, and forced water into him with an eyedropper, all the while trying to mask her growing concern beneath a cheery monologue.

When she was thirteen, those first one-sided conversations had been awkward. They still were, although admittedly, she found it easier to talk to an unconscious man than an attentive one. But since Papa believed comatose patients maintained some level of awareness, she had put aside her shyness and forced herself to become as chatty as a Calvinist before a class full of converts, hoping the patients could hear her and know they were not alone. It was vital that Henry suffer as little as possible—for her sake, as well as his. Bad enough that she hoped to benefit from his death; she wouldn't burden herself with the added guilt of having anything she did or didn't do hasten it.

"It's sunny today but quite cold." As she spoke, she ran her hand up his injured arm from elbow to shoulder, checking for heat and telltale red streaks, but finding only cool skin over firm muscle. Surprisingly firm, considering his stupor. The man's bicep must be as big around as her thigh. Her lower thigh anyway.

Realizing she was still stroking his arm, she jerked her hand away and moved to the other side of the bed. "I was told Texas was hot, but I've never been so cold. Are you warm enough? Would you like another blanket?"

He didn't respond.

"How about a cup of warm cider? Broth?" Absently, she lifted his right hand and pressed her palm to his, measuring the long length of his fingers against her own. Despite their size and the numerous scars and calluses, his hands were surprisingly elegant with broad palms, long blunt-tipped fingers, and mostly clean, square-cut nails. Strong, hardworking hands. She liked that in a man. In a woman too.

Lowering his arm back to his side, she studied his bruised face, trying to read the man behind the distorted features. "Are you a good man, husband? Am I your one and only wife, or do you have another waiting for you somewhere?"

A disturbing thought.

Where was he going? Where had he been? Whom had he left behind? He was a puzzle with too many missing pieces, yet one she felt driven to solve. "Who are you, Henry Wilkins?" she murmured, studying his battered face.

The high, broad forehead indicated intelligence. The strong limbs bore proof of years of strenuous physical activity. His abundant white teeth spoke of a lifetime of good nutrition, a lack of serious illness, and an avoidance of tobacco.

A clean-living man. And fit. Very fit.

When she had helped the doctor change Henry from his soiled clothing into that ridiculously small nightshirt that had comprised his wedding garb, she had noticed how powerfully constructed her husband was—at least on his upper torso. Murray had insisted she exit the room when he removed Henry's trousers, which was absurd since she was far too experienced to be flustered by such things.

Absently running her fingertips over the knobby knuckles of his right hand, Molly lapsed into fanciful thoughts as she often did to sweeten the endless and often distressing chores of the sickroom. "Are you a cooper, Mr. Wilkins? A blacksmith? Is that scar on your wrist from a hot branding iron?" The sun-darkened skin of his arms and face told her he spent a great deal of time outdoors; the paler skin of his forehead indicated he wore a hat when he did. "Maybe you're a miner. Maybe you've discovered gold, and the machinery you were loading was for your mine."

She brushed back a lock of hair she'd cleaned of blood, noting the soft sable brown was several shades darker than her own. "Do you have children, husband? Are they waiting for you to come home?"

Another disturbing thought.

Battling a feeling of confinement, she

wandered idly about the room, finally coming to a stop at the window. The workers were gone, the breaks in the tracks repaired, and the passengers on their way again. Even the wind had pitched in, sweeping the sky clean of smoke from the smoldering floorboards of the abandoned passenger car, and leaving behind icy dewdrops on bare limbs and cactus spines to sparkle like diamonds in the morning sun. Except for tumbleweeds bouncing down the rutted road, the streets were quiet.

All nice and tidy and back to normal. Except for two new graves on the hill north of town and the dying man in the infirmary.

She pressed her hand against the windowpane. It felt cold against her palm.

Don't die.

The thought came out of nowhere—unambiguous and irrevocable. Confusing. Even though the railroad settlement would send her and the children well beyond Fletcher's reach, she realized she didn't want it if it meant Henry Wilkins had to die.

"Oh, Molly," she murmured, her breath fogging the windowpane. "Don't let emotion rule you. Remember Andersonville."

"Fifty-six. Eighty-three."

Startled, she turned, wondering who spoke. Only she and Henry were in the room, and other than a slight rattle in his chest, he rested quietly.

She crossed to the bed and checked his pulse. A bit fast but steady and strong. His color was less gray and his brow felt cool. She studied him closely. There was no outward change, yet she sensed an awareness, as if he hovered just beyond reach—not quite there but not quite gone either—fighting for every breath, every moment he had left.

Moved by his struggle, she laid her palm against his face. "Don't give up."

His eyes flew open. His right hand shot out, the knuckles catching Molly high on her cheek. "Get it off!" he gasped and began tearing at the bindings around his chest. "Get it off! I can't bre—" Suddenly he went limp. His eyes fluttered closed, and his arm fell back to his side.

Stunned by the abruptness of the attack, Molly stood gaping, her palm pressed to her stinging cheek, ready to run if he moved.

He rested quietly, eyes closed.

Inching closer, she nudged his shoulder.

He didn't move.

"Mr. Wilkins?" When he didn't respond, she gave a gentle shake. "Henry?"

Papa said in comatose patients the first signs of awareness often showed in the mouth and eyes. But with the swelling and that heavy beard, she could hardly even tell what he looked like. "Can you hear me, Mr. Wilkins?" she asked in a loud voice.

"What are you doing?" Dr. Murray demanded from the doorway.

She looked up with a grin, unable to contain her excitement. "He woke up. Just for a moment. He opened his eyes and spoke to me. That's good, isn't it?"

Murray came to the bed and checked Henry's pupils.

Molly noted Henry's left eye, although no longer dilated, showed minute movements like quick, tiny jerks. The right showed the same random movements. An improvement, but still worrisome. After listening to Henry's chest through the stethoscope, Murray pressed a thumb against his injured arm and pinched his nipple.

Henry never moved or gave indication of pain.

"Involuntary," Murray said, removing a

vial of laudanum from his pocket. "A minor seizure. Maybe pain. Either way, this will help."

Molly frowned as she watched him fill the dropper. Was the seizure a response to pain or a reaction to too much medication? What if Henry was struggling to regain consciousness but was too drugged to do so?

"May I shave him?" she asked.

After administering the laudanum, Murray replaced the glass stopper and returned the vial to his pocket. "Don't you have children to tend?"

She ignored his surly tone. "It would make it easier to see how much water he's taking." And easier to tell if he was coming out of his stupor.

"He's dying. Leave the man alone so he can get on with it."

Molly bit back a rush of angry words. She couldn't accuse the doctor of incompetence. Henry's treatment met acceptable standards. The medications were appropriate to the injury even if the laudanum might be too freely given. Murray seemed to have a care for cleanliness and adhered to Listerian antiseptic principles, but beyond rudimentary attention, there was nothing—no sympathy, no interest, no emotion whatsoever. He gave off such an air of defeat, the room stank of it.

Without waiting for his permission, she left to get what she needed. When she returned with shaving supplies, Murray was gone. Relieved, she bent to the task.

It was more difficult than she'd expected. Because of the swelling, it was like shaving a lumpy potato, and by the time she'd finished, the poor man's face bore a half dozen new lacerations. After wiping away the last of the soap, she pushed that errant lock off his brow and sat back to admire her work. A jolt of surprise ran through her.

"Why, Henry Wilkins," she chided in a wondering tone, "what have you been hiding under all that hair?"

The man was handsome. Beyond handsome. If he managed to survive and his face healed without undue scar tissue, he might even be beautiful . . . in an overgrown, roughly masculine sort of way. Definitely striking.

She wondered what his smile was like. With all those lovely teeth, it should be a dazzler. She liked to see a man smile, especially since those with whom she normally came in contact rarely had reason to. She hoped Henry smiled often; otherwise he might seem too severe with that sharply defined jaw. Leaning closer, she noted tiny white lines in the puffy skin at the outside corners of his deep-set eyes. A squinter or a grinner. She poked his good shoulder. "You better live, Henry Wilkins. You owe me a smile at least."

Murray returned with an instrument tray, which he set beside the bed, and assorted surgical items, which he spread atop the tray. Scalpels, clamps, scissors, an atomizer, tubes of wire and horsehair ligatures, a serrated bone saw.

As Molly watched him arrange the implements on the tray, a feeling of dread gripped her. "Do you intend to amputate?"

"Probably best, although a waste of time." Motioning her aside, he lifted the atomizer to spray carbolic antiseptic solution into the air above the patient.

"It's not salvageable at all?" she asked, lifting a hand to shield her eyes from the irritating mist.

"Why bother if he can't use it? Better to be rid of a useless limb."

Molly didn't believe that. She didn't believe a man who fought so hard to live wouldn't work just as hard to save his arm. And if he couldn't fight for himself, she would have to do it for him.

She put her hand atop Murray's. "No," she said.

He twisted to stare at her, the atomizer still in his grip, his good eye round with surprise. Then anger transformed his face into a snarling mask. "Get out!"

"We must try," she insisted, using the soothing tone Papa had taught her.

"We? You're a doctor, are you?"

"I've had some . . . experience."

"Haven't we all?" With a harsh laugh, he tossed the atomizer onto the tray. "It doesn't matter," he added, brushing trembling fingers over the instruments, obsessively touching each item. "He'll die. They all die, no matter what we do."

Molly looked down at her husband's battered face. Murray was probably right; Henry would probably die anyway. But on the slim chance he didn't, shouldn't they at least try to keep him whole?

"I can help," she said.

He slammed his palm onto the tray,

sending the instruments into clattering disarray. "I don't want your help, damnit! I just want you gone!"

"Well, I never," a woman's voice snapped.

Molly looked up to see Effie Beckworth in the doorway. "The children?"

"No, no, they're fine," Effie cut in reassuringly. After sending Dr. Murray a glare of disapproval, she ignored him and spoke to Molly. "But a man is here. He says he's related to your husband. He seems very angry. I think you should come."

Lovely. Just what I need. "Thank you, Effie. I'll be there in a moment." As Effie disappeared down the hall, Molly turned back to Murray, who was carefully arranging the implements in perfectly aligned rows on the tray. In a calm, firm voice, she said, "As Henry's wife, Doctor, I have a say in whether you remove his arm or not. And I'm asking you to wait until I come back."

Murray didn't look up. His fingers continued to play across the medical instruments like those of a pianist at his piano. Sweat sheened his brow. His body gave off a sour smell. When he spoke, his voice sounded distant and weary, as if every utterance was an effort. "I'll do what I have to do."

COLD. DARK. THEN LATER—HOURS? DAYS?—A gray place of nightmare dreams and distorted echoes that sounded like the distant pounding of an ax against a hollow tree. Slowly pinpricks of light pierced the grayness, growing brighter with each beat of his heart.

Then pain.

It crouched on his chest like a demon with a hammer, driving hot spikes into his brain, his arm, between his ribs, until the unending agony sent terror roaring through his mind. Teeth clenched, eyes clamped tight against the burning brightness, he lay in shivering misery and tried to endure.

Dimly, he heard a voice. He couldn't hear the words but recognized it as a woman's voice . . . soft, soothing . . . with the sound of the South in the rolling cadence. He focused on it with all his mind, knowing as long as he could hear her voice, it meant he was still alive and not alone. Time ebbed and flowed, but the pain stayed constant. Only her voice kept him from drifting into the abyss.

After a while, the voice became two voices. A man and the woman. Arguing. It made his head hurt. *Damn them.* He turned toward them to tell them to stop.

And everything spun out of control.

Dizziness swamped him. His stomach heaved. Bile burned in his throat. Swallowing convulsively, he fought back wave after wave of churning nausea and waited for the spinning to stop.

Finally, it did. And then all that was left was the pain.

Sweet Jesus—am I dying? Dead?

Blackness pressed like hands against his chest, forcing him down into the smothering emptiness that was more terrible than pain. He fought it, but his strength was gone and the hands were too strong.

No!—I'm not ready—I want to go back!

But already he was sinking down, down in a slow, spinning fall.

Three

EFFIE AND THE REVEREND MET MOLLY AS SHE came up the steps of their small clapboard house beside the church. It was a welcoming house, boasting fresh white paint on the rails of the porch and an abundance of ruffled curtains at the windows. The kind of house Molly would have liked had she and Papa ever stayed in one place long enough to make a home.

"He's talking to Mr. Harkness then he'll see his brother," Reverend Beckworth told Molly as he held open the door. "I said you'd wait for him in the study."

"You're not leaving her alone with him?"

Effie asked in surprise. "He might hurt her. Did you see how angry he was?"

With a quelling look at his wife, the reverend turned to Molly. "His name is Brady Wilkins. Of Wilkins Cattle and Mining in New Mexico."

"Oh, my," Effie murmured. "I didn't realize."

Molly felt as if the floor had shifted beneath her feet.

Effie rallied first. "Well, I don't care who he is. He is a most unpleasant person, and I don't think you should leave her alone with him, not at all."

Molly tried to steady her breathing. It had never occurred to her that her husband might be one of those Wilkinses. Even though she was new to the Southwest, she'd heard enough to know they were not a family to cross.

Steering his wife toward the kitchen, the reverend gave Molly an encouraging smile. "Call if you need us."

With a feeling of dread, Molly went to the study. Standing at the window, she watched the children play in the side yard and wondered what she would say to Brady Wilkins. Should she tell the truth?

Try to gain his sympathy? Lie? She was a poor liar. Over the years, to ease a patient's anxiety she had learned to shade the truth a bit, but she had never outright lied. Until now.

She had no choice. She needed that money. The children had no one to protect them but her. That justification sounded a lot better than it felt.

Suddenly the door flew open. Molly whirled.

He loomed in the doorway, nearly as tall as his brother but leaner. Dressed for travel, he wore a dusty black Stetson, a sheepskin jacket over faded Levi Strauss trousers, and a large revolver in a holster on his right hip. His eyes had all the warmth of a cloudless winter sky and contrasted starkly against his weathered skin and dark stubble. She couldn't see his mouth beneath the black mustache, but judging by the furrow between his dark brows, she guessed he wasn't smiling.

"You must be Henry's brother," she said, striving for a friendly tone.

Those icy blue eyes flicked over her, a purely masculine assessment that hit all the pertinent places but showed little interest.

Automatic and uninvolved. She wondered if he was even aware of doing it.

Stepping into the room, he slammed the door shut behind him then stood braced in front of it, feet apart, jacket hooked behind big hands planted just above his low-slung belt. "You married my brother."

"Yes. I'm Molly McFarlane . . . Wilkins." She held out her hand, hoping he didn't notice the slight tremor in her fingers. When he ignored the gesture, she moved to one of the two worn leather chairs in front of the desk and sank down before her knees gave out. Folding her hands tightly in her lap, she put on a smile. "Please sit, Mr. Wilkins. I'm sure you have many questions."

He didn't move. "When?"

She looked at him, confused by the question.

"When did you marry him?"

No use lying about that. There were too many witnesses. "Yesterday."

"How convenient." He said it with a sneer. Spinning, he stomped to the window, then back, then to the window again. His ferocious energy seemed to charge the very air with menace.

Molly watched his big hands open and close, open and close, and considered bolting from the room but doubted her legs would hold her up. Instead, she sat absolutely still, hands clasped, feet flat on the floor, trying to make herself as unnoticeable as possible.

Use a calm voice, show concern, not fear. Papa's words, drilled into her over and over in those terrible months at Andersonville Prison, where violence and despair and rage had been a way of life. And death.

"You heard he was rich, is that it?" he accused, still pacing. "And now that he's hurt, you're just biding your time until he dies so you can get your hands on his money. Jesus, what kind of woman are you?"

"If."

He stopped and scowled at her. "What?"

"*If* he dies." A small, but important distinction . . . at least to her. "And I didn't realize who he was until an hour ago."

"You married a man without even knowing his name?"

"I knew his name. I just didn't associate it with Wilkins Cattle and Mining."

"Hank didn't tell you?"

Realizing her slip, Molly dumped another lie onto the growing pile. "We were, ah, busy. It didn't come up—the cattle and mining thing, that is." Heat rushed into her face. "So no, Henry didn't mention it," she added lamely.

For some unfathomable reason, he seemed to accept that. "Typical," he muttered. "Why?"

"Why didn't he mention it?"

Stopping before her, he folded his arms across his chest and glared down at her. "Why did you marry him?"

Molly hesitated, wondering how to answer. She sensed truth was not an option. This man would be a formidable enemy if he found out she had forced marriage onto his unconscious brother. But the lies were piling up fast, and shame was urging her to blurt out everything. Then she thought of the children and realized for their sakes she had to play out this wretched charade.

"He asked," she said weakly.

His eyes narrowed in suspicion. Beautiful eyes. Too beautiful for such a hard face. "Hank proposed marriage?"

"You sound surprised."

"I am." He continued to stare at her, a

muscle jumping in his bristly jaw. "Considering."

In the yard, the children's voices rose in laughter. On the street, a wagon rattled by. But inside Reverend Beckworth's study, the silence was so oppressive it felt like a weight against her chest.

Abruptly he turned and went to stare out the window, absently twisting a ring on his left hand. A wedding band by the look of it, which surprised Molly. He didn't seem like a man who would favor jewelry.

"That doctor, Murray, says he may never wake up," he said after a moment. "Says he's dying." When she didn't respond, he swung toward her. His face showed both hope and dread, an expression Molly had seen too often.

She resented the burden it put on her . . . to soothe, to take the pain away, to make the unthinkable acceptable. She was weary of it. Even so, it was against her nature to withhold comfort when it was needed. "Don't lose hope, Mr. Wilkins. Henry is strong. I don't think he's given up. Nor should you."

With a curse, he turned back to the window. "He just went to get a part for the concentrator. He was only supposed to be gone three weeks. What the hell happened?"

"Perhaps if you sat down, I could explain."

He whipped around, fury radiating from every line of his long form. "Explain what? How in less than three weeks my brother's train crashes, he gets himself married to a goddamned vulture, and now he's dying? How do you explain that?"

She didn't respond, afraid her voice would wobble. *A goddamned vulture.* How hurtful to hear oneself described in such terms. And how sadly true.

"None of this makes sense." Those cold eyes studied her thoughtfully. "Something's not right."

Molly sat frozen, the truth stuck like cotton batting in her throat.

"Where did you meet him?"

"In Sierra Blanca." Since that was where he had boarded, she thought that answer might suffice.

"When?"

"Over two weeks ago." Another safe answer. She hoped.

"Christ." With a weary sigh, he slumped into the chair across from hers. "Tell me about the derailment."

Relieved to be able to tell the truth about this, at least, Molly smoothed a pleat on her skirt and tried to gather her thoughts, "After the wreck," she finally began, "things were a mess. The caboose was on fire, mail and baggage scattered everywhere, passengers milling about like sheep. Luckily, only two men died and—"

"I don't care about them. What about Hank?"

Hank? "Do you mean Henry?"

"No, I mean Hank. Jesus, will you just get on with it?"

Pausing long enough to let him see how little she appreciated his surly behavior and foul language, she continued in as calm a voice as she could muster. "Other than the brakeman and conductor, both of whom died, and various scrapes and bruises among the passengers, your brother was the sole injury. Only three cars actually left the tracks, you see, and when the—"

"Christ! Do I have to beat it out of you? Tell me what happened to Hank!"

Molly refrained from shouting back at him. "He was thrown off the rear platform and under the baggage car," she said bluntly.

His rugged face seemed to lose color. "Then what happened?"

"It took a while to dig him out. Then he was loaded into one of the passenger cars and we continued on to El Paso. When we arrived, Harkness had him taken to Dr. Murray's infirmary."

"Where you forced the marriage yesterday."

"I didn't force it. Exactly. I just moved up the date."

"So you could marry a dying man you barely knew. A man you *say* you didn't know was rich. A man who was unconscious." His voice dropped to an ominous tone that was even more threatening than his bluster. "Again, I have to ask . . . if not for his money, then why?"

Sensing a trap, Molly gave a partial version of the truth. "Not *his* money, exactly. The railroad's." When she saw he was about to start shouting again, she raised her voice to cut him off. "The railroad seemed intent on cleaning everything up as quickly as possible, no doubt hoping to forestall an outcry like the one after that head-on in Utah last month—and within hours, their representative, Harkness, was offering cash for signed releases. Twenty dollars for an injury, a hundred for a lost limb, three hundred for a life."

"Three hundred," he said in mingled fury and disbelief.

"To some people," she added hastily, "three hundred dollars is a lot of money."

"Jesus Christ almighty."

Having said too much to stop now, Molly forged ahead. "When I heard your brother was not expected to survive the night, I told Harkness who I was and that I was Henry's intended, hoping to get the death settlement should Henry . . . well." She cleared a sudden dryness from her throat, then continued. "Henry cared about the children. He would have wanted me to get the money. For them. But Harkness balked. He said the money was for widows, not fiancées. With the Beckworths' help, I convinced him to allow for the circumstances, and by evening Henry and I were married."

There. It was out. Most of it anyway.

Scarcely daring to breathe, Molly waited for his reaction, wondering if she had gone too far.

"You lying, cold-hearted bitch."

Too far. And unjustly accused, she thought. She might be a liar, but not cold-hearted. And certainly not a . . . *that*. Seeing that he was jumping to all sorts of erroneous conclusions, she fixed her gaze to his and with firm conviction, said, "I need that settlement, Mr. Wilkins. I have two children to provide for, and when I saw an opportunity to get the money I desperately needed to accomplish that, I took it. But I'm not evil. I never meant harm to your brother and I never sought his death. In fact, I've worked hard to prevent it." Lifting her chin, she glared at him down the length of her nose. "But if he does die and there's money to be had because of it, I shall take it. Because Henry would have wanted me to."

He studied her for several moments, then looked toward the window, his jaw working. "I don't believe this. Any of it. Christ."

Molly let out a tiny sigh of relief. She had half expected him to bound from the chair and throttle her. With his attention directed elsewhere, she studied him. He had a hard face, not as handsome as his brother's but arresting, nonetheless. The family resemblance showed in the strong jaw and stubborn chin and high, intelligent forehead. But Henry's eyes were a warm chocolate brown, whereas his brother's were glacial ice. She sensed Henry would be a man easy to like, while this man would be one easy to fear.

Ruthless. Protective. Perhaps violent. Certainly driven.

He looked exhausted. The tired lines around his eyes and the deep brackets at the corners of his dark mustache made her wonder if he had ridden through the night to reach his brother's side. She also noted he gripped the armrests so tightly his knuckles lost color, which made her wonder if she had misread him altogether and what had at first seemed unbridled fury was fear for his brother instead. She hoped not. That would make him almost likable, and this would be so much easier if she thought of him as her enemy.

He exhaled wearily, and some of the tension seemed to leave him. "Don't call him Henry. He won't like it." Without the edge of anger, his voice had an unusual quality. Deep and slightly hoarse. It drew his listener closer so no word was missed, even as his hostile demeanor pushed him away. "Who shaved him?"

An odd question. "I did."

"He won't like that either." He gave her a measuring look. "But you don't know him at all, do you?"

She didn't answer.

"Yet you married him anyway." That seething anger again, so intense even his stillness carried threat. "And if he lives? What about your money then?"

Words froze in her throat.

"Goddamn you!" He bounded to his feet. "If you hurt him—if you do a single thing to—"

"I wouldn't," Molly cut in, aghast to realize where his thoughts had taken him. "I am a trained nurse, not a murderer! I would never do anything—*anything*—to harm a patient!"

He loomed over her, chest pumping. Then he lifted one shaking hand, the thumb and forefinger spaced an inch apart, and leaned closer. "I'm this close to snapping your neck, lady," he said through clenched teeth. "This close."

Molly met his gaze without flinching, sensing if she gave in to this attempt at intimidation, it would only drive him to further threats. But it was hard. The man was utterly terrifying. "I would never harm a patient," she said again.

"If you did . . ." He let the sentence hang, then after a moment, dropped his hand and straightened. "When Hank wakes up—which for your sake he better—you'll have to answer to him for what you've done. And he's not as nice as me."

A horrifying thought.

"Meanwhile I'll be watching you, so stay away from my brother."

Suddenly she felt ill. Unclean. If this conversation didn't end soon, she feared she would vomit all over his boots. But when she saw him start for the door, she remembered something else. "One more thing . . ."

He stopped. His wide shoulders rose and fell on a deep breath. When he turned to face her, his expression showed he was as sickened by all this as she was.

"I'm worried your brother is getting too much laudanum. I know he needs it for pain, but too much might prevent him from coming awake. Perhaps if you spoke to the doctor. I would, but . . . well . . . it might be more effective coming from you."

Wilkins laughed, a bitter sound without joy or mirth. "Don't underestimate yourself, lady." He yanked open the door. "You just married Hank Wilkins, the biggest, meanest, most elusive man in the territory. I'm sure you can handle one scrawny doctor."

Molly flinched as the door slammed behind him. Biggest *and* meanest? Dear God, what had she gotten herself into?

Strength left her, and she slumped back in the chair. Her head ached, her throat burned, and her stomach felt like it was filled with broken glass. But it was done. She would get her money. Then she would grab the children and run as far from this day and this place as she could.

Numbly she watched dust motes cast tiny sparkles in a shaft of sunlight. Do dust motes ever settle? Or like shame, do they linger in the air forever waiting to be exposed by the sun? Wearily she rose from the chair. By the time this was over, she would surely know.

WHEN SHE ENTERED THE INFIRMARY, MOLLY saw Murray standing over Henry, scalpel in hand. Horrified that he had already begun the amputation, she rushed toward him then saw that although the arm was prepared for surgery, no incision had been made.

Relieved, she stepped to Henry's right side, ready to assist if needed.

Murray neither moved, nor spoke. He wore an expression she'd seen at Andersonville. Empty. Defeated. Gone. It sent a prickle up her spine. "Doctor?"

"I can't do this anymore," he muttered, still staring down at the exposed arm. "I thought I could, but I can't." Lifting his head, he gave her an unnatural, almost-grisly smile. "Do you know how many amputations I've performed? Hundreds. And for what?" The smile became a grimace. He threw the scalpel onto the implement tray so hard it bounced off and onto the floor. "I'm sick of it. The blood—the dying—sick of it!" With every word, his voice grew more frantic. He began to yank at the ties on his apron. "I won't do it anymore. I can't."

Suddenly the door opened, and Brady Wilkins stomped into the room. When he saw Molly, his scowl deepened. "Why are you here?" he demanded angrily.

She ignored him. "We can set it, Doctor. We needn't cut—"

"Aren't you listening? It doesn't matter!" Jerking the apron free, he threw it to the floor. "He'll die anyway! They all die! There's nothing we can do."

"My brother's going to die?"

"We have to try," Molly insisted, pushing Wilkins aside.

Murray rounded on her. "You try! You say you have experience. You do it. Unless you want these cutting on your husband." He thrust his hands into her face. They were shaking. His whole body was shaking. Sweat ran down his face. Or was it tears?

"She's not cutting on my brother," Wilkins argued, glaring from the doctor to Molly.

"Well, I'm not doing it!" Murray shouted, starting toward the door.

Wilkins thrust out an arm to stop him. "You have to."

"I can't! I won't!" Dodging the bigger man, he stumbled from the room.

"You sonofabitch!" Wilkins shouted after him. "You get back in here!"

When it was apparent Murray wasn't returning, Wilkins turned his fury on Molly. "Damnit, I told you to stay away from my brother."

"Oh, hush," she muttered, trying to think. "We'll need more light. Towels." She glanced around the room, trying to quell her panic and decide how to proceed. "And chloroform, just in case."

"Chloroform? Christamighty! If you think I'm letting you cut on my—"

Anger sent her spinning toward him. "Do you want him to lose his arm?"

He took a step back. "No, but—"

"Then get out of my way or do what I tell you." Pushing past him, she flung open the door. "Find clean toweling."

"Where are you going?"

"To wash my hands and get a smock. Find a lamp."

"You're not cutting on my brother!" he called as she ducked down the hall.

When she returned, wearing a clean smock over her dress and a kerchief over her hair, he was waiting with two lamps, a stack of clean toweling, and a bottle of whiskey. He thrust the latter toward her.

"I don't take spirits. Besides, I just washed my hands."

"Suit yourself." He took a deep swallow, coughed, and dragged a sleeve across his watering eyes. He gave her a grim look. "You better know what you're doing."

"Or you'll snap my neck, I suppose," she muttered as she sprayed carbolic solution over the implement tray.

"Damn right." He lifted the bottle again.

"If you intend to help, put that away."

He stopped, the bottle poised above his mouth. Slowly, he lowered it. "Help?"

His face had gone pale. His eyes were as blue and round as robin eggs.

"I can't do this alone, Mr. Wilkins."

He took a step back. "You want me to help you hack off my brother's arm?"

Good Lord, did he think she intended to go at the poor man with an ax? "I want you to hold the lamp while I *repair* his arm. Surely you can do that?" *You nitwit.*

"I, ah . . ."

"Or would you prefer to do nothing and just let him die?"

The harsh question jerked him from his frozen state. “I’ll help.” As he put the bottle aside, Molly saw that his hand was shaking, but she had no time for sympathy. Even now it might be too late— Henry might have already gone too long without proper attention.

He gave her a sideways glance. “You’ve done this before, I hope?”

“More or less.” Lifting the atomizer, she sprayed antiseptic solution over her hands and the wound. “I assisted my father many times.”

“Assisted. Oh, Christ.” Retreating into bluster, he gave her a menacing glare. “Then you better do this right. I can still snap your neck.”

“With encouragement like that, how can I fail?”

Setting the chloroform near in case Henry revived, she selected a scalpel and took a deep breath. “I hope you’re a praying man, Mr. Wilkins,” she muttered as she pressed the blade into Henry’s arm and the blood began to flow.

“I sure as hell am now.”

The injury wasn’t as bad as Molly had anticipated. The ulna had a single clean break four inches above the wrist. With Wilkins pulling the arm straight, she was able to slip the broken ends back into position without too much difficulty.

The radius was another matter. Shattered in several places, it took almost an hour to fit the pieces back together. By the time she had finished, her back ached and her hands trembled with fatigue. "The hard part is done."

"Jesus, I hope so." He stared at his brother's arm. "Looks like a gutted fish."

The man was definitely odd. Maybe he'd been raised by badgers. Eyeing his wedding band, Molly wondered what kind of woman would align herself with such a volatile, rough-speaking man. A deaf-mute, perhaps. Or one that was insane.

Nonetheless, she sensed a subtle change had come about during the hours they had battled to save Henry Wilkins's arm. It was almost as if an unspoken truce had formed—not one based on trust, of course—he still thought her a liar and opportunist, which, regrettably, she was—but one based on grudging respect. Assuming she was capable of respecting Satan's minion.

"Do you have sisters, Mr. Wilkins?" she

asked as she draped a cloth over the wound. The lack of feminine influence might explain his uneven temperament.

"One. She died. And another woman who was almost a sister."

Sensing sadness, Molly didn't probe. Wiping her hands on a clean towel, she turned toward the door. "Mind the arm while I'm gone. Until it's splinted, it's very vulnerable."

"You're not going to sew him up?"

"And stay away from the whiskey," she called back as she started down the hall. "I may need you later."

"Goddamnit, you come back here!"

She found Dr. Murray sitting in the dark in his bedroom. She hoped he was lucid. "The bones are in place," she reported. "There doesn't seem to be significant tendon or muscle damage and capillary function is good."

"Still alive then. Bravo, Clara Barton." He gave a half-chuckle. "You sound quite professional. Where did you train?"

As her eyes adjusted to the dimness, she saw the vial of laudanum on the bed table. "On the battlefield of Atlanta. And later at Andersonville. My father—"

"Was a brilliant surgeon," he cut in. "Matthew McFarlane. I remember the name from his articles in the *Medical and Surgical History of the War of the Rebellion.* Suicide, wasn't it?"

The familiar bitter taste of rage rose in her throat. She would not discuss her father with this damaged, defeated man. Someday the truth would come out. Someday Daniel Fletcher would pay for what he'd done. She would see to it.

But for now, she had to put that from her mind and focus on saving her husband's arm. "Is there anything more I should do before I close the incision?" Although she had sewn wounds and assisted Papa many times, she had never performed surgery on her own. She felt certain she had followed procedure and done all she could, but she needed to make sure. A simple mistake could be deadly.

"I was at Fredericksburg," Murray said, ignoring her question. "We hacked and sawed for days and still they came. Bodies stacked up like cordwood and the ravens had a feast of limbs. The cries never stopped. I hear them still."

"Doctor?" she prodded, growing impatient. "What about the arm?"

He sighed. In a voice so weary she had to lean closer to hear, he said, "Flush it with carbolized water then sew it in layers from the inside out. Use silver wire for muscle tissue—there are several tubes in the cabinet. For the surface you can use horsehair ligatures but boil them in alcohol first. Leave four strands sticking out for drainage. Top it with carbolic dressing then splint it, but don't use plaster for now, and don't bind it too tight . . ." His voice trailed off.

She waited. Outside, the wind gusted, whipping through the eaves with a sound like a woman's cry. After a long silence, she said, "Anything else?"

"Oh, you can pray, I guess. But it doesn't help."

The stitching was tedious but not as stressful as repairing the broken bones. The motions were so repetitive they became almost automatic, allowing her occasional glances at the man across from her. He looked as weary as she felt. Yet he had remained steadfastly by her side from the moment they had begun, and she was glad of that. Oddly, having his male vitality present had strengthened her.

She knew so little about men. From the time she was thirteen, not long after Mama's passing, she had been in training at her father's side. No beaus, no girlish chatter, no party dresses for her. Instead, she had spent her youth in field hospitals, watching with trepidation as her father performed his surgeries, then cleaning up the blood when he had finished. Over the years she had gained intimate knowledge of how the male body functioned, but she had no idea how a man's mind worked. And she had a feeling the man across from her had a mind more complex than most.

"Higher, please. And a little to the left."

He repositioned the lamp.

She ran a loop, pulled it tight. Somewhere down the hall, a clock chimed the dinner hour. She hoped Mrs. Beckworth wouldn't mind tending the children awhile longer. She seemed to enjoy having them about. Molly didn't know how she would have managed without the dear woman's help.

"Where is the woman who was almost a sister?" she asked, less from curiosity than a need for distraction from the cramping in her back.

"I think she married my brother."

She looked up. "Henry?" Had their marriage made him a bigamist?

"Jack. And don't call Hank Henry. He won't answer to it. Never has."

She finished one layer, adjusted the strands left for drainage, started another.

"What happened to your husband?" he asked.

"There is no husband." When he didn't respond, she glanced up to find him studying her. The play of light across his features made him look quite severe, and for a moment she was reminded of Papa and how exacting he had been and how desperately she had tried to measure up.

She snipped one stitch, started another. "The children are my sister's. She died of lung fever last month. Their father was on the *Sultana*. After five years of war, he dies in a steamboat accident. Ironic, isn't it?" She didn't mention the children's stepfather. The less known about Fletcher, the better.

After tying off the last stitch, she dropped the needle onto the tray. The black stitches looked like a parade of drunken ants on a slab of raw meat. He would have a scar, but with luck and hard work, Henry—Hank—might regain full use of his arm. Assuming he woke up. "After we splint and bind it, we're done."

With Wilkins's help, that chore took only a few minutes. Satisfied with the results, she gave Henry—Hank—water through the dropper then did a final check.

Fingertips warm, pulse strong, color good. Once the swelling subsided and the drainage stopped and she was sure circulation was unimpaired, she would put a hard plaster bandage over the arm. But for now she'd done all she could. It was over. Finished. And the patient was still alive.

Suddenly the smell of blood and sickness made her stomach lurch. Shoving past Wilkins, she rushed to the washstand in the corner.

After emptying her stomach, she grabbed a fresh towel, wiped her face, then dropped it onto the pile of bloody rags beside the bed. "I apologize for that," she said with a wry smile. "It happens every time. Nerves, I guess."

He shrugged. "I'm used to it. My wife's pregnant. Her third. She's a good breeder." He said it with a grin that almost rocked her back on her heels. White teeth. Dimples. Dancing aqua eyes. He didn't even look like the same man.

The grin faded. "You won't tell her I said that? About being a good breeder? She's, um, prim. It's because she's English. They're different. Not as bad as the Scots, but . . . well . . . I think it's the red hair. Or the hats."

She blinked at him, beginning to think she preferred Brady Wilkins when he was angry. At least then he made sense.

Pulling a gold watch from his trouser pocket, he flipped up the lid with his thumbnail, checked the time, then snapped it closed. "I told her not to come, but she never minds." His expression indicated he considered his wife's inability to follow orders an endearing trait. "A lot like you in that respect. If she took the branch line out of Redemption last night, she won't get here until early morning. Unless she told them who she was." He slipped the watch back into his pocket.

"And who is she? Queen Victoria?"

He seemed surprised by the question. "My wife."

She laughed in his face. "You're that important, are you?"

"Our water is. The railroads can't get from here to Santa Fe without Wilkins water." This time his grin showed menace. "And they pay dearly for it."

The man's arrogance was monumental. "By giving you special privileges?"

"That, and giving my wife anything she wants."

"Or you'll shut them off?"

"Or I'll shut them off."

She studied this man who was as changeable as quicksilver, smiling one moment, threatening the next. He was beyond her experience and sorely tested her understanding. Yet she appreciated that he loved his wife enough to let it show, that he valued his brother above any price, that he hadn't faltered when she'd needed him. "You're a bit of a blackmailer, aren't you, Mr. Wilkins?"

Unbelievably, the grin stretched wider. "Damn right."

For a moment they looked at each other.

She sensed that uneasy connection again, and tried to ignore it, telling herself she would be gone in a few days. She would never see him or his brother again. She wasn't a part of the family he watched over so vigilantly. "Get some rest, Mr. Wilkins. I'll stay for a while to be sure there are no complications. If I need you, I'll send word."

"Can't . . . breathe," a voice rasped.

Astonished, Molly whirled to see Henry tugging at the bindings on his ribs.

"You big bastard, you're awake!" Brady Wilkins crowed. "You finally woke up!"

Seeing Henry's growing agitation, Molly tried to reassure him before he pulled off his bandages or reinjured his arm. "Stay calm, Henry. You're safe. We're with you. You're going to be just fine."

Brady Wilkins clapped a rough hand on his brother's good shoulder. "Hear that, Hank? She says you're going to be just fine."

Henry blinked, his eyes rolling and unfocused, his breath coming in short quick bursts through tightly clenched teeth. "Who's . . . Hank?"

Four

YOU'RE ALIVE. YOU'RE BREATHING. YOU'RE ALL right.

Then why did it feel like someone was yanking his stomach up through his throat every time he moved his head? He tried to sit up, couldn't. His chest felt trapped in a vise. Over the drumming in his head, he heard his own breathing, a hoarse gasping that didn't sound right, didn't feel right.

Nothing made sense. Nothing seemed to work.

Jesus, what's wrong with me?

Pain—relentless, spiking with every breath—in his arm, his head.

He fought to calm his panic so he could figure out what had happened to him and where he was and who these people were standing over him. But whenever he tried to think, everything jumbled up in his mind until he couldn't remember anything. And that was the most terrifying thing of all.

A figure moved closer. A woman. She bent close and spoke in a calm, soothing voice. "You're safe, Henry. Stay calm. I'm here to help you."

Who the hell was Henry?

Her voice was familiar, but her face was only a blur. He tried to remember, but the effort sent him sliding back toward the void. Terror thundered through him. "Don't go," he choked out as blackness pressed against the edges of his vision.

"I won't. I'm here."

He felt her hand on his cheek, her palm cool and soft against his skin.

"You're safe, Henry. You're all right. I won't leave you, I promise."

Her touch was his lifeline, her voice his beacon. In desperation, he clung to it with all of his mind as the smothering darkness sucked him under.

* * *

"WHAT'S WRONG WITH HIM? WHAT DID HE MEAN, 'Who's Hank'?"

Still rattled by Henry—Hank's—sudden awakening, Molly straightened to find Brady Wilkins frowning ferociously at his brother. But she knew him better now and sensed it was worry, not anger, that made him look so severe. Oddly his need for reassurance steadied her. This she could handle.

"It happens," she said, sounding calmer than she felt. "Especially with head injuries. It's called amnesia. It's a form of forgetfulness. Sometimes there are gaps, and the patient never fully remembers what happened immediately before or after he was injured, but it's rare to forget everything. If so, it's usually temporary."

"How temporary?"

"A few days, maybe a week or two. I'm not sure." When she saw his look of distress, she added quickly, "You mustn't make too much of it, Mr. Wilkins. He woke up. That's good."

"Good? He didn't even know who he was. How can that be good?"

"He could see and speak and move.

That's all good. If the damage was severe, he wouldn't be able to do even that."

"Christ." He dragged a shaking hand through his hair. "What do we do now?"

After a moment to think about it, Molly said, "We wait for him to wake up, then we get as much water down him as we can, try to keep him calm, and let his body do its work. He's strong. He should heal fast." If his arm didn't become infected. If one of his broken ribs didn't puncture a lung. If there was no bleeding in his brain. Too many "ifs" and not enough skill. She felt out of her depth and sinking fast. "Perhaps I should get Dr. Murray. He's probably more familiar with—"

"No!" Wilkins spun toward her, raw terror in his eyes. "Whatever needs doing, you do it. I don't trust him."

If the situation had allowed, she would have laughed. "And you trust me?"

"No. Yes. I don't know. You're just a liar. He's stark crazy."

She couldn't argue with that. Sighing wearily, she nodded. She would do what she could—not for this man—but for Henry. "Get some rest then. I'll watch over your brother for now. And please tell Mrs. Beckworth I'll be delayed here for a while, possibly all night."

After he left, she settled into the chair beside the bed to begin her vigil. Now that the crisis was over, every aching muscle made itself known. But she felt heartened. She had accomplished something important here, something that might impact the rest of this man's life.

Because of her, Henry Wilkins was whole. Because of her, he might live a complete life. Surely that might mitigate the terrible injustice she had done him.

Looking toward the window, where the nearly full moon softened the angular planes of El Capitan's rocky face, she realized that for the first time she felt confident in her nursing skills—not intimidated by the task put before her or overwhelmed by the burden of responsibility those skills carried with them—but proud. She had saved a man's arm. What a wonderful thing to be able to do that.

She turned back to study Henry—Hank—counting his breaths, watching to see if his fingertips turned blue, if his face flushed with fever or he opened his eyes again. If he did and questioned who she was, what should she tell him? Now that it seemed her husband might recover, what was she to do about their marriage? And the money she so desperately needed?

She would have to act quickly. Even now, Fletcher might be nearing El Paso. But how could she leave until she knew for certain her husband would survive? There could be infection or fever or seizures from his head injury. Dr. Murray was clearly incapable. Who would take care of Henry—Hank—if she left?

Sighing, she tipped her head back against the chair and closed her eyes.

You've made a fine mess of it now, haven't you, Molly?

IN THE EARLY DAWN LIGHT HE STUDIED THE woman stretched on the unmade cot beside his, trying to figure out who she was and why she was there. He had a hazy memory of a woman leaning over him, her hand on his cheek—and a man who called him a big bastard as if they knew each other. But beyond that, nothing. No idea who they were, or where he was, or what had happened to him. He didn't even know his own name.

He tried to sit up to see how bad he was hurt or if he was missing any parts, but the motion made him dizzy and nauseated, so he gave up and checked by feel.

Despite stabs of pain in his back and ribs, he could move his legs, which was a relief. His right arm seemed to work, but the left was so sore and swathed in bandages he didn't even try to move it. He felt another bandage above his left temple, which probably accounted for the headaches and dizziness and trouble seeing, and his ribs felt like a horse had rolled on him. None of which explained why he couldn't remember anything. It was as if his life had begun the moment he opened his eyes and saw those people standing over him.

How could that be? How did a man forget his own name?

"What the hell happened?" he muttered.

The woman jerked upright on the cot. Her head snapped toward him, eyes groggy and unfocused. "W-What?"

He squinted against the morning light,

pleased that there was only one of her now and that the blurriness was fading, which told him at least his vision was improving.

The first thing he noticed was her conformation—small, long legs, trim through the waist, and a lot of shiny sorrel-colored hair that tended more toward brown than chestnut. And kind eyes. Hazel, with maybe a green cast—he wasn't sure—and so charged with intelligence they seemed to shimmer in her pale face.

A pretty face. Strong. All cheekbones and deep-set eyes, with a determined chin and a mouth that might have been stern if not for the small crescent-shaped scar at the outer right corner of her top lip. Rather than disfiguring, it softened the angles of her face, making it seem she was on the verge of smiling even though her eyes told him she wasn't, and probably didn't very often.

In fact, she almost looked afraid.

Of him?

Hazy memories teased his befuddled mind—a crowded place, her looking back at him past rows of people—on a train? Then later, a gentle hand on his cheek—a soft voice with a Southern accent urging him not to give up. He wondered if it was hers.

"Say something," he ordered in a raspy voice.

She blinked. "About w-what?"

"Anything. Just talk."

"How do you feel? Are you in pain?"

Definitely her voice. "What happened? What's wrong with me?"

She finally moved, almost leaping from the bed. In the time it took her to cover the short distance between the two cots, everything about her changed—her expression, her posture, even the tone of her voice. Within an eye blink, she had slipped behind a mask of cool efficiency as if the fear had never been.

"You were in a train derailment," she said as she turned down the wick of the oil lamp sitting on the table between the cots. "Your injuries are substantial but not mortal. A broken arm, several cracked ribs, and a head wound. The head injury is why you're confused now. It should clear up with time." She looked down at him, hands clasped tightly at her waist. "Can you take some water?"

Just hearing the word awakened an overwhelming thirst. Although the effort brought wracking pain to his ribs, with her help he managed to sit up enough to drink from a cup. After two refills, he lay back, light-headed and dizzy. "Where am I?"

She set the empty cup on the table. "Dr. Murray's infirmary in El Paso."

"The man who was here earlier?"

"That was your brother, Brady Wilkins."

The name meant nothing to him. "Who are you?"

"Molly."

That meant even less. "Who am I?" He felt stupid asking it.

"Henry—Hank Wilkins."

Panic surged through him. "Why didn't I know that? Why is there an empty place in my head where all that should be? And why are these bindings so tight? I can't breathe."

"Try to remain calm, Mr. Wilkins."

"I am calm. Get them off." He tugged at the bindings on his ribs.

She pulled his hand away. "I realize you must be upset—"

"Damn right I'm upset."

"And shouting helps, does it?" They stared at each other for a moment then she looked down and saw she still held his hand and quickly let it go.

"It should." He threw his right arm over his eyes, hoping to mask his confusion. Who was this woman? And why was she in here and why was everything so jumbled up in his head? He wanted to ask her, but his stomach was churning again and he wasn't up to conversation.

Apparently she was. "I know this is difficult for you, Henry, and I'm—"

"Henry?" He lifted his arm and looked at her. "I thought I was Hank."

He saw her take a deep breath and let it out, and wished he could. "You are," she said in a strained voice. "I'm just more accustomed to thinking of you as Henry."

"Don't." He dropped his arm back over his eyes. Taking shallow breaths and speaking softly so the pain wasn't so bad, he added, "I prefer Hank, I think. I don't feel like a Henry." He thought about it for a moment then lifted his arm again. "Do I look like a Henry?" He hoped not. Henrys sounded like tea sips.

She didn't seem to have an answer.

"Is there a mirror? Maybe if I look in a mirror."

She retrieved one from a cabinet by the door and thrust it into his right hand.

He stared into it at the face of a stranger. Brown eyes, brown hair, bruises, and bandages. Just a face. Nothing familiar. "Did I have a beard?"

"Yes. Do you remember that?"

She sounded so hopeful, he hated to disappoint her. "My face is paler on the bottom where a beard would be. I must have shaved it recently."

She took the mirror from his hand. "You're handsomer without it."

As if that accounted for anything. "Why am I wearing a dress?" A Hank would never wear a dress. But a Henry might.

"It's not a dress. It's a nightshirt."

"There's flowers on it."

When she leaned closer to study the cloth stretched across his shoulder, he caught a faint sharp-sweet scent. Lemons. *Lemons?* Why would a woman wear perfume that smelled like food? *Food.* His stomach rumbled.

She straightened. "Those are shamrocks. For luck."

Bad luck, maybe. "Feels like a dress."

"Really?" She raised one gently arched brow. "How do you know?"

He squinted up at her. How *did* he know? While he pondered that, she pulled something out of her pocket, stuck one end onto his chest and the other end into her ears. "What are you doing?" he asked, alarmed.

"I'm listening to your heart and lungs. Hush." After a moment she put away the contraption—which he could now see was a stethoscope—and started squeezing the tips of the fingers on his sore arm. She must have seen his flinch. "Are you in pain? Would you like laudanum?"

"Of course I'm in pain. You're mashing my fingers. And no, I don't want laudanum. It gives me bad dreams." Suddenly he was so weary he could hardly keep his eyes open. She'd worn him down with all her fussing and mashing. Yet oddly, it had distracted him from his other pains and that smothered feeling, and although he was still a bit queasy, he was breathing easier and his headache was almost tolerable. His stomach rumbled again.

"How do you feel?"

"Hungry. And like a barn fell on me." Realizing she wasn't getting him food, he closed his eyes, feeling slightly nauseated again.

"Actually, it was the baggage car. You're fortunate to be alive."

"I don't feel fortunate." He heard her moving around him. Worried what she might be up to now, he forced open his eyes to find her looming over him with a worried crease between those almost-green eyes. It was unsettling. What was she doing? And what kind of woman carried a stethoscope in her pocket? "What are you, a lady doctor?"

Before she could answer, a voice spoke from the doorway, "You don't recognize her?" It was the man she'd called Brady. His brother.

Hank studied him closely, trying to spark a memory. He looked like an arrogant sonofabitch. Tall and lean with black hair and a mustache. Big toothy grin and strange-colored eyes that were full of mischief.

Or suspicion, whenever he looked at the woman . . . who was wearing that frightened look again. Something was not right here.

His brother sauntered closer to loom over the bed. "You look like hell, little brother."

Little? From what Hank could see, he was heavier than this man by at least forty pounds and probably even taller. "I feel like hell."

His brother pulled out a pocket watch, checked the time, then snapped it closed. "I got word Jessica's on her way, so I can't stay long."

"Jessica?"

"My wife. Her Ladyship. English, tall, red hair, crazy hats. Familiar?"

"No."

His brother's scowl deepened. "Give it time. It'll all come back. It better," he added, looking hard at the woman.

Hank decided he didn't much like his brother and he especially didn't like the way he taunted the woman. The woman. Who was she? He glanced from one to the other, which set his head pounding again, sending dagger thrusts of pain down his neck and across his shoulders. To change the subject, he asked, "How old am I?" A stupid question. Seemed he was full of stupid questions.

"Three years younger than me. Going on thirty-three."

"Are there more like you? More brothers?"

"None like me, of course. There's another brother, but he ran off."

Hank wasn't surprised. "Did I like you?"

The question startled a grin from his brother and reawakened the mischief in his blue eyes. "More than was manly, I suspect."

"Well, I don't now. So get out."

Instead of being insulted, his brother laughed. "See, you're better already." His grin fading into a scowl, he turned to the woman, who stood watching with wide eyes and a grim tightness to her mouth. "He looks hungry," he said. "Why don't you get him something to eat?" It was more of an order than a request.

As soon as she'd left, Hank said, "Who is she?"

His brother's gaze shifted away. "She saved your arm. Probably your life."

Hank frowned, not satisfied with that answer. But before he could question him, his brother headed out the door.

* * *

"WHERE'S MURRAY?" BRADY ASKED WHEN HE walked into the kitchen and found his brother's supposed wife stirring something on the stove.

"Gone." She nodded over her shoulder at a piece of paper on the table. "He left a note. Said to take any medical supplies I need and lock the door when I leave."

"Christ," Brady muttered, scanning the note. This complicated everything. Tossing the paper back onto the table, he went to peer over the woman's shoulder. Watery soup. "He prefers steak," he told her.

"He's too ill for steak. For now he'll get broth."

"He won't like it." Wandering aimlessly around the kitchen, Brady wondered what he should do now. He still didn't trust this woman. But she did seem to know her way around a sick room, so she might yet be useful. And she needed money, so he had that to keep her in line. He stopped and glared at her back. "You didn't tell him you were married. Why?"

Setting the spoon aside, she wiped her palms down her skirts and turned to face him. "I've been thinking."

There's trouble. The woman was smart.

No telling what mischief she had conjured this time. Crossing his arms over his chest, he waited.

"It appears your brother might recover, so I thought—"

"Might?" Brady cut in.

She made a dismissive gesture. "There's always the risk of infection after surgery. Or a seizure after a head injury. Or, well, any number of complications. It might be touch and go for a while, but as I said, he's strong. And a survivor."

Hank was that. Which was why seeing him laid so low had been such a shock to Brady. He'd already lost one brother, and another was missing. He couldn't tolerate losing this one too.

"So I thought," she went on, "it might be best if we had the marriage annulled."

Brady's thought exactly, but finding the doctor had left put a kink in his plans. Who would tend Hank now? And if he managed to get his brother back to the ranch, he couldn't expect Doc O'Grady to make the twenty-five-mile trek from Val Rosa every day to check on him. There was really only one solution, and he didn't like it. There were still too many unanswered questions circling in his head. "Why would you want to do that?" he asked suspiciously. "Hank proposed. You accepted. But now that you've rushed him into marriage, you want an annulment?"

She started to speak, cleared her throat, and said, "I rushed it because he was dying and I needed the settlement money. But now that it appears he may recover . . ."

"You don't want him anymore," he finished acidly.

"Or perhaps he won't want me," she countered.

The woman seemed terrified, and he suddenly knew why. "Or maybe you tricked him and he never proposed. Maybe you married an unconscious man for the settlement, and now that he's getting better, you're ready to run."

Her eyes looked huge in her frozen face. "I didn't say that."

But she didn't deny it. "What about the money?"

"I, ah . . . thought perhaps I would get it from you."

"Me?"

"You're a rich man, Mr. Wilkins. Since you seem so disapproving of this marriage, surely it's worth three hundred dollars to get me out of your brother's life."

He blinked in astonishment. "You're blackmailing me?" he finally said, more surprised than angry. "And if I don't pay?"

She gave a sickly smile. "Then I guess you could welcome me to the family."

Surprise gave way to fury. "Or I could kill you." But then who would take care of Hank?

Her smile became a smirk. "Back to that neck-snapping thing, are we?" Then the fight went out of her on a weary sigh. Turning back to the stove, she picked up the spoon and poked at the broth. "God, what an unholy mess."

And then he realized what he had to do. He'd have to keep a sharp eye on her, of course—he still didn't trust this woman—but it was the perfect solution to all his problems. "Okay, I'll give you the money."

She looked back at him over her shoulder. "You will?"

"Once Hank is fully recovered."

Her hopeful look faded. She stirred so vigorously, broth sloshed onto the hot stovetop. "But that could take months. I can't stay here that long."

"You won't have to. You'll come to the ranch, instead."

She whirled, the dripping spoon clutched in her hand. "I'll what?"

He flinched and glanced at the hall. "Not so loud. He'll hear you. We don't want him to know what you did."

She actually seemed to get bigger while he watched. "What I did?"

"You know. Faking the marriage for the railroad money." Again, he almost wished she would deny it. She didn't. "You'll get your money," he said. "After."

"After what?" She clapped fists on her hips, apparently unconcerned that the spoon dripped broth on his boots. "What are you talking about? Surely you don't want to continue this charade of a marriage?"

He backed out of dripping range and tried to keep his voice reasonable, hoping she would do likewise. Excitable women made him almost as nervous as crying ones. "Hank doesn't trust women. Hell, you shaved him. You saw. When he cleans up, they jump on him like ticks on a hound. He doesn't like it. Doesn't trust it."

"You're saying he has an aversion to women because they find him attractive?

That's absurd. And what does it have to do with my money?"

"Not an aversion, exactly. He's shy. Why do you think he grew all that hair?"

She threw up her hands, flinging broth against the wall. "Then hit him with a rock and break his nose so you can both feel better. What about my money?"

"We tried that. It didn't work." When he saw her shock, he quickly added, "It was an accident. The thing is, there was this featherbrain he had his eye on, but she ran off with a tin soldier from Fort Union and that only made it worse."

"Oh, for God's sake. You're insane. You should be chained to a wall in an asylum." Whirling, she yanked the saltcellar from a shelf above the stove.

Brady prepared to duck then relaxed when she began flinging salt into the broth with all the vigor of a woman trying to stone ants.

"I hate all this lying," she muttered.

Since when? But Brady wasn't so stupid to say that out loud. Nor did he mention the soup was probably salty enough now to cure pork. He needed her too much to run her off. "He's wary enough as it is. If he knew what you did, he wouldn't let you anywhere near him."

"That won't be a problem, since I have no intention of going to your ranch."

"You will if you want your money," he snapped, drawing her head around again. Curbing his temper, he added in a more reasonable tone, "Here's what we'll do. Because we don't want anyone accidentally blurting it out, we'll go ahead and tell him about the marriage. But not about the money. I want to get him home and well again before we pull his feet out from under him." *And by then, hopefully it'll be over and Jessica will be safe,* he added silently to himself.

She faced him, eyes narrowed in suspicion. "I don't know what scheme you have going here, Mr. Wilkins, but I am not lying to your brother."

"Hell, you already have!" He clapped both hands to his head. "Christ. You're as bad as he is, hardheads, both."

Muttering to herself, she snatched a bowl off the shelf and began spooning broth into it.

This wasn't going as Brady had hoped. He didn't want to get harsh with her, but there was more at stake here than just Hank's well-being. "Look at me," he said.

Pausing mid-scoop, she glared at him over her shoulder.

"You'll come to the ranch," he said with soft menace. "You'll stay married and tend Hank and not tell him about the money, or we can go to the sheriff right now and he can explain the penalty for fraud. What'll happen to those kids then?"

The bowl dropped. Broth sizzled on the hot stove. "You'd do that?"

He stepped closer until he loomed over her. "I'll do anything to protect my brother. He may have finally come awake but he's not out of the woods yet, and you're his best hope of staying alive."

"You arrogant—"

"I know you're running from something," he cut in. "I don't know what or why and I don't care. But if you'd rather face *that*—or jail—instead of coming to the ranch to nurse Hank a little longer, it's your choice. But decide now."

Her face went white. She pressed a hand to her stomach.

He hoped she wasn't going to puke again.

"When he realizes what we've done, he'll hate me," she said. "And you."

"But he'll be alive, won't he?"

Straightening, he took a step back. He knew his size and manner could be intimidating, and he didn't like using it against a woman, but he'd do whatever he could to help Hank. And Jessica. And this woman was exactly what he needed to do that.

He tried to soften his expression. "Hell, he may never remember, you said so yourself. And who knows? If you sweeten up to him and play your cards right, he may never care that you tricked him like a blind dog." He grinned.

She hit him in the side of his face with the wooden spoon.

For a moment they blinked at each other, then Brady lifted a hand and brushed his fingertips over the broth dripping down his cheek. He tasted it and shook his head. Chicken. "I'm telling you he'd prefer steak. And less salt."

"You are the most vile, manipulative, deceitful—"

"I know. What's your answer?" When he saw her hand tighten on the handle of the spoon, he took another step back. The woman had a formidable temper.

In the distance a train whistle blew. He glanced at the clock above the stove then back at the woman, aware that if his wife was on that train, he was running out of time. "Think of the little ones, Molly. And Hank. Come to the ranch and they'll all be safe."

He watched tears well up in those sad green eyes, and panic shot through him. "If you cry, I'll take you to the sheriff now," he lied. "I swear it."

"You horrid man." She swiped at her eyes. "You ingrate."

The whistle sounded again, closer. "If you come to the ranch, I'll protect you and the children," he persisted. "I won't let whatever you're running from reach you there. And when it's over and Hank is safe, then I'll give you your money and see that the marriage is annulled. My word."

She looked like a cornered cat. He remembered seeing that look on Jessica's face and felt something clench in his chest. Suddenly he felt so guilty for all his empty threats and manipulations he almost admitted the other reason he so desperately wanted her at the ranch.

Christ. What if Hank really had proposed? What if he really wanted this woman? Brady still didn't know what to believe. But the truth wasn't important right now. Keeping Hank and Jessica alive was.

"I'll never forgive you for this," she said, her chin wobbling.

"I expect not. But you and the children will be safe, and Hank will be alive." *And hopefully Jessica will be too.* "I can live with that. Can you?"

Brady didn't know if he'd ever seen such a desolate expression.

"I guess I'll have to."

Five

HER HUSBAND—HOW ODD THAT SOUNDED—WAS asleep when Molly returned with a bowl of broth. Not wanting to wake him, she set it on the bedside table then stood for a moment, undecided. She needed to check on the children but was hesitant to leave Hank alone in the empty house. Then she heard voices at the front door—Brady Wilkins and a woman with an English accent.

Slipping back into the kitchen, she waited until they passed down the hall to the room where Hank lay, then ducked out the side door. Cowardly, to be sure, but after a near-sleepless night, she was desperate for a wash and change of clothes, and after that wretched confrontation earlier, she had no desire to talk to Brady Wilkins or make chatty conversation with his precious "Her Ladyship."

The Beckworths had everything in hand. Effie had a picnic planned then a visit to the blacksmith's, and later in the afternoon, Thaddeus was taking the children fishing at a creek north of town. Grateful for their continued help and a blessed moment of privacy, Molly tended to her needs. An hour later, washed, coiffed, and dressed in her second best—only because everything else was wrinkled or soiled, and certainly not out of any desire to impress anyone—she returned to the infirmary.

As she hung her coat on the peg by the side door, she heard raised voices coming from the sickroom. Alarmed that Brady Wilkins might be badgering his sick brother, she rushed down the hall.

Instead, she found Hank struggling to ward off a sturdily built middle-aged woman armed with a dripping rag. "Get away from me," he rasped, swatting at her with his pillow.

Dodging the pillow, the woman deftly

yanked back the covers—revealing that the nightshirt was even less adequate than Molly had thought—and slapped the wet cloth on Hank's bare thigh.

Hank yelped, then the wrestling began in earnest as he struggled to pull up the covers and push down the nightshirt at the same time—which was quite impossible with only one hand. "Get off me!"

Ignoring him, the woman scrubbed with alarming enthusiasm, slinging soap and invectives in equal measure. "I was hired to clean you up, you stinking, overgrown goat herder, and bigod, I will. Now lift your leg."

Battling both shock and amusement, Molly stepped into the room. "Enough!"

Hank sagged back. "Thank God."

The woman whipped around. "Who are you?"

"I'm Molly, his wife. Who are you?"

"Agnes Meecham, but people calls me Bunny."

Molly couldn't begin to fathom why. "Who hired you?"

"The other one."

"Brady Wilkins?"

The woman nodded. "Said he smelled like a pig farmer, but my daddy was a pig farmer, and I have to say he smelled worse. This one's just musty and sour smelling. But Pa, whew! When he—"

"Thank you," Molly cut in, trying not to laugh. She took the rag from Bunny's rather large hand. "I can take it from here."

The woman planted beefy fists on beefier hips. "What about my money?"

"Oh, Mr. Wilkins will pay you. In fact, you should receive a bonus for your efforts." She smiled, liking the idea. "Double, I think. Tell him I insist upon it."

After the grateful woman left, Molly turned to Hank, who had the covers clutched to his chin and was looking at her as if she had grown a second set of ears.

"*Wife*? You're my *wife*?"

Heat rushed into her face. "Apparently you don't remember me," she said with a weak smile.

He just stared at her.

Fearing he was about to launch into questions she wasn't yet prepared to answer, she thrust the dripping rag in his direction. "Will you finish? Or shall I?"

He blinked at the rag, then up at her. "How long have we been married?"

"Awhile." Grabbing his right hand, she stuffed the rag into his fingers, then turned toward the door. "There's rinse water in the bowl on the bedside table," she called back as she fled through the doorway. "Call when you're done. I'll bring a fresh dress—er, nightshirt."

HE DIDN'T CALL.

Setting a pot of oatmeal aside to cool, she tasted the fresh batch of broth—less salt this time—then collected the largest clean nightshirt she could find in the examination room and went back down the hall to the sickroom.

She found Hank in his soiled nightshirt, perched on the edge of the bed, his head hanging, his breath coming in shallow bursts. He held his injured arm cradled against his chest and his right hand clutched to his bound ribs. His face was as white as the bed linens.

"What are you doing?" she cried, dropping the clean nightshirt onto the chair and rushing toward the bed, looking for signs of fresh blood, renewed swelling. She should never have left him alone. Or left him at the mercy of his horrid brother and that brutish woman, Bunny. "Are you hurt?"

"I need . . . to relieve . . . myself," he gasped, struggling to breathe against the constrictive bandages.

She stumbled to a stop beside the bed, still rattled but also relieved he was uninjured. "But you can't get up. You'll fall and hurt your arm."

"Then step aside."

"What?"

"Move."

Molly gaped. Surely he didn't intend to relieve himself on the floor? When he reached for the hem of his nightshirt, she blurted out, "Use the chamber pot," and pointed at the door in the bottom of the nightstand.

He shifted, then groaned. "I can't . . . bend."

"Oh. Of course." Stooping to open the door, she realized his feet were in the way. Swiveling to tell him to move, she found herself nose to knee with his hairy leg. She also noted that the undersized nightshirt had risen halfway up his thighs. For a moment she bridled, thinking he had done it on purpose to shock her, but one look at his face told her he was in too much pain to be thinking of her.

After asking him to move his feet aside, she quickly retrieved the metal chamber pot. When she straightened, the nightshirt was higher yet. She didn't know why the sight unnerved her. She had seen thighs before. Dozens of thighs. Dozens of pairs of thighs, even. Although few had been quite so . . . well, substantial.

"Plan on watching?" he asked, his breathing a little less labored.

She jerked her gaze from his lower limbs. "I am a trained nurse, Mr. Wilkins," she said in her most professional voice. "And quite accustomed to aiding—"

"I don't need aid. I need the pot."

She exhaled and tried for a more conciliatory tone. "I am here to assist you, Henry. You are still quite ill and weak. Should you fall on that arm—"

"Not weak. Hurt."

"Of course you are. I didn't mean that kind of weak. It's just that if you—"

"And I'm not a kid, so quit treating me like one."

"Of course you're not." Was this their first quarrel? How ludicrous.

"And I'm not Mister, or Henry. I'm Hank. Just Hank." He tipped his head to frown up at her. "But you should know that, shouldn't you? Wife."

Frozen by that stare, for a moment she couldn't respond. "I meant no offense, Hank." She held out the pot.

He took it, wincing at the pull of bruised muscles across his cracked ribs.

Seeing his struggle made her own chest ache, which was ridiculous. He didn't need sympathy, he needed assistance. And she was trained to give it. "I can see you're having some difficulty. Will you allow me to help you?"

"The day I need help to piss, shoot me. Close the door behind you."

Obdurate man. Did he not understand that with only one operable hand it would be physically impossible for him to hold both the chamber pot and his . . . himself . . . at the same time? "Can't you see this isn't going to work?" she said with strained patience. "You'll need two hands."

He went still. Slowly he lifted his head and regarded her from behind long strands of dark hair. His face showed no expression, but his eyes danced. "I'm flattered you think so. But I'll manage."

She frowned, wondering if she'd misunderstood and decided surely she had. She looked around. "Maybe there's a portable commode chair. Or a long-necked urinal jar. That would only take one hand to—"

"I know how many hands it takes. I've done this before."

"Or I could hold it for you."

He blinked.

"Unless you'd prefer I call your brother?" Even though she was trained to deal with these situations in a matter-of-fact way, she wasn't insensitive to the patient's need for modesty. "Shall I send for him?"

"If there's any holding to be done, I'd prefer you do it. Wife."

Pinhead. "Fine. Then give it to me." She held out her hand.

He stared at it, his lips twitching. "Which one? The pot or—"

"Of course the pot!" Finally realizing where his mind was, she snatched the pot from his grip. But once she had it, she wasn't sure what to do with it.

"Better hurry. Twenty-eight."

She eyed his bent head. "Twenty-eight what?"

"Panes in that cabinet over there. You leaving or not?"

What did panes have to do with anything? Fearing for the man's sanity, but determined not to let the already uncomfortable situation deteriorate into gibberish or infantile sickroom snickering, she put the pot on the floor squarely between his rather large bare feet then stepped back. "How's that?"

He gave the pot a considering look. "Too far. It's not a fire hose, you know." Then apparently overcome by his own adolescent wit, he snorted then grabbed at his ribs. "Ow-ow-ow."

And Brady Wilkins thought this man was shy?

"The chair then." In growing desperation, she picked up the pot, slapped it onto the seat of the chair with the clean nightshirt, then shoved the chair into his knees with enough force to send him into an involuntary cringe. "How's that?"

He looked at the chair between his legs then up at her. She was gratified to see his expression of amusement had changed to one of healthy respect. "Better."

"Excellent." Flush with victory, she retreated to the kitchen.

As she readied a tray, she decided to put the entire awkward exchange out of her mind. Sadly, such ribald behavior was not uncommon when women tended male patients. Despite the great strides toward respectability female nurses had made during the war, there were still those who felt any woman, nurse or no, who put hands on a strange man's body was little better than a prostitute. It irritated her to think this man—her husband—might harbor a similar opinion.

Fire hose indeed. *Wicked man*.

Wicked her. She still couldn't get that image out of her mind. So much for professionalism.

When she returned with a bowl of oatmeal and a cup of warm cider, Hank was back in bed, eyes closed, mostly covered by the fresh nightshirt. A towel covered the chamber pot.

Moving quietly, she set the tray on the bedside table, removed the chamber pot to the hall to be emptied later, then went back to the bed. "Breakfast," she said cheerfully, poking his good shoulder.

He cracked open one eye—the one with the purple bruise, rather than the greenish-yellow. "What is it?"

"Oatmeal and cider."

He sighed and closed the eye. "When can I get real food?"

"This is real food."

"Not to me. I doubt I got this size eating mush."

She doubted it too. "Perhaps tomorrow. Can you sit up?"

With grunts and grimaces, he managed. As she leaned over to prop a pillow behind his back, she could sense him watching her. It gave her an itchy, prickly feeling.

"What happened to your face?" he asked as she straightened.

Without thinking, she lifted a hand to her cheek where earlier he had accidentally struck her.

He pulled her hand away. "Is that a bruise?"

She froze, her fingers trapped in his. And suddenly everything intensified—the sound of his breathing, the smell of soap and carbolic dressing, the feel of the calluses on his fingers. It was startling, like being wrenched from deep sleep into full alertness within an instant.

"Did somebody hit you?"

She pulled her hand free and took a deep breath. "It's nothing." Avoiding his gaze, she positioned the chair so she wouldn't have to lean too far, spread a napkin over his chest, then reached for the bowl and spoon.

"Was it me?" he asked, apparently unwilling to let it go. "Did I do that?"

"You weren't yourself." She scooped a spoonful of oatmeal and held it out.

"I sure hope not." Instead of allowing her to feed him, he took the spoon from her grip, fed himself, then handed it back, watching her all the while.

The fragility of male pride never ceased to amaze her.

"Did you deserve it?" he challenged.

She refilled the spoon and passed it over. "I sure hope not," she mimicked.

His lips might have twitched, but she wasn't sure. The man guarded his emotions like a dog with a bone.

As he ate, she studied him, noting that the swelling in his face had gone down and his eyes were now fully open and he was in need of a shave again. She hoped he would let her tend to that. It would be a shame to hide that face under a beard.

"Where did we meet?"

She glanced up from her contemplation of his bristly chin to find him watching her with that same intense concentration she had noticed on the train. It made it hard to draw a full breath.

"We are married, aren't we?" he persisted.

"Yes." She almost choked on the word.

From the front of the house came the sound of voices. A man and a woman. The woman had an English accent. *Lovely.* A sleepless night, a petulant patient, and now that deceitful, conniving Brady Wilkins and Her Ladyship.

"How long?"

"What?"

"How long have we been married? Earlier, you said 'awhile.' How long is 'awhile'?"

"Two, ah, three days." Hoping to avoid further inquiry, she scooped oatmeal with a vengeance. But no matter how rapidly she shoved the filled spoon into his hand, the questions kept coming.

"Where did we meet?"

"Sierra Blanca."

"You live there?"

"No, the children and I were just passing through."

He stopped chewing. "Children? We have children?"

"They're my late sister's," she explained. "A boy named Charlie—he's eight, and his sister, Penny, who is six."

He passed back the spoon. "Hell."

"You don't like children?" Would she have to protect them from this man too?

"Yeah. Sure. It's just that—hell, I don't even remember getting married and now I've got kids. It's a lot to take in all at once."

He was silent for a moment—too silent. Molly wondered if he realized she'd been desperately dodging his questions. "Their mother is dead?" he finally asked.

"Yes." She scooped the last of the oatmeal and passed it over, watching in fascination as his lips closed over the spoon. He had a very nice mouth.

"Their father too?" he asked as he chewed.

She nodded.

He dropped the spoon into the empty bowl. "Too bad. Kids need family."

The remark hit hard, triggering a surge of emotion that constricted the muscles in Molly's throat. She didn't want to think of Nellie and Papa. That loss was too raw, and the wall she had erected to shield herself against it was a weak barrier at best.

The voices seemed louder, nearer. She set the bowl on the tray.

"Are they all the family you have?"

"Yes." Avoiding his gaze, she brushed a blob of oatmeal from her skirt.

"Except me."

Removing the napkin from his chest, she tossed it onto the tray. "Yes." She hadn't considered this man to be part of her family, which he wasn't, of course. But now that his brother was forcing her to come to their ranch for an indeterminate amount of time, she would have to pretend he was. Oddly, the notion wasn't as disturbing as it should have been. Even if their marriage was based on a lie, it was a comfort to know that, for a while at least, she wouldn't be entirely alone and the children would be safe.

Footsteps thudded in the hall. Nervously she brushed back a stray curl and checked her skirt for more oatmeal. She was definitely not looking forward to being scrutinized and found wanting by some fancy Englishwoman. Looking up, she found those watchful eyes studying her with such focused attention it was like being invaded. Snatching the cup of cider from the tray, she thrust it toward him.

"It doesn't add up," he said, ignoring the cup. "I don't remember you. Yet I do remember loading a part for a concentrator in Sierra Blanca."

Her hand jerked. Cider sloshed over her hand. "Y-You do?"

Those sharp eyes bored into her. "That scares you. I wonder why." A frown drew his dark brows together. "You wouldn't lie to me, would you? Wife?"

The cup slipped. The door opened. Cider splashed into Molly's lap just as Brady Wilkins stepped into the room, followed by a striking redheaded woman.

"We're back," the woman cried, pushing past Brady and into the room. She stopped when she saw Molly. "Oh, I see you have a guest. Are we interrupting?"

Heart pounding, Molly lurched to her feet. After a moment of befuddled panic, her gaze fell on the outrageous hat that by rights should have snapped the woman's slim neck. A huge brim, pleated peach satin on the underneath, green organza on top, with a wide matching satin ribbon, and on one side peach silk flowers and three egret plumes, the longest of which curved over the crown and down past the brim to gently brush her cheek. It was the most astounding hat Molly had ever seen.

Aware that she was staring, she lowered her gaze. Hank's words rushed back at her, awakening the panic again. His memory was returning. He knew about the machinery. How long before he realized she had deceived him? The thought almost buckled her knees.

Numbly she watched cider drip from her sodden skirts onto the toes of her shoes and wondered how to escape this room—this town—her wretched lies.

Brady Wilkins sauntered in, grinning like the devil he was. "Did that sweet Mrs. Meecham get you cleaned up? Hope so, since I had to pay her double."

Hank's normally calm voice held such a note of menace it drew Molly's attention. "In a day or two I'll get up from this bed. And the first thing I'm coming after is you, Brother. Just so you know."

Brady blinked innocently. "What? You didn't like Bunny?"

While the brothers argued and threatened each other, the Englishwoman said, "How lovely to hear them fighting."

Realizing she was staring again, Molly jerked her gaze from the hat to find the other woman regarding her with a thoughtful expression.

Did she know about the marriage? Molly wondered. The money? Was that the reason for the speculative look in her amber brown eyes?

Overwhelmed by a sudden urge to flee, Molly said, "If you'll excuse me, I seem to have made a mess." She motioned to her stained skirts. "I should go change." As she bent to pick up the tray, Hank's hand clamped over her arm.

"Stay," he said.

She stared down at the long fingers encircling her wrist. Dark against her paler skin. Knuckles nicked and scarred. A powerful hand with a gentle grip that sent prickly shocks up her arm. She met his studied look with a tentative smile. "I'll only be a moment."

"I have questions."

"Later." Forcefully pulling her arm from his grip, she picked up the tray and made her escape. But once in the safety of the kitchen, courage deserted her. Setting the tray on the counter, she pressed a hand over her racing heart.

God, now what? Did she grab the children and run? Try to brazen it out? Tell Hank the truth? She hated lying to a man who was already confused and bewildered. How could she allow this to go on?

"He shouldn't have done it," a voice said behind her.

Whirling, Molly saw the Englishwoman watching her from the doorway.

"Brady is more bluster than bite," she added, coming into the room. "He shouldn't have tried to force you to come to the ranch. If he tries to push you around again, simply ignore him. Or cry. That will send him scampering." She stopped before Molly and held out her hand. "Hello. I'm Jessica."

Molly stared at the proffered hand, her thoughts in turmoil. Hesitantly, she placed her hand in Jessica's then quickly drew back when she felt the stickiness of cider on her fingers. "I'm sorry," she murmured, wiping her hand down her damp skirt. "Cider." Pulling a piece of toweling from a hook by the sink, she held it out.

While the Englishwoman cleaned her hand, Molly studied her, feeling more inadequate and awkward by the moment.

She felt hopelessly inept in social situations. She had no flair, no interest in small talk, and no inclination to flirt. Most Southern women burst from the womb with all the correct phrases and mannerisms etched into their memories. They knew instinctively how to coo, and bat their eyelashes, and flit through life like dainty butterflies. And what they weren't born knowing, they were taught by their mothers.

But after the age of twelve Molly had no mother and no one to teach her but Papa—energetic, flamboyant, charismatic Papa. What did it matter if his shoes didn't match or the buttons on his vest didn't line up or his hair needed a trim? He was a genius and so far above such banal considerations it wasn't worth notice. Much like his awkward, too-serious daughter, his shadow in the shadows.

While other fifteen-year-olds went to finishing school, Molly went to the surgical wing of Our Lady of Mercy Hospital. While other girls painted watercolors and stitched samplers, Molly mopped blood and stitched torn flesh. While they flirted with handsome young men, Molly watched them die. From the Battle of Atlanta to the horror of Andersonville, she had seen too much, endured too much to remain unchanged. Such harsh experience had separated her forever from what she was supposed to be, and now after so many years the gap was too wide to bridge. And never did Molly feel that sense of alienation and isolation more keenly than when faced with a woman as feminine and gracious as Her Ladyship.

The woman was striking. Exceptionally tall, regal, and graceful—despite the slight evidence of her pregnancy—with curly red-gold hair; wide, intelligent eyes; and a smile that rivaled her husband's. Taken separately, her features were unexceptional. But together, and set off by that vibrant hair and her commanding height, she was easily one of the most attractive women Molly had ever seen.

Or she might have been had she not been crying recently. Not only was her nose red and her skin splotchy, her eyes were puffy and her top lip seemed double the size of the bottom.

Oddly, evidence of such honest emotion made Molly admire her all the more.

After wiping her hand, Jessica carefully folded the cloth and set it on the counter. They stood in silence until the need to unburden herself forced Molly to speak. "He remembers the machinery he was bringing back. It means he's starting to remember."

"Is he? How wonderful!"

"Yes. But—"

"But he's a long way from full recovery," Jessica cut in before Molly could make her confession . . . almost as if she knew what was coming and had intentionally headed it off. Perhaps Brady had told her of his suspicions. Another innocent drawn into this deception.

"It's most vexing." Jessica made a fluttery gesture with one graceful hand. "Hank has always been the steady one. Invincible, it seemed. It's difficult seeing him so . . ." Her voice faltered. She cleared her throat then met Molly's gaze, her expression fiercely determined. "I know circumstances hastened your marriage and that you probably would have preferred to wait. But it's done. And even if Hank doesn't fully remember you now, he soon will, and then all will be put to rights. But until then, he needs you."

Did Jessica truly not know the marriage was a sham? Or was she pretending, for propriety's sake? Molly couldn't tell. Things had gone so far beyond her control now she hardly knew what was real anymore.

"Will you help us, Molly? Will you see Hank through this? We couldn't bear to lose him."

Did she really have a choice? What had changed over the last two days—other than marrying a dying man, who didn't die, and finding herself under the thumb of Satan's sidekick? She still needed money. She still had two children to protect. And she still had Fletcher's men tracking her every move.

And then, of course, there was Hank. Beautiful, quirky, funny Hank. He needed her.

Jessica must have read her hesitation. Words came out in a rush, as if by talking fast she could overcome Molly's reluctance. "Brady said you were in difficult circumstances, that you were low on funds and had two children in your care. I understand you must do what is best for them. Believe me, I do. But we can help you, Molly. Money, a place to stay, whatever you need." She must have realized she was twisting her hands because she abruptly stopped and laced them tightly at her waist. "Help us. Please, Molly. Hank is my friend, and Brady, well . . . Brady has lost too many brothers as it is."

Molly felt that tug of sympathy that always got her into trouble. A good nurse couldn't afford that emotion. It would crush her. So she hardened herself against it by mentally stepping back. "So you want this marriage to continue? You want me to come to the ranch?"

"I want you to make him well again, no matter what it takes. And I would be so grateful if you came to the ranch. It would be lovely having another woman to talk to. Brady, well . . ." She smiled, wryly. "Although I adore him to distraction, he can be such a dolt."

Tactfully, Molly didn't agree. "But surely there's a doctor you can call."

"O'Grady." Jessica made a dismissive gesture. "A bit of a tippler, I'm sorry to say.

Besides"—she gave Molly a sly smile—"I have no doubt Hank would prefer being nursed by you than O'Grady."

Molly doubted that. But again, what choice did she really have? "Well . . ."

"Oh, thank you," Jessica cried, taking Molly's hand in her own. "You have such a kind face, I knew you would help us." Tucking Molly's hand into the crook of her elbow, she pulled her gently but determinedly toward the door. "I vow we shall be great friends. I knew it the moment Brady told me you hit him with a spoon. I daresay he deserved it. He always does. And while we get that skirt changed, I'll tell you all about my first meeting with Brady and how I almost gelded him with a parasol. It's a charming story."

Pulled along in the Englishwoman's wake, Molly wondered if she'd just been manipulated again. If so, at least this time it had been done with a gentler touch.

THE WOMAN WAS A FORCE OF NATURE. BEFORE the day was done, Jessica had everyone organized for the overnight trip to Redemption. They would travel in the accommodations Jessica had borrowed from the railroad owner, which consisted of a locomotive and tender, a caboose, and a forty-foot-long sleeping and parlor car. The two ranch hands she'd brought with her would bunk in the caboose, which also served as quarters for the brakeman, engineer, fireman, and conductor.

Coupled behind the caboose was the parlor-sleeping car, which was divided into four compartments. The small forward section contained fold-down bunks for the owner's personal staff. Molly and the children would sleep there. Next was a compact galley kitchen, and behind that, the parlor, with plush seats and a small dining area. Hank would travel there on a makeshift bed that would better accommodate his size. There was a tiny water closet that dumped directly onto the tracks, and at the end of the car, the owner's sleeping quarters, which was where Brady and Jessica would sleep.

They loaded Hank last. Because he was still dizzy from the head wound and weakened by his other injuries, Jessica didn't want him subjected to the jarring of a wagon down the rutted and rapidly thawing street, so over his strenuous objections, she had the two ranch hands, Brady, and three men she conscripted from the hotel strap him on a door they'd also conscripted from the hotel and carry him through town to the depot. Molly and the children followed with baskets of medical supplies.

The Beckworths saw them off, the reverend presenting Molly a box filled with food and Effie struggling not to cry as she bent down to hug Penny and Charlie.

Molly made a vow to come back someday and thank them properly.

By nightfall they were on their way to Redemption, the mining town that served the Wilkins silver mines. Once there, they would transfer to wagons and continue over another pass to RosaRoja Valley, the home of their high mountain ranch.

Six

"WE OUGHT TO KEEP HER. MOLLY, I MEAN."

Jessica's gaze met Brady's in the mirror over the vanity in the owner's private car. One copper brow rose. "Of course we'll keep her. She's Hank's wife."

Bracing his legs against the swaying of the rail car, Brady slipped off his shirt and tossed it onto a chair, enjoying the way her whiskey brown eyes pored over his chest. "I just meant she's a hell of a nurse. Better than O'Grady. It might be nice having her around the place. You know, just in case." He tried not to flex too much as he unbuckled his belt. The woman was pregnant, after all, and she'd had a long day. Still . . . the rocking motion of the car brought up some interesting possibilities.

Or not, judging by the way she swiveled on the stool and planted her hands on her hips. Always a bad sign.

"Is that what this is about, Brady? Why you forced her to come to the ranch?"

Avoiding her gaze, he climbed into bed. "It was her choice." Which, without going into the particulars, was mostly true.

"Oh, Brady." With a sigh, she rose from the stool, grabbing the bedpost for balance as the rail car swayed and rocked. "Just because there was some difficulty with my last confinement, there is no need to think it will happen again."

Some difficulty? Brady still broke into a sweat when he thought of those harrowing hours when she struggled to bring Abigail into the world. It had been a breech birth, and he had nearly lost them both. Now, eight months later, she was pregnant again. The woman was killing him.

Hanging her robe on the bedpost, she got into bed and began rooting around like she did every night, fluffing the pillows, pulling the covers just so, then neatly folding over the top and smoothing out every wrinkle.

Brady watched, arms tucked behind his head. He loved the way she fussed around. He loved that she was his, and he knew without her he'd die. It was that simple and that pathetic. Ever since she'd told him she was pregnant again, he'd been in a blind panic—how could nursing mothers even get pregnant? But with Molly coming to the ranch, maybe he wouldn't have to worry so much. He hoped so. He'd already had to tighten his belt a notch and Jessica was barely even showing.

"All done?" he asked when she had finally settled down, arms on top of the covers straight against her sides.

"All done."

"Good." He turned down the wick on the lamp bolted to the wall beside the bed, then rolled over, messing up her perfect arrangement, and pulled her back against his chest. "I missed you," he said against the crown of her head.

"It's only been two days." She sent him a look over her shoulder. "Do you know what Ben said yesterday?"

"Mmm, what?" Closing his eyes, he ran

his hand over her breasts, down her belly to skim the arch of her hip, learning by feel the daily changes her pregnancy brought. It was a chore he never tired of.

"He said, 'Hellfire.' He finally speaks and the first word he says is profanity."

Brady grinned into the darkness. Ben was his son by intent, if not blood, and he loved him fiercely. From the minute Jessica had blundered into his life, pregnant and on the run, he had taken her and her unborn child into his heart. They never spoke of the bastard who had fathered Ben—Jessica's brother-in-law and rapist—the sonofabitch was dead anyway—and even though his brothers and Jessica's sister knew the truth, Brady never thought of Ben as anything but his son. He was past his second birthday now and a redheaded terror like his mama. Abigail, though still a crawler, looked to be an early walker. And now they had another on the way. He would have considered himself the luckiest man in the world if he hadn't been so worried.

She pinched his roving hand to regain his attention. "The point," she said in that starchy high-toned voice he found so amusing, "is that he used profanity. Where do you suppose he learned that?"

Brady avoided another pinch by moving his hand up to cup her breast. Which by rights should be his breast, since he was a lot fonder of it than she seemed to be, a claim he was willing to restake every chance he got. "Probably from Dougal."

"As if. Dougal knows better after I threatened to send him back to Scotland if he continued to misbehave with the children."

"Speaking of children," Brady said, adroitly changing the subject as he ran his palm over her rounded belly. "How's little Thomas Jefferson today?"

"Nigel is fine."

"And you?"

"Tired. Relieved to be going home. Grateful Hank is better."

"You're sure? No pains?"

"I'm fine." She reached up to pat his cheek. "You must stop this incessant worrying, you sweet, silly man."

Sweet? Silly? "All I did was ask how you were. How is that worrying?"

She lifted his hand to kiss his open palm

then pulled his arm tighter around her. "I missed you too."

They lay in silence, lulled by the rocking motion of the car and the clickety-clack of the wheels as they rolled over the joints in the track. "I was scared, Jessica," he said after a while. "I thought we were going to lose him. After Sam, then Jack—"

"You haven't lost Jack," she cut in gently. "He's simply misplaced."

"Then why haven't we heard anything? We don't even know where they are, or if Elena is completely recovered from the surgery."

Jessica counted on her fingers. "Let's see . . . me, the children, Hank, Jack, Elena, the baby . . . is there anything you *don't* worry about?"

"Money," he said promptly.

"Well then."

"Although with all the talk about switching from the silver standard to paper money, the mines—"

"Am I going to have to spank you?" she said with mock severity.

He grinned. "Would you? I wouldn't mind. Truly. I'll even show you where."

Jessica's soft chuckle vibrated against

his chest. "I have a better idea," she whispered as she rolled toward him.

"ARE YOU DEAD?"

Hank opened his eyes to find cinnamon brown eyes staring down at him out of a tangled mess of blond hair. Penny. Molly had briefly reintroduced the children to him when they had boarded last night, but he still didn't remember either of them from before the derailment. "I don't think so." Although he did feel odd. Itchy and hot one minute, cold the next. And his arm burned like a sonofabitch. "Are we there?" he asked, realizing they had stopped moving. No more rocking and swaying, and without the clatter of the wheels on the track, he could hear the rhythmic exhalations of the idling locomotive.

"I almost had a kitty once. But he went dead. Do you got kitties?"

"Yeah. Probably." Didn't he live on a ranch and didn't most ranches have cats?

"Guess what? My kitty was white all over except for his nose. It was pink. I was gonna name him Sugar. What's your kitty's name?"

"I don't remember."

Propping her elbows beside his shoulder,

she studied him in that frank and disconcerting way children had. "I'm not supposed to talk to you."

"Why not?"

"Aunt Molly said we were never *ever* supposed to talk to strangers."

"I'm not a stranger. I'm your steppapa."

She poked her finger at his cheek. "You're blue."

"I'm bruised and that hurts."

"How come you're wearing a dress?"

"It's not a dress. It's a nightshirt." And he was burning it as soon as he found real clothes to wear. "Where's Molly?" It wasn't that he didn't like children, but this one was such a talker it was giving him a headache. A family trait, he guessed.

"Do you kick kitties?"

He blinked, taken aback by the question. "No." What a strange kid.

"Not even if they scratch your best shoes and poop under your chair?"

"No. Does Molly know you're in here?"

She pulled several strands of blond hair from a tangled knot and stuck them into her mouth. "Steppapas are mean. They hurt."

Hurt who? Kitties? Kids? Hank watched her work the rope of hair with her tongue and wondered what kind of man would do either. “I don’t kick kitties and I don’t hit kids.” And even though he couldn’t remember for sure, he was fairly certain that was the first time he’d ever used the word “kitties.” God, he hoped so.

She stopped chewing. “Ever?”

“Ever.”

“Even if they wet their beds?”

“Nope.”

“What if they’re spying little bastards?”

He tried to hide his shock. “Not even then.”

“Suppose they take something they shouldn’t and are too afraid to put it back so they hide it and then lie and say they don’t know where it is?”

Hank shook his head and smiled, masking his concern while he tried to remember every word so he could question Molly. But his mind felt fuzzy and sluggish, and it was hard to keep everything straight. “Did you take something you shouldn’t have, Penny?”

Her lips clamped shut on the strands of hair. He saw fear in her eyes.

“Penny?”

“I’m not supposed to talk about it.”

“Says who?”

"I can't tell."

"Your brother, Charlie?"

Her gaze slid away.

"I bet he wouldn't mind if you told me."

She shook her head. "The monster will get us and make us dead too." Her eyes teared up. Replacing the hair with her thumb, she said something Hank didn't catch.

Afraid she'd start wailing, he changed the subject. "Would you like a kitty?"

Her mouth formed an "O." The thumb slid out. "Of my very own?"

He nodded. The motion made his head pound. "I don't know if we have any white ones but I'd guess we have some with yellow stripes."

"Sunshine!" she squealed in a high kid voice that ricocheted around his skull like a bullet. "I'll name it Sunshine! Or Tiger! That's a good name, isn't it?"

"Yeah. Great." Hank pressed his good hand to his brow and was surprised to find it slick with sweat. How could he be sweating when he was so cold?

"I have to tell Charlie!" She darted toward the door, then stopped and turned back. "I forgot. Aunt Molly wants me to see if you're awake."

"I'm awake." And feeling worse by the minute. What was wrong with him now? Was he getting a fever?

She started, then stopped again. "Oh! And guess what, Papa-Hank!" She waved skinny arms and danced in a circle. "It's sno-o-ow-ing!"

Which was probably why he was starting to shiver. "Get . . . Molly," he muttered as weariness pulled him down.

SHE SHOULD HAVE EXPECTED IT.

With trembling hands, Molly filled a bowl from a water cask in the galley kitchen. It usually took three days for infection to set in after surgery and it had been that long. But she'd been so sure she'd done everything right, and so careful to keep the wound clean, and Hank was so strong and healthy. What had gone wrong? Was he to lose his arm, after all? She wouldn't even consider the possibility that he could die, that something she did, or forgot to do, might be the cause of his death.

As she added several clean cloths to her medicine basket, Brady came in. "The wagons are loaded. You and the little ones ready?"

"We can't go. Hank's running a fever. Take this." She thrust the bowl of water into his hands.

"Fever? How high?"

"Too high." Nudging him aside, she picked up her medicine basket and rushed down the narrow aisle toward the parlor section.

Brady crowded behind her. "What are you going to do?"

"Bathe him with cool water to bring down the fever. He won't like it."

When they'd reached Hank's makeshift bed, she set the basket on the floor and threw back the covers. Hank's nightshirt was wet with sweat. The rank smell of infection rose from the soaked bedding.

"Won't that wake him up?"

"He's not asleep, he's unconscious. Help me remove his nightshirt."

Setting the bowl of water on a table beside the bed, he pulled a long knife from his boot and cut through the cloth with savage efficiency. "He's already shivering."

"That's his body's way of trying to cool itself down. The cool cloths will help. If you'll bathe his chest and neck and head, I'll check his arm."

While Brady slapped dripping cloths on Hank's bandaged chest, Molly cut through the wrappings on his shattered arm. The incision was swollen and red, and the stink of putrefying flesh almost made her gag. Gently she tugged on the strands of horsehair she'd left for drainage. They didn't move. She pulled harder. Hank groaned and flinched as the ligatures came loose in a rush of blood and pus.

She'd try a drawing poultice first. If that didn't work, she'd have to reopen the incision and cut away any necrotic flesh. If that didn't work, she'd have to amputate. And if that didn't work, he'd be dead.

Dear God. What did I do wrong?

SHE STARTED WITH A HOT FLAX SEED POULTICE, replacing it as soon as it cooled. It worked somewhat. After adding ground mustard, it seemed to draw better. In addition, every thirty minutes she dosed him with aconite solution through a dropper to help with fever and restlessness, and with each third poultice, she flushed his arm with one ounce of carbolic acid mixed in a pint of water. Meanwhile, Brady continued with the cool compresses.

Throughout the day they worked, and by late afternoon, the swelling was down and his fever had dropped below the critical level, although it still remained high.

Taking a break to clear her mind and figure out what more she should do, she left Hank in Brady's care and, donning her coat, stepped out onto the small platform at the front of the parlor car.

It was dusk. The caboose and locomotive and tender were gone, and the parlor car stood alone on a siding next to the main track, slowly disappearing under a mantle of white. Clouds hung heavy and low, and the air was so thick with wood smoke and fog rising from a fast-moving creek nearby, it felt like the world was wrapped in a misty cocoon. Drawing no comfort from it, Molly started back inside.

"Ma'am?"

A woman stepped out of the mist, her face a white oval under a slouch hat dusted with snow. She stopped at the steps leading up to the platform. "Is Hank . . . is he . . ." She cleared her throat. "We were wondering." She gestured over her shoulder toward shadowed buildings beside the track and the darker shadows standing against them. "Will he make it?"

Dozens of shadows. Workers from their mines, waiting for word of Hank. Emotion clogged Molly's throat. Knowing she wasn't alone in this struggle, and that the man she was fighting so hard to save was beloved by so many people, brought the sting of tears to her eyes. "He's alive and holding on," she said. "We're doing all we can, I promise you."

"Praise the Lord," said a voice in the shadows.

"Told you he was too big to die," a man joked.

"Can I help?" the woman at the foot of the steps asked.

Surprised by the offer, Molly hesitated too long. The woman filled the silence with a rush of words. "I don't know much about doctoring, but I'm a hard worker and I can fetch and cook, and Lord knows I've tended men before, so there's no surprises there, if you know what I mean, and I'd be willing to do whatever—"

"Thank you," Molly cut in. "I'd be grateful for your help."

The woman's smile lit up the dark night. She rose on tiptoe and tried to peer into the glass window of the door into the galley. "Looks pretty crowded in there, so I don't know if you have room for anybody else, but there's plenty folks out here who would like to help if they knew what to do."

Molly felt that surge of gratitude again and with it an infusion of energy and hope. "I could use some cheesecloth and a length of oiled flannel or silk. Also a jar of mutton tallow. And if someone could refill the coal bin and water barrel in the galley? And we need food—broth or weak tea, maybe thin gruel. And Hank could use clean bedding if you have it."

"I'll tell them. Anything else?"

Molly thought of Dr. Murray. "Yes," she said with firm resolve. "You can pray. It *always* helps."

"We will." The woman walked back into the shadows.

As Molly opened the door, a man called out, "Good luck to you, ma'am."

"Thank you," Molly said and stepped inside.

* * *

THE WOMAN'S NAME WAS MARTHA BURNETT. After she returned with the items Molly had requested, she took over for Brady, freeing him to check on Jessica and the children, who had moved into the top floor of the Redemption Hotel. She was younger than Molly and pretty in a buxom, overblown way. And quite a talker.

"Do you know Hank well?" Molly asked during a lull between poultices. It would be interesting to get a glimpse of her husband through another woman's eyes.

Martha laughed. "Oh, sure. He's a once-a-weeker. You can set a watch by him." Squeezing cool water from a rag, she spread it gently over Hank's forehead. "And always a gentleman, not like some others I could name. Great stamina. Generous too." She laughed and sent Molly a sly wink. "And not just with money, if you know what I mean."

To her chagrin, Molly was beginning to. Aware of the flush heating her cheeks, she busied herself spreading the hot flax and mustard paste on a clean cloth. She had met prostitutes before. They were as much a part of army life as the field hospitals that followed the troops from camp to camp.

There had even been a few at Andersonville from time to time, brought in to service the Union officers.

This woman had apparently serviced her husband. How embarrassing. And curious. She wasn't at all sure what to think about it. Or say.

Martha didn't seem to note her unease but continued as if the bedroom habits of the Wilkins brothers were a normal topic of conversation. Which, if that were true, was even more disturbing. "Hank's not as inventive as his brother Jack, mind you. But then, who would be?" Martha laughed and shook her head. "Lordy Lord, the things that man could think up. We sure miss him."

I shouldn't be listening to this, Molly thought as she covered the poultice on Hank's arm with a square of oiled flannel to keep the heat in. *How will I ever look any of them in the face again?* Yet she didn't interrupt.

"And built like bulls. All of them. Why, the last time Brady—"

Molly's head snapped up. "Brady is a regular too?" How dare he put on a moral act with her while he was deceiving his wife. That lying—

"Not anymore," Martha said, cutting into Molly's mental tirade. "Not since Miz Jessica showed up. When she's around, that man wouldn't notice an oncoming train much less worn-out whores like us."

Us? Had Molly dropped even lower in status without being aware of it?

Martha's gaze flicked over her, pausing on Molly's less-than-opulent bosom. "How do you know Hank? You one of Hillsboro's new girls? I heard he was having some sent in from New Orleans."

"Ah, no." She felt the other woman studying her, apparently expecting more of an answer. "I'm Hank's wife."

Silence. Molly could sense Martha's astonishment. Or was it disbelief? Amusement? Would it be so unusual that an unremarkable woman like herself would garner a proposal from a man like Hank? Which, of course, she hadn't. But still . . .

Martha finally burst into action, hands flapping in distress as words rushed out. "Oh my Lord. I'm so sorry. I didn't know, ma'am—I mean Miz Wilkins. No one said—holy Christ—I mean—Jesus. I didn't even know Hank was courting—I mean after he went after that girl from the fort—oh ma'am,

I didn't mean nothing, and as for Hank and the girls, that didn't mean nothing either. Just scratching an itch, that's all it was, I swear it. He's a good man. The best. Once he said his vows, he would never break them, I just know it."

Feeling somewhat appeased, Molly patted her shoulder. "It's all right, Martha. All that was before I even met Hank. Water under the bridge. If it's acceptable to you, we'll forget this conversation entirely."

"Oh, yes, ma'am. It never happened. And if it did, I already forgot it."

"Thank you. Hmm. We're out of hot water. Would you mind heating more?"

As Martha happily escaped to get more water, Molly pressed a hand to her flushed cheek and struggled not to laugh. That had to be the most uncomfortable conversation she had ever suffered through. Wouldn't the brothers die if they—

"You need to know more, just ask," a hoarse voice said.

She jumped back, almost crashing into the table beside the bed.

Hank blinked up at her, his expression wryly amused. "Although I doubt there's much you don't know about me by now.

Wish I could say the same . . ." His voice trailed off. His eyes opened and closed in slow, sluggish blinks. "I don't feel so good."

Embarrassment forgotten, Molly studied him, noting the flushed cheeks, the sweat, the too-bright eyes. His fever was rising again. Hurriedly she dampened a cloth in the cold water and draped it over his forehead.

"What's wrong with me?" he mumbled.

She debated worrying him, then realized she had lied to the man too many times already. "Your arm's infected and you're running a fever."

He lay still for so long she wondered if he'd lost consciousness again. With mounting alarm, she dampened another cloth and spread it over the bandages on his chest. Where was Brady?

"Then cut it off."

She jerked her gaze back to his. "What?"

"If it's killing me, cut it off."

The words sent terror pounding through her chest. It was a moment before she could find the breath to respond. "No. Absolutely not. Not unless I have to."

He looked at her. She recognized in his eyes a man who saw his own death and wasn't afraid. It made her want to scream at him for giving up so easily. "No!" she said again, louder, sharper. Leaning over him, she took his face in her hands. His cheeks were rough with whiskers and felt hot against her palms. She could almost feel the life ebbing from him. "You will not die," she said fiercely. "I will not allow it! Do you understand?"

His fever-cracked lips split in a slow, crooked smile—the first he'd ever given her. "Sweet Molly," he whispered. Then his eyes rolled back into his head.

"No!" she cried, shaking him. "Don't leave me!"

Martha appeared at her side. "Lordy, what's wrong?"

Seeing the fear in the other woman's face helped Molly gain control of her own. Thoughts raced through her mind with sudden sharp clarity. This was good. He was insensate. He wouldn't feel pain when she opened up his arm.

She rummaged through the medicine basket for what she would need. "Boil these," she ordered, handing Martha a pair of scissors, two scalpels, and tubes of needles and horsehair ligatures. And this." She added a roll of gauze to the pile. "Cut it into six-inch strips first. And find another lamp."

As Martha rushed out, Molly called after her. "And send someone for Brady. I'll need him in case Hank wakes up. Tell him to hurry."

MOLLY HAD NEVER WANTED TO BE A NURSE. SHE had never felt that compelling need to tend the sick or do battle with disease that drove others into the healing professions. She had simply wanted to be with Papa.

After Mama died and her older sister moved to Savannah, he was all she had left. And she knew with a child's certainty that he would leave her too if she didn't make herself so useful he would have no reason to move on without her.

So she became his apprentice, his unwilling assistant within the nightmare walls of the surgical room. She never liked it. She never grew accustomed to the sickness and blood, or the pain she often brought to patients already in agony. And no matter how hard she tried, she couldn't harden herself to the suffering or step back far enough to see the good that might come from her clumsy efforts. In misplaced sympathy, she writhed along with her patients, which did them little good and left her trembling with nausea. But because of Papa she muddled through, trying to do less harm than good and vomiting in despair when it was over. It ripped a hole in her soul every time.

But now with Hank . . . something had changed. She felt no doubt. No flinching uncertainty. No will-sapping sympathy.

She would do this. She would save Hank because he needed her and she owed him and she couldn't bear that he should die. She wouldn't weaken this time.

When Brady came back, she was ready.

"I'm going to reopen the incision," she told him. "I have to cut away the dead tissue and clean out the wound. Every two hours it must be flushed with bromine solution then repacked with gauze and mutton tallow."

As she spoke, Brady's face lost color, but he didn't interrupt.

"We must keep him from injuring his arm while it's exposed," Molly went on. "Strap him down if necessary."

"He won't like that."

"Then you'll have to restrain him. Can

you do that? If not, I'll have to administer chloroform, which might be a risk in his weakened state."

"I'll hold him."

Molly studied him, seeing the lines of fatigue, the terror in his ice blue eyes. He looked like he'd aged a decade in the last few days. But she couldn't worry about that now.

Pushing sympathy aside, she rested her hand on his arm. "Don't fail me, Brady."

He met her gaze without flinching. "I won't. My word."

"Good. Let's get started."

Seven

HANK AWOKE TO BRIGHT SUNLIGHT AND THE awareness that something had changed. The pain wasn't so bad, and he no longer felt like he was fighting his way through swirling black fog. He could think again. And the first thing he thought of was his arm. Was it gone? Had she cut it off?

He didn't want to know.

Not yet.

But he looked anyway.

Still there. Still whole.

Relief hit so hard, he shuddered. He still felt weak, but not sick and not trapped in that empty place that made him feel like he was drowning.

He was alive. He was going to make it.

Movement against his right side startled him, and he looked down to see a woman in a chair next to his bed. She was asleep, bent forward with her head resting on her crossed arms beside his hip. He recognized the sorrel hair. Molly. His wife.

When had he taken a wife?

He remembered confusing dreams broken by times of wakefulness when he rose out of the void to find her gently stroking his brow, or whispering words of reassurance in her soft Southern voice, or one time crying softly while she did something to his arm. He remembered watching her across a crowd of people sitting in benches on a train, then another time, seeing her asleep in the bed beside his. He remembered wanting to tell her he was sorry, although he wasn't sure why or for what. He remembered his brother and Jessica. He remembered . . .

Sweet Jesus.

He remembered.

Heart pounding, he watched a kaleidoscope of images flash through in his mind.

Jack laughing. Sam trying to teach the hound to dance. Brady watching Jessica cross the yard. His parents. Elena, Sancho's sister and the daughter of the previous owner of the ranch. The way the sky turned brown when the ranch burned. The hillside rushing toward him when they dynamited Sancho's cave.

Faster and faster the images came. The new house. The mines. Laying the first section of track on the spur line. Loading the part for the concentrator then boarding the passenger car in Sierra Blanca, then . . .

. . . nothing . . .

. . . until he woke up in El Paso at that doctor's house.

It was all there. Everything but her.

How could that be? What happened during that train ride?

He looked down at the woman sleeping at his side. How could he forget some things and remember others? And how could he meet a woman, marry her, then lose all memory of her during the time it took to travel from Sierra Blanca to El Paso? It made no sense.

Lifting his right hand, he brushed a glossy curl from her cheek, wanting her to wake up and look at him, hoping when she did, it would free the memories trapped somewhere in his head.

He wanted to remember her.

The way she smelled, the way her breasts fit his hands, the look on her face when he moved inside her. He wanted to remember the sound of her laughter. He wanted to know if he loved her and why he had taken a wife when he'd come to accept that he would live his life alone. He wanted to know where all those memories had gone and how he could get them back.

He needed to remember her.

"Look at me," he said.

With a jerk, she opened her eyes. She sat up, blinking groggily until her gaze focused on his. He watched emotions flit across her expressive face—joy, relief, then worry, and finally something that almost looked like dread.

"You remember," she said.

He sensed her withdrawal, and it confused him. He didn't know what to say to her, how to tell the woman with whom he'd exchanged vows and shared a bed that she was a stranger to him. Reaching out, he cupped her cheek, tracing the smooth arc of her cheekbone with his thumb. "I do," he said. "Everything but you."

"Oh."

He wasn't sure what he'd expected—tears, anger, disappointment—something more than "Oh." Instead, she seemed to turn to stone. It concerned him the way she stared at him without blinking, without even breathing. Wanting to dispel that feeling of distance growing between them, he gave her a half-smile. "So I guess we'll have to start over. Make new memories."

She moved then, her mouth opening and closing twice before any words came out. "Is that what you want? To stay married?"

Surprised, he let his hand fall back to his side. "Why wouldn't I want to stay married?"

She looked down and began fussing with her skirts. "Since you don't remember me, I thought, well, perhaps you'd prefer to just forget the whole thing."

"Forget we're married?" Which was exactly what he'd done, although not in the way she meant it. Suddenly his defenses came up. "Why? Don't you want to stay with me?" He'd heard that excuse before.

Her gaze flew to his, then quickly away. "It's not that, it's just that, well, if your feelings have changed . . ."

"Changed from what? Do you think because I don't remember you, I can't still care for you?" He had no memory of whether he had cared for her or not, but judging by the way he felt about her now, with her being almost a stranger to him, he must have cared for her a lot when she wasn't. A stranger, that is. Before he forgot her.

Jesus. He was getting a headache with all this thinking and wondering and not remembering. He had to put an end to it before he was too confused to think at all. "Let's just let it ride for now, okay? Get to know each other again if that would make you feel better. Maybe my memory will return, and we can go on as if nothing happened. If not, we'll start over. Pretend we're courting or something."

It was starting to sound less fun by the minute. He didn't like courting. He didn't know how to act or what to say, and the one time he'd tried it—other than with Molly, apparently—he'd felt big and awkward and clumsy. So much easier if he could just say, "We're married. Take off your clothes." Neat and simple.

He glanced at her, wondering if he should give it a try.

Her expression said not.

Just as well. He wasn't feeling that perky.

"Well, I suppose we could do that," she finally said. "If you're sure."

He wasn't sure of anything but nodded anyway. He was just relieved to have most of his memory back. And if he had to court a wife for the second time he didn't remember from the first time, well . . . he'd do it . . . and hope they got to that taking-off-the-clothes part before he was so old he started losing his memory all over again.

With a weary sigh, he closed his eyes, wishing he had his strength back and was free of this stinking nightshirt. "When can I go home?" he asked, trying not to whine.

"A couple of days if you have no fever and you're up to it."

Real clothes. Real food. Thank you, Jesus. "I'll be up to it."

THEY LEFT BY CARRIAGE TWO DAYS LATER, bundled in their warmest clothes and flanked by the outriders Brady insisted accompany his family whenever they were away from the ranch. Jessica, anxious to return to her children, had left the day before. Brady planned to follow later that day, after tending to mine issues his brother wasn't up to yet—apparently Hank ran the mining business, while Brady oversaw the ranching and cattle interests. So it was just she and Hank and the children riding in the large, well-sprung closed carriage, which, judging by the garish décor, Brady must have borrowed from the madam at the local brothel—how did he explain *that* to his wife?

With so many people inside, the coach stayed fairly warm despite the gusty November wind that rattled the small glass windows from time to time. It was no longer snowing, but the higher they rode into the mountains, the lower the temperature dropped until the muddy track gave way to frozen ruts.

Molly could see that the constant jarring bothered Hank. To distract him as well as introduce the children to the place where they would reside for the indeterminate future, she asked what the name "RosaRoja Rancho" meant.

"Red Rose Ranch," he explained. "It was

named that in '39 when the previous owners planted a hundred rosebushes along the foundation of the house to commemorate the birth of Sancho, their son."

"How lovely."

"Not really," he said dryly. "They were destroyed by that same son when he burned the ranch to the ground thirty years later. Jessica planted yellow roses when we rebuilt."

"Then why isn't it called Yellow Rose Ranch?"

This time he almost smiled. "We changed the name to Wilkins Cattle and Mining to make a new start. But everybody still calls it RosaRoja."

"Why did he burn it?"

He shifted and resituated his injured arm. "It's a long story."

"You'd rather I recite poetry? Or sing?"

Even in their short acquaintance, Molly had learned Hank wasn't much of a talker. In fact, he volunteered as little information as possible. But rather than attribute it to shyness, as Brady did, she had decided Hank was just naturally reticent. When he had something to say, he spoke. When he didn't, he didn't.

But she had no intention of traveling for several hours in silence, or worse, listening to children squabble over the least little thing to relieve their boredom. Either Hank would talk, or she would. And since she'd already heard everything she had to say, she preferred to listen to him.

"Tell us why he burned it," she prodded.

"Yeah, tell us, Papa-Hank," Penny seconded. She loved stories.

With reluctance, he did. "It was all part of a feud that started years ago," he began, "over a tract of land granted a century earlier to the Ramirez family by Charles the Second of Spain. Not a big grant. Eighty-eight thousand six hundred and forty acres—or one hundred thirty-eight-and-a-half square miles, to be precise."

And Molly had noted that Hank was markedly precise whenever numbers were involved. In fact, during his crisis, when his temperature had risen so high it had brought on feverish dreams, she had heard him mumble numbers several times. When she had asked Brady about it, he had told her his brother often did sums in his sleep—sort of Hank's way of calming his mind whenever something preyed on him.

"He can do all kinds of calculations in his head," Brady had expounded, then had gone on to add, "Besides being a looker with a talent for growing hair and a gift for numbers, he also has a magical touch when it came to fixing things or gentling horses or knocking a fractious mule to its knees with a single punch. Helluva thing."

She had thought he was joking. He wasn't. The man had the oddest sense of humor, which was definitely a family trait.

As was their love for their land. As Hank described his ranch to her and the children, his eyes sparkled and the words flew, proving her supposition that he could be quite talkative when the subject was important to him.

"It's got good water and grass, which is a rarity for this country," he continued. "Which makes RosaRoja more valuable than a lot of the larger grants, especially now that it has two silver mines and its own spur line to the transcontinental."

Two mines *and* a spur line? No wonder Brady assumed she'd been after Hank's money. "How long have you owned it?" she asked.

"More than twenty years." He turned to

look out the window. "Our pa first saw the RosaRoja Valley back in '48 when he joined up with the Missouri Volunteers and left Saint Joseph to fight in the Mexican War. It was all he talked about in his letters home . . . the high emerald valley where a man could be his own king." His expression hardened. "We didn't know at the time that he'd set his sights on more than just the land."

He frowned at the distant mountains for a moment, as if lost in thought, then with a sigh, resumed his story. "After Mexico lost the war, the Hildalgo Treaty required the owners of all the old grants to refile their patents with the provisional government in Santa Fe and pay their taxes. But Pa figured the owner of the valley, Don Ramon Ramirez, wouldn't do it. Too proud. The old man considered himself Spanish, not Mexican. He didn't think he should be bound by any treaty between Mexico and the United States. But he was wrong. When the deadline passed and Don Ramon didn't reregister, Pa filed a claim, paid the back taxes, and that was that. RosaRoja became Wilkins land, free and clear. And that was when all the trouble started."

"Did he fight your papa?" Penny asked.

"Don Ramon? Not much." Hank looked at the child for a moment, although Molly sensed he was focused not on her, but on his newly found memories. By his expression, she guessed they weren't pleasant ones. "But his son, Sancho, did."

Penny frowned and stuck a twist of hair into her mouth. "Was he mean?"

"He was. Crazy too."

Charlie turned from the window and looked at Hank, but said nothing.

"Did he kick kitties?" Penny asked.

"Mostly he kicked his sister, Elena." Hank must have seen Penny's fear because he quickly added, "But she's fine. In fact, we think she married our brother."

Hoping to turn the conversation to more pleasant thoughts, Molly asked how many brothers there were in the family.

Hank seemed surprised by the question. "Four. Brady, then me, then Jack. Jack is the one who followed Elena when she went to California to have her hip operated on. Haven't heard from them since. Sam was the youngest." His tone suggested she should already know that, which if they had truly courted and married, she would have.

Molly met his gaze without wavering or offering explanations. She was through lying to this man. If asked, she would tell him the truth. If not . . . well, until he figured it out on his own, she would, as he suggested, let it ride.

"Is Sam at your ranch?" Penny asked.

"He is." Hank turned back to the window. Molly watched his breath fog the thin glass, and wondered what memories plagued him now. "He's buried there."

They rode in silence for a time, then Penny said, "I almost had a kitty once."

"Sugar." Hank turned to smile at his stepdaughter. "With the pink nose."

"He went dead."

"I remember."

"Did the bad man hurt Sam?" Penny was chewing her hair again.

"He did."

Molly didn't like where this conversation was going, but before she could steer it to a less upsetting subject, Charlie blurted out, "Did you hurt him back?"

She looked at him in surprise. Those were the first words he had uttered since the initial bickering with Penny when they had boarded. For the last two hours he had huddled against the door beside her, staring out the window, his face set in that perpetually worried scowl.

If Hank was surprised, he didn't show it. "If I'd had the chance, I would have."

The boy's face paled. "He's still out there?"

"No. He's dead. Your Aunt Jessica killed him."

Molly was appalled.

The hair slid out of Penny's gaping mouth. "Aunt Jessica killed him?"

"I bet she shot him," Charlie said savagely. "I bet she stuck a gun in his mouth and pulled the trigger and shot him dead. That would have killed him good."

Molly was too shocked to speak. Why had Charlie said such a horrible thing? Didn't he know that's how his grandfather died? Anger blasted through her—anger at Charlie for being so unfeeling—anger at all those who so readily believed her father would take his own life—anger at Papa for leaving her.

"Molly?" Hank touched her arm. "Are you all right?"

Anger faded so abruptly she felt shaky and disoriented. She saw faces staring at her and forced a smile. "I—I'm fine. A bit weary. The rocking motion—"

"I'll have them stop." He turned toward the small door above his seat that opened into the driver's box.

"Don't." Leaning forward, she pressed her fingertips on his knee. "It's not necessary. Let's go a bit farther, then have the lunch Jessica had the hotel prepare." Removing her hand, she sat back. She was flattered by his concern. But also a bit troubled. She didn't want him to take his husbandly duties too seriously.

"Meanwhile," she said brightly to her niece and nephew in an attempt to dispel the gloomy mood, "you two should try to nap. We've a long way to go, and if there is any daylight left when we arrive, I know you'll want to play in the snow." Glancing at Hank, she explained that, being from Atlanta, they didn't often see snow. "Penny's been talking about building a snowman since the first flake fell."

"Maybe we can have a snowball fight," Hank suggested.

Penny pressed against Molly's side. "I don't like fighting." She stuck her thumb into her mouth. "It hurth."

Hank regarded her for a moment. Then he leaned forward and said quietly, “I’ll watch out for you, Penny. I’ll make sure it doesn’t hurt.”

The child met his gaze solemnly, her cheeks working. “You promith?” she asked without taking the thumb from her mouth.

“I promise.”

“Okay.” Snuggling closer to Molly, she closed her eyes.

And as simply as that he won over a worried, fearful child. Molly wondered why it was so difficult for her to do the same. She loved these children. She was desperate to keep them safe. Why couldn’t they see that?

An hour later, when the sun was high overhead, reflecting off the snow in blinding sparkles, they stopped for the picnic. Molly encouraged the children to play in the snow to wear off excess energy, but the cold soon chased them back into the coach. A half-hour later, they resumed their journey. Lulled by the rocking coach and their full stomachs, the children finally slept, Penny tilted against her right side, Charlie sitting on her left as far away from her as he could get. Hank sat across from them, lost in thoughts as he watched the snowy landscape bounce past the window.

With a nurse's eye, she studied him, checking for the flush of fever, swelling in the fingers of his bandaged arm, signs of increased pain. When she detected none, she studied him as a woman—more than a nurse, but not quite a wife. He was so big his shoulders spanned more than half the bench seat. His long legs and big feet took up most of the narrow space between the benches, and his dark hair almost brushed against the tufted ceiling. Even weakened by illness and rendered virtually immobile by his injuries, he seemed capable of handling any crisis.

What was it Jessica had called him? The steady one.

The beautiful one. With his size and stern demeanor, he should have been overpowering. Instead, with just a few words, he had gained a wary child's trust.

With sudden and frightening clarity, Molly realized she had come to care for Hank in ways that would only bring her pain. If she allowed herself to, she could become deeply attached to this man, and that would never do.

As if sensing the direction of her thoughts, Hank turned from the window and looked directly into her eyes.

She froze, pinned by that sharply focused gaze. It felt like he was seeing into her mind, as if he were trying to read a message written on the back wall of her skull. What did he see when he looked at her that way? A wife he didn't remember? Or another woman he couldn't trust, just like the one who had betrayed him at the fort by running off with another man?

I'm not like that, she told him silently. *I wouldn't betray you.*

But she already had, hadn't she?

"I didn't mean to upset them." He spoke softly in deference to the sleeping children.

"I know."

"But I won't lie to them."

She held back a bitter smile. No, Hank would never lie. He would never feel the need to deceive or manipulate or coddle to achieve his ends. Life would never hand him more than he could handle.

"This is hard country," he said when she didn't respond. "And sometimes we have to make hard choices. It's not civilized like in the city. The rules are different here. If a dog goes bad, you shoot it. No vote, no trying to make it better, no calling someone else to take care of it. You do what you have to, then you move on."

Molly watched, unable to look away as his expression became brutally cold. It was in the eyes, his beautiful, warm, chocolate brown eyes. They seemed to darken until she couldn't tell pupil from iris, until they looked as hard and unfeeling as dark polished stones. They held no softness. No forgiveness or mercy.

And it terrified her to know that someday when he realized how she'd deceived him, that implacable expression would be directed at her.

He leaned forward. "Sancho killed a lot of people, including his parents," he said in a low, clipped voice. "He tortured Sam and left him in the desert to die. He tied Brady in the burning barn. When he stole Jessica away, she realized she couldn't wait for someone to come rescue her. She had to take care of herself. So she hit him with a lit lantern and set him on fire. Harsh times call for hard choices, Molly. And sugar-coated half-truths won't change that." He sat back.

She thought of the suffering Sancho had brought to this family and felt faintly ill. But to burden Penny and Charlie with that knowledge would destroy their innocence. “They’re just children, Hank.”

“Sam was twelve when he died. Maybe if we had warned him, taught him to be less trusting and more cautious . . .” He shrugged, then continued. “The point is, Jessica was prepared. She knew what she had to do and she did it. That’s why she survived.”

Molly sensed his guilt and despair. She didn’t know what she could say to make it go away, so she said nothing.

“I’m just saying the children need to be aware,” he said. “For now, I’ll leave that to you. But if they ask, I’ll tell them the truth. I won’t lie.”

Beside her, the children began to stir, so Molly said no more. And really, what could she say? Hank would never understand that when it came to hard choices, lying might be the best one.

It was early afternoon when he turned from the window with a big grin. “We just crossed the boundary line.”

Molly felt as if someone had knocked

the breath from her lungs. "Oh my," she said when she finally found her wits again. All those lovely teeth.

His grin faded. "What's wrong?"

"You should do that more often."

"Do what?"

"Smile."

He blinked at her. "I smile all the time."

"No you don't, Papa-Hank," Penny chimed in.

Now he looked disconcerted—another new expression. "Well, I mean to."

"Mean-tos don't count. Isn't that so, Aunt Molly?" In her delight to be instructing someone much older and many times larger, Penny drummed her heels against the front of the bench seat—in the exact tempo of the pounding throb that bounced between Molly's temples. Resting a hand on her niece's knobby knee, she said quietly, "Would you please stop that, dear?"

"Stop what?"

Charlie leaned forward to glare past Molly at his sister. "Hitting your feet on the seat, you stupid baby."

"I'm not a baby!"

"Charlie," Molly began, reaching for his arm.

He jerked it from her grip. “Leave me alone!” Turning toward the window, he sat with his shoulders hunched, his wiry body as far from Molly’s as he could get it.

Humiliated by the rebuff, Molly didn’t pursue it. Instead she gave Hank an apologetic smile. “He’s just tired. We all are.”

Hank didn’t respond. But that hard look was back in his eyes.

The tension within the coach built with every turn of the wheels. Sandwiched between the two children, Molly had no escape from it. Too weary to attempt conversation and too embarrassed by her ineptitude with the children to face Hank, she stared past Penny’s blond head toward the window.

It was a daunting view.

They were descending into a vast, snow-covered valley that stretched for miles in each direction. Winding down the middle was a tree-lined creek. The trees were bare now, their branches bowing under a burden of snow. Tall evergreens bordered the valley, spilling down from deep canyons carved into the steep slopes rising on all sides. Above the timberline, folded slabs of weathered rock, gouged and scored as if giant talons had been dragged through clay, ended in snow-capped peaks that cut a scalloped edge against the cloudless sky. It was savagely beautiful, and Molly easily understood how a man from the flatlands of Missouri might risk everything to own it.

Two hours later they passed under a high wrought iron arch with back-to-back R's across the top. Suspended below it and waffling in the wind hung a thick wooden plank with the words WILKINS CATTLE AND MINING carved in foot-high letters.

Craning her neck to see as far ahead as she could, Molly noticed a rambling two-and-a-half-story log and stone house at the end of the drive. Rising behind the house was a hill dominated by a single drooping tree. Beside it, half-hidden under a mantle of snow, was a small fenced cemetery, the white-shrouded tombstones silhouetted against the lowering sun.

A sense of isolation, of being thrust into an alien place, assailed her. In another week, a carriage would never make it back through the pass to Redemption. They would be trapped here until spring with people they scarcely knew. What if Hank remembered and called her to accounts for what she'd done? What if he really did have the nasty temper Brady mentioned? And what if he unleashed that temper on her and the children? She wouldn't be able to escape him or this place until the thaw.

Frowning, she glanced over to find Hank watching her, his face revealing nothing of his thoughts. She forced a nervous smile. "It's a beautiful place."

"It is."

A space opened between them, growing wider with each thudding heartbeat. She told herself to stop being fanciful. Hank had never given her reason to fear him.

But she'd never seen him angry either.

The coach shuddered to a stop. A moment later, footsteps crunched in the snow, then the door opened. Their driver grinned at them. "Still alive, I see."

"Barely," Hank muttered. He exited first, holding the doorframe for balance as he stepped onto the icy surface. As he moved aside, the driver reached in for Penny. She hung back until Molly whispered it was all right, then she reluctantly let him scoop her up by the waist. Handling her like a prized vase, he set her carefully on the frozen ground then turned back for Molly.

Hank was there first. Reaching past him, he extended his right hand, palm up. Molly took it. Once she touched ground and found her footing, he let her go. Charlie refused his help, jumping down unaided and almost slipping on the ice before he grabbed the wheel. Molly started to steer the children toward the house when Hank rested his good hand on her nephew's shoulder.

"I need to say something to Charlie," he said in a calm tone that belied the hard glint she saw in his eyes. "You go on. We'll be there directly."

She hesitated, glancing from Hank's determined face to Charlie's scowling one. She sensed a confrontation brewing, perhaps over Charlie's earlier rudeness. He was her responsibility—she should take care of it, not Hank. But, God forgive her, she didn't have the strength for it just then.

Hank read her concern. "It's all right, Molly. We'll only be a minute."

Hoping she wasn't making a mistake, she followed Penny toward the house.

ONCE MOLLY WAS OUT OF EARSHOT, HANK turned Charlie to face him and hunkered down so their eyes were almost on the same level. "Don't do that again," he said.

Charlie shot him a sullen glare. "Do what?"

"What you're doing now. Being a rude little sonofabitch."

Hank saw the word shocked the boy, which was why he'd used it. Having gained the kid's attention, he continued. "When I married Molly, you became part of my family whether you like it or not. And the men in my family don't treat women the way you treated your Aunt Molly. It's unworthy and cowardly."

The boy stared at the ground, a flush inching up his neck until the tips of his ears were as red as beets. "I'm not a coward."

Hank didn't agree or disagree. He just looked at the boy, waiting to see if he had anything else to say. When he didn't, Hank continued, keeping his tone conversational but determined. "I know you're angry. If you want to tell me why, I'll be glad to listen. But right now that doesn't matter. What matters is not taking that anger out on people weaker than you, like your sister and Molly."

Charlie gave him a look of disbelief. "Aunt Molly's much bigger than me."

"But she's a girl. They're not as strong as us. Which is why we have to protect them and be gentle with them even when they make us mad." He allowed a tight smile. "Especially when they make us mad."

Charlie studied his feet, but Hank noted his ears had faded to more of a peach color. "So find a better way," he told the boy.

"Like what?"

"Chew jerky. Kick rocks. Cuss up a streak when they're not around to hear you. Just don't take it out on them."

"I'm not allowed to cuss."

"Me neither. That's why I wait until I'm past the corrals before I start."

The kid's stony face almost cracked into a smile.

Satisfied, Hank rose. He looked down at the bent head, and for one stark moment saw Sam in the dark auburn curls and the square set of the skinny shoulders. The image brought such a tightness to his chest he couldn't draw a full breath.

Or maybe that was the bindings around his ribs. Soon as he got inside, he was cutting them off, no matter what Nurse Molly said.

"We understand each other?" he asked.

Charlie continued to stare at the ground.

"No? Yes?"

Still, nothing.

Hank sighed. "I need an answer, Charlie, before I freeze my balls off."

"Okay."

"Okay, what?"

"Okay, I understand."

"Then let's go get something to eat."

FROM THE PORCH, MOLLY WATCHED THEM COME toward the house, trying to gauge their moods by their expressions. Neither seemed angry, although Charlie carefully avoided looking at her as he came up the steps. Hank had the satisfied look of a man pleased with his own competence. Molly refrained from snorting at the notion.

After Charlie went inside, Hank looked back at her. "You coming?"

For some perverse reason she hesitated, sensing that once she crossed over that threshold, she would be moving away from everything she knew toward something unknown and unexpected. "In a minute," she answered, needing a bit more time before she took that irrevocable step.

Hank went inside.

As the door closed behind him, she turned to look down the valley. Stark, unrelieved white. Not a single cloud softened the icy blue of the sky. Not a single sound interrupted the stillness. The vista was immense. The silence deafening. The emptiness as stifling as a hand at her throat.

With a shiver, she stepped inside.

Eight

IT WAS AN IMPRESSIVE HOUSE, EQUAL TO SOME of the plantation homes that had risen out of the cotton fields throughout the South before they were destroyed by war. However, this dwelling was no reflection of graceful Georgian architecture, but more in keeping with the raw landscape of towering mountains and up-thrust ridges and piney canyons that surrounded it. This home was a reflection of the family that built it. Massive. Sturdy. Commanding.

The structure was laid out in a rectangular design, the center having three stories, with two-story wings jutting out on either side. A broad porch stretched across the front of the house, shaded by the overhanging second and third stories. As Molly stepped into the entry, she saw a log-banistered, U-shaped staircase rising along the entry wall on the left, and on the right, rows of hooks and shelves, now filled with jackets, hats, tall boots, and snowshoes. Beside the staircase, a long, open hallway ran past a dining area and through an archway that Molly assumed led into the kitchen. To the right of the entry, the hall stretched past a reading area and through another archway into the east wing. But the heart of the house was the huge open room across from the double entry doors.

After removing her coat and hanging it on a peg, Molly crossed toward it, stepping down onto slate floors over which lay woven Indian rugs in striking geometric designs. Half of the room was covered by a second-story mezzanine. The other half extended twenty or more feet up through two levels of exposed beam work that supported both the mezzanine and the third story. On the back wall stood a massive rock fireplace, flanked by banks of mullioned windows and French doors that framed a breathtaking view of snow-capped mountains. The mantle was an eight-foot-long, two-foot-wide slab of timber supported by two carved bighorn rams' heads. Before the fireplace stood several oversized chairs, a rocker, couches, and assorted tables, arranged for comfort rather than symmetry. Footed oil lamps lit the room, as well as a huge, ornate chandelier made of antlers and entwined ironwork. It would have looked absurd in any room but this, Molly thought. But here, with the combination of stone and log, it fit perfectly.

The reading area at the east end of the room boasted bookcases and a smaller rock fireplace on the interior wall, and overhead, a smaller version of the antler and iron chandelier. In addition to a long reading table and a pair of wingback chairs, there was a low table with children-sized chairs beside a small bookcase overflowing with primers and children's books. In the western end of the room, the dining area also had its own fireplace and antler chandelier, as well as a table that would easily seat twenty and two glass-fronted china hutches on the interior wall. All along the back of the giant room and interspersed between huge log support posts, the French doors opened onto the back porch, which was uncovered, except where cantilevered balconies jutted out from the second-story bedrooms.

The scent of pine permeated the air, giving the sense that the house was a living, breathing thing. Oddly, despite its daunting proportions, this huge open room had a welcoming feel to it, and judging by the clutter of tables and shelves throughout, it was less a showcase room than a well-used family gathering place.

"Rather much, is it not?"

Turning, Molly saw Jessica walking toward her.

"I certainly thought so when I first arrived," Jessica added with a chuckle as she stopped beside her. "Brady designed it, you see." She gave the room an assessing look, then shrugged. "But really, where else could the Wilkins brothers live? It so perfectly suits them. I had to make a few changes, of course. But once I removed the guns and tack and dead things, it was much better."

"Dead things?"

Jessica wrinkled her freckled nose.

"Taxidermy. It's all the rage since the war. Ghastly. Why men think having decapitated animals leering down from the walls would enhance a room is beyond me. I managed to move out everything but the buffalo in Jack's bedroom, which I hope he will remove when he comes home, and the ten-foot grizzly in Brady's office, which he insisted on keeping despite the smell. Shall I give you a tour now, or would you prefer to go directly to your room?"

Recovering from her astonishment at the idea of having large dead animals in one's bedroom, Molly looked around. "I'm more concerned with finding the children. I seem to have lost them."

"They're fine. Dougal took them upstairs to meet Ben and Abigail." Taking Molly's arm, she steered her toward the staircase. "Molly, I'm so glad you're here. It will be like having a sister again. I so want to chat with you, but I can see you're tired, so we'll talk later. Let's get you and the children settled, then a long hot bath. How does that sound?"

"Heavenly."

Molly hadn't slept well the last few nights, worrying over Hank and the children and whether she was doing the right thing coming to this remote ranch. The prospect of a bath and a real bed rather than a fold-down cot in a narrow train car would go a long way to restoring her spirits.

At the top of the staircase, Jessica turned right along the mezzanine. On one side, it overlooked the main room, and on the other, it was lined with several doors. She explained that this section was hers and Brady's area, and it consisted of a master suite and water closet at one end of the hall, with a small adjoining bedroom that had been converted into an infant room, and at the opposite end, a linen pantry and two small bedrooms separated by another water closet.

"This is Hank's section," she said as they continued through the archway into the east wing of the house. "The west wing is Jack's."

"The missing brother?"

Jessica frowned and shook her head. "He's not missing. He's simply busy. I'm sure he will find his way home soon. There are four bedrooms in this wing," she went on briskly. "These two"—she pointed to two doors on the right—"have their own dressing rooms and share a water closet. Penny and Charlie can sleep there unless you'd prefer they stay in the children's nursery upstairs."

She must have seen Molly's surprise. "I know. It does seem rather too grand for a ranch house . . . three sprawling stories. But I do so love having the family together under one roof rather than spread out in several smaller houses. That's the way Bickersham Hall is laid out—that's my home in England—and I wanted the same here, so we converted the attic into a nursery. Family is so important, don't you think? And what could be lovelier than a house full of life and laughter? Especially," she added with an impish smile, "if the children's rooms are on another floor entirely."

"Your children don't stay with you?" Jessica was such a mother hen, Molly couldn't imagine her being separated from her children for long.

As they passed a hall table, Jessica swept her hand across the top then checked her fingers for dust. Apparently she found none.

"They stay in the room next to ours,"

she went on, "until they are able to sleep through the night. Abigail moved upstairs about a month ago. I still sleep fitfully, expecting to hear her awaken, but I'm doing better."

Pausing to straighten a lovely floral watercolor, she sent Molly a rueful smile. "However, *she* is doing beautifully, which is a bit lowering, I must say. One would think she would be sad to leave her mum, but alas, not."

"The children sleep on the top floor?"

Jessica chuckled. "Not alone, I assure you. Ben is entirely too wild to be unsupervised, even at night." Bending, she picked up a gingham doll and set it on a hall chair. "There is a large dormitory-style sleeping area, a water closet adjoining a suite for the Garcia sisters, Lupe and Maria, who look after the children, and also a play area with books, art supplies, a piano, some horrid tom-tom drums Brady bought, and entirely too many toys. I'm sure Ben and Abigail would love having Penny and Charlie stay up there with them."

Molly wasn't certain she wanted them that far away, especially in a strange house with people they scarcely knew. Charlie was still having nightmares, and she felt she should be near if he awoke. "I'll check with them, then we can decide."

As they continued through Hank's wing, Jessica nodded to a door on the left. "That bedroom also has its own dressing room, although it shares a bath and water closet with the master bedroom. And this," she said, pushing open the double doors at the end of the hall, "is the master bedroom for this wing." Stepping back so Molly could precede her into the room, she added with a smile, "It's one of my favorites."

Molly could see why. It was a lovely corner room, full of sunlight. The colors were muted and calming, pale yellows and beiges with soft pastel blue touches in the rug on the polished floor, and on the quilt atop the oversized bed, and in the woven tie-backs on the pale beige drapes. On one side of the bed, a French door opened onto a balcony. On the other exterior wall stood a rock fireplace bracketed by bookcases and two large windows. On the wall to the left of the door, a wardrobe and bureau framed the doorway into the dressing area and bath. The room was a subtle blend of the masculine and feminine—the log walls adorned with pastoral paintings, the upholstered wingback chairs dressed up with ruffled pillows and lace doilies, the wood floor softened by a thick rug in a subtle floral design.

"It's beautiful," Molly said. She looked around, trying to picture Hank in this luxurious room. The bed would certainly accommodate his height, but the ruffled pillows seemed unlike him. In fact, she saw little of Hank in the room—no knickknacks, no books waiting on the nightstand, no boots by the bed—nothing to indicate a man resided here. She wasn't sure what she expected, but certainly not this restrained elegance with its soft feminine touches. "It's a very comfortable room."

Jessica looked pleased. She moved silently through the room, her hands reaching out to touch this, straighten that. "I'm glad you like it."

Molly noticed atop the fireplace mantle the scattered remnants of what had once been an ornate shelf clock. "Is that an Ormolu clock?" she asked.

"It was." Jessica came to stand beside her. "Until Hank tinkered with it." She sighed and shook her head. "The man has an insatiable curiosity about how things work and will dismantle anything he can get his hands on. I suggest you keep an eye on your belongings." Moving toward the French doors beside the bed, Jessica stared past the balcony to the hilltop cemetery and the mountains rising beyond it. "Some people might find a view of a graveyard off-putting, but I . . . I find it comforting." A momentary sadness crossed her face. Then with a determined smile, she turned and said, "I furnished this room as the master suite, but Hank thought it too grand for him, so he took the smaller room that adjoins the bath."

"So no one uses this lovely room?"

"I hope you will. I thought under the circumstances, you might prefer your own room."

"Under what circumstances?" a deep voice asked.

Startled, Molly looked over to see Hank in the doorway, her traveling case under his good arm, his saddlebags thrown over his shoulder.

"There you are." Jessica crossed to the wardrobe. "Put Molly's things in here, Hank. She can sort through them after her bath."

Turning to Molly, she asked, “Shall I show you how the bath works? It’s quite ingenious, I assure you. Hank designed it himself. He has such a talent for building and fixing things.” Her smile clearly showed the pride and affection she felt for her brother-in-law.

“I’ll show her,” Hank said, still standing in the doorway.

“Then I shall attend to supper.” Jessica crossed the room, speaking as she went. “Dress warmly. Log houses can be quite drafty this time of year. If you want, I can send Penny and Charlie down, although I daresay they’re having a lovely time up there with all the toys and games.” When Molly said to let them play until supper, Jessica nodded and slipped past Hank into the hall. “Enjoy your bath,” she called with a wave of her hand.

As Jessica’s footfalls faded, Molly glanced at Hank, waiting for him to say something. When he didn’t, she motioned toward the connecting door. “You were going to show me how the plumbing works?”

“Right.” After he dumped her traveling case by the wardrobe, he led her through the dressing area into a large tiled room dominated by an outsized wooden tub. Two cast iron pipes emptied into it, while more pipes ran along the ceiling to a sink mounted on the far wall, with drainpipes running through the floor. Behind a screen stood a fixed toilet stool with a flush tank on the wall above it. It was the most modern water closet Molly had ever seen.

He turned one of the faucets over the tub. "This is hot water. It's really hot, so be careful." Steam burped out, then a trickle of water. "Cold is on the right." He put a wooden stopper in the drain hole in the bottom of the tub then straightened. "It's not as dangerous as it looks, no matter what Brady says."

Molly watched in alarm as the pipes knocked and wobbled, then the trickle of water became a gushing stream. Several of the hospitals where she and Papa had worked had boasted their own steam rooms, but to have such a luxury in one's home was almost decadent. "You did this yourself?" she asked over the noise of the pipes.

"It's not that complicated. A boiler in the basement heats water into steam until it creates enough pressure to force hot water up through these cast iron pipes. Nothing new about that."

Molly thought of Nellie's first husband, who had perished, along with over a thousand others, when his steamship blew up. "Couldn't it explode?"

Hank answered with a shrug. "That's why we only fire it up twice a day. We also make regular checks to be sure there's water in the boiler and the pop valves that release steam are working. It's probably safer than carrying buckets of scalding water up the stairs every time you want a bath. Considering what circumstances?"

Startled by the change in subject, she looked up to find him studying her with that sharply assessing look. She sensed that with the return of most of his memory, he was fretting over the gaps where she and the children should be. He was an intelligent man. It wouldn't be long before he figured out there was more going on here than just minor lapses of memory. For the umpteenth time, she regretted allowing Brady to talk her into keeping the truth of their marriage a secret from Hank.

His frown deepened. "Jessica said considering the circumstances, she thought you would want your own room. What did she mean?"

Molly felt heat inch up her neck and wondered how to answer that without further arousing his suspicions. "Well, there's your arm to consider," she said in her nurse's voice. "Even though it's splinted, it's still quite vulnerable until I put a hard plaster cast on it." When he gave no response, she hurried to fill the lengthening silence. "And then there's the fact that you don't remember me. That I'm a stranger to you. More or less."

He continued to watch her, as if expecting her to say more.

The man had the strangest way of controlling a conversation without saying a word, using silence to compel one to speak while he said nothing. It was a bit unnerving, although normally such a thing wouldn't bother her. She wasn't that talkative herself and preferred to observe rather than participate in conversations. But with Hank she often found herself rambling on like a nervous schoolgirl, which was quite out of character for her. "Perhaps she thought, in view of that, it would be awkward if we were to share, er, private quarters," she offered lamely.

He studied her for such a long time Molly was forced to look away.

"You're afraid of me," he finally said. "Why?"

Her gaze darted to his.

"Have I given you reason?" he persisted.

"No," she said quickly, which was the truth. It wasn't Hank she feared so much as the idea of him, of a husband. She never thought she would be married, and now that suddenly she was—and to a stranger—well, it took some getting used to.

"Then what's wrong, Molly? What's really going on?"

Realizing she had clenched her hands, she straightened her fingers and pressed them against her skirts. "Nothing's going on. But we haven't known each other for long, and now you don't even remember me. It's awkward."

"Hell," he muttered. "You want to me to court you again, don't you?"

Actually, that wasn't what she'd been thinking at all. She had never been courted—proposals from dying men hardly counted—

and she'd long reconciled herself to it never happening. But now that he mentioned it . . .

"Would that be so bad?" she asked, warming to the idea. "Courting?"

"For how long?" he asked with such a put-upon look she almost laughed.

Had he truly expected her to simply toss up her skirts, even though they didn't even know each other? Didn't he need at least a *hint* of an emotional attachment before he took a woman to bed? Or perhaps any woman would suffice as long as she had the correct anatomical accommodations. Honestly. Men were so . . . basic.

"Two days ago you were at death's door," she reminded him. "You should heal a bit before you exert yourself."

"I don't have to exert myself. There are ways—"

"Be that as it may," she cut in, horrified that he was about to give her instructions on how to service him, "you should at least know who I am before we"—she cleared her throat—"that is to say, you . . . assert your husbandly rights."

His face showed nothing, but she could see amusement in his eyes. "I already know who you are. You're Molly. My *wife*."

She waved a hand in dismissal. "That's a name and a title. It's not *me.*" Suddenly inspired, she covered her eyes. "What color are my eyes?"

He hesitated. "Green, sort of. Or maybe brownish-something."

"See?" Dropping her hand, she looked up with a smirk. "You don't even know the color of my eyes, or what color I prefer, or what I do in my spare time, or if I have a favorite food. In fact, you know nothing about me at all."

He gave that some thought. "I know you're a good nurse, you're smart, you're trying to do well by your niece and nephew, and you're . . . earnest."

Earnest? Good Lord, she sounded like a yapping terrier. And wasn't *earnest* somewhere between "well-meaning" and "desperate"? What woman wanted to be thought of as *earnest,* for heaven's sake?

"Beets," he said, interrupting her mental rant.

She blinked at him.

"Me, neither," he went on, taking her silence for consensus. "Blue."

"My favorite color?" Molly was having trouble keeping up. "No."

"Orange. Purple. Yellow."

"No to all three." Biting back a smile, she shook her head. "It's not going to be that easy, *husband.* You'll have to do more than list colors. You'll have to get to know me, and then maybe we can talk about . . . the other."

One corner of his mouth quirked. "My husbandly rights."

"Exactly. Now please leave, so I can take my bath."

His expressive eyes lit up at that. "If I helped, I could get to know you faster."

"Go," she ordered, hoping he didn't see the laughter she was barely able to hold in check.

But instead of moving away, he leaned closer. Then closer still, until his face was mere inches from hers and her eyes lost focus and started to cross.

Oh, Lord, she thought, frozen somewhere between shock and anticipation. *He's going to kiss me*. Just an inch more and—

"Almost green," he said and straightened. "So I was almost right."

Molly swayed, disoriented and oddly off balance.

With a nod of satisfaction he turned toward the door, then stopped and turned back. He was frowning again. "At least tell me you can add and subtract."

"Y-Yes, of course I can."

"Well, there's that then." With a sigh, he turned and walked out, closing the door behind him. Which somehow made the room seem suddenly quite a bit larger.

By the time Molly had left her room an hour later, bathed, dressed, and ravenously hungry, she had come to the conclusion that being courted by her husband might not be a bad thing.

At one time she had dreamed of being courted, of having a husband and children of her own. Then somewhere between pinafores and a surgical smock, that dream, much less the opportunity to make it into a reality, had simply withered away. But the instant Hank had planted that idea into her mind, all those hopes and fantasies had come roaring back. Suddenly, she had another chance—probably a *last* chance—to experience the merry chase other women whispered about and authors of romantic novels described in such eloquent detail.

Plus, she thought as she headed downstairs, it had the added bonus of keeping her husband at arm's length until she decided what to do about this sham marriage.

Courting. What did that mean, exactly? What was she supposed to do? Did she even have the proper clothes? It was ludicrous, really, that at the spinsterish age of twenty-six all those adolescent yearnings and doubts should grip her so strongly.

Would he recite poetry? Tell her she was beautiful?

The notion almost made her laugh. Romantic words from the man who had wrestled her over a chamber pot? Not likely.

As she stepped across the entry into the main room, Molly found it teeming with children and an odd assortment of people. Seeing them interact, she decided the Wilkins family was every bit as unorthodox as any Southern household with its mishmash of relatives, friends, hangers-on, and beloved servants.

In addition to Brady's family of four, and now Hank's family of four, there were seven other people who either lived in the house or spent so much time there they might as well: the Mexican housekeeper, Consuelo; the Garcia sisters, who tended the nursery; two young Mexican girls, who did a bit of everything—all of whom spoke limited English with such strong accents Molly had difficulty following them—an ancient Negro woman named Iantha, who supervised the kitchen; and Dougal, an elderly Scotsman who did little but argue with Brady, sleep sprawled out on the couches, and harass the children, to their utter delight. None of these seven was actually family, but all were treated as such.

"There you are." Smiling at Molly, Jessica hitched the toddler she carried higher on her hip, then shot a warning look at a small boy dangling upside down off the arm of a chair. With reluctance, he righted himself and came to stand dutifully beside his mother. "Children, this is your Aunt Molly," Jessica said, then beaming proudly at the children, added, "And this is Abigail and Ben."

"Hello," Molly said, which apparently was the release signal for Ben because he immediately ducked beneath Jessica's arm and climbed back into the chair.

Jessica's smile became strained. "He's

still in his twos," she explained, as if that might mean something to Molly, which it didn't. "And Abby, here, is getting ready to walk. Saints preserve us."

Molly smiled tentatively at the infant in Jessica's arms. The child was already a beauty, with her mother's ready smile and her father's striking eyes and dark hair. She would be a heartbreaker someday. Ben took more after Jessica in appearance, with dark auburn hair and intelligent brown eyes, but in temperament he seemed all Brady—boisterous, stubborn, and fearless. And apparently quite a climber.

"Well then. I see supper is served," Jessica said, setting off a stampede toward the dining area.

Supper was a lively affair, with Dougal arguing with Brady, Brady teasing the children, and Jessica striving in good-humored exasperation to maintain a semblance of polite discourse. Hank said little, ate enormous amounts of food to make up for his sickroom fare, and spent far too much of his time watching Molly. Penny was in such delight to have so many people to entertain, she was either giggling or shouting, and Charlie was his usual quiet self.

After the meal, the family gathered by the fireplace for cakes served with coffee, tea, or hot chocolate. While Jessica read aloud to the children and the brothers discussed how the dissolution of the silver standard in favor of the greenback might impact their silver mines, Molly watched thick, white snowflakes drift past the mullioned windows. Already the porch railing held an inch of new snow. If it snowed through the night, the roads would be impassable, which meant they wouldn't be able to leave until spring. But that also meant Fletcher couldn't come after them until spring either. They would be safe for a while, at least.

Molly's gaze drifted across to Hank. He was still talking to his brother, slouched in a leather chair beside the fireplace, long legs stretched out toward the crackling logs, his booted heels propped on the hearth. Firelight played over his face, softening the sharper angles and highlighting the strong arc of his jaw.

My husband, she thought, still amazed. A feeling of contentment stole over her, and she smiled, thinking if she and the children had to be snowed in somewhere for several months, this was a lovely place to be.

Abruptly Hank turned his head and looked at her.

Molly's smile faltered. Trapped by those eyes, she stared back. A heaviness seemed to settle against her chest. One moment. Three. Then five. When finally he turned back to his brother, she almost gasped for air, feeling suddenly so weightless, she might have floated up to the beams.

"YOU'RE STILL UP," HANK SAID FROM THE DOORway of his brother's office.

Brady looked up from the booklet spread open on his desk. His gaze dropped to the apple in Hank's hand, and he shook his head. "Do you ever quit eating?"

"I went a week without. I'm just making up."

Brady went back to his booklet.

Hank wandered over to the French doors opening onto the back porch. It was still snowing. The children had long been in bed, and Molly and Jessica had retired about an hour ago. A light from the other end of the house, probably Dougal's room off the kitchen, cast a yellow wash over the gentle drift of snow. Dropping the apple core into a trash basket, he wiped his hand on the grizzly then settled into one of the leather chairs in front of the desk. "What are you reading?"

Brady held up the pamphlet for Hank to see. "*The Causes and Prevention of Screw Worm Infestations North of the Rio Grande*."

"Sounds exciting," Hank said dryly.

"It is. Did you know the fly that lays the screw worm larvae mates once, lays its eggs, then dies?"

"That would sure take the fun out of it." Hank didn't want to think about mating. Yet lately, ever since he found out he was married, that seemed to be all he did think about. Picking up the letter opener Jessica thought would look nice on Brady's desk, he scratched an itchy place under the bandage on his arm.

"But if they can figure a way to sterilize it," Brady went on, "then it won't lay any eggs and there won't be any larvae. What do you think of that?"

Hank tossed the opener back on the desk. "I think the cows will be glad."

Brady returned to his reading.

"It's snowing."

"I saw."

"Six, maybe eight inches so far."

Brady turned the page.

Hank propped his ankle across his knee, picked up the letter opener again, and dug at a crust of dirt in the seam between the leather and sole of his boot. "Buck says it won't last long, since the flakes are so big and the wind is out of the east." Buck was Iantha's husband. Both were runaway slaves who had been with the family for over twenty years. He had been a gifted carpenter until rheumatism crippled his hands. Now he was the ranch barometer. He read clouds the way a cartographer read maps, and by Hank's recollection, he'd never missed a blizzard. "He figures it'll be done by morning. Still ought to be enough for a snowman."

His brother glanced up.

Hank returned the opener to the desk and lowered his foot to the floor, wincing at the pull of muscles across his sore ribs. "Penny wants to build a snowman."

Brady continued to watch him, a thoughtful frown on his face.

"They're from Atlanta," Hank reminded him. "Not much snow in Atlanta."

Closing the booklet, Brady sat back.

Hank tucked a loose end back under his bandage, then scratched the mostly healed cut on his temple. "Charlie doesn't seem to care, but Penny's real excited about it. I told her maybe we'll have a snowball fight."

"What's wrong with you?"

Hank quit scratching and looked at him.

"Why are you talking so much?"

"I'm practicing."

"Practicing talking? I thought you already knew how."

"I need a drink." Hank wasn't sure how much he wanted to reveal to his brother. Brady had an annoying habit of sticking his nose in where it didn't belong, and Hank had learned years ago the best weapon against his interference was silence. But this had him baffled, and he didn't know who else to ask.

His brother rose and went to the crystal decanters and glassware artfully arranged on a silver tray atop a dainty claw foot table by the bookcase. Another of Jessica's additions. Now, instead of sharing a jug of Buck's potent home brew, he and Brady were treated to fine Scotch sipping whiskey in cut crystal glasses.

Neither of them complained. But if something stronger was needed, there was always a jug in the barn and another in the loafing shed. Hank thought he might be heading out there fairly frequently in the days to come.

After pouring an inch of whiskey into each glass, Brady handed one to Hank, then returned to his chair. "So what's going on, Hank?"

Leaning back, Hank propped his boots on the corner of Brady's desk. He figured with Jessica asleep, he was safe enough. "She wants me to court her."

Brady stared at him for a moment then shook his head. "Hell."

"I know."

They drank in silence for a time then Hank said, "I'm not so good at courting. I only did it that once—other than Molly—and we know how that turned out."

"You talking about Melanie Kinderly? You never told me what happened."

Hank stared silently out at the snow.

Brady sighed. "And I guess you're not going to."

"How'd you go about it with Jessica?" Hank asked after a while. "Whatever you did seems to have worked." And Hank was still amazed that it had. Brady was a rough cob, and Jessica, well . . . Jessica was all starch and fancy hats. And rules. Lots of rules.

"It's a confusing process," Brady admitted. "Not at all what you'd expect."

Studying his brother over the rim of his glass, Hank waited.

Brady spread his hands in a helpless gesture. "I went to save her from tripping over my saddle, and she tries to geld me with a ruffly umbrella. I grab her before she falls down a cliff, and she gouges my arm bloody. I tell her I'm going for help, and she nearly knocks out my tooth. And that was just the first day. A dangerous undertaking, courting is. Like juggling porcupines."

Hank gave it some thought. "I don't think I'm up to that. Not with this arm." On top of which, his ribs were still pretty sore and headaches plagued him from time to time. He didn't need to be beat up any worse. Besides, he shouldn't have to do any courting anyway. He was already married, for crissakes.

"Women do tend to complicate things," Brady agreed.

Hank sighed. “I wish I could remember what I did the first time. Doesn’t seem fair to have to go through it all again.”

Brady studied him, his expression troubled. “You don’t remember any of it?”

Hank shook his head. “Seems odd, but I don’t.” And the harder he puzzled on it, the more confused he became. Nothing about his marriage—or his wife—made sense.

“If you want,” Brady said in a hesitant voice, “we could settle some money on her and cut her loose. No use staying married if you don’t want to.”

Hank frowned. “Cut her loose? Why would I do that? And who said I didn’t want to stay married?”

“Whoa,” Brady said, raising a palm in a placating gesture. “Don’t get yourself worked up.”

“I’m not worked up.” Regretting his outburst, Hank studied the glass in his hands. “All I’m saying is she’s a decent woman. She doesn’t deserve to be cast off just because my memory’s confused.”

“So you like her.”

Hank thought back to the times she’d surprised him with her wit and her earnestness and those blushes that brought out the sparkle in her almost-green eyes. The woman definitely had him interested, and to his way of thinking, that was a step past "liking." "Why wouldn't I like her?"

"Well, for one thing, she hit me in the face with a spoon."

Hank grinned. "Why? What'd you do?"

"Nothing. We were just talking." Brady studied his fingernails then shrugged. "Maybe I said something about you she took exception to."

"See? Pretty *and* smart."

"You like her."

"She's my wife."

"But you like her."

Swirling the amber liquid in his near-empty glass, Hank debated answering, then thought, why not? He must have liked her at one time if he'd gone to all the trouble of marrying her. "Yeah. I guess."

His brother tugged at his mustache with his thumb and forefinger, a thoughtful look on his face. It was an expression Hank had seen often, and it never boded well.

"Well, I don't trust her," Brady finally announced. "There's something she's not telling us."

Anger sparked in Hank's mind. "*Us?* Now she's your wife too?" Why did Brady have to elbow his way in, then try to take charge of everybody else's business? "She's *my* wife. If there's any telling to be done, it'll be to *me*."

"I'm just saying there's something not right about all this."

"Goddamnit, Brady," Hank warned.

"Okay, okay." His brother made a hands-off gesture. "But don't come crying to me when everything goes to hell."

"Believe me, I won't." It struck Hank as odd that he was defending a marriage he had no memory of, and protecting a woman he hardly knew. But she was his wife, so he must have known her well at one time. *Damn that Brady.* Now his head was starting to hurt again.

"Well, if you're so insistent on going through with this courting thing," Brady said after a lengthy silence, "I figure you've got three things going for you. First"—he held up his index finger—"you're hurt. I know it's a bother, but women seem to like fussing over a man when he's hurt. And what woman wouldn't like a big strapping fellow like yourself at her mercy? Especially if he's feeling weak."

"I'm not weak."

"Second"—he held up another finger—"you've got the Wilkins smile. Of course, you'll have to keep your hair cut and the beard shaved so she can see it, but if you use it wisely, it'll get you a long way. Remember the Norton twins."

Hank would rather not. He'd felt like a lone pork chop caught between two starving dogs.

"And third . . ." This time it was the finger sporting the wedding band Jessica had given him, which he proudly wore even though it drove him crazy.

Hank frowned, realizing neither he nor Molly wore a wedding band. Why was that? He didn't care so much about himself, but why didn't she wear one? Had she removed it? Or had he never given her one?

"Since you're already married—or so she says," Brady went on, regaining Hank's attention, "even if this second courtship is a complete failure, there's nothing she can do about it. She's stuck with you." He showed his teeth in that big grin that always made Hank wary. "In fact, when you think about it, little brother, this is the perfect way to court a woman because nothing you say or do matters in the least since you're already married. I wish I'd thought of it with Jessica. Could have saved me a lot of pain. What do you think?"

Hank shook his head. "I think I'm not surprised you got hit in the face with a spoon."

Nine

"Good morning, Dougal," Molly said as she walked into the kitchen. The room was empty but for the old Scotsman, who sat at the long center worktable, which also served as a family dining area on less formal occasions.

"Morning? 'Tis nigh afternoon, lass. I dinna ken if ye'd died in the night."

Smiling, she plucked a muffin from a plate on the warming shelf above the stove. "I haven't slept so well in weeks. Where is everyone?"

Before Dougal could answer, Brady came in behind her, tracking snow and carrying a protesting bundle that sounded like Abigail—it was difficult to tell under the wooly scarf and hat.

"Finally up," he said when he saw Molly. "You better get out there. You're missing all the fun." Depositing Abigail on the counter, he anchored her with one gloved hand and grabbed a rag from a peg with the other.

"What's going on?" Molly mumbled around a bite of muffin.

"Snowball fight." He unwrapped the scarf enough to expose Abigail's red cheeks and runny nose. "Blow," he said, holding the rag to her face. While his daughter wiggled and squirmed and made snorting noises against the cloth, Brady grinned at Molly. "Hank's team is losing. They could use your help."

"You have teams?"

"Hank and Penny versus me and Ben and Abigail."

"What about Charlie?"

Brady shook his head. "He's just watching." Having cleaned up his daughter, he tucked the towel in his jacket pocket, then began rewrapping the squirming infant.

"You and Dougal ought to come out. It's a beautiful day."

"Tae cold," Dougal protested. "Colder than a well digger's donkey, I'll warrant."

"Ass," Brady said, adjusting Abigail's wool cap. "Colder than a well digger's ass in the middle of winter in the Yukon. Can't you get anything right?"

Dougal glared up at him from beneath his bushy eyebrows. "That's what I said, ye great lummox. Ass, donkey, 'tis the same."

"Arse then."

"Och, mon, have ye nae sense at all? There's a lass and wee bairn present." He turned to Molly with a sigh. "My apologies tae the tew o' ye. The bumble-headed maundrel wed above himself and doesna ken how tae behave wie the lassies."

Brady smirked. "Strong words for a man who wears a dress." Holding his daughter under one arm like a squirming bundle of laundry, he left the room.

"It's no' a dress," Dougal yelled after him. "It's a kilt."

Fighting a smile, Molly asked, "Are you sure you won't come out with me?"

"Nae, lass. The cold makes me bones

ache." He made a show of looking around. "Dae ye ken where that bonnie lassie, Consuelo, might be?"

Bonnie lassie? By Molly's reckoning, Consuelo must be fifty years old—long past the "lassie" age—and although she had a kind face and lovely eyes, the missing teeth kept her from being what might strictly be called "bonnie." But then, Dougal, with his contentious nature and more hair in his ears than on his head, was no blue-ribbon catch, himself. "Isn't she married, Dougal?"

The Scotsman gave a dramatic sigh. "A widow, more's the pity. A puir lonely widow wie a need for the companionship of a fine braw lad."

"Like yourself, perhaps?" Molly teased.

"I'll nae turn me back on a puir soul in need, lass. 'Tis no' the Scots way."

Relenting, Molly said, "I think I saw her go into the pantry."

Moving with surprising spryness for a man of his years, Dougal trotted from the room.

After donning her coat, mittens, and a scarf, Molly went onto the front porch.

Jessica sat in a rocker, holding a steaming mug in both mittened hands while directing the fracas between bouts of laughter. Charlie leaned against a post by the steps, watching, his sullen expression softened by a look of longing. The outsider looking on. Molly knew the feeling.

In the yard, the battle lines were drawn, with Hank and Penny half-hidden behind a mound of snow, lobbing snowballs at their opponents, Brady and Ben, who crouched behind another mound of snow. Abigail wallowed in the drifts between the warring camps, giggling and flailing at the snow, unperturbed by the snowballs flying over her head. Deep male laughter and children's squeals filled the crisp air.

After exchanging words of greeting with Jessica, Molly went to stand beside Charlie at the top of the steps. "Why aren't you helping Hank and Penny?"

"I don't want to."

Aware that Jessica was watching and that the fight in the yard had slowed, which meant Hank was probably watching, too, she forced a smile. "It might be fun, Charlie."

"I don't care."

Determined to get the child involved,

she scooped a handful of snow off the railing, shaped it into a ball, and held it out. "Here, try it."

"I don't want to. Just leave me alone!" Spinning, he stalked away.

From the corner of her eye, Molly saw Hank shoot up from behind his snow bank, arm swinging. A moment later a fat snowball spattered between Charlie's shoulder blades.

He whirled, a scowl on his face.

"What do you say to that, Charlie?" Hank challenged.

The boy glared at him, his mouth pressed in a tight, grim line.

Molly fought the urge to rush to his defense, sensing he wouldn't appreciate her interference. Instead, she sent Hank a warning look.

He responded by loosening another snowball.

Charlie ducked, but it still caught his shoulder, showering his face with snow. Furiously, he wiped it off. "You better stop that," he yelled.

"Says who?" Hank fired again.

Charlie threw an arm over his face as the

snowball smacked against the post beside him.

Needing to do something to help the boy, Molly quickly grabbed a handful of snow and thrust it into his hand. "Actions speak louder than words."

Charlie threw. The snowball went wide, but before it landed, Molly had another waiting. Within moments, amid laughter and shrieks, the fight was on, with only Charlie taking it as anything other than a game. He seemed oblivious to the snowballs plopping all around him, but retaliated with a single-minded determination. Soon he was down the steps and into the yard, scooping snow with both hands, firing a constant barrage as he crossed to where Penny and Hank huddled. By the time he'd reached them, he was covered with snow and grinning as he hadn't in months.

"Get him, Charlie!" Penny shouted, loyally switching sides in favor of her big brother.

With a whoop, Ben scrambled out from behind his hill and joined the attack, while Brady stood safely out of range shouting encouragement.

Laughing, Hank fell backward, all but disappearing under a cloud of snow as Charlie and Ben breached the wall and landed on top of him. With a squeal that could have ruptured eardrums, Penny leaped into the fray.

"Molly, help me," Hank called, his voice muffled by thrashing children and flying snow. "They're hurting me."

Laughter instantly forgotten, Molly shot down the steps. "Brady, get the children!" she cried, slipping and sliding through the snow to get to Hank. "Penny! Charlie! Get off! Now!" Dragging the children from the heap, she flung them toward Brady, who stood laughing over his brother. By the time she got Hank uncovered, she was panting with exertion and fear.

If he reinjured that arm, she might not be able to save it a second time. She might never be able to restore circulation, or the damage to the torn tissue might be so severe she would have no choice but to amputate. Why had she relied so long on wrapped splints, rather than putting on a hard plaster cast?

"Be still, Hank," she said, trying to keep her voice from betraying her alarm as she ran shaking hands over his arm. But with the heavy jacket and the bandages, she couldn't tell if he had rebroken it. "Where does it hurt? Here? Here? Can you move your fingers? Oh, I knew I should have put on the hard cast. Why did I—"

"Molly, Molly," Hank choked out, his voice vibrating with laughter. "Calm down. I'm all right. They didn't hurt me."

"We didn't hurt him, Aunt Molly," Penny defended. "Did we, Charlie?"

Molly froze as the words penetrated. She reared back to find Hank grinning up at her.

"See? I'm fine." He lifted his bandaged arm and wiggled the tips of his fingers to prove it. Drawing back her fist, she punched him on the shoulder. Then burst into tears.

"Come on, kids," Brady said, hastily. "Let's see if Consuelo will fix you some warm milk."

"With chocolate in it?" Penny shouted.

"Chocolate *and* green beans," Brady teased.

"Beans," Ben crowed.

Shrieking in delighted disgust, the younger children clambered over Brady as he picked up Abigail and headed toward the house, Charlie following more sedately behind.

As soon as they were out of earshot, Molly rounded on Hank, who was still stretched in the snow. “How could you do such a thing? Don’t you know how hard I worked to save your arm—to save *you,* you big lout. How could you tease me that way?”

“Now, Molly.” Hank tried to put his good arm around her.

She threw it off and swiped tears from her cheeks, furious with him for frightening her so badly, and furious with herself for overreacting. But after a week of constant worry and sleepless nights, she was in no mood for cruel jests.

“I’m sorry, Molly. I thought you knew I was joking.”

“You’re hateful. See if I ever worry about you again.” She started to rise.

He pulled her back down. “Molly, don’t.”

“Don’t what? Worry about you? Be upset that all my work and effort and constant attendance on you could have been for nothing?”

His gloved hand moved to her shoulder,

then around and under the scarf over her head. It was cold and wet against the back of her neck.

"Stop that!" She tried to shrug it off.

"Shh." He pulled her head down toward his. "I didn't mean to worry you."

"Well, you did, and I don't appreciate it. If you ever do that a—"

He kissed her.

His lips were icy. His tongue was hot.

Molly was too shocked to react.

She had been kissed before. Fumbling sickroom kisses from men desperate to feel something other than pain and sickness and encroaching death. Grateful goodbye kisses from men recovered enough to walk away and die another day.

But they were nothing like Hank's kiss.

Whatever indefinable and invisible connection existed between them, it flared tenfold the moment his mouth touched hers. Like a shock of energy, it moved through her, tingling along her nerves, vibrating under her skin.

It was just a kiss.

But oh . . .

When he finally released her, she drew

back, feeling shivery and breathless and so confused she couldn't think. "Why did you do that?" she asked in a shaky voice.

His smile was slow and sweet. "Can't a man kiss his wife?"

His wife.

How lovely that sounded.

Heart twisting in her chest, she looked down at him . . . the man she had wronged and had lied to . . . the man who made her heart race simply by being in the same room with her. She saw laughter in his dark eyes, affection in his smile . . . and guilt almost choked her.

"Is this your idea of courting?" she snapped, desperate to distance herself from the feelings churning inside her. "Scaring a woman half to death and making her cry, then kissing her as if nothing is wrong?"

His smile faded. "Is something wrong?"

Of course something was wrong. Everything was wrong. What she was doing—what she was feeling—what she wanted from this man was wrong. She knew that.

But her heart didn't.

It hammered in her chest and sent blood shushing past her ear, whispering of temptation, second chances, a way to make up for all the lost, lonely years she'd spent at her father's side. For just this one moment she could be like other women, feel what they felt, know what they knew.

"Molly?" He had risen up on his right elbow and was studying her in that intense way he had. "You don't want to kiss me?" he asked.

Dare she? Dare she not? She stared back at him, wanting . . . wishing . . . until guilt melted into something hot and urgent and undeniable, and all the doubts fell away. Breathless from the pounding of her heart and her own boldness, she bent closer. "As a matter of fact . . ." she whispered and pressed her lips to his.

JESSICA LOOKED PAST BRADY AS HE CAME UP the steps with Penny under one arm, Abigail under the other, and Ben wrapped around his leg. Charlie hung back, no longer laughing but not as sullen either. "Oh, look," she said, smiling at the couple kissing in the snow.

After unloading the children and shooing them into the house, Brady turned back to see his brother helping Molly to her feet. "I know. I hope he knows what he's doing."

Rearing back in surprise, Jessica searched his face. “What’s that supposed to mean?”

“I’m not sure. It’s just . . . something feels off.”

“They’re newly wedded,” Jessica defended. “In addition, Hank has suffered a grievous injury, so of course, something is off. Heavens, I’m amazed Molly will even let him touch her at all in view of the fact he doesn’t even remember her. I certainly wouldn’t were I in her place.”

Smiling, Brady tucked a curl back under her scarf. “I’d never forget you.”

“Apparently you did for a year, when you sent me back to England after the ranch burned.”

“The worst year of my life. And I didn’t forget you. Not for a second.”

“Of course not.” Leaning up, she kissed his cold cheek, then led him into the house. “Now stop worrying about your brother and tend to your own knitting.”

“I don’t knit.”

“Oh?” She sent him a look over her shoulder. “Then come upstairs and I’ll teach you.”

* * *

"IT'S HEALING WELL."

Molly ran her fingertips gently over the ridge of puffy skin where the incision was. "I hope removing the stitches didn't hurt too much."

"I hardly felt it."

It was late evening. Everyone else had retired for the night. They were in the tiled bath between their rooms, Hank seated on the edge of the wooden tub, while she sat on a stool by the sink, soaking gauze strips in a bowl of plaster of paris. After that scare earlier, she was determined to get the arm protected before it could be reinjured.

"The nerves near the surface are probably damaged," she said. "It might be numb for quite some time. Maybe forever." Realizing that she still stroked his arm, she dropped her hand back to her lap. "You'll have an ugly scar, I'm afraid."

"I still have an arm. Did I thank you?"

"You lived. That's thanks enough." Avoiding his gaze, she dug dried plaster from beneath her thumbnail. "Not all my patients do, you know."

"Not from lack of trying, I'd guess."

She shrugged. "A lack of skill, perhaps. Or knowledge. Or courage. But no, not from lack of trying." After brushing flakes of plaster from her skirt, she folded her hands in her lap and put on a smile. "You'll have to remove your shirt. Or we can cut the sleeve, if you prefer."

He removed his shirt.

She almost sighed. So entranced was she by that perfectly sculpted torso it was a moment before she noticed the wrappings around his ribs were gone. "When did you remove the bandages?"

"Last night."

"Why?"

"So I could breathe."

Without the thick wrappings, his musculature showed in starkly delineated slabs across his chest and down his abdomen. She took a moment to observe how they flexed and relaxed with each breath he took. An inspiring sight. And even though there was a new gauntness to him and the loose waistband of his trousers indicated he had lost weight during his ordeal, he was still the most powerfully built man she had ever attended. Most of the men she had nursed had been on the brink of starvation. Or death. But Hank was so vibrantly alive, he seemed to fill the room with his energy.

Realizing that he was noticing her noticing him, she adopted an expression of mild irritation. “If I wrap them more loosely, will you let me rebandage? It’s important to keep the cracked ribs protected until they heal.”

He didn’t respond.

She sighed and glanced up at him through her lashes. “You’ll just take them off again, won’t you?”

He didn’t speak, but the answer danced in his eyes.

“Then no more wrestling with the children,” she ordered in her nurse’s voice. “Or riding horses, or playing in the snow, or doing anything that would jostle your ribs or your arm or risk a fall. Do you understand?”

He smiled.

“I’m serious, Hank.”

“I can see that.”

“So?”

He blinked innocently. “So?”

“So, will you do it?”

“Do what?”

She wanted to punch his arm again. Instead, she bent closer to study his ribs. The bruises had faded to a yellowish green.

The abrasions and lacerations were healing nicely. Where he was uninjured, his skin was the color of clover honey and felt warm and solid beneath her hand.

Realizing she was stroking him again, she abruptly sat back. "Well," she said lamely, feeling his gaze on her once more. "Since you'll just remove them, I won't rebandage. But promise me you'll be careful."

When he didn't answer, she looked up. The laughter was gone, replaced by that intense probing stare. "You worry too much, Molly," he said with a small, crooked smile.

She truly did almost punch him that time. "How can I not worry? Do you know how close you came to dying? How frightened I—your brother—all of us were?" Realizing her outburst had revealed more than she was willing to admit, even to herself, she fussed with the gauze strips. "Just be careful. That's all I'm asking."

"I will."

"Thank you."

"You're welcome."

She didn't have to look up to realize he was laughing at her again. But this time, rather than rising to the bait, she attended to the task at hand.

Positioning his arm on a folded towel along the edge of the sink, she wrapped a thick cotton pad around his arm from his bicep to the second knuckle of his hand, then began laying the plaster-coated strips over it.

"You don't like it, do you?" he said after several minutes had passed.

She glanced up to find his expression curious rather than teasing. "Like what?"

"Doctoring. I can see it bothers you. So why do you do it?"

"For Papa." She smiled to hide the surge of painful memories. "If he needed me enough, he wouldn't send me away." She gently pressed out the wrinkles on one gauze strip then reached for another. "But you're right. I don't like the suffering."

"Part of the healing process, I'd think."

"Perhaps. But when you're thirteen, it's difficult to separate the two."

"Thirteen? That's pretty young."

He sounded indignant, and that surprised her. No one had ever commented before on the appropriateness of her tending the wounded or sick. But now that she thought about it, it was a bit much to expect of an adolescent girl. But then, she had never protested, had she?

Out of loyalty to Papa, she tried to explain. "After Mama died and my sister moved with her husband to Savannah, it was just Papa and I. He traveled a great deal, studying under different surgeons. I didn't want to be left behind, so I went with him."

"Still. You were a kid. Too young to deal with all that."

"Apparently so," she agreed with a rueful smile. "The first time Papa asked me to dispose of an amputated limb, I thought it moved, and it scared me so badly I tossed it on the floor and fled shrieking. Papa was furious."

When he didn't respond, she glanced at him, expecting him to see the humor in the situation, however macabre.

Instead, he was glowering at her with such a ferocious expression she drew back, almost knocking the bowl of plaster of paris off her lap.

"How could he do that to you?"

"He didn't mean to upset me," she quickly

defended. "He just didn't . . . think. Papa was like that."

"He was your father. He should have protected you from all that, rather than dragging you into the middle of it."

Molly looked away, both pleased and confused by the strength of his reaction. No one had ever stood up for her before. Or questioned Papa's treatment of her. As a child, even when she'd felt almost crushed by the responsibility of tending the wounded or ill, she had never doubted Papa's right to put the task before her, only her ability to carry it out. It was strange that Hank would be the first to see it from the child's point of view. Strange and . . . nice.

"Okra."

It took her a moment to figure that out, then she smiled. "Back to that are we?" she asked, cutting more strips and dropping them into the bowl. "Too slimy."

He chuckled, a lovely, welcome sound. "Not the way Iantha makes it. How about collards?"

"They're edible with bacon and vinegar, but not my favorite."

"I like beef."

"I know." She didn't add that it wasn't experience that told her that, but his brother. "I prefer chicken."

"With potatoes?"

"Rice."

"I'm getting hungry."

His voice was a low rumble that bounced off the tile walls and swirled around the small room like a gentle whirlwind of sound. No other noise intruded. It was as if the world had narrowed to these four walls and her and Hank. There was an intimacy to it that made her want to edge closer and touch his hair or run a fingertip down his bristly cheek. Perhaps she was becoming ill.

"He'd be proud of you, I think," he said, jarring her back to reality.

"Papa?" She covered her discomfiture with a nervous laugh. "Have you seen your arm?"

"It's there and it works. What would he have done differently?"

She thought about it for a moment, then shrugged. "Not differently. Better."

"Would he have talked to me and slept on the cot next to mine and told me not to give up?"

She laughed self-consciously. "You heard? I didn't know you were awake."

"I wasn't very often. Most of the time I felt like I was dying, like I was buried alive. Then I would hear your voice and I'd know I wasn't. Would your father have done that?"

Feeling that rush of pleasure again, she smoothed the strips over his arm, not sure how to respond. Expressions of gratitude always made her uncomfortable; she was never convinced she deserved them. And Hank's had her almost in a dither. How deflating. She had always thought dithering beneath her.

"Papa wasn't much of a pillow fluffer," she admitted with an embarrassed smile. Then quickly changing the subject, she said, "Thank you for getting Charlie to join in today. He hasn't laughed like that in a long time."

Hank didn't respond.

"He's lost a great deal for one so young," she went on. "His father, mother, grandfather. I've not been much help to him, I fear. I can't seem to—"

"It's not about you," he cut in. "He's afraid. But not of you. How does that work?"

She looked up to find him eyeing Papa's stethoscope, which was tied to the underside lid of her medicine basket. Remembering what Jessica had said about him dismantling things, she flipped the top closed with her toe. "It magnifies sound."

"It does? How?"

"I don't know. Penny seems very taken with you."

He shrugged. "She's afraid too. Just not as angry about it. Can I see it?"

"Perhaps later," she hedged. Leaning down, she picked up another handful of gauze strips and dropped them into the bowl on her lap.

They sat in silence while she smoothed more strips over the cast. It wasn't a comfortable silence, but then Hank's silences rarely were. He always seemed to be watching, assessing, observing, but gave little indication of what he thought.

Molly knew he was still trying to fit together the puzzle of his missing memories. She had no doubt that his sharply analytical mind would soon tell him there were too many missing pieces, and those he'd been given didn't fit. Perhaps that was why he had stopped asking questions about their marriage. Perhaps he was waiting for her to tell him the truth, rather than forcing a confrontation.

She wished she had the courage to tell him. But the more time she spent with Hank, the more time with him she wanted. Her clinging to the lie wasn't just because of her promise to Brady, or even her need to find a safe place beyond the long reach of Daniel Fletcher. It was about time—time to savor the sense of belonging to a family again. Time to rest and let the children heal a little. Time with Hank, whose smile sent all the lonely yearnings of all the empty years rushing into her mind.

"Why don't you wear a wedding ring?"

The question so startled her, she dropped a plaster strip onto the tiled floor. After she retrieved it then wiped up the mess, she was able to answer calmly. "I don't have one." Holding up her dripping left hand, she added, "Jewelry interferes with my work."

She felt him studying her as she laid the last of the strips over the hardening cast, then daubed it with a final coat of plaster.

"There," she said, rising to rinse her hands in the sink. "Once that hardens, your arm will be fully protected. But you must tell me immediately if there's any pain, or a feeling of tightness, or if you notice any swelling in your fingers."

"How long until it dries?"

"Not long. It'll dry more quickly and you'll be warmer if you come into the bedroom and sit by the fire."

As soon as the words were out, she wanted them back, realizing he might take them as an invitation to . . . what? Assert those husbandly rights?

For one frantic moment, she cast about for an excuse to put him off should he make advances. Then she realized it was right in front of her, covered with wet plaster. He couldn't do anything with that arm. Not that he'd be using his arm, precisely, but—*God, I am such a ninny.*

As Molly directed him toward one of the two upholstered chairs flanking the fireplace, she realized that even though as a nurse she had long abandoned the rules of propriety and had in fact become quite accustomed to the sight of sick men in various states of dishabille, it was vastly different to have a healthy, half-dressed, incredibly attractive man lounging in a chair in her bedroom. Especially when his gaze tracked her every movement as she pulled a quilt from the chest at the foot of her bed and came to drape it over his long form. She was almost sweating by the time she settled in the chair opposite his, her feet squarely on the floor, her hands clasped in her lap.

Unable to tolerate another of his probing silences, she looked around for something to spark a conversation. Her gaze came to rest on the disassembled clock on the mantle. "Why did you take that apart?"

"I needed parts."

"For what?"

"A toy train I was making for Ben."

"Did it work?"

"For a while."

Silence again except for the pop and hiss of the fire. Molly tapped a fingernail on the arm of the chair in tempo with an inane tune she hummed in her head.

"I wanted to build a stuffed bear with a movable head," he said after a while.

"Oh? Why didn't you?"

"Jessica couldn't spare the clocks." He smiled.

She smiled back, enjoying his droll humor.

She wondered if he felt it, too, that unseen bond that seemed to have grown even stronger since the kiss in the snow. She wondered if he was as confused by this new intimacy as she. She wondered if he would kiss her again. But mostly she wondered why he stared at her that way.

Looking down, she saw her hands clenching and made herself straighten her fingers until they lay flat against her thighs. "I wish you wouldn't do that," she said.

"Do what?"

"Stare at me."

He continued to watch her. She could feel it.

Lifting her head, she looked directly into his eyes. "You're doing it now."

"You're talking to me. I can't look at you when you talk to me?"

"It makes me nervous."

"Why?"

She wasn't sure what to say. "I'm not accustomed to it," she finally admitted. "I feel like I'm being scrutinized, censured . . . like I've done something wrong. I don't like drawing attention to myself."

He snorted. "Then you better start wearing a potato sack."

She frowned, not sure what he meant.

"You're a beautiful woman, Molly. I can't have been the first man to notice."

Beautiful? She blinked at him, astonished. She had always thought of herself as unremarkable. Hair an undecided mix of too many colors. Eyes not quite green, but not completely hazel either. Average height, average weight, average face. Nothing to attract notice. Undecided, unremarkable Molly.

Up until now, that had suited her fine. She liked the invisibility it brought, because when one went unseen, no response or participation was required.

Until now. Now, it mattered. Because now a man had noticed her—a man she could care about thought she was beautiful. How shocking was that?

"Well, it's late," he said, pushing the quilt aside.

"No," she blurted out. "It's still too soft."

"Too soft?"

"The plaster hasn't had enough time to set properly."

A hint of a smile tugged at one corner of his wide mouth. "Oh, I think it's hard enough." He pushed to his feet.

She rose, too, and moved forward to examine his cast. "You must be careful not to roll on it. Perhaps I should wrap it in something."

Hank put his hand on her shoulder. "It's all right, Molly. I'll be careful."

She looked up at him, realizing this was the first time she had been this near him when they were both standing. He was taller than she had thought. Even taller than his brother. And he stood so close she knew if she tipped her face forward, she would almost be able to taste the warm, male scent of him on her tongue.

"Molly." His right hand moved slowly from her shoulder, up her neck, to slide beneath the heavy braid hanging down her back. A warm hand now, instead of an icy glove. He bent toward her. "Maybe next time, you'll take your hair down for me," he said as he brushed his lips over hers. "That's all I ask. For now." Then he straightened and, smiling, turned away.

She watched him cross the room, wanting to call him back. But then it was too late and the door was closing behind him, leaving her standing dazed and breathless in the silent room.

Next time?

Ten

THANKSGIVING WASN'T A TRADITION MOLLY AND Papa usually celebrated. Not for political reasons—Papa had no particular feelings for President Lincoln one way or the other, and as for his Proclamation of 1863 designating a national day of thanksgiving, he thought that was downright silly. Orchestrating gratitude? Absurd. No, Papa's political beliefs were characterized less by societal ideals than a general dislike of government interference, a natural outcome, Molly supposed, of the cadaver procurement difficulties of his medical apprenticeship days. Even donating his skills at Andersonville Prison had been less about humanitarian concerns than an interest in furthering his medical pursuits.

Consequently, they never celebrated that holiday. Immersed as they were in the carnage of war, they had never felt moved to celebrate a day of thanksgiving—Papa, because he couldn't be bothered—and Molly, because it was hard to feel grateful when sewing up a man who was screaming in agony. War rather dampened the holiday spirit.

So Molly was both delighted and a bit surprised that Jessica was making such a to-do about it, especially since Thanksgiving was more of an American tradition than a British one. She suspected it might simply be an excuse for Jessica to do something special for the family.

The morning before the last Thursday in November, almost two weeks after coming to the ranch, Molly walked into the warm kitchen to find it crowded with busy women and filled with the scents of baking bread and simmering vegetables. At the far end of the large room, Iantha worked on sweet potato pie while supervising the two kitchen girls as they chopped vegetables for sage dressing and dirty rice. Consuelo sat at one end of the long center table, humming and peeling potatoes, and Jessica kneaded bread dough at the other end.

"May I help?" Molly asked Jessica.

"Absolutely." After outfitting Molly with an apron and a tin shaker of flour, Jessica retrieved a ball of dough from the towel-covered bowl on the warming tray above the stove. "Have a go," she said, plopping it onto a floured breadboard.

They worked in silence, Molly enjoying the smell of spices and yeast and the quiet companionship of the women around her. When Mama was still alive, she and Nellie often helped in the kitchen, making corn fritters and pecan pie and apple dumplings while Mama sang hymns in her soft contralto voice. Molly smiled, not realizing how much she missed those times until walking in here today.

"This is a lovely kitchen," she said, rolling the dough under the heels of her hands. "So roomy."

"More so since the explosion."

Molly glanced over to see if Jessica was joking. She didn't appear to be. "Another of Hank's inventions?" she ventured.

Jessica nodded. "A pressurized cooking apparatus for Iantha. It took out a bank of cabinets on the back wall. Luckily no one was in the room at the time."

Not knowing what to make of that, Molly changed the subject. "What meats will you be serving tomorrow?"

"Whatever the men can find. If not turkeys, they'll bring deer or elk or wild sheep." She wrinkled her flour-streaked nose. "Hopefully not bear. Bear meat is quite strong. In my condition I simply couldn't tolerate it."

"Why not beef?" Molly asked, patting the dough in a loaf. "They seem to have plenty of that on hand."

"Too easy, I suspect. Hunting Thanksgiving dinner is something the men of the Wilkins family have always done, even when they lived in Missouri. Much like the Christmas tree hunt." She chuckled and shook her head, sending copper curls sliding from her topknot. "Now, there's an ordeal. The first year I was here, I accompanied them, and I have to say, I have never seen two people argue so over a silly tree. If Jack had been there, I daresay it would have disintegrated into a family brawl. Meanwhile, I'm sitting in the sleigh, freezing my toes, while they tromp around, discussing tree after tree until finally settling on the first one they had seen. Needless to say, I haven't accompanied them since. Although I probably should have gone on today's meat hunt, just to make certain they got something edible."

They? "Hank went with Brady?"

Jessica must have heard the snap in Molly's voice. Lifting an arm to brush the curls from her eyes, she looked at her. "Shouldn't he have?"

"I specifically told him not to ride horses or do anything that would jostle his ribs or arm."

Jessica's lips twitched. "Did he agree to that? Because if he didn't give his word, then it doesn't count." She resumed kneading. "That's how they dodge my edicts. I've learned if I get a promise, I get results."

"I'll remember that," Molly muttered.

Jessica added more flour and punched down the dough. She shot Molly a worried look. "If you didn't know Hank was going, then I guess you don't know about Charlie."

Molly whipped her head around. "Charlie? Charlie's with them?"

Jessica gave her a reassuring smile. "And Dougal—don't worry, his gun isn't loaded—and several of the ranch workers and their sons. As I said, a male family tradition. Ben is still too young to participate, thank God. I can't imagine what will happen when Brady puts a gun into that child's hands."

Molly scarcely heard her, worry over Charlie eclipsing all else. Her nephew had nightmares enough. What new night terrors might a "meat hunt" bring out?

"Don't worry, Molly," Jessica added. "They'll watch over him."

"I'm sure he'll be safe physically. It's just that he's so fragile right now. After the death of his mother . . ." She let the sentence hang.

"Hank knows that. He won't push the boy. He has a magical touch with children."

Children too? Molly thought peevishly. As well as fractious horses, balky mules, and any kind of machinery? The man should join a traveling circus.

It was late afternoon before the hunters

returned. Molly had positioned herself in the rocker by the main fireplace and was practicing what she would say to Hank when she heard deep voices and heavy footfalls on the front porch. A moment later, the door swung open and the man with the magical touch entered with Charlie in tow.

A smiling Charlie, Molly noted. With a bit of a swagger in his walk.

So maybe she'd been foolish to worry. But magical touch aside, she was still piqued that Hank would take her nephew on a hunting excursion without discussing it first with her. Although, as his "supposed" stepfather, he probably thought he had the right to make the decision on his own. But still.

She waited for them to remove their outer wear, all set to confront him, when Hank turned and saw her sitting there. He gave her that bone-melting smile, scattering her thoughts like thistledown on the wind, and before she could gather them up again, he walked over and kissed her as if he had a perfect right to do that as well. Which, as her "supposed" husband, he probably thought he did.

Molly didn't complain. In fact, she was so befuddled she couldn't speak at all, and it wasn't until he left the room, trailed by Charlie, that she even remembered what she had wanted to say. Letting out a rush of air she wasn't even aware she'd been holding, she turned to find Brady looking thoughtfully down at her.

"He's shaving," he said.

She blinked at him, still addled. "Charlie?" Surely Hank wouldn't put a straight razor into the hands of an eight-year-old.

"Hank. He never shaves unless he's courting."

"Oh?" She feigned nonchalance. "And does that happen often?"

Brady scratched his chin in thought. "Maybe once in ten years."

That girl from the fort that Martha Burnett had mentioned. "What happened?" she asked, trying to sound only marginally interested.

"Ask him." Then with a last probing glance, he strolled from the room.

THAT NIGHT SCREAMS SENT MOLLY BOLTING upright in bed.

Charlie!

Terrified that Fletcher had found them, she leaped out of bed, half-asleep and so disoriented she almost stumbled into the door before she got her bearings. Rushing across the hall, she burst into Charlie's room to find him huddled against the headboard, sobbing.

"It's all right, Charlie. I'm here." Taking his rigid body into her arms, she rocked him while he wept. "You're safe. It's just a bad dream. You're all right."

"H-He's coming—I s-saw him—he's c-coming to get us."

"No one is coming, Charlie. We're safe here. It's just a dream."

Charlie drew back. "Is P-Penny all right?" He swiped the sleeve of his flannel nightshirt across his running nose. "W-Where's Papa-Hank?"

"Right here, Charlie," a deep voice behind her said.

Turning, Molly saw Hank coming through the doorway, struggling one-handed with the buttons on a shirt with a split left sleeve. He looked tousled and sleepy and such a welcome sight to her frantic mind, she sagged in relief.

"Hey, fellow, what's wrong?" Crossing to the opposite side of the bed, he settled beside Charlie. Immediately the child lifted his thin arms and threw himself against Hank's broad chest, causing Hank to wince as a bony elbow hit his sore ribs.

Looking rattled, Hank frowned across the boy's auburn curls at Molly as if asking what he should do now.

Molly shrugged, as surprised as he.

Moving awkwardly because of the cast, he patted the small body almost dwarfed by his own. "I'm here, Charlie. I'll keep you safe."

"P-Penny too?" Charlie asked, his voice muffled against Hank's chest.

"Penny too."

"A-And Aunt M-Molly?"

Hank's gaze found hers again. "Always."

Charlie wiped his face against Hank's shirt, then pulled back to look up at him. "You promise?"

"I promise."

Molly looked away, blinking hard, weakened by a confused mix of emotions. Although she was moved by Hank's tender care of the boy, and grateful that Charlie drew comfort from it, she was also a bit disturbed by Charlie's sudden dependence on a man with whom they had such an uncertain future. What would happen when the truth came out? Would Charlie's brittle trust be another casualty of this deception?

Sickened by the prospect of the additional heartache the boy might suffer because of her actions, she turned to the door. "I'll check on Penny."

Once in the hall, guilt overcame her, and she leaned against the wall, one hand pressed to her stomach. How could she let this go on? How could she allow them all to become attached to a man destined to send them away?

Anguish churned in her belly. She wanted to explain, to tell him how in a moment of desperation she had made a terrible decision, and then had compounded it with silence because . . .

She bent over, teeth clenched, as realization burned through her.

Because she was so afraid. So weak. So loath to return to the lonely sterility of her life.

Tears burned hot on her cold cheeks.

Selfish, selfish fool.

* * *

ONCE HE WAS SURE THE BOY WAS SLEEPING, Hank left Charlie's room and stepped into the hall. For a moment he stood listening, but all was quiet and dark except for the soft light coming from Molly's room. Resolved, he crossed toward it.

The room was empty, lit by coals from the dying fire and a single candle burning on her night table. Stepping into the room, he closed the door quietly behind him and went to stoke the fire. He had something to ask his wife and he wanted enough light to see her face when she answered.

After stirring the embers, he added kindling until it caught, then more logs. By the time it was crackling, Molly returned. He didn't see her come in, but he felt her watching from the doorway into the dressing room, her gaze like a warm hand sliding over his back. Adding more logs to a fire already blazing, he waited for her to speak.

"How is he?" she finally asked, moving to one of the chairs flanking the hearth.

Hank looked over at her, saw the puffiness of her eyes, and knew she'd been crying. He wondered why. He wondered what she would do if he walked over and put his arms around her and kissed the haunted look from her eyes. He wondered what her skin felt like beneath that silky robe.

"Asleep," he said and turned back to the fire.

Unfolding the throw laid across the back of the chair, she sat and draped it over her hips and legs. "Thank you for helping him."

"He's my responsibility, too, Molly." As he said it, he shot her a glance, but she didn't meet his gaze. He thought she might be hurt because Charlie had turned to him after his nightmare, rather than her. Most likely she was upset that he hadn't told her about the hunt and probably thought that was the reason behind the nightmare. He decided to put that to rest first.

"I guess I should have asked you before I took him hunting."

"Yes. You should have."

He studied her, trying to gauge the level of her anger, but she was looking down at a pleat she was working on in the blanket on her lap. He decided to wait for her to speak first.

It didn't take long. "You know how fearful

he is," she said. "I'm not sure I want him playing with guns at such a young age."

Definitely mad. Which sparked his own anger. "We don't *play* with guns, Molly. We hunt."

"Charlie's too young—"

"Charlie didn't hunt and he never touched a gun," he cut in. "He wasn't even there for the shoot or when the other men dressed out their kills."

She looked so surprised, it felt like an insult. "Did you think I'd bring harm to the boy, Molly? Have you so little faith in me?"

He watched a flush move up her neck and across her high cheekbones. Her eyes were great wounded pools that shimmered in the firelight.

"I worry," she said.

"Don't." Regretting that he'd snapped at her, he jabbed at the fire with the poker. How could he have forgotten this woman? How could he feel about her the way he did now, and not have a single memory of her from before the derailment?

Unless there were no memories.

The thought came from nowhere—so sudden and shocking he mentally recoiled from it, unwilling to examine it too closely or acknowledge that there could be any truth in it. But like a scrap of tune that wouldn't let go, it kept circling in his mind until finally he had no choice but to face it.

If there were no memories, then it was all a lie and everyone around him was in on it . . . even his brother. But why would they do such a thing? To what end?

There was no logical reason for it.

It made no sense.

Still, the doubts ate at him, leaving a dark emptiness where trust used to be.

The fire popped and hissed, sounding loud and intrusive in the quietness of the room. Somewhere out in the valley a coyote yodeled.

Staring into the dancing flames, he tried to calm his turbulent thoughts. Brady would never lie to him. The one unshakable truth in Hank's life was his faith in his brother. Since the day Brady finally told him the truth about Sam's death, Hank had never doubted him.

And he wouldn't start now.

Rising gingerly so he wouldn't jar his ribs, he moved to sit in the chair across from Molly's. He studied her. In the firelight she looked tired and sad and defeated. He focused on that, rather than the doubts, and posed the question he had come to ask. “What aren’t you telling me, Molly?”

She wouldn’t look at him, but stared down at her clenched fists instead. He watched them loosen, the fingers straightening one by one, as if each movement was forced rather than a slow release of tension. When they lay stick-straight on her thighs, she still hadn’t spoken.

“Why is Charlie so troubled?” he persisted.

Her head flew up. “Charlie?” She shot him a quick glance before her gaze shifted to the fire. But in that single instant when their eyes had met, he had seen profound relief. Why? Again, that feeling that she was hiding something.

He waited, having learned that Molly, like most people and especially his brother, found his silences intolerable and, when confronted with one, felt compelled to fill it with words. This time was no different.

“After the children’s father died,” she began in a faltering voice, “my sister remarried. It turned out he wasn’t a very nice man. Nellie learned to distrust him, and the children grew to fear him. Before Sister died, she made me promise to keep Penny and Charlie safe and take them someplace far from his reach."

Hank remembered Penny saying "step-papas hurt." Now he guessed why, and he didn't like it. "Did he hurt them?"

"I think he hit them, but I'm not sure. Nellie said he was 'up to something bad,' was the way she put it. Something about a new war. She didn't explain what she meant and was too ill to question, so I didn't press it. That night, I took the children and left Savannah. That was six weeks ago."

Savannah? Savannah was thousands of miles away. Yet they'd been back at the ranch for almost two weeks, and the week before that, he'd been in the infirmary in El Paso. Could that be right? He counted again. He and Molly had gotten married within days of meeting each other? That made no sense either, but he put it aside to puzzle through later. "Where were you headed?"

"There's a doctor in California—a

colleague of my father's—I thought maybe I could work in his clinic."

"Then you met me." In Sierra Blanca. Thousands of miles from Savannah. Only days before the derailment.

Her fists clenched again. "Yes."

The questions were piling up fast, but for now, Hank concentrated on the children. "Is their stepfather trying to find them?"

"Charlie believes he is. If not him, then someone he sent. Penny told me she thought someone was following us, but she has a rather vivid imagination sometimes." She looked up, her face showing confusion. "My sister said Daniel lost some papers. He thought the children had them, but when I questioned them, they seemed to know nothing about it. So I don't know why he would come after us."

A memory skirted Hank's mind . . . something Penny had said when he was sick. But the thought faded before he could grasp it. "Did I know him?"

"Fletcher?" The question seemed to rattle her. "No. You never met."

Daniel Fletcher. Hank reminded himself to remember that name.

"You tell Charlie he's safe here," he said. "You're all safe here."

She nodded, but didn't say anything.

He thought of something Charlie had said a few minutes ago when Molly had left to check on Penny. "The hunt today didn't set off his nightmare, Molly. After you left, he asked about Penny again, then you. Even me."

She watched him, her almost-green eyes reflecting back the firelight.

"He seems worried that something will happen to us," he went on. "That he'll lose us like he's lost the other people in his life. I think he feels powerless to save us, and that's what makes him so afraid and angry."

"Save us from what?"

He shrugged. "His stepfather? Who's Mappa?"

She seemed to draw into herself. Her gaze dropped to the hands clasped in her lap. "His grandfather. My father. His name was Matthew, but when Charlie first learned to speak, it came out 'Mappa' instead."

Hank watched her hands clench again and knew she was upset. He was learning to read the signs. "He's dead?"

"Three months ago."

"How?"

"Supposedly he shot himself."

"Supposedly?"

When she looked up, he saw anguish in her eyes, and beneath it, a smoldering anger. "Papa would never take his own life. He was too . . ." She hesitated, searching for the right word. "Focused," she finally said. "Medicine was everything to him. His work was too important to him to leave behind."

His work? Not the daughter who apparently gave up everything to stay by his side? A log collapsed in the fire. Idly Hank watched sparks rise in a swirling dance and thought of his wife's sadness and Charlie's fear and Penny's need for attention. Families were so complicated.

"What did he say about Mappa?" Molly asked.

Hank looked up to meet his wife's troubled gaze. She had pretty eyes. Mysterious. They made him think if he just looked into them hard and long enough, he would know all her secrets. "He thinks the monster got him. And we'll be next."

"Oh, God."

"But we can fix that," he added quickly. "We just have to build up his confidence. Show him how to protect himself so he won't feel so powerless."

"How do you plan to do that?"

"Oh, I'll think of something." No use getting her upset again. She had a tendency to overprotect the boy. He waited to see if she would argue. Molly wasn't one to be easily led or condescended to. He admired that. And even though he wished she would allow herself to rely on him more, he understood why she didn't. Her father, for whatever misguided reason, had done a good job of teaching her to depend on no one other than herself. But she'd come around. Already she trusted him enough to come at him head-on, not cowed in the least by his size, or manner, or probing silences. She wasn't afraid to question him and demand her answers. And she was smart. She wouldn't be as easy to play as Brady, and he admired that most of all. But he still expected to win most of the time.

"Before you do anything you think I won't approve of, talk to me," she said.

Only a fool would agree to that one, and

he didn't consider himself a fool. "If you think that's best." He showed his teeth in a sincere smile.

"I want your promise, Hank. Say it."

He sighed. "I promise." Maybe too smart. "Now you do something for me."

She watched him, waiting.

"Take down your hair."

Her eyes widened. The tips of her ears turned red. But she was too wise to pretend she didn't remember his words the last time he had been in this room.

Hesitantly she lifted her arms and tugged loose the ribbon tied around the end of her braid.

He watched, hands gripping the arms of the chair, amazed that such a simple movement could be so . . . inspiring. Then her fingers combed through the loosened mass, drawing the shiny waves forward over her shoulder until the ends curled over her breast like a cupping hand. And his mouth went dry.

His gaze traveled up to meet hers. A shock of awareness shot through him when he realized that while he had been watching her, she had just as intently been watching him. And reacting, judging by that flush on her cheeks. The idea of that made his heart thunder in his chest.

He forced himself to stand while he still could. As he looked down into those almost-green eyes, he realized this woman had taken ahold of him in a way he'd never expected and in a way no other woman ever had. And he knew with certainty that whatever had passed between them before he lost his memory of her couldn't have been any stronger than what he was feeling now.

If it was all a lie, he didn't want to know.

Not yet.

Maybe not ever.

Bending, he slipped his hand beneath her forceful chin and tipped up her head. He kissed her. She didn't move, so he did it again. "I don't know what to do with you, wife," he murmured. Then still holding her chin, he put his mouth next to her ear and whispered, "But maybe next time, you'll take off the robe and we'll find out."

He heard her sharp intake of breath. Felt the flutter of her pulse against the fingertips still holding her jaw. Felt it all the way down into his chest.

Letting his hand fall away, he straightened. “Apples.”

A moment of confusion, then that slow, sweet smile. “No.”

“Blackberries.”

“Close.”

“Thank God. I’m getting tired of waiting.” And turning, he made himself walk from the room.

THANKSGIVING WAS A JOYOUS FEAST—NO BEAR meat, but plenty of elk and grouse and even a turkey, along with an assortment of English puddings and pastries, Iantha’s “down-home vittles,” and a few Mexican dishes contributed by Consuelo. Molly had never eaten so much.

But she almost cast it all back up when well-meaning Jessica asked how she and Hank fell in love.

“Yeah, Molly,” Brady seconded in a challenging tone once Molly had stopped coughing. “Tell us all about how my little brother proposed.”

Still clutching her napkin to her mouth, Molly snuck a glance at Hank, hoping he would step in and tell his brother it was none of his business. He didn't. And in fact, he wore as curious an expression as all the other faces staring and waiting patiently for all the sordid details.

"Yes, well." She coughed again, mostly for effect, but also in a frantic attempt to buy time to formulate an answer. And then, happily, somewhere during the time it took to carefully fold her linen and place it neatly beside her plate, inspiration arrived—and with it came all the half-imagined daydreams that had seen her through endless bloody days and countless lonely nights.

Her perversity was beyond belief.

Nonetheless, she graced her audience with a dramatic sigh. "It was quite romantic, really. Most definitely love at first sight. I—we, that is," she added with a smile at her rather confused-looking niece and nephew, "were standing on the train platform when I looked up and there he was."

"But Aunt Molly—" Penny began.

"Not with your mouth full, dear," she cut in quickly before continuing. "He was so tall and handsome—"

"You were able to tell that through all the hair?" Brady cut in.

"Hush, Brady," Jessica admonished. "Let's hear her tell her story."

Oh yes, let's. Molly took a deep breath, let it out, then forged into fantasy.

"Later that evening, I saw him again," she went on, the story unfolding in her head. "The children were in bed. I was too restless to sleep, so I went downstairs to get a pitcher of water. It was so hot. The air felt thick as molasses. I longed for cool water to rinse the dust and heat from my body . . ."

Her thoughts drifted. She could almost feel the perspiration beading on her neck, trickling slowly down between her breasts. Then she realized that was her hand, and the tips of her fingers were sliding down past the loosened buttons at the collar of her dress. Shocked, she pulled her hand away, but noticed that both Brady's and Hank's gazes remained fixed on shadowed cleavage where it had been.

"But the dining room was closed," she went on in a voice that sounded breathless in her own ear. "So I went outside onto the boardwalk, desperate for a breath of fresh air. It was so hot and sticky, I could scarcely breathe. I felt like ripping off my clothes and sinking into the water trough in front of the hotel . . . anything to cool my overheated body. But of course, I couldn't. Instead, I stood there, the darkness wrapping around me like a lover, the night so still it seemed a thousand crickets were singing just for me."

She paused and looked around at the rapt faces—Jessica, smiling dreamily, Brady's blue eyes round in his slack face, and Hank . . . dear Hank . . . he looked almost flushed. Locking her gaze on his, she smiled lazily and dropped her voice almost to a whisper.

"I didn't see him at first, sitting so quietly in the shadows . . . watching. But I knew he was there. I could feel him"—her hand started wandering again—"feel his eyes move over my body as surely as if he'd reached out and brushed his hand over my—"

"Well, all right then," Brady said, abruptly rising from his chair. "How about we all go into the main room for cookies and cakes? Jessica, can I see you upstairs for a minute?"

"But I want to hear the rest of the story," she argued as he pulled back her chair.

"No you don't. We'll be back in a minute," he called, ushering her from the room.

As the children stampeded into the main room for dessert, and Dougal trotted after Consuelo into the kitchen, Molly sat back in her chair, feeling a bit unsettled and oddly short of breath. And when had the room become so stifling? she wondered, fanning her face with her hand.

"Over what?"

Pretending to be startled, as if she'd forgotten she wasn't alone, she glanced at the other end of the table, where Hank slouched in the chair watching her, his good arm hooked over the high back. That intense look was back in his warm, chocolate eyes. His masculine energy seemed to crackle in the air like fire.

She resisted the urge to fan harder.

"You said it felt like I'd brushed my hand over your . . . what?"

She saw the laughter in his eyes and realized he was teasing her. It made her feel wicked and daring and braver than she was. Rising slowly from her chair, she sauntered toward him. "Strawberries," she said, drawing out the word on a sigh. "Ripe, luscious, pink strawberries, so deliciously sweet on the tongue."

His eyes widened. The teasing light in his eyes flared into something else.

Pausing behind his chair, she bent to whisper in his ear. "They're my favorite food."

Eleven

A WEEK AFTER THANKSGIVING, A WARM CHInook wind swept down the eastern slopes of the mountains, melting most of the snow and turning the road to mud. Overnight, the creek that cut through the RosaRoja Valley became a raging river, churning up rocks and brush and fallen trees before it finally crested and started back down. Two days later, the road into Val Rosa was dry enough for wagon traffic.

Taking advantage of the warm break in the weather, ranch workers checked on the cattle scattered throughout the valley, moving those that had wandered too far into the mountains back to the valley floor. As the unseasonably warm weather continued, Hank and Brady planned a trip to Redemption to check on the mines, while Jessica organized a jaunt into Val Rosa to do last-minute shopping for Christmas gifts and to arrange bonuses for Boxing Day. Having two additional children in the family to shop for had her in a dither of excitement.

Molly was reluctant to go. If the roads were passable for them, they were also passable for Fletcher. If he had tracked them to El Paso, it wouldn't be difficult for him to learn they had left several weeks ago for the Wilkins ranch. Even now, he might be in Val Rosa, knowing it was the nearest town, and if they left, that would be where they would go.

Hank must have noted her concern. "If you're worried about Fletcher," he said as he stood at the kitchen table, loading rations into his saddlebags for the ride to Redemption, "you needn't be. You'll be safe."

"I'm more worried about your ribs," she said, which was partly true. But it was more than that, and more than worry over

Fletcher. She'd known he was leaving for the mines that morning, and had wanted to see him before he left. She wasn't sure why. She'd checked his arm the night before and had pronounced him well enough to travel—not that he would have remained home if she hadn't. They'd said goodbyes. He'd even given her another of those slow, teasing kisses that always left her feeling so disoriented and yearning for more. She had nothing more to say to him. Yet as soon as she awoke this morning, she had been driven to see him.

One more time.

Ridiculous, but there it was. She was becoming besotted with the man.

After buckling the strap on the bulging saddlebag, he hefted it over his right shoulder and turned to face her. He looked big and indomitable and utterly beautiful to her. Sunlight streaking through the kitchen window highlighted the strong angle of his jaw, the long corded tendons down his neck, the warm fire in those deep brown eyes. Just looking at him made her heart tremble.

"We've doubled the riders with your

wagon," he told her. "And Brady and I will be waiting for you when you get to Val Rosa. No need to worry."

"I know." It wasn't her safety or that of the children that concerned her. It was his. What if he slipped on the ice and fell on his arm? What if it started snowing again and they became lost or stranded miles from help?

"Promise me you'll be careful," she said.

He reached out to brush his fingertips across her cheek. "Sweet Molly. You worry too much."

"You give me cause."

"I try not to."

A mere foot separated them but to Molly it felt like an immense distance. Despite the gentle kisses and whispered words, Hank had never taken her into his arms. He always kept a space between them, held a part of himself back.

Why? Was it her? Had she ever been held in a man's arms?

With a shock, she realized she hadn't. Not truly. Her father had occasionally given her a one-armed hug, a brief, friendly squeeze of camaraderie rather than deep affection. Papa had been a passionate man, but not a demonstrative one. She'd understood and accepted that.

But with Hank, well, she wanted more.

As if it had a will of its own, her hand came up to rest against his wide chest. She watched her fingers splay as she pressed her palm against the soft flannel of his shirt, seeking the muffled vibration of the heart beating within. "Just come back."

When he didn't respond, she looked up. And while her mind floated in emotion, her body took action on its own, her fingers sliding up his chest and around his neck to comb through the crisp curls on his nape. Pulling him closer, she rose on tiptoe and pressed her mouth to his.

She tasted coffee, and caught a drift of his pine-scented shaving soap, mingled with the tang of old smoke and the mustiness of his shearling jacket. Tentatively, she ran the tip of her tongue over the seam of his lips, then drew back.

But he followed her, kissing her again, then again. By the time he lifted his head, they were both a bit out of breath. "Jesus," he said in a long exhale. "How could I have forgotten that?"

And with those words, guilt stole the joy

away. She stared back at him in mute misery, unspoken words clogging her throat. The urge to blurt out the truth overwhelmed her, and she knew she couldn't hold it back any longer.

"Hank, I need to tell you—"

The bang of the door cut her off as Brady came in with a whoosh of cold air. "There you are," he said, slamming the door shut, then stomping mud off his boots onto the rug inside the threshold. "The horses are saddled. Morning, Molly."

Reason returned and the moment passed. Molly stepped back from Hank and brushed a hand over her hair. Now was not the time for confession. She couldn't send him off on a long, hard ride with worry—or anger—on his mind.

At least, that was the excuse she gave herself for her continued silence.

Hank studied her for a moment. Then adjusting the saddlebag over his shoulder, he gave her a final nod and followed his brother out the door.

Molly watched them ride out, thinking she still hadn't gotten her hug and sensing time was running out.

* * *

THE DAY OF THE TRIP INTO VAL ROSA DAWNED crisp and clear.

Hoping the weather would hold for the few days they intended to be gone, Jessica and Molly helped the Garcia sisters herd the children into a high canvas-covered wagon with wheels that could be fitted with sled runners if necessary—another of Hank's innovations. Bundled in blankets and fortified with the two baskets of food Iantha had packed, they headed down the drive for the six-hour wagon ride to Val Rosa.

The countryside spread before them like an illustration in a storybook. Rolling hills dotted with glistening patches of snow, sugar-frosted evergreens, soaring white-capped mountains reaching into the cloudless sky. Distant herds of elk and mule deer browsed at the mouths of the canyons. Overhead, eagles and hawks rode the currents looking for smaller prey. Occasionally their wagon scattered small groups of cows and calves from their path, and once along the tree line, Charlie spotted either a buffalo or a very big bear. As the day passed, the sun dipped lower toward the mountaintops, and the angle of sunlight highlighted an intricate maze of tracks crisscrossing the remaining snow. Penny thought it looked like a giant, sparkly spider web.

They made good time, and even though clouds began to build to the north and the wind picked up, they arrived on schedule in midafternoon. The warm weather had the town bustling, the muddy streets lined with wagons and carts, the boardwalks filled with people restocking winter supplies and making Christmas purchases. True to their promises, Hank and Brady awaited them in the Val Rosa Hotel lobby.

The Wilkins family took over the top floor—Brady and Jessica in a parlor suite, their children sharing rooms with the Garcia sisters. Hank had his own room, and Penny and Charlie shared a suite with Molly. She wanted them near in case Charlie needed her, although since the night after the hunt and his talk with Hank, he hadn't been troubled by nightmares. But she also wanted them close in case Fletcher had tracked them this far.

After sending the children off with the Garcias, Molly freshened up, then stood at the window of their corner room, studying the street below. She saw neither Fletcher nor the scarred man Penny said she'd seen in Omaha and later in Utah. But she did notice the Wilkins riders lounging here and there on the boardwalk within shouting distance of the hotel, and felt safer knowing they were there.

The family took an early evening meal in a private parlor off the dining room. After they ate, Jessica, who knew nothing about Fletcher or his trackers, suggested they take a turn along the boardwalk before the shops closed for the night.

Molly was about to offer excuses when Hank pulled her aside. “It’ll be all right,” he assured her. “If Fletcher is here, he’ll have to get through six men to get to you, and I won’t let that happen.”

“You’ll stay close?”

He gave a crooked grin. “As close as you’ll let me.”

She looked away, her cheeks warm, a smile tugging at her lips. For a man who didn’t talk much, he certainly knew how to charm.

The evening was crisp but not overly cold, with a gentle breeze just strong enough to clear the air of wood smoke but not harsh enough to chill. Wearing an outrageous ribbon-and-feather-bedecked hat almost the size of a small wagon wheel, Jessica led them past the shops like the proud flagship of a grand flotilla, escorted by her formidable husband, their children, and the Garcia sisters.

The town was in full Christmas celebration. On a large wooden platform in front of the corner building that housed The Peoples Bank stood the town Christmas tree, a twenty-foot-tall blue Douglas fir topped by a tin angel. All the ornaments decorating the tree were made of wood and tin, and after dark, the dozens of candles in wooden hoops that hung from the tips of the branches lit up the boardwalk. It was magical.

The storefronts were dressed up as well, with garlands of spruce in the windows, as well as crocheted snowflakes and tin stars and little bouquets of dried spices and flowers hanging from the beams. The scents of pine and spiced cider and cinnamon sticks filled the air. The children were agog with excitement.

The Wilkins family was well known and obviously well liked, if the number of people calling greetings and giving friendly waves was any indication. Or perhaps that was just curiosity about Hank's wife. It was apparent news of his marriage had reached Val Rosa. Amid all the stares and well-wishes, Molly felt like a prize cabbage. No one was rude, of course, not with Hank looming so attentively by her side, but after years of being invisible, she found all the attention a bit unnerving.

Perhaps sensing Molly's unease, Hank steered her and the children away from curious eyes and into Milford's Emporium and General Store, where he bought strings of rock candy for the children and a paper cone of sugared nuts for Molly. While Hank and the children wandered the aisles, Molly made a careful study of the skeins of yarn on the back wall, thinking she might knit hats and scarves for the children for Christmas. Pulling out her coin purse, she counted the few coins she had left. Just enough. Satisfied, she closed the purse and looked up to find Hank watching her, a troubled frown on his face.

"Thinking to buy something?" he asked.

Avoiding his eyes, she tucked her near-empty purse back into her coat pocket. "Yarn. The children could use warm hats." Picking up a skein of green yarn and another of yellow, she held them up. "Which do you think Charlie would prefer?"

He studied them a moment, then shrugged. "The red. More manly."

The red? She frowned at the twists of yarn she held, but before she could question him about it, he said, "Are those all the coins you have, Molly?" When she didn't answer, his frown deepened into a scowl. "Have I been that stingy with you?"

"No, not at all. It's just that . . . well . . . lately there's been no need."

"I'm not a miser," he said gruffly, reaching into his pocket. "You shouldn't be without spending money. And you shouldn't have to ask me for it." Before she could stop him, he dumped a handful of coins into her hand. "Go buy what you need for yourself and the children."

When she started to protest, he closed her fingers over the coins. "It's Christmas, for crissakes. If you won't get something for yourself, buy presents for the children. For everybody."

The coins felt heavy in her hand. There were probably enough to keep her and the children for a month, maybe more. Out of habit, she almost stuffed them into her pocket as insurance against the hungry days ahead.

"There's more if you need it."

Kind, generous Hank. She had stolen his name. Why not his coin?

Filled with self-disgust, she put the money away. "Thank you."

While Hank took the children to the feed store, she made her purchases—a beautifully painted tin of imported tea for Jessica, a braided leather hatband for Brady, and a book on inventions for Hank. In addition to the hats and scarves she planned to knit, she bought rag dolls for Penny and Abigail, toy soldiers for Charlie and Ben, and taffy and apples and oranges for all their stockings. For the Garcia sisters, she purchased lengths of cloth and matching ribbons, for Dougal, a pair of warm gloves in case he ever ventured outside, and for Consuelo and Iantha, bright calico aprons. As she paid for her purchases, she asked the proprietor who in town did small-item repair.

"That would be Gruber's Fix-It," he said. "Across from Helen's Haberdashery. Small place. Careful, or you'll miss it."

After thanking him and arranging for her purchases to be delivered to the hotel, she stepped outside into a chill gust that almost ripped her bonnet from her head. The day had faded to twilight with shadowed gray clouds hanging low in the sky. Hoping she wouldn't run into Hank and the children, she hurried to the Fix-It Shop.

Mr. Gruber was a wiry little man with a shiny bald head, a short white beard, and startling black eyebrows. When she entered his shop, he peered over half-spectacles with the impatient expression of a man who didn't tolerate interruptions well. Knowing he was probably anxious to close for the night, she got straight to the point. "I need parts."

"Parts."

She nodded. "Various sizes, more small than large, and in good condition."

Setting aside the timepiece he'd been working on, he regarded her with a skeptical eye. "Parts. Small, not large. In good condition."

"Yes." She spaced her hands a foot apart. "A box of this size will do."

He continued to stare at her as if she were speaking in tongues. Then a smile of understanding broke across his face. "You are the new wife of Hank Wilkins."

"You know him?"

"She asks if I know him." He rolled his eyes. "I know him. He comes all the time, touching this, touching that. So many questions. What a tinkerer, that one." Rising from his stool, he held aside the curtain draped over a doorway behind the counter. "Come. I maybe have just the thing."

Molly could see why Hank would find Gruber's workroom fascinating. It was a cluttered mess of items in all stages of disrepair, stuffed onto shelves that were already overflowing with tools and parts and more parts. A tinkerer's dream.

"Will that do?" Gruber pointed to a squat, round, wooden container the size of a small nail keg—approximately eighteen inches tall and ten inches across—that was filled to the brim with screws and springs and nuts and bolts and gears and all manner of metal and wooden parts.

"Are you sure you can spare all that?" Molly asked, mentally counting the coins she had left. "It must be very expensive."

"For you, not so much." He gave her a twinkling smile. "If it keeps your husband out of my shop for a while, I will consider it a wise investment."

By the time she'd paid, made arrangements to have the keg delivered to the ranch, and exited the shop, the street was dark except for the checkerboard patterns of lamplight shining through store windows onto the wooden boardwalk. And those were fast disappearing as shopkeepers began pulling down shades and locking their doors for the night. The saloons and cantinas at either end of the main street were the only establishments that seemed to have increased their business, judging by the number of horses tied at the rails outside.

Pausing in the recessed doorway of Gruber's shop to tighten the bow on her bonnet, Molly looked around. She saw no ominously familiar faces or lurking watchers, although two women standing in the window of Helen's Haberdashery seemed to be staring at her. One she recognized as the storeowner, a middle-aged matron with improbably dark hair that Hank had introduced earlier when they'd passed by the shop. The blond woman she didn't recognize.

They were definitely staring.

Molly looked to see if there was anyone else who might have drawn their interest, but she was the only one in their line of vision. It bothered her to be watched that way, and sent that rush of heightened awareness tingling beneath her skin.

Could Fletcher have sent a female tracker after them, thinking a woman might be more difficult for Molly to detect?

Growing alarmed, she tucked her head against the wind and their prying eyes and moved quickly down the boardwalk. Her footsteps sounded loud and lonely on the wooden planks. Hearing them triggered imaginings of other footsteps coming up behind her, and she quickened her pace until her breath fogged the air and frost collected damply in the bow tied at her chin.

As she passed a dark alley, she caught movement in the corner of her eye, and whipped her head around in time to see a dark shadow ducking into the darker shadows behind the building. Panic flooded her mind.

She shouldn't have left the ranch. She shouldn't have let the children out of her sight. They should have stayed at RosaRoja, where they were safe. She was so intent on putting distance between herself and the watchers, she didn't see the figure looming before her until she rammed into it.

Rebounding off a big, solid form, she staggered for balance until a hand gripped her shoulder to steady her. "Whoa," a familiar voice said.

"Hank." She sagged against him in relief. "It's you."

"Who'd you think it was?" When she didn't answer, he gently held her away with his good hand and peered down into her face. "What's wrong?"

She felt him waiting, probing. Then a new panic assailed her. "Where are the children?"

"I sent them back to the hotel with Jessica and Brady. The Garcias will see that they're readied for bed." He gave her shoulder a gentle shake. "Now tell me what's wrong."

Suddenly she felt foolish and melodramatic. Before Fletcher, she had never feared anything but failure, but now she saw a threat around every corner. This sense of helpless panic was new to her, and she didn't like it.

"Nothing. Some women were staring at me, and I—"

"What women?"

"In the Haberdashery." She didn't mention the figure in the alley.

Releasing her shoulder, he turned back.

Realizing he intended to go over there, she grabbed his arm. "It's unimportant. They didn't do anything. I—" Her words stopped when she looked past him to see the blond woman standing on the boardwalk in front of the shop, staring at them.

Hank turned to see what had drawn her notice.

Molly still gripped his arm, and even through the thick leather and wool interfacing of his jacket, she could feel the ripple of tension that went through him.

"Hell."

"You know her?" The woman was now focused on Hank, rather than her.

Instead of answering, he pulled his arm from her grip and gave her a gentle push. "Go back to the hotel, Molly."

The woman stepped off the boardwalk and started toward them, her gaze never leaving Hank's face. Even in the fading light, Molly could see she was pretty and petite and smiling. At Hank. Her husband.

A feeling Molly didn't recognize coursed through her.

Another nudge regained her attention. "Go on, Molly. I'll be there directly."

Lips pursed, Molly spun. Head high, looking neither right nor left, she marched toward the hotel, furious that her husband had dismissed her as if she were a child. And who was that woman that he would so easily cast aside his own wife—

Her steps faltered as realization came.

Filled with dread, yet unable to stop herself, Molly looked back.

They were standing where she had left him. Standing close, talking. As Molly watched, the woman raised a gloved hand and touched Hank's cheek.

An intimate, telling gesture. One Hank didn't try to avoid.

Something coiled in Molly's chest and constricted her lungs. She gulped in air, felt the cold bite of it in her throat, the icy sting against her damp eyes. Blinking hard, she forced herself to move on—past the General Store—dark now—and the milliner's shop, the assay office—her entire being focused on reaching the bright squares of light spilling from the hotel windows—then through the lobby and up the stairs and, with a last burst of strength, through the door into her room. Closing it behind her, she leaned against it, her heart pounding, her mind in tatters.

It was her. The woman from the fort—the woman Brady said had chosen a tin soldier over Hank—the woman Hank had been in love with before Molly had trapped him in this sham of a marriage. *What have I done?*

A hollow ache spread through her chest. She felt the burn of tears on her cold cheeks and didn't know whom she wept for—herself or Hank.

IT HAD BEEN TWO YEARS, BUT AT FIRST GLANCE, Melanie didn't appear to have changed at all. Same small, round-cheeked face, same wispy blond hair, same soft gray eyes. But as he watched her draw closer, Hank saw that though the changes were subtle, the years had marked her. Those gray eyes seemed a bit weary now, and faint worry lines marred the smooth forehead. The smile was the same, although less open and eager. More subdued. Wiser.

But the biggest change was within himself. She moved him not at all.

"Hank," she said in that breathy, childlike voice he remembered. "It's really you." Reaching up, she brushed her fingertips along his cheek.

He steeled himself not to pull back.

She must have sensed it. Taking her hand away, she motioned to the cast showing below his left cuff. "I'd heard you were in a derailment. Are you all right?"

"Fine. What are you doing here?" It came out more sharply than he had intended, but he was rattled, by both Melanie's sudden appearance and Molly's obvious anger. He hadn't meant to upset his wife by sending her away so abruptly. He'd only wanted to save her from an uncomfortable confrontation. But he'd done it badly, and now . . . hell, before this was over, he'd probably have both women mad at him.

"I was on my way back to Baltimore," Melanie said.

"Taking the long way, are you?" Val Rosa was at least fifty miles the wrong way. When she didn't respond, he looked around.

"Traveling alone?" What he wanted to ask was where was her husband.

She brushed a tendril of blond hair from her eyes and peered up at him. "I don't know if you heard, but there was an outbreak of smallpox at the fort last spring." A hard look crossed her normally placid features. "Brought in by one of those filthy Indians, I'm sure."

He didn't remind her that someone from the fort had probably infected those "filthy Indians" in the first place. "I heard."

"Mama died. And Paul. He was my husband."

"Sorry to hear it." And he was. Whatever animosity he'd once felt for this woman was long gone. She seemed a stranger now. And a little lost. He watched her gloved fingers worry the fringe on her shawl and felt that familiar surge of protectiveness that always gripped him whenever he was in her presence.

It was a failing of his. Probably because of his size, he felt compelled to watch out for those who were weaker and smaller. Even now, he fought the urge to shelter her as if she were a helpless child.

Which in many ways, Melanie was—in

temperament and intellect and that cloying need to please that he'd once attributed to a gentle nature, but had come to recognize as weakness of character. He'd forgotten how burdensome that dependence could be. And tiresome. Molly had spoiled him.

Molly. What was she thinking right now?

Impatiently, he shifted his weight from one foot to the other, wishing this conversation would end so he could get out of the cold. He glanced toward the hotel and wondered how to explain Melanie to his wife, or if he should say anything at all.

"I was pregnant."

Startled, he looked back at the woman before him. "Not by me." His memory might be faulty, but he was positive he'd never taken Melanie Kinderly to bed.

"No, it was Paul. He was Father's adjutant. I was lonely, and he . . . well, it just happened. Before you came to the fort and asked me to marry you." Her sentences were short and choppy. Hesitant. "I never loved him, not like I did you."

Not knowing what to say, he remained silent. None of this mattered now. He was married to another woman. A better woman.

"When Mama found out about the baby," she went on, "I told her it was yours. I wanted it to be yours. I wanted it so bad. But she still wouldn't let me marry you."

"You were a grown woman, Melanie. It was your choice."

"I know, but I was afraid, Hank. Can you understand that? Besides, Father said he would throw you in the guardhouse if I didn't make you leave." Her voice turned bitter. "He wanted me to marry Paul, you see. Keep up the military tradition."

Hank had wondered. When he'd first arrived at the fort, Melanie had seemed so glad to see him—frantic, almost. He'd proposed, she'd said yes, and then suddenly, she was marrying another man.

He'd felt stunned. Then betrayed. And finally so furious it had put him off women for over a year, until, well, Molly came along.

In his rage, he had assumed Melanie's mother had forced her into it—he knew Maude Kinderly had no love for the Wilkins family—or that Melanie's affection had all been a sham, just another fabrication of her overworked imagination. There had always been a fantasy quality about Melanie, an emotionalism that shielded her from reality. Life was a dime novel adventure to her, complete with heroes and damsels in distress and happy endings. She saw what she wanted to see, believed what she wanted to believe. Given enough time, she might have even convinced herself that he really was the father of her baby. Thinking back on it now, he had to wonder if he *had* married her, would he have ever known otherwise?

Feeling like a man who had survived his own hanging, he thought how lucky he was to have avoided binding himself to this woman forever. No Molly. No Charlie and Penny. A life built on a lie. The idea of it left a sour taste in his mouth.

"The baby was stillborn."

He studied the toes of his boots. "That's too bad."

"I just wanted you to know what happened . . . why I did what I did. And to tell you that I wish I had done it differently."

Hank was glad she hadn't.

They stood in silence for a moment. He noted the wind had picked up and carried a bite that foretold snow. They'd be lucky to make it home before the roads were buried in snowdrifts. "Well—"

"Actually I was headed to your ranch," she blurted out before he could finish the sentence. "To see you. I was hoping . . ." She gave a forced laugh and made a fluttery gesture with her hand. Hank could see it was shaking. "But the lady in the haberdashery said you were married. Is that true?"

He nodded.

"I see."

Another awkward silence. She cleared her throat. "Then I wish you well. Do give my regards to Jessica and your brothers." She held out her gloved hand.

He gave it a brief squeeze then released it. "Have a safe journey."

Blinking hard, she nodded. "Thank you."

As Hank watched her move quickly down the boardwalk, he felt the past slip away—the months of doubt and bitterness, the disappointment, the wondering "what-if"—and by the time she faded into the gloaming light, all that was left was a deep sense of relief.

He turned toward the hotel, wondering if

Molly would be waiting to ambush him, or if she'd punch him like she had after the snowball fight. Perversely, the thought of her being mad at him made him smile.

Being unafraid of confrontations but hating to wait for them, he went straight up to her room. Mentally bracing himself, he knocked on her door.

The knob turned on his third knock, which told him she'd either been asleep and he'd awoken her, or she'd had a hard time deciding whether or not she wanted to open the door.

She was fully dressed, so she hadn't been asleep. Judging by the puffy eyes, she'd been crying instead. The fight went out of him. Reaching out, he pulled her against his chest. She felt smaller than she looked and smelled like lemons and the cinnamon and sugarcoated nuts he'd bought her. "I didn't mean to upset you."

"I'm not upset."

Even though her voice was muffled against his chest, he still heard the quaver. "She means nothing, Molly."

She drew back to glare at him through damp eyes. "How can you say that? She was in love with you. You were in love with her. How can that mean nothing?"

"I mean *now*. She means nothing *now*."

"So you *did* love her."

Accused and condemned. Hank let his arms fall back to his sides.

"Do you still have feeling for her?" Before he could answer, she rushed on. "Because if you do, my offer still holds."

"Molly—"

"We don't have to stay married, you know. We can still call this off."

Anger spiked through him. "Is that what you want? To call it off? Because that's sure as hell not what I want."

She blinked like a startled owl. "It isn't?"

"No. It isn't."

"You want to stay married?"

How could she be so smart and ask something so stupid? He considered whipping her clothes off and showing her exactly what he wanted. Instead, he struggled for patience and tried to keep his voice calm. "Molly, if I didn't want this marriage—and you—I wouldn't be standing here." He was amazed that she would think otherwise.

She looked away, but not before he saw the smile in her eyes. It made him want to shake her. Then hug her. Then shake her again.

She brushed at her skirts. "She's very pretty."

"A china doll," he agreed, feeling contrary again.

"And petite."

"A strong wind would blow her over."

"She seems a lovely woman."

"She is."

That brought her head up, those almost-green eyes snapping fire.

He met them with a smile. "But she's the wrong woman, Molly."

"Oh." The fire faded to a warm glow. "You're sure?"

"I'm sure."

This time, she reached for him, hugging him with a vigor that made his still-sore ribs creak in protest. Which bothered him only a little.

Twelve

"I PUKED UP THE CANDY."

Startled from a deep sleep, Hank opened his eyes to find Penny looming over him, her wild curls backlit by the muted light coming through the hotel window.

"Jesus!" he choked out, yanking the blanket over his bare chest.

"But I'm not supposed to say that."

His heart racing in his chest, he looked down to be sure he was fully covered. The kid must be part Apache the way she snuck up on a person. "Say what?" he asked groggily.

"That I puked."

He squinted up at her, trying to make sense of her words. Conversations with Penny were always a challenge. "Why not?"

"Ladies aren't allowed to say 'puked.'"

"You're a lady, are you?" He wondered where Molly was, and what time it was, and how he could get Penny out of his room so he could dress.

She giggled. "Not yet. I'm only a baby lady. I won't be a real lady until I grow bosoms." She stretched her flannel gown over her puffed-out chest. "Do you think they're growing? I think they're growing, don't you?"

He embarrassed himself by checking before he realized what he was doing. "Give them time," he muttered, quickly looking away. "Where's Molly?"

"Getting dressed. She says it'll take years."

"To get dressed?"

"To grow bosoms. She's been growing hers a long time. That's why they're great big."

He blinked at her. Not *great* big. More like gently rounded. Definitely sufficient. An idea came to his befuddled mind. "Did

Molly send you in here?" Be just like her to try to get even for Melanie.

"They're really soft too."

"Are they?" Suspicions giving way to pleasant musings, he grinned up at the ceiling. "Remind me to check."

"And bouncy."

"Bouncy." An interesting word. One that conjured interesting images.

"What's thirty-seven?"

The images faded. He turned his head to find his stepdaughter picking at a scab on her elbow. "Thirty-seven what?"

"I don't know. When I came in, I thought you were asleep then you said thirty-seven and fifty-nine and leventy-something. What's that mean?"

"It means I was sleeping."

She paused in her scab excavations to give him a wondering look. "You talk while you're sleeping?"

"I work numbers. Or so I've been told. Aren't you hungry? I bet you're hungry. Why don't you go see if it's time for breakfast."

Having completed her surgery, she wiped her finger on the blanket and grinned at him. "I might get pukey."

He eyed the smear on his blanket and felt a little pukey himself.

"Where's your dress, Papa-Hank? Last time you were wearing a dress." She lifted the corner of the blanket.

He quickly pinned it to the mattress with his arm. "It wasn't a dress. It was a nightshirt. Don't I hear Molly calling you?"

"Where's your nightshirt then?" She tugged at the blanket, then froze, her eyes as round as marbles. "You're not wearing anything, are you? You're naked!"

Before he could answer, she let loose a high-pitched squeal that would deafen the hounds of hell and fled the room. "AuntMolleee PapaHanksnaked!"

Ten minutes later, he was dressed, shaved, and knocking on Molly's door, primed for battle. He suspected confrontations with Molly would be almost as much fun as conversations with Penny.

She didn't disappoint, flinging open the door on the first knock.

"Morning, Molly."

"Please tell me you did not invite my niece in for a visit while you were lying in bed nude."

He smiled.

"Hank!"

Stepping past her into the room, he closed the door behind him, then turned to face her. "In the first place, I didn't invite my stepdaughter in, she snuck in. And it wasn't for a visit, so much as a cozy chat—very informative, your niece. And as you well know, that's how I sleep—nude. At least I hope you know," he added with a rakish grin.

She blinked at him.

Amusement faded. "You *do* know, don't you? Tell me you do."

"I—ah. . . ." She cleared her throat. "Ch-Chat about what?"

Sweet Molly. So shy. His confidence happily restored, he attacked hers. "Bosoms." He sauntered across to the window, speaking as he went. "Yours, mostly. Your great big, really soft, bouncy bosoms. Her words, not mine—that faulty memory, you know." Pulling aside the lacy curtain, he scanned the sky. No snow yet, but low clouds promised it was on the way. "They sound so . . . perky." He let the curtain drop and turned to face her. "Brings to mind a French postcard I once saw."

"Oh, Lord." She lifted a palm to her

flushed forehead. "That child will be the death of me."

"Death of *you*? Try waking up to her looming over you."

She chuckled.

Enjoying the sound of it, he pressed for more. "The kid would make a fine burglar. Or spy. Remind me not to sleep with my pistol nearby and to get some sturdy door locks."

"Oh, Hank." Dropping her hand to her stomach, she let chuckles give way to laughter.

It was an infectious laugh, with a throaty, sexy quality that made him want to tickle her to keep it going. He appreciated that she didn't even try to stifle it. And appreciated even more the jiggle of motion it set off under her shirt.

Penny was right about the bouncy bosoms.

He waited until she had finally regained control of herself, then walked closer and said, "I like to hear you laugh, Molly. It's the second-best way to greet the day." Bending forward, he nuzzled the soft skin below her ear. She smelled like lemons. Why did she always smell like lemons? "At least I think it is," he added, sliding his lips over her cheek toward her mouth. "You'll have to refresh my memory. Soon." He kissed her, felt her lean into him, and kissed her again.

"Morning, wife," he whispered against her lips. Then in a louder voice, "Morning to you, too, Charlie."

She jerked back.

Straightening, he smiled over her shoulder. "Had breakfast yet, son?"

"No, sir."

"Better get to it then. I suspect we'll be leaving shortly."

As soon as the door closed behind the boy, he reached for his wife. "Now where were we?"

She sidled away. "I was packing. I don't know what you were doing."

"Fending off your niece. Where is she, by the way?"

"The Garcia sisters took her down to breakfast a while ago." Retrieving a garment from a pile on the couch, she carefully folded it and slipped it into the open valise by her feet. "I'm surprised they haven't quit already."

"Brady pays them a fortune." Moving to

the upholstered chair beside the window, he sat, crossed his outstretched legs at the ankles, and settled back to watch her. "He'd have to with Ben to tend."

Having finished with the clothing, she moved to the bureau and began sorting through hairbrushes, bottles with glass stoppers, jars of this and that. "Oh, he's not that bad."

"If you like tyrants."

That throaty chuckle. "Well, he is Brady's son."

An odd comment, Hank thought, since in actuality Ben wasn't Brady's son and Molly surely knew that. But he lost that thought when she bent over to pick up her medicine basket and the action hiked her skirt up the backs of her calves. The woman did have a nice pair of legs.

She straightened, moved the items on the bureau to the basket, then studied her reflection in the mirror. Apparently, she saw flaws undetectable to the male eye. With a frown, she leaned forward to thumb a smudge from the corner of her mouth, then straightened to pat a few hairs back from her temples and smooth a brow.

The rituals of women. They enthralled

him. Having grown up in a predominately male household, he didn't often get a chance to observe them, and when he did, he was completely captivated. All the little gestures—the stroking, dabbing, patting, smoothing—each movement so alien and feminine and so quick to draw his eye. And when she raised her arms to repin the coil of hair at her nape, lifting for his contemplation those round, bouncy bosoms he and Penny so admired, he was lost.

"What are you staring at?" she asked, her eyes finding his in the mirror.

"Nothing." He tugged at the knees of his trousers, then recrossed his legs. "I was just thinking I sure miss my memories."

A shadow crossed her face before she masked it with a wistful smile. "Is it so bad?" she asked, turning to face him. "Having to start over and make new ones?"

He thought about it for a moment then shook his head. "It's the not knowing. Like I've lost something important and I don't know how to get it back. Makes me feel . . . stupid, I suppose."

"Oh, Hank." Her eyes clouded. "I'm so sorry."

Regretting that he'd upset her, he

pasted on a smile. "I'm alive. And I still have you and Penny and Charlie to help me make new memories. I'm a lucky man."

And he was. Looking at his beautiful wife, he had no doubt of that. But still it bothered him, that last niggling doubt that something more was missing than just a few memories, and things were not exactly as they should be. It was like looking into a flawed mirror and getting back a distorted reflection of himself. He didn't like distortions. They were almost as bad as lies.

THEY WERE AN HOUR OUT OF VAL ROSA WHEN the first flake fell. And by the time they rounded Blue Mesa, there was enough accumulation that they had to stop and bolt on the sled runners. After switching horses twice with the outriders to relieve the flagging wagon teams, they rode under the arched gate ahead of a howling wind that sent snowflakes into such a swirling frenzy, visibility was reduced to mere feet. They covered the last half-mile at a crawl, nearly blind in a world gone eerily white, and finally reached the house ten hours after leaving Val Rosa.

The Wilkins brothers thought it a grand adventure, Jessica was pale with exhaustion, and Molly near ill from worry. The children slept through most of it.

The snowstorm lasted three days, and when they awakened to clear skies on the fourth morning, the landscape had been redrawn into a rolling white vista that sparkled in the sun. "Oooh," Penny breathed, pressing her face to the frosty window by the grand fireplace. "It looks like sugar. Or fairy dust."

"Hellfire," Ben seconded, earning a look from Dougal that sent him scurrying from the room.

Muttering something in a language Molly didn't know, Dougal hiked his jacket to toast his backside at the roaring fire. "And I gave up Scotland for this?"

He may have given up Scotland, Molly noted from her place on the couch, but not his kilt, under which, in deference to his rheumatism, he now wore jaunty red unions and high-topped woolly boots. An eye-catching ensemble.

"Looks like we're snowed in for a while," Brady announced, entering from the porch with an armload of firewood. "Buck says there's another storm on the way. Dougal, if you want roasted nuts," he said, elbowing the Scotsman aside so he could drop the wood on the stone hearth, "there's store-bought in the pantry. No need to cook your own."

While Dougal and Brady traded barbs, Molly looked past Penny at the unbroken white landscape beyond the porch railing. Maybe by spring Fletcher would give up and call in his trackers. Maybe by spring this deception would be over and all would be forgiven and they would never have to leave.

The couch groaned as Hank eased down beside her, favoring his sore ribs. "Don't suppose you play poker," he asked with a hopeful grin.

"Sorry. But if you're bored, stop by my room later"—she leaned toward him to whisper into his ear—"and I'll teach you how to knit."

When she drew back, she found him studying her in amused speculation.

Dusting his hands, Brady rose from the hearth. "Charlie," he called toward the library end of the room, where the boy sat reading. “Get your coat. There’s something I want to show you.”

“Can I come?” Penny shouted.

“Not this time, imp.”

“Why not?”

Brady gently thumped her head. “Don’t be so nosy. It’s Christmas.”

Dejected, Penny watched them leave then crawled onto Hank’s lap. She thrashed around, making Hank flinch and groan, before finally settling down against his chest. “What’s an imp, Papa-Hank?” she asked, idly plucking at a few dark chest hairs showing at the vee of his shirt collar.

“A squirmy little kid with sharp knees and elbows who likes to sneak into people’s rooms when they’re sleeping. That tickles.”

“I’m not little. Aunt Molly, am I little?”

“Certainly not.”

“See, Papa-Hank? I’m not little.”

He reared back to study her. “You’re right,” he finally said. “You’re very big for your size. And heavy.”

“Maybe pretty soon I’ll be too big to sit on your lap.”

“One can only hope,” Hank muttered, deflecting a knee from his groin. “Hadn’t you better go see how the hot chocolate's coming along?"

"Hot chocolate," Penny shouted, bounding off Hank's chest and charging toward the kitchen. "AuntJessicaismyhotchocolateready?"

Dougal grimaced and rubbed his ear. "That lass could wake the dead."

"She does have a gift," Hank allowed. He sent Molly a scolding look. "And some pretty disgusting habits you might want to work on."

"Oh, dear. Not of a digestive nature, I hope."

"Not yet."

"Be grateful."

After lunch, the brothers, Dougal, and Charlie left on the Christmas Tree Hunt, another all-male affair, which had Penny in a pout until Jessica herded her and Ben and Abigail into the kitchen, where they joined several of the younger ranch children to make Christmas treats—drop cookies, gingerbread men, cut-out cookies, taffy, and little cakes with sugar and butter frosting. Even with Iantha, the Garcias, and several other mothers on hand, it was chaos. Molly hadn't had so much fun in years.

But Jessica didn't seem to be enjoying herself, Molly noted. Her face was pale and a frown of worry—or pain—furrowed her brow.

"Is something wrong?" she asked quietly, not wanting to alarm the others.

Jessica lifted a shaky hand to her brow. "Simply tired, I think."

But Molly could see the strain of fatigue around her mouth, the worry in her eyes. "Perhaps you should stretch out for a bit."

"Yes. Perhaps I should."

Quietly motioning Iantha to take over, Molly took Jessica's arm and steered her from the room. Once out of the kitchen, Jessica's steps slowed and she leaned into Molly for support. "I don't know what's come over me," she said, clinging to the railing as they slowly mounted the stairs. "I just feel so out of sorts. None of my other pregnancies was this exhausting."

Trying to keep the concern from her voice, Molly asked, "Have you been sleeping well?"

"Not particularly. Nothing specific. Simply restless." On the landing she stopped and turned to Molly. "Please, don't tell Brady. He worries so, the dear man. And I'm sure this is not beyond normal for a woman in my condition."

When Molly nodded, they continued down the hall to Jessica's room. After settling Jessica on a chaise by the fire, Molly moved across the hearth to sit in an oversized wingback chair that had to have been Brady's. Leaning forward, she rested her elbows on her thighs and clasped her hands together. "Now tell me what's wrong. And don't think to hide anything from me, Jessica. I'm a nurse. I can see something is bothering you. Perhaps I can help."

Jessica took a long time to answer. "I'm sure it's nothing, Molly. Nothing physical, at any rate. I just worry."

"About what?"

Sadness clouded her eyes as she stared into the flames crackling in the hearth. "Ben was a twin, you know. The other baby was a girl. Victoria. She died inside me long before the birth." She met Molly's gaze. "You mustn't say anything to Brady, but I saw Dr. O'Grady when we were in Val Rosa. He thinks I may be carrying twins again."

Molly tried to keep her expression from

betraying her concern. She knew how dangerous bearing twins could be. She had never assisted in a multiple birth, but she'd read of complications in Papa's medical papers. "What happened last time?"

"They came early. Dr. O'Grady said that was not unusual with twins. Ben was small but healthy. But Victoria . . ." Her voice trailed off.

"And you think that will happen again?"

"I don't know. I worry that it will. It was difficult losing Victoria."

"Well." Clapping her hands to her knees, Molly straightened. "It won't happen this time. That's why I'm here."

"You're here because my husband coerced you."

"He's concerned." But Jessica's words sparked a sudden shocking realization in Molly's mind. It wasn't just because of Hank that Brady had forced her here. It was because of Jessica too. *That liar.*

"And we'll not add to his burden, will we?" Jessica said pointedly. "Promise me you won't say anything to Brady unless it's absolutely necessary."

Oh, she had plenty to say to Brady. And all of it necessary. But not wanting to worry Jessica, she pasted on a smile. "On one condition."

Jessica arched one coppery brow, haughty as a banker's wife. If Molly hadn't known better, she might have been intimidated. "And what would that be?"

"You must do everything I tell you."

"A rather broad edict, wouldn't you say?"

If not for the British accent, Jessica could have passed for a Southern lady of quality. Steel wrapped in velvet, draped with a smile. "Just let me do the worrying," Molly told her. "And before you know it, there will be two more beautiful babies for you to fuss over."

For the first time, Jessica smiled. "Won't that be lovely?"

Molly was determined that it would be. She owed this family so much. She knew she hadn't the right, but she felt they were her family, too, and even though delivering babies was not part of her usual nursing tasks, she would do everything she could to see that this delivery was perfect.

"Now that we have me taken care of," Jessica said. "Let's tend to you."

"Me?"

Jessica gave her a speculative look. "How goes it with you and Hank? I've sensed a bit of awkwardness between you. Is all well?"

Uncomfortable under Jessica's probing gaze, Molly rose and walked to the window. It was another beautiful sparkling day. Spun sugar clouds floating above a diamond-crusted earth. So white, so pure, so untainted. A fairy tale.

If only . . .

Irritated at her own imaginings, she turned away. "You know him better than I. Do you think he's happy in this marriage?"

"I wouldn't say I know him better. Longer, perhaps. Hank isn't that easy to know, since he shares so little of himself."

"Why is that?" Molly asked. "He does seem guarded."

Jessica shrugged. "Perhaps because he's the middle brother and is easily overlooked. Especially around Brady and Jack. Those two seem to draw all the energy from a room."

Molly wasn't sure she agreed. She didn't know Jack, but it was her observation that more often Brady revolved around Hank, much the way the quicksilver moon circled the larger, stabler Earth. Besides, how could anyone overlook a man like Hank? Beauty aside, the man filled a room with his indomitable presence, charging the air with his male energy and creating an aura of safety that drew people like moths to flame. Drew *her*, anyway.

"I met the woman from the fort when we were in town," she said.

Jessica's eyes widened. "Melanie? What was she doing in Val Rosa?"

"I'm not sure. Hank sent me back to the hotel while he spoke with her."

"Surely she didn't think to rekindle his interest."

"I don't know. But he assured me he didn't harbor feeling for her."

Jessica waved a hand in dismissal. "Well, how could he, really? Melanie is a lovely girl but utterly cowed by her mother—a vicious woman at best—and certainly no match for Hank's sharp mind. He would have been bored in a month." She arched that brow. "And he certainly never looked at Melanie the way he looks at you."

Molly felt a blush of pleasure inch up her

throat. She had often felt Hank's gaze on her. Sometimes puzzled, sometimes amused, sometimes showing that intensity that sent her heart into chaos and left her feeling confused and anxious and wanting . . . something. Forcing a bright smile, Molly pushed those thoughts aside. "Back to you." Donning her nurse persona, she said in a firm, no-nonsense voice, "Naps twice a day, small frequent meals, and no lifting. Agreed?"

"Agreed."

"Excellent." As Molly turned toward the door, Jessica's voice called her back.

"I'm so glad you're here, Molly," she said, her eyes suspiciously bright. "And not solely because of your excellent nursing skills. But because I need a friend. A woman friend. They add so much to one's life, don't you think?"

Molly felt an answering sting in her own eyes. "Indeed they do." Especially to one who had been blessed with so few.

Later that afternoon, the men returned with a fifteen-foot-tall spruce, which, with a great deal of muttering and cursing, they set up beside the grand fireplace. Molly waited until the task was completed and Hank left to tend chores in the barn, then as soon as she saw Brady head toward his office, she marched after him.

"You lying scoundrel!" she accused, charging into the room on his heels.

He looked around, his face showing surprise. "What'd I do this time?"

"It's not just because of Hank you blackmailed me into coming here! It's because of Jessica too! That's why you wouldn't tell him the truth. You were afraid if he knew what I'd done, he wouldn't let me come, and then there would be no one to tend Jessica!"

His look of surprise gave way to a wary look. "As I recall, it was you blackmailing me," he said, easing down into his chair. "Something about three hundred dollars to get you out of my brother's life."

"You really are a bastard, aren't you?"

"I told you I'd do anything for my brother. You think I'd do less for my wife?"

"God." Sinking into a chair in front of the desk, she propped her elbows on her knees and dropped her head into her hands. "He'll never forgive me or trust me again.

He'll hate me." She thought of Melanie, and how easily Hank had put her from his mind. Would he do that with her too?

"Not if he doesn't find out," Brady said, almost as if he knew her thoughts.

She lifted her head and frowned at him. "He already suspects the truth, Brady. He's not stupid. He'll realize we've been lying to him all along."

"Where's the lie? You did marry him. Beckworth showed me the certificate that proves it. So where's the lie?"

"He was unconscious. I doubt the marriage is even legal."

"How will he know if you don't tell him?"

Molly stared at him, not seeing the reaction she'd expected. No surprise. No fury. Not even confusion. "You knew," she said in startled disbelief. "You knew he never proposed, that it was all a sham from the beginning, didn't you? You knew!"

"Not from the beginning," he said in a placating tone that made her want to leap over his desk and throttle him. "Not until I saw you working so hard to keep him at arm's length. A true wife wouldn't have done that."

"Damn you, Brady." Tears rose in her throat, making her voice high and wobbly. "What have you done?"

"What I had to. For him and for Jessica."

She couldn't get her mind around it—the manipulation, the deceit, his utter disregard for anything other than his own aims. "He'll hate me. He'll never forgive me or trust me or . . ." Realization hit so hard, she rocked back, one hand to her chest.

Or what? Love me? Was that what she had been hoping for? She wanted to laugh. Then cry. Then scream at her own stupidity. She had fallen in love with the man she had set out to deceive. How sad and ironic and pathetic was that?

Tears filled her eyes, ran unchecked down her face.

"Don't do that," Brady muttered, tossing a kerchief across the desk.

Molly ignored it. "How could you do this to me, Brady?"

"Do what?" He dragged both hands through his dark hair then let them fall back to the armrests. "What exactly have I done, Molly? You're safe. Your children are safe. Hank is alive and recovering. What the hell have I done?"

Hopeless despair defeated her. Pressing her hands to her face, she let the tears flow.

"Aw, hell." There was a long, tense pause, then Brady sighed. "You care about him. You want it to be a real marriage, don't you, Molly? Sonofabitch."

Molly lifted her head and glared at him. "No chance of that now, is there? Thanks to you and my own stupidity." Snatching the kerchief from the desk, she wiped her eyes and blew her nose. "I should have told him the truth as soon as I knew he would recover. Instead, I let you talk me into coming here and continuing this despicable farce." She flung the kerchief back onto the desk and rose to her feet. "Well, no more. I'm done." She turned toward the door.

"No wait! Listen!" Brady shot to his feet and came around the desk. "It can still work, Molly. We can both still get what we want."

"How?" she asked, disgusted with herself that she was still in the room, still listening to this man . . . still hoping.

"I'll vouch for you, tell him the marriage is real. He never needs to know about the money or that he never knew you before."

Hope curdled. “You don’t understand, Brady,” she said wearily. “Hank is not like you. He doesn’t even think the way you do. Lying about the marriage was one thing. But covering it up these last weeks . . . ? That’s what he’ll never forgive.”

As she turned back toward the door, Brady grabbed her arm. “Don’t, Molly. Wait a minute. Just listen.”

She whirled, prepared to flay him alive. Then she saw his face.

He looked panicked and worried. The man was clearly suffering—not that he didn’t deserve it—but such a show of vulnerability seemed so alien to Brady’s character, it shocked her.

“You’re right. It’s Jessica,” he blurted out “I need you to stay because of Jessica. She’s—” He faltered, then rushed on. “Doc O’Grady says she’s carrying twins.”

“I know that. So does she.”

“She does? Why didn’t she tell me?”

“Because you’re a worrying nitwit.” Pulling her arm from his grip, Molly opened the door.

He reached past her to shut it, and held it closed when she tried to pull it open. “Did you know she almost died when Ben was born? And that Abigail was breech? What if it happens again? Women die in childbirth all the time."

Swallowing back her irritation, she whirled to face him, arms crossed over her chest. "And you think I can keep that from happening to Jessica?"

"You can try." His eyes were pleading now. His face was so tense a tiny muscle jerked in his jaw. "Stay. I'll make it right with Hank. I'll tell him it was all my idea, that I forced you into it. I'll do whatever you want, Molly. Just don't leave her."

Molly thought of Jessica—her friend—and the sadness in her eyes when she spoke of her lost daughter.

She thought of Penny and Charlie—safe here, and so happy. And Fletcher—waiting to pounce the moment they left.

She thought of Hank—who had kissed her and asked her to take down her hair, and who made her feel more like a woman than she ever had before.

Dust motes in sunlight.

Did they ever grow weary and long to settle too?

"I won't lie to him, Brady," she finally said. "Ever again."

"But you'll stay? At least until the babies come?"

"For Jessica. Not you." Pushing his arm aside, she flung open the door and stalked from the room.

Thirteen

Jeanerette, Georgia

GORDON HENNESSEY WATCHED WITH DISPASsionate interest as Edward Rustin struggled to propel his rolling chair across the thick carpet of his dimly lit office.

It was obvious the man's kidneys were failing fast. He stank of decay, and the fingers gripping the wheels were so swollen they looked ready to split like sausages roasting on a fire.

It was too disgusting. Dying by the inch. Ghastly.

Moving his feet out of the path of the wheels, Gordon pressed a perfumed handkerchief to his nose as the blind old man fumbled and bumped his way past him toward his fine cherrywood desk. It was amusing in a macabre sort of way. Like watching a trussed and blindfolded child try to find his way out of a cage. It might be fun to send the old man careening down a hill or bouncing down a flight of stairs. *Higgledy, bouncity, pop.* Gordon smiled, picturing it in his mind. What a mess that would make.

Once Rustin was situated behind the desk and his labored breathing had settled into rapid, shallow gasps that reminded Gordon of steam escaping the pop valves on a locomotive, he leaned forward and said, "Well, Hennessey? Have you found them?"

Gordon watched the palsied fingers move restlessly on the desktop like fat, blind worms. "I have. They're at a ranch in New Mexico Territory. It's heavily guarded and snowbound for now, so I haven't had a chance to talk to them yet."

"But you will."

"As soon as the roads clear."

"No. Don't wait. If you can't go in after them, lure them out to you. I want that book!" The vehemence in Rustin's voice brought on a hacking fit that had him rocking and clutching the armrests of his chair.

Gordon eyed him in distaste. The old fool should just die. Really, he should. He was much too disgusting to be around other people. And just what was in this book Rustin was so frantic to find? Gordon loved puzzles.

He waited until the old man had regained control of himself before speaking. "Of course, Edward," he answered, using Rustin's given name because he knew how much it upset him. "And my money?" Because of the old man's condition, Gordon had insisted on being paid his monthly fee in advance. Be just like the maggot to choke to death on his own blood before settling his bill.

Rustin fumbled with the drawer, extracted an envelope, and shoved it across the desk. "Just get that book, Hennessey. Soon."

"Oh, I shall." Rising, Gordon slid the envelope into his coat pocket. "And Edward," he added, as if in afterthought. "When it's finished, might I ask a favor?"

Rustin's milky eyes stared at Gordon as if he could actually see him. "What?"

"The children. I'd like to have the children, if that's okay with you?" *Or even if it isn't.* The children were the only reason he had taken this assignment.

"Bring me the book. Then you can have anything you want."

"Thank you, Edward." After silently positioning his chair directly in the path the blind man would travel from his desk to the door, Gordon left, whistling, as best he could with his damaged face, a lively Christmas tune.

DRESSING THE CHRISTMAS TREE WAS A GRAND event.

The first layer was a series of ribbons and garlands strung with dried berries and glass beads, laced with sprigs of rosemary and sage. Then the children added their own decorations of colorful cones of sugared almonds, strings of rock candy, paper stars, and snowflakes. And finally came Jessica's fancy ornaments—silver angels, painted glass balls, miniature china dolls, tiny musical instruments, German tinsel, and hand-sewn silk gift pouches with gold and silver stitching. It was a lovely sight when it was done and the finest Christmas tree Molly had ever seen.

After spending most of the day preparing the ornaments and dressing the tree, the children were too tired to stay up long after supper. Brady, concerned that Jessica was overdoing, insisted they retire early too. With Dougal no doubt chasing Consuelo through the pantry, Molly and Hank found themselves alone in the great room.

Retrieving her sewing basket from beneath a side table, Molly settled in to finish the scarves she was knitting for the children while Hank sprawled in an adjacent armchair, his gaze fixed on the fire, his long legs crossed at the ankles.

As she worked the needles, Molly studied him from beneath her lashes, all manner of questions floating through her mind. After insisting that he learn about her, she realized how little she knew about him.

Did he have a favorite color? A favorite food? Did he sing? Dance? Did he like having a wife?

"Say something," she said, breaking the long silence.

He looked over, his dark eyes reflecting back the firelight. "About what?"

"You." At his look of confusion, she gave

him a chiding smile. "You don't talk about yourself much, do you?"

He shrugged.

"Brady thinks it's because you're shy."

"Shy of him maybe. Give my brother an opening and he'll be on you like a pack of starving chiggers."

Wrapping a loop of yarn around her finger, she slipped the needle through. "I didn't realize chiggers came in packs."

He smiled. "A pack of heelers then. He likes to herd people around. Manage them. I've found the only way to keep him from trying to take control of my life is to tell him nothing about it."

Molly wished she'd known that strategy earlier. She might not have let Brady manipulate her into this mess. But then, if she hadn't, she wouldn't be here now, sitting before the fire with Hank.

"I would never try to control you," she said.

He snorted. "Hell, you already do."

Letting her hands fall to her lap, she frowned at him. "How?"

"By walking into the room. Saying good morning. Breathing." He grinned. "But I don't mind."

Feeling a rush of heat into her face, she picked up the knitting again. "I'll remember that," she murmured, her heart dancing in her chest.

"See that you do."

Silence again. But it was a comfortable, companionable silence, as if they were a long-married couple no longer plagued by awkward silences or moments of uncertainty or unanswered questions.

"A small hand loom could do that faster," he said after a while.

She looked up to find him watching her work the needles. "Is there such a thing?"

"Not yet."

Ah. Another innovation. Molly smiled. "It's not about speed," she explained. "Needlework can be very relaxing. Hand me that red yarn and I'll show you."

He leaned over to study the balls of yarn in her sewing basket, then picked up the green one and tossed it into her lap. "I'd rather watch you."

She looked at the green yarn, then back at him to see if he was teasing her. He didn't appear to be. Watching him closely, she held up the green yarn. "Do you think this red is too bright for Penny?"

He shrugged.

She unrolled several inches of yarn and made a.show of studying it. “It is a rather bright red, don’t you think?”

“It’s not red.”

She let the yarn fall back into her lap. “Then why did you say it was?”

“I didn’t. You did. You’re not very subtle, you know.”

“Then why—”

“I get my reds and greens mixed up sometimes.”

“Just reds and greens? No other colors? What about blues and yellows?”

He sighed and tipped his head back to study the ceiling high overhead. “You sure ask a lot of questions.”

“It’s called communication. It’s how people get to know one another.”

“Why do we have to get to know each other? We’re already married.”

She was about to scold him when he shot her that startling grin. “Mostly reds and greens,” he explained. “It’s a bother sometimes, but it helps when I’m hunting.”

Molly was enthralled. She had read about

Daltonism in her father's medical journals. "How?"

"I see patterns others don't. Like game hiding in the bushes. Or shadows that someone else might not notice."

Setting her knitting aside, she dug through her sewing basket until she found the small magnifying glass she used for tatting. "May I look at your eyes?"

"You won't poke at them, will you?"

She rose. "Sit up straight."

When he did, she nudged his knees aside and stepped between them so she could look directly down into his right eye with the light from the overhead chandelier behind her. "Look up at the ceiling."

When he complied, she leaned closer to peer into his eye with the glass.

"You smell like lemons," he said.

"That's from the rinse I use on my hair. Be still."

"Four. Sixteen. Two hundred fifty-six."

She drew back. "What are you doing?"

"Squaring numbers." At her questioning look, he added, "It calms me."

"Why do you need calming?"

"I've got a piece of glass an inch from

my eye and a woman's bosoms resting on my chin. I find that unsettling."

She jerked back. "I was not resting my . . . anything . . . on your chin."

"Would you like to?"

"Don't be impertinent." Suddenly feeling overheated, she turned away. "I'll have to read up on it."

"Bosoms?"

"Daltonism." Horrified that she might burst into nervous giggles like some tittering schoolgirl, she busied herself stuffing the yarn back into her basket, and making a fine mess of it in the process. "Well." She straightened, the basket clutched before her like a shield. "I believe I'll go to bed."

He rose, towering over her, so close she had to crane her neck to look up at him. "Want me to go with you?"

"To bed?" It came out more of a squeak than a voice.

"I was thinking up the stairs, but if you want to take me to bed, I—"

"Good night." Turning before he could see her smile, she fled the room.

Hank watched her go, pleased with the way things were progressing. It wouldn't be long before he had her right where he wanted her. Right where she belonged.

It was taking longer than he had expected, this second round of courting, but it wasn't as awful as he'd thought it would be. In fact, he was almost enjoying himself. He hadn't laughed so much in a long time, and he was sure he hadn't used so many words in at least two years.

It was odd having a family to look after. That sense of detachment he'd always felt even when surrounded by brothers and people who knew him well was fading. Sometimes all his new responsibilities weighed heavily upon him. Other times they filled him with purpose. He liked that Molly and the children depended on him. He liked being a father. And he was pretty sure he was really going to like being a husband.

Again.

WHEN HANK ENTERED THE BARN A FEW MORNINGS later, he heard raised voices and sounds of a struggle coming from the last stall. Hurrying forward, he yanked open the stall door to find Amos Logan, one of the younger RosaRoja hands, straddling

Charlie, who was down in the straw, flailing at the older boy with his fists.

With a muttered curse, Hank yanked Amos off his stepson and pinned him with his right hand against the wooden wall. He glared from one boy to the other. Both were bloodied, but neither seemed seriously hurt. "What the hell's going on?" he demanded.

"He hit me," Amos shouted. "He jumped on me and hit me, the coward."

Hank looked down at his stepson, who was rising stiffly to his feet. "Charlie?"

The boy glared at him, then at Amos, but said nothing.

Hank gave Amos a shake. "You got anything more to say?"

"The kid's crazy," he muttered, swiping a sleeve over his bloody nose.

Hank pointed him toward the door. "Get to the bunkhouse. I'll talk to you later." As Amos left, he turned back to Charlie. He could see the boy was fighting tears, even though his expression and posture showed his usual angry defiance.

"You're bleeding," Hank said.

Charlie dabbed at the cut on his lip and winced.

"You want your Aunt Molly to tend it?"

Charlie didn't answer.

"Then I guess I will."

With a hand clamped to the boy's shoulder, Hank steered him out of the barn and into a chill wind that sent a swirl of powdery snow into their faces. "We have a low tolerance for fighting," he said as they crossed toward the house.

Charlie didn't respond.

Hank looked down at him. The tears were gone, and his lip had stopped bleeding, but if they crossed paths with Molly, there was little chance he could convince her everything was all right.

Luckily they reached Charlie's room without being seen. Pointing the boy to the chair by the bed, Hank told him to stay, then went to get Molly's medicine basket.

It wasn't a bad cut and would probably heal before the bruise darkening the boy's right eye faded. But Hank was more worried about what was going on inside the kid's head. He didn't know how to convince the boy to talk to him, or let him help him with whatever was troubling him. It was frustrating, and he was beginning to understand how Brady must feel when

Hank treated him to one of his long silences.

Once he'd tended the cut, Hank set the basket aside and sat on the end of the bed. He studied his stepson, trying to figure a way past that wall of anger. He'd thought they'd made progress. After the hunt and the subsequent nightmare, the boy had seemed less touchy. So what had set him off this time?

"He's bigger and older than you," Hank said. "Why'd you take him on?"

Charlie stared silently at the floor, his face hidden by a flop of deep auburn hair sliding over his brow.

"He said you started it," Hank prodded. "Is that true?"

Charlie shrugged.

"Why?"

Another shrug.

Sighing, Hank rose. "I can't dismiss you, but I can dismiss him. Unless you think that wouldn't be fair."

No response.

"Guess I'll have to let him go then." He started for the door.

"What about the dog?"

Hank stopped and turned back. "What

dog?" When Charlie didn't answer, he lost patience. "Charlie, talk to me. Now! What dog?"

"The one in the barn." Having finally broken his sullen silence, words came tumbling out in a shaky rush. "He's just a pup and he's got no one to look after him and he's so scared . . ." His voice trailed off. He stared at the floor again.

Hank waited to see if the boy would say more. When he didn't, he motioned for him to rise. "Show me."

It took some hunting before they found the dog in one of the stalls. It was a pitiful little thing, a half-starved stray with a lame front foot and an attitude every bit as defensive as Charlie's. Yet Charlie seemed unafraid, and despite the dog's bared teeth and warning growls, he knelt before the shivering animal and held out his hand.

"It's all right, boy," he said in a soft, soothing voice. "He's gone. No one's going to hurt you anymore."

Hank watched the dog cower against the slatted wall, eyes wary. "Who hurt him, Charlie?"

"Pup wasn't doing anything. He was just afraid, that's all. When Amos went to grab him, Pup snapped at him. But he didn't hurt him, I swear. Pup never even touched him. But Amos jumped up and tried to kick him. So I shoved him." Charlie leaned closer then jerked back when the dog snapped, hackles rising. "Why is he so mad?"

Hank wasn't blind to the parallels between the dog's lack of trust and Charlie's. He wondered if there was a way he could use it. Hunkering down beside his stepson, he said, "He doesn't trust you."

"But I wouldn't hurt him. Can't he see that?"

"Trust is earned, Charlie. Show him you're not a threat to him. Don't crowd him. And maybe he'll lose some of his fear."

"You think so?"

Hank studied the animal for signs of illness or damage. He saw no foam around the mouth, no blood, no crust at the nose and eyes. Just a rail-thin, scared dog that probably needed this boy as much as the boy needed him. "It'll take patience and persistence and a lot of work. Think he's worth it?"

Charlie's glare told Hank what he thought of that question.

"Well, you started this, so you finish it." Hank rose, hoping he was doing the right thing and he wasn't setting the boy up for another disappointment or loss. "If you can heal him in body and spirit, I think he'll make a fine companion."

"Really? I can keep him?" Charlie looked up, his scowl transformed into a wide grin. It was the first smile he'd ever given Hank and a wondrous thing it was.

"He's yours," Hank said. "So what do you plan to do with him?"

Charlie's mouth twisted from side to side as he thought about it. "I guess I should feed him first. Do you think Iantha or Consuelo have some scraps?"

"I expect they do."

"And he'll need a bed. Something warm." He shot Hank a hopeful look. "Unless you think he could sleep in my room?"

"Let's let him get used to you first," Hank hedged. "He seems comfortable here. Maybe you could make this stall his pen for a while."

"What about a blanket?"

"I bet he'd like that."

"And a name." Charlie thought it over,

then nodded. "You're going to be my buddy," he told the dog. "So that's what I'll call you. Buddy. You like that, boy?"

Lowering his head to his outstretched paws, the exhausted animal watched them with unblinking black eyes.

"Look. He's not shivering anymore. I think he likes it."

"I think you're right." Hank hesitated. "Charlie?"

Tearing his attention from the dog, the boy looked up.

"What you did—taking on a bigger boy to protect this dog—that was a good thing. A brave thing, son. I'm proud of you."

Charlie looked away, that telltale flush inching up his cheeks and turning the tips of his ears red. But Hank saw his pleased grin, and for the first time, he felt like a father.

"But no more fighting. Understand?"

"Yes, sir."

Resisting the urge to ruffle the boy's red brown hair, Hank opened the stall door. "I'll be back shortly."

As he closed the latch behind him, Charlie said softly, "You don't need to fire him, Papa-Hank. Amos isn't mean. He's just afraid of dogs."

"I'll keep that in mind."

He found Amos sitting on his bunk, a worried look on his face. As soon as he saw Hank in the doorway, he jumped to his feet and started talking as fast as he could get the words out.

"I didn't mean to hit Charlie, Mr. Hank. He startled me is all, shoving me like that. I won't do it again, I swear it. Sir."

Hank stopped at the foot of the bunk and studied the stammering boy. He couldn't have been more than fourteen, big for his age and gangly. A thatch of wheat-colored hair and a chipped front tooth made him seem younger, and with that anxious look in his blue eyes, younger still. "And the dog, Amos?"

A moment of confusion, as if he'd forgotten, then the boy blurted out, "The cur went to bite me, Mr. Hank. I didn't do nothing but try to pet him, and he comes at me, snarling like he had the rabies."

"So you kicked him?"

"Not to hurt him. Just to get him away. I knew a man once who caught the rabies, and a terrible thing it was. He scared me, is all. Sir."

Hank studied the fidgeting boy but saw no meanness in him, only a lack of experience and an earnest desire to please. Sort of a pup himself. "We don't kick dogs here." He thought of Penny and bit back a smile. "Or cats."

"Yes, sir."

"Since this is your first misstep, and because Charlie admitted he swung first, I'll go light on you this time."

"Yes, sir. Thank you, sir."

"Bathe."

"W-What?"

"You smell like a goat. Bathe. That's your punishment. But if I hear of one more misstep, you and I are going to the woodshed. Understand?"

Some of the color faded from the boy's flushed cheeks. "Yes, sir."

"Head on over to the washhouse then."

A long sigh. "Yes, sir."

That night, the children ate early and went upstairs to work on Christmas gifts, so after a blessedly quiet supper, the adults retired to the great room for drinks and coffee.

The storm Buck had predicted was hung up on the peaks of the mountains, gray ominous clouds churning fitfully as though anxious to sweep down the slopes. But inside, the house was warm and cozy, scented with the sharp woodsy tang of the Christmas tree and the boughs Molly and Jessica had draped over the mantle.

Hank noticed that Molly seemed as thrilled as the children about all the Christmas doings, which made him wonder what Christmases with her father had been like, or if they'd even celebrated the season. There was so much about his wife he didn't know, and it seemed every piece he added to the puzzle only opened the way for a dozen more.

He had his concerns about their marriage. In many ways, they seemed strangers. In other ways, the connection between them was so strong he felt like he'd known her forever. Whatever happened in the past, he wanted it to be right this time. No doubts, no unanswered questions. They were bound together, and the wedding ring he'd bought that was waiting under the Christmas tree was his way of showing her that's how he felt and how it was going to be. Hopefully her gift to him would be along the same lines. But involving fewer clothes.

"Does the wind e'er stop blowing in this ice bowl?" Dougal muttered, standing as close to the fire as he could. "I canna feel me own arse nae more."

"Oh, it's there," Brady mumbled. "We heard evidence of that earlier."

"Gentlemen," Jessica chided gently without looking up from her sewing.

Dougal opened his mouth to say something more then caught sight of Consuelo moving past the open door into the kitchen. Immediately he perked up. "Mayhap a bit 'o warm milk might take the chill off these old bones," he said, starting across the room.

"The man's incorrigible," Jessica said, watching him scamper into the kitchen.

"If that means randy old goat, you're right," Brady agreed.

Lifting his right arm, Hank draped it along the back of the couch where he and Molly sat. "They don't have snowstorms in Scotland?"

"Yes, certainly," Jessica said. "But rarely ones of such violence."

Brady rolled his cut-glass tumbler in his

palms to warm the whiskey, then tossed back the last swallow. "Buck said give it a day or two then bar the doors." He set the glass carefully on the tiny pedestal table by his overstuffed chair. "Says we'll definitely have a snowy Christmas."

"Penny's worried Saint Nick won't make it if we have another blizzard." While he spoke, Hank gently stroked the nape of Molly's neck. She had the softest skin, warm and growing warmer as a flush crept up her throat and spread across the curve of her high cheekbones. He was anxious to see if the rest of it was as soft. And warm. And—

"Papa-Hank," came a high-pitched shout from the entry stairwell.

Penny. With a sigh, Hank let his hand drop to the back of the couch.

Tiny footfalls clattered on the stairs. Then more footfalls, so many they sounded like a herd of calves racing across hard ground. "Papa-Hank!"

Hank glanced at Molly. "Hadn't you better see what she wants?"

"She's calling for you, not me."

"Kid sure seems taken with you," Brady observed. "Charlie too."

Hank wondered why he sounded surprised. He was their stepfather. Why wouldn't they be taken with him?

Penny rounded the corner, legs churning. "Papa-Hank, Papa-Hank!"

Charlie raced after her, trailed by Ben, then both panting Garcia sisters, one of whom held a thrashing Abigail.

Jesus. A full-out frontal assault. Hank braced himself, lowering his left arm with its hard protective cast over his unprotected lap.

"Ben says Charlie got a dog!" Penny shouted, coming to a stop at Hank's knees. "Where is it? Can I see it? How come I don't have a dog?"

"A dog?" Molly turned her head to look at him. "What dog?"

Hank felt the beginnings of a headache. "Well, I—"

"My word!" Jessica cried out. "Charlie, what happened to your poor face?"

For a moment all eyes went to Charlie, who stood red faced and frozen by the sudden attention.

"He was fighting," Molly said, sending another hard look in Hank's direction.

"Hell of a mouse you got there, Charlie,"

Brady said, admiring the purple bruise under the boy's right eye.

"You should see Amos," Hank said proudly.

Charlie grinned and stared at his shoes.

"Fighting isn't funny," Molly told her nephew.

"No, ma'am."

Brady winked at Charlie. Jessica scowled at both of them. Hank's headache settled like a cap over his skull.

"I want a dog too!" Penny shouted, climbing into Hank's lap to resume the battle. "Why can't I have a dog?"

"You're too little for a dog, Penny," Charlie said.

"What dog?" Molly asked again.

"I'm not little!" Penny poked Hank's chest. "Tell him, Papa-Hank!"

"Now, Penny—" Hank began, before Molly shouted him down.

"Children! Enough!"

"But I want a dog!" Penny wailed, too far into the fray to retreat now. "Or a kitty. Where's my kitty? You said I could have a kitty, Papa-Hank."

Molly rounded on him, clearly as out of patience with him as with the children. "A kitty? First a dog, and now a cat? When did you tell her she could have a cat?"

Hank rubbed his fingertips against his temple. "I don't remember."

"You don't remember? How can you not remember promising a cat to a child?"

"Hell, I don't even remember my own wedding," he muttered.

"That's because you were asleep, Papa-Hank. Mrs. Beckworth told me all about it." Tipping her head back, Penny glared up at him. "And you were wearing your dress," she added in a tone of contempt only a six-year-old could get away with.

"It wasn't a dress," Hank said wearily. "It was a nightshirt. How many times do I have to tell you . . ." Words died as realization struck.

Asleep? Why had he been asleep at his own wedding? He turned his head to find Molly staring at him. "What's she talking about?"

She stared back at him, color fading from her face, her eyes round and full of dread.

And in that instant he knew. It was as if a floodgate had crashed open in his mind, and all those niggling doubts that had pestered him for weeks came pouring in.

It wasn't real. They weren't married. She wasn't really his wife, and these weren't his stepchildren.

Was it all a lie?

A red mist formed behind his eyes. His head pounded so hard he could hardly move or breathe or think. He looked at the faces staring back at him—Molly, Jessica, Brady. They knew. They all knew. They let him think his memory was faulty when they knew it wasn't. They let him think his mind was damaged. *Why?*

"Hank," Brady said.

Hank looked at him and saw the truth in his eyes. "You sonofabitch."

"Hank, please," Jessica said softly. "The children."

With jerky movements, Hank lifted Penny from his lap and set her on the floor, a distant part of him amazed that he could still function despite the chaos in his mind. "Go upstairs."

"But what about my kitty?" Penny asked, her voice starting to wobble.

"Not now, Penny. Charlie, take your sister upstairs."

"But I want my—"

"Now!" he thundered.

In round-eyed silence, Charlie led his protesting sister from the room, trailed by the Garcias with Brady's children.

As their footsteps faded up the stairwell, Brady's voice cut through the tense silence. "Hank, it's not what you think."

Hank looked at him, too furious to speak.

Lies. The whole time. All lies.

It was Melanie all over again. And Brady's lies about Sam's death. And the hundred deceptions his father had spun when he had allowed the feud ravaging his family to continue because he'd fallen in love with his enemy's wife.

The red mist churned and swirled as he looked from one face to another. His family. His whole goddamn family. "You did this," he choked out. "On purpose. Why?"

They stared silently back, tintype figures frozen in place, their stricken expressions telling him the truth. They'd all been in on it, and that knowledge—that *betrayal*—was like a bullet to his chest. For a moment it hurt so bad he could hardly breathe.

He turned to Molly—his wife—his lying, treacherous wife—and felt something dark take hold of his soul. Moving his hand along the back of the couch, he gripped her neck, not hard enough to hurt but enough to keep her from moving. He felt her rapid pulse beat against his thumb and was glad she was afraid.

Bending close, he put his mouth next to her ear. "Tell me why. *Wife.*" He gave her neck a quick, hard squeeze. "Now!"

Tendons flexed under his fingers as her head came around until her lying almost-green eyes looked directly into his. He saw fear, regret, then a flash of anger that was so unexpected his mind couldn't even accept it.

"Not in front of the others, Hank."

He was astounded. Didn't she know how precarious her position was? How easily he could crush her throat? Didn't she realize how furious he was?

Hearing movement, he looked over to see Brady rising from his chair. "Hank, it's my fault. I—"

"Go to hell."

From outside came the whinny of a horse. But inside, it was as still as a tomb where they sat like mute, immobile statues trapped in rigor for all time. Hank remained so intently focused on his wife, he could hear her rapid breathing, see the tremble of her lips, almost taste her fear. He wanted to shout at her, demand she tell him the doubts weren't real. But he couldn't form the words, couldn't give voice to the questions careening through his mind.

Distant voices seemed to crack her frozen shell. Her gaze flitted about the room as if seeking escape, then paused on Brady. Hank sensed silent communication between the two, but when Brady opened his mouth to speak, Molly gave an almost-imperceptible shake of her head before turning back to Hank.

The fear was gone. In its place was an expression of resignation and dread.

Mentally bracing himself, Hank waited for more pain to come.

"I have done you a terrible wrong, Hank," she said.

"Christ," Brady muttered.

Jessica made a soft sound of distress.

Molly's head whipped toward her. With a falsely bright smile, she said, "It'll be all right, Jessica. You mustn't worry. Brady, make her rest." Abruptly, she rose, a fist clenched to her stomach. “Now, if you will excuse us, Hank and I need to talk.”

“Molly, you don’t need to do this,” Brady said, frowning at her.

“Yes. I do.” Head high, she turned and walked stiffly from the room.

A part of Hank admired her for her courage. A darker part hated her for not being afraid.

Fourteen

DON'T CRY, DON'T CRY, SHE CHANTED IN SILENT tempo with each step she took up the stairs. It was an effort not to run. Not to give in to the anguish burning in her chest. She felt Hank looming behind her, a dark, furious mass, his rage so intense it pressed against her back like a shoving hand.

Oddly, she wasn't afraid. At least, not of Hank. The worst had happened. What more could he do to her?

It was over, her idyllic dream life, her sham of a marriage, her hope of something more than endless years of tending other women's husbands, other women's children, other lives less barren than her own.

The bleak injustice of it rocked her, sent a blast of anger through her mind. She wanted to whip around and strike the man behind her, shake him until his eyes bounced from their sockets, force him to understand.

Yes, she had done a terrible thing.

Yes, she had lied.

But she'd also saved his life. Didn't that account for something?

Loud voices drifted up from the entry. Fearing Brady and Jessica might come to intervene and cause an even greater scene, Molly increased her speed. Flinging open the door into the bedroom with enough force to bounce it against the logs, she whirled to face her husband as he slammed the door shut behind him.

"You weren't supposed to survive the night," she blurted out before he could speak. "The railroad was offering widows' portions to the wives of men killed in the derailment. I was desperate for money, so I married you to get it."

He stopped before her, his chest heaving,

his clenched teeth a white slash against his flushed skin. "How disappointing for you that I didn't die."

She slapped him. Tried to slap him again, but he grabbed her wrist to stop her. "Don't ever say that!" she cried, wrenching from his grip. "Don't even think it! I saved your life! Your arm! I did everything I could to—"

The door crashed open. Brady stood on the threshold, his face stark and white.

"We have to go. There's been a cave-in at the mine."

"WHERE DO YOU THINK YOU'RE GOING?" BRADY asked when Molly rushed into the kitchen a few minutes later. He was stuffing provisions into his saddlebags and was dressed for travel in a heavy shearling jacket and long oiled duster. A muffler covered his ears and neck, and over it he wore his Stetson. Hank stood beside him, filling his own saddlebags. Other than a quick glance, he ignored her.

Molly plunked her valise and medicine basket on the table. "With you."

"No you're not," Brady said.

"There will be injuries," she argued. "I can help. It's what I do."

"We have a doctor."

"The Irishman?" Molly had heard about O'Grady, who had a better reputation as a drinker than a doctor. "And what if there are more injuries than he can handle?"

Brady's scowl deepened. "I didn't drag you here to tend miners."

Hank looked up. "You dragged her here?"

Ignoring him, she tried to reassure Brady. "I've spoken with Jessica. I checked her yesterday and everything is proceeding well. Consuelo is making her an herbal tonic, and Iantha will see that she eats properly. She's fine."

"Why'd you have to drag her here?" Hank persisted. "She didn't want to come?"

"Later, Hank," Brady snapped.

Molly watched fury flash across Hank's face. Fearing an eruption, she laid a hand on his good arm. "Hank—"

He jerked away as if her touch burned him. Or disgusted him. With a last glare at his brother, he picked up his saddlebags and stalked out the back door.

Molly pressed a hand to her chest, stunned at how badly his rejection hurt.

"Jesus, what a mess," Brady muttered.

"Don't sound so surprised." Blinking back

tears, Molly picked up her valise and basket. "We knew this day would come." Even so, she wasn't prepared for the pain that closed like a fist around her heart. She started for the door.

Brady snagged her arm. "If you're coming with us, you'll have to wear more than that," he said, eyeing her worn wool coat. "Come into the entry. We'll see what we can find."

Five minutes later, dressed in wooly boots, a scarf, a hat, another scarf over the hat, fur mittens, an oversized shearling jacket that reached past her knees, and an oiled duster buttoned to her chin, she was ready to go. Bundled as she was, she needed Brady's assistance to get down the porch steps to where Hank sat atop a tall bay, the reins of two saddled horses in his mittened hand. In the yard, three other mounted men waited. As soon as Brady hoisted her onto her horse, they were off.

Molly still couldn't believe they were traveling at night with a storm brewing. Apparently these people were so accustomed to treacherous weather, nothing held them back. Luckily there was a near full moon rising out of the clouds to the east, and if the weather held, they would have good visibility at least through the same pass she had crossed only weeks ago when she had first come to the ranch.

Brady led, setting a hard pace. Molly rode behind him, sandwiched between two outriders she recognized from their jaunt into Val Rosa, while Hank and the other man brought up the rear. She was soon glad for all the extra padding. She wasn't that accomplished a rider, and certainly had never attempted it under these conditions. Fortunately the gelding Hank had chosen for her seemed well trained and even-tempered and moved with a smooth, mile-eating gait.

They rode in silence except for the jangle of harnesses and the sounds of the horses' hooves crunching through the icy crust on the road. Since riders traveled between Redemption and the ranch several times a week, the snow was packed down and the horses didn't have to slog through deep drifts. But still it was hard going.

An hour out, Molly's horse began to limp. Hank called to Brady to stop, then dismounted and tossed his reins to the rider beside him. Without a word, he wrapped his good arm around Molly and pulled her from the saddle, then bent to check the gelding's hooves. Molly could see that the underside of the right front was clogged with a hard ball of icy snow. Hank knocked it loose, then taking off his glove, retrieved a tin from his pocket, opened it, and scooped out a gob of what looked like axle grease. He smeared it on the underside of the hoof. After wiping his fingers clean on the horse's shaggy belly, he tossed the tin to the waiting rider, pulled on his glove, and motioned for Molly to remount.

She tried, but with so many clothes, she couldn't lift her leg high enough to reach the stirrup. Hank hoisted her into the saddle, handed her the reins, and walked back to his own horse.

Not a word. He never even looked directly at her. It was as if, as far as he was concerned, she had ceased to exist.

One hour bled into two. The wind rose and the temperature dropped. Barely staying ahead of the clouds crowding behind it, the moon arced across the dark blue dome of the sky, casting ghostly white light on the rolling snow-covered valley. It was odd riding through a world with no color, no sound or movement except for the six riders cutting a dark trail through the snow. An hour later they left the valley, heading up through a piney canyon where snow-laden trees bordered the road like hooded, white-caped sentinels.

Molly burrowed deeper into her scarf, wishing she could still move her hands enough to retie it. But she'd lost feeling in her fingers, her feet ached, and her cheeks were so cold they burned. She tried to remember what Papa's medical books said about frostbite, but her mind was as numb as her body. By the time they cleared the pass and started down the other side, she was so chilled she was beyond shivering. Just staying in the saddle took all her concentration. Every breath she took made the walls of her throat ache. She was so weary she could scarcely keep her eyes open, and the urge to just let go and sink into the snow was almost overpowering. The analytical part of her mind knew she was in trouble. The rest of her didn't care. If she could only stop for a moment, just close her eyes and—

"Molly. Molly! We're here."

She opened her eyes to find Hank standing beside her horse, scowling up at her. His cheeks were as red as apples, and the muffler over the lower half of his face was crusted with ice and snow. She wanted to ask him when it had started snowing, and why he wouldn't talk to her, and tell him she was sorry, so very, very sorry . . .

"Lean toward me," Hank ordered, peeling her hands from the saddle horn.

She tried, but ended up falling against his chest instead. He scooped her up with his right arm and slid his bent left arm with the hard cast under her knees. Pressing her face against the scarf around his neck, she tried to draw in his heat as he carried her up steps, then through a door.

Sudden bright light, then a blast of heat that was so intense it made her eyes hurt. Dimly, she heard a woman's voice as he carried her down a darkened hall into another brightly lit room that smelled like roses. Roses in winter. How could that be?

He lowered her onto a bench and began unwinding the scarf around her face, making her flinch when the frozen folds scraped against her chaffed chin. The warm, rough palm of his right hand cupped her cheek.

"She's too cold," he said to someone behind her. "Get a basin of warm water—not hot—and some cloths. Hurry. If we don't get her blood moving, she'll start losing fingers and toes." Kneeling before her, he began yanking off her gloves.

As the heat penetrated her chilled body, she shivered harder, her teeth chattering so uncontrollably she bit her tongue. But that discomfort was mild compared to the pain that shot through her fingers when Hank began rubbing her hand with his. It felt like needles jabbing into her flesh and grew even more painful when he thrust her hands into a bowl of boiling water.

"Not boiling," he argued over her whimpering protests. "Barely warm."

Hunched over with pain, she pressed her forehead against his shoulder, trying not to cry as circulation returned and hot blood flowed into her icy fingers. After a while, the burn in her hands eased, and she was able to relax a bit. Then he started on her feet.

At some point during that agonizing warming process, her mind began to function again, and she became aware of her surroundings. They were in a well-appointed water closet with the same array of piping as the water closet in the ranch. Had Hank designed this too? She looked around, seeing little details—a shaving mug on a tall cabinet, oversized boots in the corner, a homespun shirt hanging on a peg by the door. A man's things. Except for the tub of steaming rose-scented bathwater.

She looked back at Hank, who knelt before her, pouring warm water down her shivering legs into the basin in which she soaked her feet. He'd removed his hat and muffler, and his cheeks had lost their redness. A stubble of beard darkened his strong jaw. She wanted to lay her cheek against the crown of his bent head, stroke the worry from his brow, feel the hard, steady beat of his heart beneath her hand.

But he was no longer hers to touch. In truth, he never really had been.

"Is th-this house y-yours?" she asked, still fighting shivers.

He nodded and poured.

"Why d-do you have a second h-house?"

He took so long, she thought he wouldn't answer. "For when I'm here tending mine business."

"I'm s-sorry to be such a b-bother."

Finally he lifted his head and looked at her. He wore that hard, implacable expression she had dreaded. "I suspect you're sorry about a lot of things, aren't you, wife?"

A wrenching sense of loss gripped her as she realized the truth of it no longer mattered. The reasons, her excuses, all the "sorries" in the world, would never mend his broken trust.

"You warming up, Miz Wilkins?" a familiar voice said from the doorway.

Molly looked over to see the prostitute who had helped her when Hank was so sick after the train ride from El Paso to Redemption. "M-Martha," she said, smiling—at least she thought she smiled—she was shivering so much the muscles in her face wouldn't behave. She wondered what Martha Burnett was doing in her husband's house and if the rose-scented oil was hers, then chided herself for questioning it. Martha had serviced him before. No doubt he would turn to her again, now that the marriage was over.

"Stew's on the stove," Martha said. "There's wood by the hearth and a fresh loaf of bread on the warmer. Anything else before I go?"

"Any news?" Hank asked.

"They're still digging out rubble. It won't be long."

Hank resumed pouring. "Tell Brady I'll be there soon. Thanks for helping."

"We knew you and Miz Molly would come. Just wanted to warm the place up for when you got here." She shot Molly a rueful smile. "You get some rest, ma'am. I got a terrible feeling they'll be calling for you soon."

HANK CONTINUED DRIZZLING WATER OVER Molly's legs, buying time until he could get his thoughts together. He didn't know why he was still here, tending a woman who had lied to him and deceived him and played him for a fool. Maybe because he still couldn't believe it. Didn't want to believe it.

Were they married? Not married? And what was Brady's part in all this?

All through the long ride from the ranch he had struggled to bring his fury under control so he could think clearly. But he still could make no sense of it. Usually he wasn't this indecisive, but with Molly he didn't know what was real and what was not, and that uncertainty kept the anger burning.

Damn her.

He could sense her watching him, waiting for him to speak. But he didn't. He could barely even look at her. What he was feeling couldn't be put into words, and he was so raw and ragged he wasn't sure what he might say or do. One minute he wanted to shake her, the next he wanted to lay her down. Either way, he wanted to get his hands on her, and no good would come of that.

Dropping the rag into the bowl of water, he motioned for her to lift her feet. When she did, he slid the bowl to the side then rose. "Stand up."

She did and stood shivering before him, her gaze pinned to his shirt.

She was so close he could feel her breath against his chest, smell the lemon rinse she used on her hair, count each dark eyelash that fanned across her flushed cheek. He wanted to choke her, kiss her, use her body until the fire inside him burned out and the lies no longer mattered. He wanted the pain to end.

With his right hand, he began awkwardly undoing the buttons on her shirt.

Her hand flew up to grip his. "W-what are you d-doing?"

"You have to get in the tub."

She pushed his hand away. "I c-can do it."

He stepped back and watched her work the buttons. She was shivering so badly she was making a mess of it. He suspected it was as much from fear as cold, and felt some gratification in that.

"Y-you don't n-need to stay."

He didn't answer.

"I c-can undress mys-self."

That darkness rose inside him again. "What are you afraid of, Molly?"

"I'm n-not afraid. I'm c-cold."

Another lie. It was one too many. Suddenly the need to hurt her the way she had hurt him overcame him. "Are you worried I'll demand my *husbandly rights*? That I'll do this?" In a savage motion, he shoved her hands aside and tore through the buttons, sending them in clattering disarray across the tile floor.

She stumbled back, clutching at the edges of her shirt. "What are you doing?"

"You're my *wife*," he snarled in her face. "I can do with you whatever I want."

"S-Stop this!" Eyes wide, she backed away from him toward the door.

He stalked after her, teeth bared. He no longer recognized himself, no longer knew the man he had become. Fury was roaring through his mind, demanding release. She had tricked him, deceived him, made him believe he could have it all. Lies. All of it. "You *are* my wife, aren't you?" he demanded, hoarsely. "I've seen the paper that says you are. Or was that a lie too?" When she bumped up against the closed door, he kept coming until he pinned her body with his.

She twisted beneath him and whipped her head away. "H-Hank, d-don't."

A distant part of himself was appalled at what he was doing. But the anger was so strong he couldn't stop. "Don't? But isn't this what you wanted, *wife*?" Trapping her face with his right hand, he brought his mouth down hard against hers, tasted salt, and wondered if it was blood or tears. "Isn't this what you lied to get?"

"No!" She shoved hard against his chest. "Hank, no!"

"Damn you, Molly!" Jerking his hand from her face, he forced himself to step back before he did her real damage. He stood shaking, dragging in great gulps of air, and tried to cool the rage churning inside. Wiping the back of his hand across his mouth, he felt a sting where her teeth had cut his lip. It scared him, and told him he had to stop this. He had to get away from her. If he didn't, he wasn't sure what he might do. Taking another step back, he tried to ignore the stricken look on her face and the tears streaming from her almost-green eyes. "Right. I forgot," he growled, as something cold and bitter wrapped around his heart. "It was never me you wanted, was it, *wife*? It was just the money."

Pushing her aside, he yanked open the door and left the room.

MOLLY STAYED IN THE TUB UNTIL THE WATER cooled and she started shivering again. She dressed, then went into the kitchen and filled a bowl with stew. She ate all of it without actually tasting it, then rinsed the bowl and put it back into the cupboard. Returning to her chair, she sat and waited.

Time passed but she was unaware of it. Years of discipline enabled her to go through the motions of whatever task was before her, while her mind wandered elsewhere. Anywhere. It was a skill she had learned in the surgical room when the smell and the blood and the horror of it were too much, and which she later had perfected at Andersonville when her mind turned the world into a flat, colorless tableau, like a faded photograph on a distant wall in a faraway room.

Wind swirled around the eaves, sending snow and sleet pinging against the windowpanes. Downdrafts drove puffs of smoke back down the chimney, where it hung in the air, collecting in stagnant layers against the ceiling of the still room. Her sluggish thoughts moved like cold molasses through her numbed mind.

It was over. He would never forgive her.

Maybe if she told herself that often enough, she would finally accept it and cut that invisible bond tying her so securely to a man who had no room in his heart for forgiveness. She was alone forever. The starkness of it settled like a stone in her chest. She wanted to weep. She wanted to rail at the unfairness of it. She wanted . . . she wanted. Him. *Stupid woman.*

The stove ticked as it cooled. After a while, the growing chill penetrated her dazed mind, and she realized the wind no longer moaned around the eaves and snow had begun collecting in white crescents on the bottoms of the frosted windowpanes. She rose, put more wood on the fire, then returned to her seat. As she waited, that hideous scene with Hank continued to play through her mind until slowly self-pity hardened into indignation and finally anger. Didn't he owe her something for saving his life? Didn't he owe her at least a chance at redemption?

The Seth Thomas day clock on the mantle had wound down to silence when a knock startled her out of her dismal thoughts. Rising stiffly after sitting for so long, she went and opened the door.

A man she didn't know stood on the porch. "They need you, ma'am."

"YOU'LL ANSWER MY QUESTIONS NOW," HANK said.

Brady looked up from the foreman's desk in the shack by the mine. "Now?"

"Now."

"Hell." Pushing aside his paperwork, Brady sat back. "All right. Ask."

He looked as weary as Hank felt. After two days of digging through rock and splintered timbers to reach the trapped miners, the missing were all accounted for, and the injured were being tended by Molly and Doc in the church behind the livery.

Two dead. Eleven hurt. A horrendous count.

Tomorrow the cleanup would begin, and hopefully within a few days they'd learn why the new shaft had collapsed. Not that it really mattered how it happened or whose fault it was. As an owner and the man in charge of their mining operations, Hank knew he was responsible.

He was so tired, he felt numb. Each day he'd worked from dawn to midnight. Each night he'd dragged himself back to his empty house to lie awake, staring at the ceiling and wondering how his life had moved so quickly from hopeful to dismal. He should have been paying better attention to the mines, rather than chasing after a woman who had never wanted him in the first place. He should have remembered what happened with Melanie and kept himself on guard. And he shouldn't have lost his temper. It wasn't like him to lose control that way. It sickened him to realize how close he had come to hurting a woman. He didn't know who he was anymore, and that scared him.

So now he stood before his brother looking for answers. Maybe if Brady explained how this farce of a marriage had come about, he might be able to find his equilibrium again. Since that scene with Molly, he'd felt as alien to himself as he had the morning he had woken up with no memory.

But now that he had the opportunity to pose the questions that had preyed on him since they had ridden in with the snow two days ago, he wasn't sure he wanted to hear the answers. He sensed that once everything was out in the open, things between him and his brother might be forever changed.

Too restless to sit, he stood with his back to the woodstove on the rear wall, arms crossed over his chest. "Was it your idea to marry me off to Molly?"

"Hell, no." Brady sighed and dragged a

hand over his jaw. His usual stubble was longer, giving his face a haggard appearance, and it seemed to Hank there was more gray in it than he remembered. "By the time I got there, it was already done."

Brady explained about the railroad settlement, and how the doctor had said Hank wouldn't live through the night, and that apparently Molly was so desperate for money she'd forced the marriage so she could get the widow's portion if he died.

Listening without interruption, Hank watched snow drift past the window and tried to ignore the sick, hollow feeling in his gut. It was hard hearing the sum total of his life reduced to a dollar value. Especially by someone he'd come to care for. Someone he'd trusted.

"As soon as I rode in and heard about it," Brady went on, "I confronted her. Said some things, made some threats. The usual. But it was too late. The marriage was done, although I doubt it's legal, since you were unconscious during the vows. Then you woke up, and we knew you'd make it."

"To her disappointment," Hank put in, trying to act as if it didn't matter.

Brady shook his head. "You would have

thought so, but that's the odd thing. The woman was hell-bent that you were going to live, even though she knew it would cost her the settlement money. That doctor, Murray, a crazy bastard if there ever was one, wanted to cut off your arm. Molly thought they should try to fix it. Murray said, 'What did it matter, since you'd die anyway,' then dumped it all on her and left. So she did it herself. It was the most godawful, horrific, bloody . . ." Brady ran a hand over his face, as if trying to brush away the memories. "I don't know how she does what she does. No wonder she pukes."

"Pukes?"

"After doctoring someone. Nerves, she says."

Hank felt a spark of sympathy and quickly smothered it out. None of this explained why he was still married or how Molly and the children ended up at the ranch. "Then what happened?" he prodded.

"She tried to blackmail me." Brady sounded amused. "Said since it looked like you were going to recover, if I paid her the amount of the settlement, she would get out of your life. I convinced her to come to the ranch instead."

Hank studied his brother, rankled at how Brady kept trying to manage his life for him, doing whatever he thought best, no matter who he stomped in the process. Hank was sick of it. "Convinced her or threatened her?" Hank knew his brother.

"Actually, I gave her a choice."

Hank knew about Brady's choices, like the time he gave their old enemy Paco Alvarez a choice between a quick hanging or a slow dismemberment. Hank was never quite sure how serious Brady's threats were, and the idea of his brother using such brutal tactics on Molly sent his anger up a notch.

"If she and the kids came to the ranch," Brady explained, "and she tended you until you were well, then I would give her the money and she could go on her way."

"Or what?"

"Or she could go to jail for fraud. Not that I would have taken her to the sheriff," he quickly added, "but she didn't know that. That's when she hit me with the spoon."

Good for her. "And the marriage?"

"I'd see that it was annulled."

And life would have gone on as it always

had. Hank thought of the wedding ring he had bought when they had been in Val Rosa and thought he must be the biggest fool there ever was. "I'm well now. So why is she still here?"

It was a long time before Brady answered. "You have to understand, Hank. You came within a breath of dying. After Sam's death then Jack going missing . . . it scared the hell out of me. But she pulled you through." Clasping his hands on the desktop, he lifted his head and met Hank's gaze straight on. "She's a good nurse, Hank. Better than Doc."

Hank waited, knowing there was more.

"And Jessica will need a good nurse."

And finally Hank understood. "Christ, Brady."

Brady studied his clenched hands. "Doc thinks she's carrying twins. She almost died when Ben was born, and you remember how bad it was later with Abigail." When his brother looked up again, his blue eyes were filled with an anguish Hank had never seen. "I know you probably think it's weak-minded, but if I lost her, Hank, I don't think I could go on."

Hank regarded him in silence. Brady's

devotion to Jessica was total. Hank had found it puzzling at first, then amusing, then enviable. His own feelings for Melanie had been mild in comparison. Comfortable and predictable, no ups and downs—until she married another man, that is, then it went down fast.

But with Molly it had been different. There had been a connection there he still didn't fully understand, and from the very beginning, it had felt . . . right.

Wrong again.

Anger sent him pacing across the small room and back. "Why didn't you tell me all this from the start, Brady? Why did you lie to me and let me think my mind was damaged? We could have ended this farce weeks ago."

"I know, I know. But then I saw the way you looked at Molly and I—"

"Stand up."

With a look of confusion, Brady did. As soon as he was upright, Hank drove his fist into the side of his face with enough force to send him toppling backward over the chair. "You should have told me."

"Christ." Brady struggled to his feet, one hand on his cheek. "You—"

Hank hit him again. This time the plank desk went over with him.

"And you shouldn't have threatened her," Hank added.

Brady sat against the wall, using his shirt-sleeve to mop blood streaming from a split lip. "Any other points you care to make?"

"Stay the hell out of my life."

"It's because of me you still have a life," Brady shot back. Rising stiffly, he righted the desk and chair.

"You should have told me. Let me decide what to do about it. You shouldn't have lied to me."

"And what would you have done, Hank?" Brady challenged. "Run her off. That's what you'd have done."

Hank glared at him.

"The truth is if she hadn't *lied* to marry you, and we hadn't *lied* to keep it from you, you'd be dead. Twice over. It's that simple."

"It wasn't your decision."

"I made it my decision. I wanted you to live."

"*You* wanted. When do we do what *I* want, Brady? When do *I* get to decide how to live my life?" Hank stalked across the room again, years of resentment and frustration churning inside him. "Christ, you let me think my mind was failing. That I was permanently damaged. How could you do that to me?" Of all the parts that made up who he was, the part Hank valued most was his intellect. That's where his imagination dwelled, and all the ideas and inventions he thought up, and all the quiet observations that brought meaning to his life. Without it, he was just a big man with a strong back and a smile women liked.

He stopped pacing and faced his brother. "How do I ever trust you again?"

Something moved behind those sky blue eyes—regret, sadness, maybe even fear. "You can always trust me, Hank. Especially when your life is at stake."

Pressing the heel of his hand against his pounding temple, Hank sighed. "And the truth be damned."

"The truth, little brother, is that you're alive with two good arms, and my wife's got a helluva nurse watching over her. As far as I'm concerned, that's the only truth that matters."

"As far as *you're* concerned. Jesus, do you ever listen to what you say?"

Suddenly Hank didn't want to talk anymore. He didn't want to think or decide or fret about what to do. So weary every step was an effort, he turned toward the door.

"Just stay out of it, Brady. Or I'll keep hitting you until one of us can't get up again. And it won't be me."

"What are you going to do about Molly?" Brady called after him.

Hank slammed the door without answering. He didn't know what he was going to do about Molly. He didn't know what to do about the shambles his life had become. He felt so confused and off balance he didn't even know what he wanted anymore. But for some reason he wasn't ready to walk away.

Fifteen

When Hank arrived at the small house he'd built for those times when he stayed in Redemption to oversee the mines, he saw a horse and a small covered carriage waiting outside. Judging by the amount of fresh snow on the canvas top, it had been there awhile. After he tended his horse and left him eating oats in the small lean-to behind the house, he went inside to find Anna Strobel in his kitchen, stirring a pot on the stove.

"Mr. Hank!" Anna rushed over to hug him, her plump arms barely reaching around his back, her wispy gray hair catching in the beard stubble under his chin. “Bless you, bless you!” she cried in the thick accent of some Central European country the name of which Hank could never remember. “You save my Hans.” Grabbing his right hand, she began covering his knuckles with kisses. “With this hands, you pull him from that black hole and give him back to me. I thank God for you.”

As gently and firmly as he could, he set her away from him. “Is Molly here?”

“Still at the church.” Pausing to dab at her watery blue eyes with the corner of her apron, she made a clucking noise. “She never rest, that one. All day, all night she work. Go.” She waved him toward the door. “Bring her home. I have nice sausage soup and strudel waiting. Make her rest. Go. Take my carriage.”

Hank went.

As he tied Anna’s horse to the rail outside the church fence, he wondered what he would say to Molly, or if she would even talk to him after that scene two days ago. Jessica called him the calm one, the steady one. But around Molly he found himself slipping into an unfamiliar role. He felt reckless, illogical, distracted. He teased, he laughed, he felt more involved and less an observer than he ever had. Just watching her walk into the room made him smile. Maybe that's why her betrayal hurt so much. All his life he'd been "the big one," "the one with the beard," "the second brother." But when Molly had smiled at him, those almost-green eyes crinkling at the corners and that tiny scar on her top lip curving in a crescent, he had felt like the most important man in the room.

He pushed open the tall arched door of the church. Unlike the other times he'd been by, tonight the church was quiet. Over the past two days, he'd made several trips, delivering injured men. He'd paused in the doorway to watch Molly work with Doc at the surgery table set up on the altar, or move from pew to pew, bringing a calm assurance to frightened men.

Had she touched him that way? Brushed his hair back from his brow? Looked down at him with that same sad, gentle smile? Or was it all just part of the role she played?

But now, as he stood in the doorway at the back of the church, he didn't see her, and that sent a jolt of alarm through him, which showed him how confused his feelings for her were.

The room was dim and quiet. The smell of blood and sickness wasn't as strong as it had been before, and there were fewer injured men stretched in the pews. A few women he recognized from around town moved quietly down the aisle or sat vigil at a man's side. Doc slouched in the pastor's chair up front, dozing. But no Molly.

He started down the center aisle.

"I hope you came to take her home."

He turned to find Martha Burnett angling toward him from a side pew. Without her face paint and with her blond curls hidden under a headscarf, she looked worn and weary. But despite the tired slump of her shoulders and the hard knowledge behind her blue eyes, she looked prettier than he'd ever seen her.

"She's had a bad time of it, Hank. I don't think the poor woman has slept two hours in the last two days." She motioned toward a small door to the right of the altar. "She's out back."

Hank nodded and crossed to the door.

The moon was hidden behind low clouds, but enough light spilled through the tall arched windows for him to see her standing in snow past her hems, her face lifted to the night sky. She wore no coat and her hands were clenched at her sides. She was breathing hard, and even in the dim light, he could see she was shaking.

He walked toward her, his boots crunching in the snow, furious with himself for still caring enough to make sure she was all right. "Molly?"

She turned. Her eyes looked as empty as the glass eyes of a china doll.

"What are you doing out here?" he asked, stopping beside her.

She blinked at him for a moment as if she didn't understand the question, then looked down at her clenched hands. With careful deliberation, she straightened her fingers, then said, "Screaming." Her voice was so soft he had to bend to catch it. "You just can't hear it."

He took off his coat and draped it over her shoulders, then stood there, unsure what to do. She seemed brittle and broken, not the high-spirited, stubborn woman he'd come to know, and he was half afraid to touch her. "Well," he said after a pause. "Let's get you home."

"Home." She made a soft, choking sound that might have been the beginnings of a laugh. Or a sob. "Where would that be, I wonder?" She made that sound again, then clapped her hand over her mouth and stumbled several steps before she suddenly bent double and retched into the snow.

Grabbing her before she tipped forward, Hank held her shoulders while her body shuddered with heaves, but nothing substantial came out. He remembered what Brady had said about her vomiting after doctoring someone. He wondered how many times she had done this over the last two days and if she'd eaten anything during all that time. After a moment, she straightened. But when she tried to step forward again, her legs buckled. Hank caught her before she hit the ground. Swinging her up into his arms, he carried her around to the carriage out front. He settled her on the seat then climbed up beside her.

They rode in silence. When they had reached the house, he lifted her down and, over her weak protests, carried her up the porch steps to where Anna Strobel held open the door.

"I have a bath ready," Anna said, following Hank down the hall toward the water closet. "Good and hot." As Hank set Molly onto the stool by the tub, Anna gently pushed him aside. "You go. Eat. I will tend the poor angel."

Hank retreated to the doorway, then stood watching as Anna untied Molly's stained apron and began loosening the row of buttons down the front of her shirt.

Molly just sat there, her face expressionless.

A glint of metal caught the lamplight, and Hank saw a tiny brass button on the floor. One of Molly's buttons that he'd torn loose two days earlier. The memory of what he'd done left a bad taste in his mouth, and he looked away to find Molly watching him. That feeling of connection shot through him, bringing with it a surge of emotion that shocked him.

She looked so sad.

Trapped by her gaze, unable to move or look away, he watched her almost-green eyes slowly fill with tears.

"Hank," she whispered. "I'm sorry."

Heart pounding, his chest so tight he couldn't take a full breath, he whirled and left the room.

IT WAS PAST MIDNIGHT. HANK WAS LYING UNDER a blanket on the kitchen table—the only piece of furniture other than his bed that was long enough to accommodate his length—watching firelight flicker across the ceiling when he heard a sound from the bedroom.

He sat up and listened.

The wind had died down, and outside sound was muffled by a foot of snow. Inside, it was quiet except for the crackling fire and the tick of the clock on the mantle. When he heard no other sound from the bedroom, he lay back, trying to ignore the itch coming from under the plaster cast on his arm.

Anna Strobel had left hours ago after feeding Molly and settling her in for the night. He had stayed scarce splitting firewood. A weak excuse, but he didn't trust himself around his wife. Given enough time, he could probably see his way past the circumstances of the marriage, but her silence about it afterward still ate at him.

Or maybe that was something under his cast. *Christ.* Just looking at it made him mad. He wasn't weak. He wasn't helpless. But every time he looked at the damned thing, it reminded him of how out of control his life his become.

He wanted it off. Now.

Rising, he padded barefoot and clad in his half-unions—he was too tall to wear the full suit and had to settle for bottoms that barely reached his ankles—to the wooden toolbox by the hearth. After digging out his hacksaw, he returned to the table, settled on the bench beside it, and began sawing down the length of the cast.

As he worked, he tried to reason through why he was still so angry. That's what he did best; he analyzed, dissected, broke things down into manageable parts to see what they were made of and how they worked. But this had him baffled. This wasn't something he could hold in his hand and examine dispassionately. This was all emotion, and he'd spent too many years walling off that part of his mind to understand what he was feeling now.

Mostly he felt like hitting something, although hitting Brady hadn't been nearly as satisfying as he'd hoped. Maybe he should try again after he got the damn cast off.

Or he could walk away. Put it behind him like he'd done with Melanie. Hell, maybe he should hunt her up and try again. There would be no surprises with her. No betrayals, no pain. Living with Melanie would be easy because he didn't care.

It took almost an hour and several pieces of skin to get the cast off, then he regretted doing it. His arm looked skinny and pale and felt like it didn't quite belong to him. There was no feeling on the surface and the scar was lumpy and puckered. His wrist and elbow felt stiff, and when he tried to wiggle his fingers, they seemed slow to react. But his arm was still there and it moved when he told it to, so he guessed he should be grateful for that.

From the bedroom came that sound again.

Rising from the bench, he stood for a moment, undecided. An image flashed through his mind—Molly, curled in his bed, her hair fanned across the pillows, her face innocent in sleep. The urge to go in there was strong inside him, but he knew if he did, he might not be able to walk away. He went anyway.

The plank floor felt cold and gritty under his bare feet as he walked down the hall to his bedroom. Stopping outside the door, he listened but heard nothing.

Lifting the latch, he eased open the door and looked inside.

The room was cold, the fire down to glowing embers. He assumed Molly was under the mound of blankets piled in the center of his bed. He could hear her breathing, not the slow rhythmic breaths of deep sleep, but the quick, rapid exhalations of someone under tension or maybe dreaming.

Moving quietly, he crossed to the hearth and added a log to the fire. Flames leaped up, brightening the dark room, and the hiss and pop of heating wood sounded loud in the silence. He stared into the fire, trying to convince himself to leave before he did something else he might regret. This woman wasn't for him. She'd already stolen his name, his trust, his belief in himself and the man he'd always thought himself to be. He couldn't give up his pride as well.

Resolved, he turned, then froze when he saw her sitting bolt upright in bed, looking at him.

MOLLY STARED AT THE TALL FIGURE SILHOUETTED against the flames, not sure if she was awake, or if he was real, or if it was one of the dead who haunted her dreams. Then he moved, and she knew who he was. "What are you doing?" she asked.

He didn't answer. With his back to the fire, his face was in shadow, but she knew he was looking at her; she could sense it the way a blind person sensed a presence nearby, or a deaf person noticed a vibration a hearing person couldn't. She felt it as surely as if he had reached across the room and put his hand to her cheek.

"I heard a noise," he finally said.

She wasn't surprised. After a bloody day in surgery, the dead frequently came calling, pulling her into a nightmare world of severed limbs and broken bodies and all the horrors she had blocked during the day. She often awoke crying. "I'm sorry I woke you."

"I wasn't asleep."

She studied him, sensing something

about him was different, then realized what it was. “Where’s your cast?”

“I cut it off.”

Concerned, although it had probably been long enough for healthy bones to knit, she threw back the covers and rose. After looking around for a robe, she realized she hadn’t brought one, so she reached for the shawl she’d draped over the foot rail earlier. Throwing it around her shoulders, she crossed toward him. “May I see?”

He held out his arm.

She angled it toward the fire to catch the light. “What did you use?”

“A hacksaw.”

“That explains the gouges.” She traced her fingertips over the scar. The incision had closed well, although there were lumps of scar tissue under the skin.

“How does it feel?” she asked.

“Itchy.”

She rotated his wrist and bent his elbow. “Does that hurt?”

“No.”

She checked his fingers, joint by joint. Everything seemed to be working as it should. “I’ll sew a sand-filled ball for you to squeeze. That will help restore strength and mobility. If you rub coarse cloth along the surface twice a day, some of the numbness will pass." She released his arm. "Do you have any questions?"

"Why were you screaming? Out back, behind the church."

It wasn't the question she had expected, and for a moment she wasn't sure how to answer. The screaming was a private thing, and she considered it a weakness, just another indication of her unsuitability as a healer. But he had asked, so she would answer, if only to keep him talking. After two days of being apart from him, she wanted to know how he was, if he was still angry, or if that connection between them had been severed forever.

"When I first started helping my father," she said, "it would overwhelm me—the blood, the sickness, all that pain. Papa didn't like emotional displays. But there were times when the suffering would fill me up until I felt like I was choking on it. So I would run to the tallest point I could find—a hill, a roof, one time a water tower—and I would look out to the far horizon and let all that pain go."

"By screaming?"

She gave him a half-smile at the absurdity of such a thing. "Not as prosaic as working numbers, but it probably works as well."

"Why were you screaming this time?"

Realizing she was clenching her fingers, she made herself stop. "I had to amputate a child's leg."

"Billy Hartnet."

"He died anyway." Saying the words aloud added fuel to the simmering anger that had sustained her during the long hours she had spent at Billy's side watching him die. "Why was a child even in a mine? Why wasn't he home doing normal things like climbing trees or fishing or—" Her voice cracked. She battled for composure, found it, then added in a calmer tone, "He was too young to be a miner. He shouldn't have even been there."

For several moments, Hank didn't speak. Then in a flat, hard voice, he said, "He was fourteen. His father died of snakebite last year, and Billy was supporting his mother and little sister. He wasn't a miner. We don't hire kids to dig ore. He carried messages down the hole for us, that's all."

She should have thought before she

spoke. Knowing what she did of the Wilkins brothers, she should have realized they would never use children to labor in their mines. "What will happen to his mother and sister?"

"We'll take care of them. We'll take care of all of them, even if we have to gut the ranch to do it."

She should have realized that too. Now she had made him angry again.

"Which reminds me," he went on in a harsh, angry tone, "what does a dead person go for these days?"

If he thought to hurt her, he was too late. She already felt flayed to the bone. Trying to make her feel guilty wouldn't work either. She had thought about it a great deal over the last days and had come to the realization that she had no regrets about their marriage. If she hadn't married him and been there to take on the responsibility for his care, he would have been left to die. Instead, he stood before her, alive and whole. How could she regret that? Still, she should have told him once he recovered. That was the greater sin, and the one that haunted her most. A terrible mistake. But surely a forgivable one. Hiking her chin, she looked directly into his eyes. "The railroad pays three hundred."

"We're thinking five."

"That's quite generous." She held his gaze, unwilling to be the one to look away first. She might be sorry, but she would never grovel for him; pride was all she had. Then she realized this wasn't a contest or a battle of wills. This was Hank. Her husband. And they were both in pain. She sighed. "I should have told you."

"Yes. You should have." His words were clipped, the tone, cold.

"I'm sorry for that."

"Are you?" Lifting his hand, he pulled the shawl from her shoulders and let it fall to the floor. "Show me how sorry you are."

She stared up at him, not sure she'd heard right and not recognizing the Hank she had come to know in that hard expression. Suddenly she remembered what Brady had said about Hank's temper. She edged back.

He came after her. "Are we married? Are you my wife?"

"Yes, but—"

"Then act like it. Take off your gown."

"Hank, don't do this." She crossed her arms over her chest.

He loomed over her, so big he blocked the light of the fire, so angry she could feel it, see it in the rigid muscles of his face. "I've waited, Molly. I've courted you. I've tried to be the man—the *husband*—you pretended I was. I've played my part in this farce. Now you play yours." Reaching out, he pushed her arm aside and laid his hand over her breast. "Take off your gown."

She shrank back, seeing in him the same man who had pinned her against the door in the water closet. "Hank, I—"

"Aren't you curious, wife? Haven't you wondered?" His voice softened. His hand grew bolder. Something shifted behind his eyes. "Isn't this what you wanted?"

She watched him look down, his gaze following the movements of his fingers as he stroked her, and something clenched deep inside her. Her heart hammered. Everywhere he touched, her skin quivered. Beneath the fear, desire built.

This is what other women know. This is how it feels to be touched by a man.

His gaze rose to meet hers. His eyes

shimmered like golden pools in the fire-light, filled with an expression she couldn't define. Not anger. But a stranger's eyes. A stranger's smile. "I want to taste your skin, wife. I want to look into your eyes when I come inside you. Take off your gown."

"Hank . . ."

"Take off your gown."

She could hardly breathe, hardly think. "Will you forgive me then?"

He looked at her without answering, his fingers hot and insistent.

Needing to stop him before she lost all reason, she put her hand over his, anchoring him against her breast. Her heart was beating so fast she wondered if he could feel it. She wondered if the rush of arterial blood into her head would cause her to faint. She wondered if she had the courage to do what she wanted to do.

"Will you forgive me then?" she demanded, her throat so tight it came out a whisper.

She waited. One second. Two. A lifetime.

"I don't know," he finally said.

His honesty was her undoing. She would have believed no other answer, no matter how badly she might have wanted to hear it. But the pain of it almost crushed her. She stepped back.

His hand fell to his side.

Instead of forgiveness, he offered lust. Instead of love, he would give her passion. He wouldn't force her. The decision would be hers. But she instinctively knew if she pushed him away now, whatever fragile thread still bound them together would be forever broken.

An hour of passion. And perhaps a lifetime of regret. But a lifelong memory as well.

Moving quickly before her courage failed her, she pulled the gown over her head and dropped it to the floor. "Come on, then," she said and walked to the bed.

MOLLY WAS FAMILIAR WITH THE FUNCTIONING OF the human body, both male and female. She understood the mechanics of sexual congress through her medical books and conversations with camp prostitutes, but none of it by personal experience. She knew about the various physical responses to erotic stimulation. But she didn't understand about the emotions and how necessary they were to mask the realities of the actual act of copulation.

He came at her like a man in desperation. His hands were everywhere. His mouth touched her everywhere . . . except on her mouth. His heat fanned an answering fire within her own body. It was exhilarating and arousing and created within her a breathless wonder and shivery need.

Then something began to change, nothing she could pinpoint at first, but a subtle shifting. Or perhaps it was a growing awareness within herself. Even though they were as physically close as two people could be, he wasn't truly with her. He didn't kiss her. Or speak to her. Despite the closeness of their bodies, there was no intimacy at all.

"Hank," she whispered, trying to reach out to him, to slow him down, to bring him back to her. But he wouldn't allow even that, pinning her hands at her shoulders so she couldn't touch him.

Ardor instantly cooled. She stiffened beneath him in confusion. "Hank?"

His dark gaze never left her face as he rose above her and, in one quick motion, thrust inside her.

Her body recoiled. Her mind splintered in panic. This wasn't a joining, or a chance for them to overcome the pain they'd caused one another. This was a cold, loveless coupling. Anguish swept through her, burned against the back of her eyes. Old feelings of inadequacy crowded into her mind, driving her back into the shadows, back into that safe sepia world where she could observe without feeling and drift without pain. Dry-eyed and detached, she looked up at him looking down at her and felt something wither inside. This wasn't even passion. This was punishment.

Hank. What have you done?

As if from a distance, she watched sweat bead at his temples and roll down his straining neck to drip onto her breasts. She watched muscles flex in his chest, felt the tremble of tension in his braced arms, saw the flash of his clenched teeth as spasms shook his big body. And through it all, his gaze never left her face.

Never a word, a kiss. Not even a look of regret.

Somewhere in her mind she stood on a hilltop and screamed.

Then finally it was over, and he rolled away from her and onto his back. His breathing sounded harsh and ragged in the stillness. Cold air prickled skin that was slick with his sweat. His scent cloaked her, choked her. Unable to move, she lay as he had left her, staring blindly up at the ceiling, too numb to cover herself. After a while, without his heat, she began to shiver.

He leaned over, pulled up the blanket, then lay back. "Why are you crying?"

She wasn't aware that she was. She turned her head to find him watching her.

He was stretched on his back, nude. His hair clung to his forehead. Damp skin gleamed through the faint dusting of dark hair on his chest. She wanted to hit him, claw him, mar his perfect beauty. "I don't know," she answered and turned her face to the ceiling again.

"Did I hurt you?"

"No." At least not in the way he meant. He hadn't raped her. She had come to him willingly. She had wanted this joining and had no one to blame but herself. But to be used so dispassionately . . .

God. She wished he would go so she could wash.

Abruptly he rolled away from her to sit on the edge of the bed, fists planted on the mattress by his hips. His head drooped and firelight gilded his shoulders and the long sloping curve of his back with gold. "Why, Molly? Why did you marry me, then lie about it?"

For a moment she hated him, wanted him to suffer as he had made her suffer. But she hadn't the energy or the will to sustain such a strong emotion, so it quickly faded, leaving her feeling drained and empty. "I told you. For the money."

He didn't respond. For a long time he sat staring at the far wall. Finally, "I didn't mean to hurt you. Earlier. That wasn't . . . I'm not usually so . . ." His voice trailed off.

"Selfish?" she snapped, anger coiling in her chest.

He turned his head and looked at her.

"Distant? Cold? Uninvolved?"

"Damnit, Molly."

Damn you she wanted to shout back at him. *How could you do this to me? To us? How do we go on from here?*

He rose, pulled on his unions, then sat back down on the edge of the mattress, as if undecided what to do next.

Molly watched firelight shadows dance across his broad back and felt some of her anger ease. He wasn't a bad man, although he'd treated her badly. Nor was she bad because she'd withheld the truth. They both deserved a second chance. But she was still too angry to allow him that.

"Why didn't you tell me truth?" he said after a while. "Why did you string me along and make me think we were a family? That we cared for each other?" He looked back at her over his shoulder. She could see the hurt in his eyes.

Because we do care for each other and we can still be a family. But she wasn't sure she still wanted that. Suddenly impatient with her own confused emotions, and desperate for this to be over, she said in clipped impatient tones, "At first I didn't tell you because Brady asked me to wait until you were stronger. Then later, I was afraid of what would happen when I did. I felt safe, and the children were happy. It was . . . nice. I didn't want it to end."

He looked at her, silent and brooding.

What did he see when he looked at her that way? What thoughts did he hide behind that expressionless mask? Resentment eddied through her. How long was she to pay for that sin? Wasn't what just happened punishment enough?

"Has Brady never lied to you?" she asked.

"Once. He had his reasons."

"We all have our reasons, Hank."

He bent and fumbled with the tab closures on his unions, then sat facing the wall, his hands resting on his thighs.

"You've forgiven him," Molly persisted. "Why not me?"

"It's not about forgiveness, Molly. It's about faith. I trusted you."

"And once broken, that trust can never mend. Is that what you're saying?"

"No, that's not what I'm saying." He swiveled to look at her.

He looked drawn and defeated. A man trapped between his implacable nature and his own desires. She sensed a battle raging inside him, could almost feel his indecision and confusion.

"But it'll take time, Molly."

And she was to meekly wait for him to finally forgive her? Hardly.

"Take all the time you need, Hank," she said wearily. "But don't come to me again like you did tonight. There's no place for anger or distrust in my bed."

"Molly . . ."

"Good night, Hank." Rolling away from him onto her side, she stared at the fire, waiting, hoping for . . . something. Instead, she felt the mattress shift as he rose, then heard the sound of his footfalls across the floor. A moment later the door closed.

Pressing her face into the pillow, she let the tears come.

Sixteen

MOLLY WAITED UNTIL SUNLIGHT CREPT ACROSS the floor, then rose and washed. She studied her reflection in the mirror above the bureau, expecting changes, evidence of the emotional seesaw she had been on over the last days.

She looked tired and pale and worn around the edges. But the greatest change was in her eyes. She had seen that expression of weary resignation in Andersonville and more recently in Martha Burnett's eyes. Had she fallen to a point where just to endure was the most she could hope for?

She had dreamed of so much more.

Hearing no movement from the other part of the house, she assumed Hank had left. She hoped so. She didn't know if she could bear facing him this morning. That scene last night had left her heartsick and angry, and she was too edgy right now to hash it out with him.

And hash it out they would. He would give her a just reason for his treatment of her. She would allow no stony silence this time. By heaven, she would make him talk to her.

Then she would decide what she must do.

Meanwhile, she would somehow get through Christmas and see that Jessica's babies were safely delivered. Then she would gather her strength for whatever lay ahead. She couldn't leave now if she wanted to, not in the dead of winter with two children in tow. She still had no money and no place to go. And Fletcher's men were still out there. Besides, she wasn't ready to give up on Hank. On them. On all those lovely dreams.

After dressing and setting the room to rights, she wandered through the empty house, wondering if anyone would come to take her back to the church or if she should strike out on her own. She wasn't sure she knew where it was, having come and gone in the middle of the night. She supposed if she walked through town, she would eventually find it. She certainly wasn't going to sit in Hank's house like a dutiful little wife and wait for him to come home. She would rather perform surgery on herself. With a rusty penknife. Resolved to bring some order to the mess she'd made of things, she donned one of Hank's spare jackets—her borrowed shearling was still at the church—and left the house.

The day was crisp and bright, a cloudless sky above and a dazzling blanket of pristine snow below. As she walked, she breathed deep, enjoying the bite of cold in her throat, feeling her spirits lift with every lungful of clean mountain air. She would get through this. She would find a way to heal the wounds they had dealt each other. After all, that was what she did best, wasn't it?

"What do you mean it was deliberate?" Hank demanded.

Brady shoved a piece of wood across the foreman's desk in the mine shack. "This is from the main crossbeam over the entrance to the new shaft. Those are saw marks."

Hank studied the markings, ran his thumb over the edge. Wood never broke that clean on its own. He returned it to the desk. "But why?"

"Hell if I know."

"Blake." Franklin Blake had been nosing around the Wilkins holdings for months. He had a reputation for shady deals and brutality toward his workers, which was why Hank and Brady had refused to consider his offers to buy the mines or the ranch water rights. But this was too blatant, too obvious, even for Blake.

"It's not your fault," Brady said.

Hank looked up and met his brother's eyes—the right one anyway. The left was nearly swollen shut. His top lip was swollen as well, with a nice split disappearing under his mustache. Hank took some satisfaction in that. "You ought to have Molly tend that cut."

"Is that an apology?"

"Hell, no." Movement caught his eye,

and Hank looked through the window behind his brother at a figure moving along the boardwalk. Molly. He would recognize that stride anywhere. The woman didn't walk. She marched. Chin first, head high, like she had a brass band playing in her head and her footsteps were the drumbeat. A woman of purpose. A hollow feeling opened in his chest. How could he have used her so badly? What kind of man had he become?

"She'd try to stitch it," Brady muttered, fingering the cut. "And that would mean shaving my mustache, which I won't do, of course."

Hank watched Molly step into the alley between the boot shop and O'Hara's Apothecary. A moment later she came back out and stood for a moment, looking down the street in one direction, then the other. Probably looking for the church. He ought to go help her, but the thought of facing her made his head hurt. Last night had been disastrous. He hadn't meant to be so . . . what had she called it? Selfish and cold. He'd been that and more. *Christ.* It seemed whenever he was around her lately he humiliated himself.

He didn't like it—that feeling of regret—of loss—of missed chances. He wasn't accustomed to such uncertainty, and the emotional turmoil she had brought into his carefully ordered life was intolerable to him. It would be best for both of them if he let her go. Ended it. Got the annulment, gave her enough money to salve his bruised conscience and set her and the children up in California, then sent her on her way.

But as soon as that idea formed, a sudden image of himself filled his mind—alone, still living in Brady's shadow, still in turmoil over these same regrets and missed chances. *Damn her.* For one unreasonable moment he almost hated her for exposing the lonely sterility of his old life. Because now, after these weeks with Molly and Penny and Charlie, he could never go back.

"I see you're still shaving."

Hank glanced at his brother.

"I half expected you to start growing the beard again."

"Why?"

"Usual reason." Brady tried to sneer, then winced at the pull on his lip. "To hide behind."

"You want another black eye?"

"You're welcome to try. Now that you don't have your cast as an excuse, I'll feel better about beating the hell out of you."

"Best bring a friend then."

Looking back to the window, Hank saw Molly hesitate outside the livery. She seemed ridiculously small in his jacket. And why wasn't she wearing gloves or a hat? Didn't she know she had a low tolerance to cold? He'd have to remind her . . . if they ever spoke to each other again.

A man in a slouch hat approached her. From this distance Hank couldn't tell who he was, but there was something about the way he moved. A lot of hand flapping. A weak sister. Molly didn't seem to like him either and tried to back away. But when he leaned down to say something to her, then took her arm to lead her in the direction of the church behind the livery, she went with him.

"The cave-in wasn't your fault," Brady said again.

Hank turned from the window, suddenly feeling restless and on edge. "I should have been more vigilant. Posted a guard. Something."

"You had no cause to. It wasn't negligence, Hank. Or an accident you could have foreseen. It was deliberate sabotage."

"I'm the man in charge. It's my responsibility."

Brady threw his hands up in exasperation. "Damnit, Hank. Haven't you made enough mistakes lately? Why are you looking for more?"

"What mistakes?"

"Christ." Brady started to scratch the stubble on his cheek then winced when he got too near the bruise by his eye. "I saw you go past here with Molly last night. Then later you come stomping back like you've got a burr up your tail. Not the behavior of a well-satisfied man."

Aware that his brother was watching him, Hank picked up the piece of wood and rolled it in his hands. "So you don't think it's Blake?"

Brady sighed. "You are one close-mouthed sonofabitch."

Hank tossed the wood back onto the desk. "And you're an interfering bastard."

"I'm observing. There's a difference."

"Right." Hank turned toward the door.

"I'll ask around, see if anyone's seen a stranger in town." Like the man outside the livery with Molly. He opened the door.

"What about Molly?" Brady asked.

Hank stopped on the threshold, one step shy of escape. The man was goddamn relentless. "What about her?" he snapped.

"What are you going to do about her?"

That was a question Hank had wrestled with since he'd left the house the night before, and he still didn't have an answer. The woman had him doubting himself, in a constant state of confusion, and so furious he could hardly form a thought.

Yet he didn't trust himself to stay away from her.

He was that doomed.

He sighed. For her safety and his peace of mind, there was really only one thing he could do. "I'll think of something." Then before his brother could question him further, he closed the door and went to tell his wife he was sending her back to the ranch.

THE SCARRED MAN SHOVED MOLLY INTO THE last stall. She hit hard against the wall and crumpled to the hay-strewn floor. Fighting to catch her breath, she crouched in the corner staring up at the man who had followed them through Nebraska, then Utah, to Val Rosa, and now Redemption.

"You're a hard woman to track down, lovey."

He was even more hideous than Penny had said, and not just because of the puckered burn scar that covered the left side of his face from hat to chin. There was an aura of evil about him that aroused within her a level of fear she had never known.

He began to pace the small enclosure, his steps kicking up puffs of dust that danced in the bands of light coming through the gaps in the planks of the exterior wall. She wondered where the stable owner was and if anyone would hear her if she screamed and what the scarred man would do if she tried to run.

He was thin, almost cadaverous, and moved with a sensuous hip-rolling gait, like she imagined a snake might move if it had legs. When he spoke, he gestured in the exaggerated way of an actor on the stage, and his voice was a lisping hiss that made her wonder if the flames that had marred his face had damaged his vocal chords as well. There was a wrongness about him that went deeper than the scar.

Trying to focus past the fear, she looked around for a way to escape or a weapon she could use against him. Nothing, not even a bucket or a halter on a peg. If he came close enough, she could go for his eyes with her nails. Or kick him in the groin. If she could butt him in the sternum and momentarily paralyze the vagus nerve, she might have enough time to get to the door. But if she failed . . .

Despair swept through her. Thank God the children were at the ranch. Whatever it was he had planned for her, at least they would be safe.

Don't argue. Do what he says. Stay alive, she chanted silently.

He stopped before her, his elegant, almost-feminine hands spread on his narrow hips. He gave her a scolding look. "Do you have any idea the trouble I had to go through to lure Nurse Molly away from that backwoods ranch?" He waved a languid hand in exasperation. "Mercy, I almost died in that cave-in."

At her look of horror, he laughed, a high-pitched trill that vibrated along the nerves under Molly's skin. "Close your mouth, lovey. You look like a trout." Hunkering down in front of her, he cocked his head to one side and studied her through eyes as dark and empty as an abandoned well.

Molly pressed back against the wall. "W-What do you want?"

"Me?" With an expression of exaggerated innocence, he splayed his fingers on his chest. "I don't want anything. But your brother-in-law is most anxious that you return what you took from him."

"I didn't take anything."

His hand shot out and struck the side of her face, driving her head back against the wall. Pain ricocheted down her neck.

"Please, love, don't interrupt. Don't let's lie to each other either. It would get messy and I abhor messiness. And you wouldn't want to upset me, would you?"

Stunned, Molly blinked at him, her senses reeling from the blow.

He leaned closer. His breath stank of cloves. "That was a direct question," he said in his hissing voice. "You can answer."

"N-No."

"No, what?"

"No, I d-don't want to upset you."

"Excellent." He settled back on his heels. "Now where were we? Ah, yes. I was explaining to you what you need to do. It's quite simple, really. Return the book. That's all. And voilà!" He snapped his fingers. "I disappear from your life, Fletcher disappears, and we all live happily ever after."

"W-What book? I don't have any book."

He slapped her again. "Then you had best start looking for one, hadn't you?"

Molly recoiled, one hand pressed to her stinging cheek. "I d-don't have anything of his, I s-swear it."

He drew back his hand.

She ducked, her arm over her face. But instead of the blow she'd expected, she felt his fingers stroking her hair. She shuddered with the effort not to scream.

"You have beautiful hair, lovey," he murmured. "I once did too. But dear old mommy set it on fire. Would you like to see?" Before she could answer, he whipped off his hat and thrust his bald head inches from her face.

She stared in revulsion at the ropy web of puckered scar tissue that rose in wine-colored ridges across his ruined scalp.

"Nasty, isn't it?" With a dramatic sigh, he replaced the hat on his head. "Children are rather afraid of it. Which, of course, makes it almost worthwhile."

He studied her as though lost in thought, one long finger idly tapping the twisted flesh of his lower lip. "Now where were we? Oh, yes, the children. I love children. Properly trained, they're so eager to please, aren't they? But oh, so breakable." He smiled, although it was more of a grimace because of the rigidity of the scarred flesh. "Now Charlie and Penny seem a sturdy pair. When I saw you with them in Omaha, I was so taken with their beauty I just wanted to eat them up. But then you left and I couldn't find you." Reaching out, he tweaked her bruised cheek. "Naughty girl. You won't do that again, will you?"

When she didn't respond, he tweaked harder. "Answer, please."

"N-No."

That grimace again, his twisted lips pulled flat against crooked yellow teeth. "Of course you won't. And you know why?" He leaned close to whisper in her ear, the perfumed reek of his body almost as nauseating as his breath. “Because I will, you know. Eat them up.” He made smacking noises and stuck his tongue in her ear.

With a cry, she shrank away from him.

He laughed. “Oh, don’t be so squeamish. They’re really quite tasty. Now hold out your hand.”

Molly stared at him, her heart racing like a wild thing in her chest.

“Hold. Out. Your. Hand.”

Panting with terror, she lifted her left hand. It shook so hard, it looked palsied. He took it in both of his, patted it reassuringly, then savagely twisted her thumb.

A popping sound, then white hot pain shot through her hand and up her arm. She sucked in air, so stunned by the searing pain, tears flooded her eyes.

“Shhh, lovey,” he whispered, clapping his hand over her mouth before she could cry out. “We wouldn’t want to draw attention, would we? Answer, dear.”

She shook her head.

He removed his hand, gave his palm a look of distaste, then wiped it on his shirtfront. “Oh, do stop crying. It’s not broken, just dislocated.”

Cradling her injured hand against her chest, Molly swallowed back bile.

"Now listen carefully," he said in his whispery voice. "You have one month, and I'm being generous here because Fletcher is frantic to find you. But I have other business in Mexico—did you know they sell children down there? Not on the street, of course, but if you know where to look—well, never mind that. But when I come back, you'll have what I want, won't you?"

Molly stared at him, numb with pain and terror, her mind so sluggish she couldn't concentrate. What was he talking about? What book?

He tapped her bruised cheek. "Stay with me here, Molly. I don't want to have to repeat myself."

Suddenly he tensed, ducking his head to peer through the gaps in the outside wall as footfalls crunched through the snow in the alley.

"Well, hello," he whispered. "Isn't that your husband, lovey?"

Molly lunged toward the wall. But before she could reach it or call out, he grabbed her by the throat and yanked her back.

She kicked, trying to hit the slats, but they were just out of reach.

His grip on her throat tightened.

In choking desperation she twisted and flailed, her lungs burning for air.

"Shhh," he hissed in her ear. "Not a word, Molly, or your fine strapping husband will end up like him." Forcing her head around, he pointed her face toward the rails of the next stall.

It was empty. But in the one past it, she saw a horse standing along one wall, a splintered door on the other, and a limp figure sprawled between.

"I tried to make it look like an accident. One of my talents, even if I do say so myself. But you already know that, don't you, lovey? Poor daddy."

An image of Papa's ruined face flashed through her mind. Despair drained the last of her strength and she sagged in defeat. When she stopped struggling, he let go of her throat and she fell onto her back in the straw, sucking in great gulps of air.

Stepping over her, he bent and peered through the gaps at Hank's retreating figure.

He made that smacking sound with his twisted lips. "My, my. Isn't he delicious. Shall we call him back?"

Molly rolled onto her side and gagged.

"Oh, pooh. You're no fun."

With her hand cradled to her chest, she crawled over to lean against the wall. Shaking and nauseated, she watched him pace back and forth. She had seen madness before. She had seen the horrors one human could inflict on another. But she had never known true terror until now.

This man was beyond madness. He was less than human. A monster.

He stopped pacing and stared down at her. "Now where were we? Ah, yes. You were going to promise to get me that book. Because if you don't, lovey, here's what will happen." He dropped onto his haunches before her. "First your husband will die. Then his brother. Then, after they've served their purposes, or my purposes, really, those delicious little children will die. Do you see where I'm going here?"

Numbly Molly nodded, tears burning hot streaks down her cheeks.

He cocked his head and studied her.

"I'm not sure you do. Perhaps you're not taking me seriously."

"I am," Molly said weakly.

Do what he says. Don't argue. Stay alive.

"Truly?" He gave her a doubtful look. "Because I don't sense resolve, Molly. I'm sorry, but I don't." He sighed. "Hold out your hand."

Molly cringed against the wall. She heard a whimpering sound and realized it came from her own throat.

"You'd rather I call your strapping husband back? Because you know what will happen if I do, and he won't even see it coming. Is that what you want, lovey?"

She shook her head.

"Then hold out your hand."

Sobbing hoarsely, she lifted her injured hand.

"The other one, silly. That one's already done. And do hurry. He's coming back this way."

Molly held out her right hand. He gripped her thumb. "Let's count together, shall we? But quietly. We mustn't let him hear. One, two, snap, pop."

Molly gasped as pain exploded. Bile spewed out her throat and into the straw.

"Well, that's disgusting," he said, rising quickly and stepping back.

Curling over her ruined hands, Molly dropped her head onto her knees, her body wracked with shudders.

"All right then." He rubbed his hands together. "I'll see you in a month, lovey. Don't disappoint."

She heard him start toward the door, then stop and turn back. Bracing for more pain, she looked up as he stopped in front of her.

"I really hope you'll keep this"—he made a fluttering motion with his hand—"just between us. If you went whining to your husband or his brother, why it would upset me so much I just don't know what I'd do. Something terrible, I suppose. For their sakes, you'll keep it quiet, won't you, lovey?"

When she didn't answer, he bent over and tapped her dislocated thumb with his index finger, sending a scream up her throat. "Answer me, Molly."

"Y-Yes," she choked out, dizziness spiraling through her head.

"That's my girl. One month. Oh, and Merry Christmas."

"YOU SEEN MOLLY?" HANK ASKED.

Brady looked up from the latest assay report he had spread over his desk in the mine shack. "Run her off already, have you?"

Ignoring the well-aimed barb, Hank scanned the street. "She went by here a minute ago. I figured she was headed to the church, but Doc hasn't seen her." He thought of Fletcher and felt a prickle of unease. "I saw her talking to a man outside the livery, but no one's there now." Which was odd, now that he thought about it. Ezra Cooper all but slept with his horses.

Brady must have read his concern. Setting the report aside, he pushed back his chair and rose. "You're really worried, aren't you?"

Hank turned and headed back down the street.

A few seconds later Brady fell into stride beside him. "She couldn't be far. Redemption's only two streets wide and a quarter-mile long. Did Ezra see her?"

"I didn't talk to him. I called out, but he didn't answer."

"Strange."

"That's what I'm thinking. Let's look there first."

They saw her as they passed the alley on the south side of the livery. She was heading toward the church, bent like an old woman, her steps halting and uneven. Hank hurried toward her. "Molly?" he said, laying his hand on her shoulder.

She cried out, wrenching away so forcefully she almost lost her balance.

Hank froze, stunned by the rejection. Then he realized she had turned away out of pain, not anger. "Molly?" He stepped in front of her, careful not to touch her, then sucked in his breath when he saw her bruised face and swollen hands.

"Holy Christ," Brady said, moving up beside him. "What happened?"

"Take me to Dr. O'Grady," Molly said in a hoarse whisper.

Hank started to pick her up, but she pulled away again. He turned to his brother. "Get a wagon."

"A wagon? But the church is right there."

"No," Molly choked out. "I'll walk."

Hank and Brady hovered on either side of her, wanting to do something but not sure what. The fifty yards to the church stretched like a mile in Hank's mind.

What happened? Had she fallen on the ice? In the livery? Did one of Ezra's horses kick her? Is that why she had straw stuck in her clothes and hair?

Brady went ahead to alert Doc, and by the time Molly made it up the steps and through the door, the doctor was coming toward them down the center aisle. One look at her hands and he reached for the laudanum. Molly protested, but after Doc explained he would have to palpate the thumb joints to check the damage and that would be painful, she took a goodly dose.

Hank helped her stretch out on the altar/surgery table then stood silently by while they waited for the drug to take effect. The place smelled of chemicals and sickness. An occasional moan came from one of the pews where the injured lay, but it was a lot calmer than it had been when he'd come looking for Molly the previous night. Not wanting to think about the fiasco that followed, Hank watched Doc settle Brady in one of the empty pews and set to work on his split lip. A dozen questions bounced through his mind. Who was that man outside the livery? And how could she injure both thumbs at the same time in the same way? And where was Ezra?

"Hank?"

He glanced down to see Molly looking up at him. The pupils of her eyes were dilated and the lines of strain around her mouth had lessened, so he knew the drug was starting to work.

"I need to go back," she said in a slurred voice that made her soft Southern accent even more pronounced. "I need to be with the children."

And away from me, he thought grimly. Not that he blamed her. He'd proven he wasn't fit to be around her right now. "All right. Soon as Doc says it's okay."

"No. Today." She blinked sluggishly up at him. "I need to go today."

He nodded, wondering how he would manage that, since she couldn't hold on to reins or a saddle horn with those hands. "I'll borrow a buggy." It would have to be covered and well sprung, and he'd need to load it with blankets and warming bricks, and bring along extra horses in case the wheels got bogged down and they had to ride partway. He should bring extra riders too. And maybe figure a way to refit the seats into a reclining bench so she—

"I'm sorry," she said, cutting into his thoughts.

He looked down at her, feeling that bitter regret that had hounded him all day. He was the one who had made a mess of things . . . although some might argue that since she started it all in the first place with her lies, it wasn't completely his fault. But he decided not to mention that. He might be a fool but he wasn't stupid.

"When this is over, Molly, we need to talk." He had apologies to make too.

"I know. Just . . . be careful." Then before he could ask her what she was worried about, her lids fluttered closed and she was out.

He motioned Doc over, then stood back as he set to work.

Her thumbs weren't broken, nor were they as dislocated as they could be, which Doc explained meant the ligaments hadn't been torn loose, so she wouldn't need surgery. She would have to wear splints for a month, but if she allowed the joints to heal properly, Doc didn't think she would suffer any lasting damage. Meanwhile, until she got the hang of eating and dressing and tending herself without use of her thumbs, she would need a lot of help.

Hank, having already sunk lower than a snake's belly in his own estimation, wasn't surprised that his whole body tensed up at the prospect of helping his wife with those personal chores. He really was a sonofabitch.

Judging by the warning frown his brother sent his way, Brady had reached the same conclusion. "I'll hire another Garcia sister to look out for her."

"Stay out of it," Hank said with soft menace. "It's my wife, my problem." He could almost see his brother choking on words he was holding back, but eventually he nodded.

"I just hope you know what you're doing."

Hank did too.

Seventeen

IT WAS LATE AFTERNOON WHEN MOLLY AWOKE.

She felt awful. Her head hurt, her mouth was so dry her tongue felt like a brick, and her hands throbbed with demonic persistence. Squinting against bright sunlight, she carefully raised her arms to assess the damage.

Her hands were in plaster half-casts stretching past her wrists, with gauze strips holding her thumbs in fixed positions. No incisions, so the ulnar collateral ligaments hadn't been ruptured.

She was grateful for that, at least. As she lowered her hands, she thought of the poor man in the stall at the livery. Ezra-something. She didn't even know his full name, yet he had probably died because of her.

A sick feeling washed over her. If she had what Fletcher wanted, she would gladly hand it over. But neither she nor the children had packed any books, so how could she return something she didn't have?

A month. That's all she had before the monster came back. A month of lies to Hank while a killer tracked his family? She couldn't do that. The brothers had a right to know what they were up against—what she had brought into their midst.

Turning her head to the left, she saw Hank standing in the fourth pew, talking with Dr. O'Grady and one of the injured men. Sunlight edged his hair in gold and brought out the strong curves of his jaw and cheekbones. He stood with his weight on one foot, shoulders relaxed, his big hands planted low on his hips.

Those hands.

Images of the previous night drifted through her mind. She had felt the power in those hands. She had tasted the salty texture of his skin and learned the breadth and strength of that body. And despite the pain they had caused each other, as she watched him standing in the sunlight, she longed to touch him again.

"You look like hell," a male voice said.

She turned her head to the right and saw Brady sprawled in the pastor's chair, watching her. How long had he been there? Her gaze took in his black eye, the bruised chin and bandaged lip. "As do you," she countered.

"We found Ezra Cooper. Appears he was kicked in the head by one of his horses. Know anything about that, Molly?" He wore that same distrustful expression she had seen on Hank's face since he'd learned the truth about their marriage.

She didn't answer.

"Strange, though," he went on in his husky voice. "Ezra's horses are as gentle as lambs. Never even threatened another horse, much less a human. Then you show up with two busted hands and a bruised face. Makes me wonder if the two aren't connected somehow."

"I had nothing to do with his death."

"Probably not. But maybe you could tell me who did."

She opened her mouth, then closed it. The scarred man could be out there watching right now, waiting to see if she said anything. He would know if she did, because the Wilkins brothers would immediately ride after him, and he would see them and draw them into a trap. But if she could get them all back to the ranch, where they would be safe, then she could tell them and they could decide what to do. But she had to get them to the ranch first.

"I want to go home, Brady. I want to get back to the children."

"Hank's taking you tomorrow."

"You come with us."

He shook his head. "We still have the cave-in—"

"No," she cut in sharply. "You come too."

He frowned, his gaze boring into hers. "What aren't you telling me, Molly?"

"Get me—all of us—to the ranch. Then I'll tell you everything."

He studied her for a moment more, then stood. "All right."

"And, Brady," she added before he walked away. "Bring all the men you can."

* * *

THE WEATHER HELD, AND THEY MADE IT TO THE pass without incident. Hank had sent ahead to have a ranch wagon with a canvas top and bench seats there to meet them, and once he'd transferred Molly from the borrowed buggy into the wagon, he climbed in after her. As the buggy headed back the way they'd come, Hank signaled the wagon driver to go on, and they continued the long ride down into the valley. Brady and the three riders who had gone with them to Redemption rode alongside on horseback.

She and Hank had hardly spoken since leaving Redemption. Molly was relieved. She wasn't yet ready to discuss what happened with the scarred man in the livery, and Hank didn't seem that anxious to open the subject of his harsh treatment of her two nights earlier. It was as if a silent truce had been called, allowing them both time to sort through what happened.

The wagon wasn't as well sprung as the buggy, and Molly had a time of it trying to keep her balance without being able to hold on. Hank, seeing her problem, moved across to her bench. Sitting with his shoulders against the side rails, he pulled her back against his chest and, mindful of her injured hands, anchored her with an arm across her waist. He wasn't as soft as the padded buggy seat, but he was a great deal warmer, and before too many miles she drifted to sleep.

It was late evening when they reached the ranch. Apparently the rider Hank had sent back for the wagon had told Jessica of Molly's "accident," but rather than flooding them with questions as might be expected, she took one look at Molly, standing exhausted and shivering in the entry, and rushed her straight up to a warm bath.

"Your poor hands," she said, helping Molly out of her clothes. "A fall, was it? Ice is so treacherous. I can't tell you how many times I've almost had my feet fly out from under me."

Molly let her run on, so weary she could hardly move, much less think up plausible excuses for her injuries. After helping her into the tub to soak, Jessica went back downstairs to tend to the men, promising to have a tray sent up later.

Molly had stepped out of the tub and was pulling on the robe Jessica had left for her when Hank came through the connecting door. She froze, fear flitting through her mind.

He saw it and frowned. "You needn't be afraid of me."

"I—I'm not." Which was almost true. "You startled me is all."

"Need help?" He gestured toward the robe she struggled to hold closed with her forearms. Before she could answer, he walked over, pulled the robe closed with a snap, then tied the sash in a double knot. He stepped back. "Hope that'll do. I'm not so good with bows."

Still rattled, she looked down at the huge knot, wondering how she would ever get it undone without the use of her thumbs. "Thank you."

"Jessica sent food." Turning away, he walked back through the dressing area and into her bedroom, speaking over his shoulder as he went. "I set the tray here by the fire. Come eat before it gets cold."

She tried, but with him sitting in the other chair watching, plus the awkwardness of holding the fork between her splinted hands, she was so clumsy she made a mess of it.

"You're worse than Ben," he muttered,

taking the fork from her hand. He speared a bite of carrot, and held it out. She took it, but before she could swallow it down, he had a forkful of green beans dangling in front of her face.

"Demoralizing, isn't it?" he said, shoving a slab of roast beef into her mouth. "Not being able to feed yourself . . . having to rely on another person for all your needs . . . feeling so helpless . . ."

"You're enjoying this, aren't you?" she mumbled through bulging cheeks.

"I am. If only Bunny were here. How'd you hurt your hands?"

She choked on a green bean. Then coughed to clear it. Then burst into tears.

The fork clattered to the tray. He jumped up and started pounding her back. "Jesus, are you all right?"

No, she wasn't all right. She'd had to amputate a child's leg then watch him die. She'd been treated like a whore by her husband. She'd been terrorized by a murderous deviant who had threatened everyone she cared about and left her so battered she couldn't even feed herself. Of course, she wasn't all right!

Dragging a sleeve over her eyes, she took a deep, hitching breath and tried to gather what shreds remained of her tattered dignity. "I'm fine."

"You don't look fine."

If her hands hadn't been bandaged, she might have struck him. "It's been a difficult few days." She sent him a pointed look. By his expression—or lack thereof—it missed its mark. "I think I'll retire now," she said wearily.

By his hesitation, she guessed he had questions to ask. But she was in no mood for an interrogation. "I'm very tired."

"There's still food left."

"I don't want it." *Just go. Please.*

"You're sure?"

"I'm sure."

He carried the tray to the hall table then came back. "Anything else?"

Dear God. Did she have to drive him out with a pitchfork? "My brush," she said in desperation. "It's on the bureau."

He brought it to her. But when she tried to take it from his hand, it slipped from her thumbless grip and clattered to the floor. She blinked at it in defeat, a new wave of tears stinging her eyes.

He picked it up and, before she could stop him, dragged the bristles through her hair, sending hairpins flying and pain burning across her scalp.

"Ouch!" she cried, raising an arm to ward him off.

He stepped back, the hairbrush gripped in his hand like a stick of firewood. "Sorry."

When he started forward again, she vigorously shook her head. "No. It's all right. Really. I think I'll leave it as is for tonight."

"If you're sure."

"I am."

He started toward the door, paused, then turned back. "Molly, you needn't be afraid of me," he said again. "I just want to help."

She gave a wan smile. "I know."

"You'll call if you need me?" He nodded toward the connecting door that led through the dressing room and water closet into his bedroom. "I'll leave my door open so I can hear you."

"Yes. Thank you." Oddly, even after his treatment of her the other night, it was a comfort knowing he would be nearby.

His gaze sharpened into that probing stare. "Maybe tomorrow, after you're rested, we can talk."

"Yes. Tomorrow." And she dreaded it.

After he finally exited the room, Molly sank onto the edge of the bed, exhausted, in pain, and wondering how she would ever get to sleep with a double knot the size of a billiard ball digging into her stomach and two-dozen hairpins poking into her head.

"I KNOW YOU'RE AWAKE, PAPA-HANK."

Hank flinched as a tiny finger that had been God-knows-where pried up his eyelid. "I can see you seeing me."

He turned his head away. "Don't poke my eye. Or my ear or nose or anything else," he quickly added, trying to cover all the pertinent areas. He really did have to get a lock on the door. And maybe a tin-can alarm system. Or a bucket of ice water over the door. That would send her running.

"Why don't you want us anymore?" Her voice sounded wet and wobbly.

Coming fully awake, Hank looked up at the face peering down at his. Tear tracks scored her cheeks, more tears were on the way, and her nose was running. Alarmed, he edged out of dripping range. "Who said I didn't want you anymore?"

"Charlie. He says you're nothing but a big fat liar and now we have to leave." Lifting a wad of blanket, she wiped her nose.

"Why?"

"'Cause Aunt Molly's hurt, and the monster will get us next."

"No, why am I a big fat liar? And don't wipe your nose—or anything else—on my blanket."

She sighed heavily. "'Cause you *lied*, Papa-Hank."

"About what?"

Splaying her tiny hands in the universal gesture of female impatience, she explained with careful enunciation as if he was the dumb one in the room, which he was pretty sure he wasn't, "Because Aunt Molly's hurt and you said you would keep us safe and now we aren't." She let her hands fall to the bed and glared at him. "But I'm not leaving until I get my kitty. You promised."

"No one's going anywhere, and you'll get your kitty. Where's Molly?"

"Getting dressed."

"By herself?" Thinking he might help with that, he sat up, the blanket clutched at his waist. It felt damp and sticky. He shifted his grip.

"She said Maria Garcia would help her."

"Oh. Well, run along so I can dress."

"I wanna stay."

"Go."

"But—"

"Now."

After he dressed, he went to Charlie's room first. He found the boy sitting on the foot of his bed with a battered wooden box open on his knees. When he saw Hank in the doorway, he slammed the lid shut and thrust the box behind him. Something that looked a lot like a dog scurried under the bed. "What do you want?" Charlie asked in a surly tone.

Hank looked at him and kept looking at him until the boy's ears turned red and his gaze slid away. It was an effort to keep from shaking the sass out of the kid. And even more of an effort to keep his voice from betraying how badly he wanted to do it.

"You're safe," he said in clipped tones. "As long as you're under this roof and under my protection, you're safe."

"But Aunt Molly—"

"Aunt Molly's *accident* has nothing to do with you, and I don't want you worrying her about it. She's safe. You're safe. Penny's safe. And no one is going anywhere. You understand?"

Some of the color left Charlie's face. His lips trembled.

Hardening himself to sympathy, Hank went on. "And if you ever speak to me or your Aunt Molly in that tone again, you and I are going to the woodshed. I won't tolerate disrespect. Do you understand *that*?"

Blinking hard, Charlie stared down at his hands as if they were something new and interesting. "Yes, sir."

"Now get that dog out of here before your Aunt Jessica finds him and bathes him again." Without waiting for a response, Hank left the room and crossed the hall.

Molly was standing fully dressed by the bureau when he swung open the door. Startled, she whirled, her hairbrush slipping from her bandaged hands to clatter on the wood floor. "Drat," she muttered.

The anger went out of him. "Need help?" he asked, walking toward her.

"Like you helped last night? My scalp still hurts." He thought she might have smiled at him, but the swelling on her face made it look more like a grimace.

He picked up the brush. “You should have told me about the hairpins.”

“You thought my hair just curled up on top of my head all by itself?”

“Don’t be pert. Turn around.”

After first checking for stray hairpins, he pulled the brush through her long, glossy hair as gently as he could. It felt smooth and warm and smelled like lemons, and made him want to wrap it around his hands so he could bind her to him forever.

Seeing her hurt had shaken him like nothing ever had. The instant he saw her injured hands, all his closely held anger had shattered at his feet, and he realized he no longer cared how the marriage had come about, or that she’d withheld the truth of it from him. He just wanted to keep her safe. That was all that mattered. And she did save his life, after all. He owed her for that.

Hearing a soft sigh, he looked past her head to her reflection in the mirror. Her eyes were closed, and she wore a faint smile, and even with the bruises, she was the most beautiful thing he’d ever seen. How could he have ever treated her so badly? Fearing he might do something to weaken this brittle trust growing between them, he set the brush on the bureau and stepped back. "There. All done."

She opened her eyes and smiled at him in the mirror, then winced at the pull of muscles across her bruised cheek. Studying her reflection, she shook her head. "I look a sight." She turned to face him, that imp in her eyes coming awake with a twinkle. "But not as bad as Brady. Should I feel bad about that?"

"He deserved it."

"No doubt. But I wouldn't want to be the cause of friction between you."

"There's always friction. We're brothers." He motioned toward her shirtfront. "You missed some buttons."

She looked down and sighed. "Penny."

"That explains the smudges. Want me to fix it?"

Her gaze flew up to his, then away again. That telltale flush inched across her cheeks. Still afraid, he guessed. Nonetheless, she nodded, which surprised him.

While she stared stoically at his chest, he undid and redid the mismatched buttons and buttonholes. He took his time, and only allowed his knuckles to brush across those soft, bouncy bosoms a couple of times. Maybe three. “I thought one of the Garcias was helping you,” he said to distract her from wondering why he was taking so long.

“She had to leave. Ben got into some mischief with the Christmas tree.”

“Climbed it. Brady was supposed to rope it to the wall so it won’t tip over on him like it did last year.”

“That’ll go nicely with Jessica’s imported tinsel.”

“Sometimes Jessica outfancies herself. Christmas is for kids. There.” Regretfully he let his hands drop to his sides. It was nice being able to talk to her again, to put the anger aside and forget for a few minutes there was unfinished business between them. He wished they could skip all the “I’m sorries” and just start over again. But there was too much still left unsaid, and too many questions waiting for answers. If they were ever to wash the slate clean, they’d have to deal with that.

“Molly, we need to talk.”

“Yes. I suppose we do.” Molly wondered if this was to be the beginning of the end. If he would send her away, or tell her he was dissolving the marriage. She wondered how she could convince him they each deserved a second chance.

"Brady told me you saved my life. Twice. I owe you for that. And I understand why you did what you did. I don't like it, but I understand. So I'm willing to let bygones be bygones and start over."

"Are you?"

He nodded. "I think we can get past this. But you'll have to promise you won't lie to me or keep secrets from me. I have a low tolerance for that."

"I see." Molly crossed her arms over her chest, lest she reinjure her hands by striking him. *The nitwit.* Did he think to dump it all on her? What about what *he* had done? But in the interest of peace, she decided to meet him halfway. "And what will you promise me?"

"Me? Well . . . I'll keep you safe."

She smiled sweetly. "From yourself too?"

She watched confusion then understanding flit across his face. At least he had the grace to blush.

"That . . ." Hank suddenly felt like a wad of cotton had gotten lodged in his throat. He coughed to clear it and started again.

"What I mean is . . . what happened the other night . . . that's not who I am."

She tilted her head to study him. "And who are you?"

"For one thing, I'm not a man who hurts women. Especially women I care about." *Jesus, that didn't come out right.* "I mean, a *woman* I care about. *You*, that is."

"So why did you?"

Damn her for wanting her pound of flesh. Hank sighed and studied his boots. He wasn't used to being in the wrong and having to explain himself. He didn't like it. He liked even less talking about personal things. But he owed her, so he would.

"All my life I've felt like the odd man out, but with you . . ." He shrugged. "It was different. Then I found out it wasn't real. And I thought you'd just been using me, playing me for a fool, like I was the butt of a joke everybody was in on but me. It made me feel stupid." He forced a laugh. "Hell, I feel even stupider admitting it out loud. But I just . . . just . . ."

"I forgive you."

He lifted his head.

She was smiling up at him—well, as

best she could with the swelling—and her beautiful eyes were shiny with tears. Relief clogged his throat. He breathed deep to clear it, then nodded several times, wondering what to say. "Well. All right then."

"Do you forgive me?" she asked, still watching him. "Do you think you'll be able to trust me again?"

He didn't want to lie to her. "In time." When he saw the light in her eyes fade, he quickly added, "I'm trying, Molly. Can't we just leave it at that for now?"

She studied him for so long his nerves started to fray. Finally she nodded.

"No more secrets?" he pressed.

"No more secrets."

"Good. Then start by telling me how you hurt your hands."

"ACTUALLY, I DIDN'T HURT THEM," MOLLY TOLD him once she'd settled in the chair across from his by the hearth in the bedroom. "Fletcher's man did. After he killed Ezra Cooper."

As dispassionately as she could, she related everything, from Papa's death, which she now knew for certain wasn't a suicide but murder, to her suspicions that Fletcher had sent trackers after them, to the horrible things the scarred man had done and said to her in the livery.

Through it all, Hank had remained motionless and silent, his gaze never leaving her face, his hands gripping the armrests so tightly she could see the indent of his fingers in the woven upholstery. The only other reaction he gave was a grim tightening of his jaw and the return of that hard, implacable look in his eyes.

When she had finished, he didn't speak. The silence grew, broken only by the snapping of the fire and the raucous call of a raven hopping along the balcony railing. Uneasy under Hank's probing gaze, but unwilling to speak first, Molly looked out the French door. Everything looked so clean and pure—the white-shrouded valley giving way to timbered canyons that stretched up to rocky peaks now softened by a new topping of snow. The sky was such a bright intense blue it almost hurt her eyes.

Somewhere out there a madman waited. And she had shown him the way.

"You have no idea what this book is that Fletcher wants?"

She turned back. “No. But it must be important if he’s willing to kill several times over to get it.”

“Who has he killed besides Ezra?”

She looked down at her bandaged hands, wishing she could clench them to relieve the tension. “He caused the cave-in. And there could be more incidents at the mines. He’s capable of anything.” She looked up, feeling again that stab of regret that she had brought such trouble to this family she had grown to love.

Love. How odd that now, after all these years, she would find it in such an improbable way. “He says he’ll kill you too. Then your brother, the children—” Her throat constricted and her voice rose in that high, trembly way it did when she was about to cry. She waited a moment then tried again. “He’s coming back in a month. If I don’t have the book Fletcher wants, he’ll . . . he’ll . . .” This time she couldn’t hold back the tears. “I’m so sorry, Hank. I never wanted to bring this trouble on you and your family.”

“Molly.”

“I’ll go. Try to lead him away. The children can stay here where they’ll be safe. It’s not them he wants—”

"Shut up."

She realized he had moved and was now hunkered beside her chair. He looked calm and unperturbed except for the muscle dancing in his cheek and the feral gleam in his eyes. "I'll take care of it."

"How? What are you going to do?"

He gave her a smile that would strike fear into Satan himself. "I'll think of something." Then before she could question him further, he rose and left the room.

"WHAT WAS THAT?" JESSICA ASKED, GLANCING up from the tiny night sack she was sewing. "Was that the front door?"

Brady set aside the veterinary pamphlet he'd been reading and rose from his chair in their bedroom. Crossing to the window overlooking the front of the house, he wiped frost off the glass and peered out to see his brother headed toward the barn.

"Hank. He's upset."

"How can you tell?"

"He's stomping." Brady could guess why. Molly had him running in circles.

Jessica made a derisive sound. "I'd think he'd be feeling better after taking out his anger on your poor face."

"He had reason."

"Nevertheless, brothers shouldn't fight."

"I'll tell him that the next time he comes at me."

As Brady suspected, Hank continued past the corrals and into the woodshed. A moment later he came out with an ax and stomped to the snow-covered mound of log rounds piled beside the shed. After kicking snow off the splitting block, he set a round on top, stepped back, and swung. The log exploded into kindling. He picked up another, set it on the block, and swung again. "I guess Molly told him how she hurt her hands," Brady said. "And he didn't like hearing it."

Jessica moved up beside him. He lifted an arm to fit her against his side and pulled her close, enjoying the soft warmth of her body against his, and the gentle stroke of her hand on his back.

She studied the figure toiling in the snow. "I thought it was an accident."

"Maybe." Brady didn't mention Ezra Cooper or Molly's odd behavior.

"Could he still be that upset about the marriage? Surely he understands why Molly felt compelled to do what she did."

Brady glanced down at her. "You knew, didn't you? From the beginning."

"Of course I did. She had children to protect. She needed money and she did what she had to do to get it. It's what any mother would do." A frown brought her copper brows together. "What I don't know is if your brother is too hardheaded to accept that and forgive her for it."

Hearing the note of worry in his wife's voice, Brady turned her away from the window and pulled her close against his body. Or as close as he could with that ever-growing belly between them. "You slept better last night, didn't you?"

She tipped her head back to give him a teasing look. "How do you know? Do you lie awake watching me?"

Brady didn't want to admit that he did. Or that he hardly slept a night through anymore, fretting the hours away worrying about her, and his brother, and the mines . . . and her. "Just trying to keep the spiders off."

He felt her body tense. "Spiders?" Eyes wide, she glanced at the ceiling then around the room. "You saw spiders?"

He put his lips against her ear. “Shh. You’ll upset little Thomas Jefferson.”

“Nigel, you big dolt. And stop teasing me.” Shoving away from him, she went back to the chaise and folded the night sack into her sewing basket. “Have you finished attaching the tree to the wall?”

“I have. Two stout ropes high enough that he can’t reach them.”

“That’ll go lovely with my imported tinsel.” She crossed to the door, waggling fingers in farewell. “I’m off to make gingerbread houses. Wish me luck.”

“You’ll need it. Don’t overdo.” As she disappeared into the hall, Brady turned back to the window.

Hank had taken off his jacket but showed no sign of tiring. His brother did some of his best thinking at the blister end of an ax, and Brady knew he’d keep at it until he’d worked through whatever was troubling him, no matter how long that took. He was sorry Hank was upset, but he surely didn’t mind having the extra firewood.

HANK SPLIT WOOD FOR MOST OF THE AFTERnoon, stopping only when his weak arm started cramping so bad he could no longer hold on to the ax handle, and his ribs were burning like a sonofabitch. After returning the ax to the shed, he picked up his jacket and headed to the house.

Brady met him as he came through the front door. "Should I send the boys to cut more trees?" he asked with that smirky grin.

"I need to talk to you," Hank said as he hung up his jacket and hat.

Brady's grin faded. "My office or yours?"

"Yours. You've got the whiskey. Ten minutes. Bring food." He started up the staircase, stopped, and turned back. "Don't bring Jessica."

Hank found Molly sitting in her chair by the fire, an unopened book in her lap. He stopped before her, feet braced, hands planted on his hips. "You're not leaving. The marriage stands. We'll work this out. No more discussion."

She blinked up at him. "Did we discuss? I thought normally in discussions, both sides get to participate."

"Say your words then. But don't think to argue with me about this, Molly."

"Yes, but—"

"And don't worry about Fletcher or his henchman. He's one man against two dozen, and we have the advantage of knowing when he's coming."

"I never—"

"We'll take care of him, don't worry about that. Meanwhile, keep looking for the book Fletcher wants. Can you do that?"

"I'll try, but—"

"Good." He put on a smile. "Anything else?"

"Else?"

Was that sarcasm? Hank studied her, wondering if pain was making her snappish. "You look tired."

"I am. Probably all this discussing."

Definitely sarcasm. Which baffled him. What had he done now? "Did you eat? If not, I could get you something." He always got cranky if he didn't eat.

She sighed. "I'm fine. But I think I'll turn in early."

"Good idea. Stand up and I'll unbutton you."

She looked down at the buttons on her shirt, then at her bandaged hands, then sighed again. "This is getting tiresome," she muttered as she rose.

"Not for me." He undid the skirt first, let it slide over her hips, then held her arm while she stepped out of it. He removed the blouse next, then two petticoats with little lacy bows, than a short vest-corset thing with lacing up the front. Finally she was down to a knee-length underdress that was so sheer he was amazed it stayed together. And more than a little disappointed that it did. Especially when she wouldn't let him take that off as well.

Surprised to find that his palms were sweating, he wiped them on his shirt and stood back to admire the wonders he had uncovered, enthralled all over again at how beautiful she was and how perfectly formed and how her skin glowed in the firelight.

"You're doing it again." She turned, giving him an inspiring view of her butt, which shimmied like two armadillos doing a slow dance under a silk scarf as she walked toward the bed. The woman did know how to move.

"Doing what?"

"Staring."

He laughed. "Jesus, how could I not? You prancing around half-dressed—"

She looked back with a laugh that set off a chain of motion beneath that flimsy underthing that made his tongue curl. “Good night, Hank.”

“No hugs?”

She slipped under the covers, but not before he saw her smile. “Good night, Hank.”

Eighteen

THAT NIGHT THE DEAD CALLED TO HER, REACHING up from their blood-soaked beds, their skeletal fingers grabbing at her skirts as she rushed by. She tried to avoid them, walking faster and faster until she was running. But still they cried out, calling her name, begging . . . begging . . .

MOLLY AWOKE TREMBLING AND NAUSEATED, HER throat aching with unshed tears. Rolling onto her back, she stared blindly up at the ceiling, where firelight shadows danced over the rafters like demon figures cavorting in the flames of hell. "Leave me in peace," she whispered.

Irritated at her own imaginings, she sat up. The room was cold, making the ache in her hands even more pronounced. Her stomach felt sour and empty. Knowing she wouldn't be able to go back to sleep and feeling suffocated by the very emptiness of the room, she pushed back the quilts and rose. After donning her borrowed robe and using her teeth and fingertips to tie the sash, she stepped into her slippers and left the room, not sure where she was going but needing to move.

As she descended the staircase into the entry, she saw lamplight shining beneath the kitchen door and another light coming from Brady's office. She turned toward the kitchen. Pushing open the door with her elbow, she looked inside.

Dougal sat at the long kitchen table, a bottle of whiskey in one hand, a half-filled glass in the other. When he saw her in the doorway, he gave a jerk then let out a huff of air when he recognized her. "Ye shouldna go sneaking up on an auld man that way, lass. My heart near stopped."

She sent him a smile as she crossed to the cupboard. "I'm sorry I startled you."

Using her splinted hands like tongs, she lifted a cup from the cupboard and carried it to the table, then went back for the tea caddy. Luckily there was a spoon already in it. Wrapping a cloth around her hand to protect it from the hot metal, she hooked the unbandaged tips of her fingers under the handle of the kettle and carried it to the table.

When she started to pour, Dougal, who had watched her efforts with blurry-eyed interest, finally felt moved to help. "I'll do that, lass, e'er ye scald us both."

At her direction, he also added a spoonful of tea leaves and stirred in the requested amount of sugar. Standing by the table, she lifted the cup in both hands and took a sip. Perfect.

"Can't sleep, lass?"

"No. You?"

"Nae." A deep sigh. "Consuelo's off tae her sister." He held up the bottle, showing a drawing of a woman on the label. "Just me and Hannah Goodman."

"May I join the two of you?"

He squinted at the face on the bottle and burped. “She says aye.”

Molly settled onto the bench across from him. Sipping her tea, she looked around. Even though she wasn’t much of a cook, she loved a well-appointed kitchen, and this was certainly that. A huge combination cookstove, cabinets and cupboards galore, running water in sinks at either end of the long room, window vents high on the outside walls to draw out the hot air in summer, and a waste chute that emptied directly into a covered barrel outside. With the vent windows closed for winter, the kitchen was comfortably warm and filled with the lingering scents of cooking. It was a space full of life and energy, and the perfect refuge against the lonely chill of her empty room. Sighing contentedly, she looked over to find the old man studying her from beneath his bushy brows, no doubt wondering what she was doing afoot in the middle of the night. She saved him the bother of asking.

“Bad dreams,” she said with a wry smile.

Dougal nodded sagely. “Aye. I ken it.”

“You too?”

"A soldier's curse," he said, rolling his R's even more than usual.

"You were a soldier?"

"For more years than I care tae remember, lass."

She hadn't known that about Dougal. In fact, she knew little about him other than he had been part of Jessica's family in England and had followed her to America when she married Brady. But now that she thought about it, she recognized signs of his military days in the way he walked, in his stiff posture when he dressed down Brady or tried to bring the children in line. And there was also the puckered scar from a bullet wound that she'd glimpsed above his knee before he started wearing a union suit beneath his kilt. "What drew you to the soldier's life?"

He shrugged. "I wanted tae see the world. And the only way tae dew that was indenturing meself or soldiering. Being as I'll no' slave for any man, I chose tae follow the pipes." He took a long swallow and coughed.

She waited for him to catch his breath then asked, "And did you see it?"

"Aye. At its worst."

"So why did you continue?"

He smiled at her in a gentle way, giving her a glimpse of the man who had caught Consuelo's eye. "The same reasons ye stay wie the doctoring, I'm guessing." He took another long swallow, coughed, then wiped a sleeve over his watery eyes. "Bad as it is, ye get comfortable wie it," he said once he had found his voice again. "O'er time, even proficient at it. And somewhere 'neath all the ugliness and destruction, ye think maybe ye're doin' some guid."

She stared into her cup. "Yet we still have nightmares."

"Och, lass. The nightmares just give voice tae the pain, e'er wise we'd choke on it and die." He reached out a gnarly hand and patted her arm. "I ken it's hard, lass. But ye're a healer. 'Tis yer gift. And using it is the task ye've been given."

"It feels more like a burden sometimes," she admitted.

"Aye." He sat back. "But ye'll do it anyway, because that's just how it is."

Suddenly the door opened with a bang that made Molly and Dougal jump. "Jesus Christ, woman!" Hank boomed. "You scared the hell out of me."

"Scared yew!" Dougal blubbered, clutching at his kilt. "I near wet meself!"

"What's wrong?" Molly asked, her heart still hammering from fright.

"Wrong?" Hank waved a hand like he was flagging down a carriage. "You tell me a madman's lurking around, then you disappear from your room—what the hell were you thinking?"

Molly blinked in surprise. "I couldn't sleep. I thought a cup of tea might help."

Muttering under his breath, he called back down the hall, "She's in the kitchen talking to Dougal."

"Better her than me," Brady called back. "I'm going to bed."

Holding open the door, Hank motioned impatiently to Molly. "You're going to bed too."

"I am?"

"You are. It's late and I'm tired and I don't want to have to worry about you wandering around the house in the dark."

Still bemused by Hank's odd behavior, Molly rose. "Good night, Dougal. I enjoyed our chat."

Dougal belched, then coughed.

"You be careful with that stuff," Hank

warned the old Scotsman as he followed Molly through the door. “It’ll make you impotent.”

“Egad.”

“Will it really?” Molly asked, intrigued.

“If it doesn’t, it should.”

As soon as they entered Molly’s room, Hank crossed to the hearth and knelt to relight the fire. Taking advantage of his distraction, Molly quickly slipped out of the robe and under the covers. Stretched on her side, one hand tucked beneath her pillow, she watched him, admiring the way the firelight played over his strong features. Her wariness of him had faded over the last days. Now what she remembered most was the way his hands had felt on her body. She wondered if she would ever feel them again. “I’m sorry I worried you,” she said after a moment. “I had a dream and couldn’t go back to sleep.”

He turned his head and looked at her. “You have bad dreams?”

“Sometimes.”

“About Fletcher?”

“Mostly about patients. The ones I lost.”

He turned back to the fire. “You fret too much, Molly.”

"This from a man who almost caused a riot over an empty room."

He was silent a long time before he spoke. "I didn't know where you were."

An unseen hand seemed to grip her heart. How long since anyone had worried over her, or even knew her well enough to care where she was or what she did? She smiled into the dark. It was nice.

Once the fire was going strong, Hank rose. "New rules," he said as he began unbuttoning his shirt. "No one leaves the house, day or night, without telling me or Brady first." Shrugging out of the shirt, he tossed it onto the chair, then sat on top of it and began tugging off his boots.

"What are you doing?" Molly asked, caught somewhere between fascination and astonishment.

He tossed the boots into a corner, rose, undid his belt, then started on his trousers. "There'll be no trips to Val Rosa or Redemption or anywhere else until Fletcher and Scarface are caught." He stepped out of his trousers and was starting to loosen the closure on the front of his half-unions when Molly finally came to her senses.

"Stop!"

He stopped, hands still gripping the tabs. “What?”

In the flickering light he was all shadow and rounded muscle and gold-tipped hair—strength and power and masculine grace come to life—and he was so beautiful, just looking at him stole her breath away.

“Molly, what’s wrong?”

“W-What are you doing?” she finally managed.

His hands fell back to his sides. “You don’t want me to stay?”

“Well . . . I . . . ah . . .” She wasn’t sure what she wanted. But what she *didn’t* want was a repeat of the other night.

He walked toward her. “I’m not going to jump on you if that’s what you’re worried about.” He sounded amused. Not threatening at all. “I’m too tired. But if that’s what you want, maybe after I rest some, we—”

“No! No. I’m tired too.”

Moving to the other side of the bed, he threw back the covers and plopped down, making the mattress sag with his weight. “What a day,” he said with a deep yawn. “At least we won’t be running out of firewood for a while.”

Molly stared blindly into the fire, every

sense focused on the movements on the other side of the bed. "Did you talk to Brady?" she asked, needing to fill the silence.

"I did."

"Did you tell him about Fletcher?"

"I did."

"Was he upset?"

"He was." Another yawn.

"Did you tell him how sorry I am to bring this trouble—"

"He knows, Molly. He's not upset with you. Go to sleep."

"Is he going to tell Jessica? He shouldn't tell Jessica. She'll just worry."

"He won't. Stop fretting. It'll all work out."

How could she not fret? Everyone in this house was in danger because of her.

The fire popped. Somewhere on the snowy flats, coyotes howled and barked. Molly tried to keep her breathing even while he rolled over, then back, then stretched and yawned. She was thankful this wasn't one of those newfangled mattresses with the steel coils, else she'd be bouncing up to the rafters with all his tossing and turning.

Finally he grew still. Silence. Was he asleep?

She wanted to roll over and see. She wanted to move her foot and maybe accidentally brush a toe against him so she would know where he was. She wanted—

"You cold?" he asked, his sleepy rumble startling her.

"A little." And before she realized what he was doing, he draped his thick arm across her waist and pulled her back against his chest. Molly went utterly still. Unsure what to do with the hand not tucked beneath her pillow, she tentatively let it rest against his arm.

He sighed, his breath tickling her scalp at the crown of her head. His male scent wafted around her and beneath her palm, his arm felt solid and warm and slick with fine, silky hair. Staring at the dying fire, she waited . . . expecting . . .

Then he began to snore.

HANK AWOKE TO A GENTLE SNUFFLING SOUND and a warm body pressed against his shoulder. *Sweet Molly*, he thought sleepily. He lifted his arm to pull her closer, and instead, encountered something damp and sticky.

Jerking his hand back, he raised his

head to see Penny crowded between him and Molly, sucking her thumb and blinking at him through teary eyes. With a groan, he slumped back to the pillow. "What are you doing in here, Penny?"

"Where were you, Papa-Hank?" she accused in a wobbly voice. "I looked in your room, but you weren't there and I couldn't find you and it scared me."

Touched by her distress, he reached out and patted her arm. "I'm right here, Penny." As aggravating as she could be sometimes, the kid did have a way of reaching right inside him and wrapping her sticky little hands around his heart.

"Why?" she asked.

"Why what?"

Rolling onto her side, she burrowed into him, one tiny hand resting on his neck. "Why are you here in Aunt Molly's room?"

"It's not really her room. It's mine."

"Then what's Aunt Molly doing in here?"

"She's been borrowing it."

"Are you taking it back?"

"No."

"Then why aren't you in your other room?"

Looking past Penny's blond curls, Hank

saw Molly watching them, her eyes full of laughter, her cheeks tinted the rosy blush of sleep. Unable to help himself, he leaned over Penny and kissed his wife. "Morning," he said.

"Morning," she answered, smiling in a way that—

"You're squishing me!" Penny yelled, thrashing between them. But when he started to straighten, she kicked her heels harder. "Me too! Kiss me too!"

After a quick scan for a clean spot, Hank kissed her forehead, then quickly drew back when he tasted something sweet and minty. "Don't you ever bathe her?" he asked, wiping his mouth on his arm.

"Every night."

"Then why is she so sticky every morning?"

"She wanders."

Molly leaned over and sniffed her niece, making the little girl giggle and kick in glee. "Today, it's peppermint."

"Where did she get peppermint?"

"Uncle Brady gave it to me!" Penny shouted, unable to stay silent for long. "He has lots. He hides it in a special drawer in his bedroom so Ben can't find it. But you can't tell. He said I could have it because guess what? It's Christmas Eve!"

"When were you in Uncle Brady's bedroom?" Hank asked her.

"I couldn't find you. And guess what else?" Putting her sticky mouth next to his ear, she whispered loudly, "He sleeps naked too."

"Oh, Lord," Molly muttered.

Hank grinned, picturing the scene. "You peeked?"

"Uncle Brady didn't like me to."

"And what was Aunt Jessica doing all this time?" he asked.

"Don't encourage her, Hank."

"I'm just asking."

"She was laughing," Penny said. "And guess what? She was naked too!"

"Penny!" Molly sputtered.

"And her bosoms are even bigger than Aunt Molly's."

Hank grinned. "Are they?"

Molly sat up. "That's enough. Both of you." She sent Hank a scolding look. "See what happens when you interrogate a child?"

Ignoring her aunt, Penny snuggled closer to Hank. "She must have been growing them for a real long time," she whispered. "They're great big—"

"Penny! Enough."

"But not nearly as bouncy as Aunt Molly's."

Rolling onto his back, Hank laughed out loud. Waking up to these two was the third best way to greet the day.

CHRISTMAS DAY BEGAN WITH A BANG. FOLlowed by a rattle and a thud. Then silence.

Hank turned his head on the pillow and grinned at Molly. "So far, so good."

"You're mean."

"Shh. Listen."

A few seconds later, another rattle and more thuds, this time coming from the connecting door into the dressing area. Then silence again.

Hank laughed and raised a fist in triumph. "And the foe is vanquished."

"Foe?" Molly smirked at him. "A six-year-old. How brave you are."

Rolling over, he grabbed his wife, pulled her over on top of him, and began nuzzling her neck. "Brave *and* smart," he said between nuzzles. "Wiley. Clever. Too clever for a—" The French door crashed open.

Hank jumped, his head colliding with Molly's. "Holy—"

"Papa-Hank Papa-Hank!"

Something cold and wiggly bounded onto the bed, shouting at the top of her lungs. "SaintNicholascameandthere'spres entsevery where!"

Molly rolled out of his arms. "Vanquished, is she?"

"And look what I brought you, Papa-Hank! I made it all by myself!"

With a yowl, Hank lurched upright, slinging snowball remnants off his chest.

"Oh no, you broke it."

"Penny, I swear to God—"

"Sweetie," Molly cut in, pulling Penny out of Hank's reach. "Why don't you put on your robe and slippers so we can go downstairs to see what Saint Nick brought?"

"I can't. The door's stuck."

While Molly rose to unlock the useless lock Hank had spent an hour yesterday bolting to the door, he stared up at the ceiling, his heart still hammering from the shock of having a ball of ice plunked onto his bare chest.

"I'm going to chain her to her bed," he muttered after the door closed on tiny footfalls pounding down the hall. "Build a cage. Or maybe a room in the barn. No, a separate house. With bars on the windows and—"

"Good morning, Hank," Molly murmured, bending down to give him a kiss.

Instantly anger dissolved in a wash of desire. Wrapping his arms around her before she could get away, he pulled her down for a proper kiss, then another and another. By the time they came up for air, he was ready to discard his plan to wait until Molly was wearing the wedding ring before he took her to bed again. It was a stupid plan. There was no reason to wait when—

"Are you playing horsey?" Penny asked inches from his face.

God give me strength. With a groan, Hank let his arms fall back to the bed.

MOLLY DIDN'T WANT TO ADMIT IT OUT LOUD, BUT she was as excited about Christmas morning as the children were.

Christmas with Papa had always been a sedate affair. He presented his gift to her; she gave hers to him. They opened them one at a time, traded thank-yous, then sat down to their normal Sunday breakfast of one egg, grits, and a thin slice of ham, but with the festive addition of apple fritters to mark the occasion. Then a visit to church and an afternoon at the hospital.

Christmas with the Wilkins family was a chaotic explosion of candy and toys and everyone speaking at once. Or in Penny's case, shouting. Molly loved it.

It began with the opening of presents in the great room, and Molly took as much delight in watching everyone else open their gifts as she did in opening her own. And what gifts she got!

From Penny, a colorful watercolor painting of herself and her brother, Charlie's dog, Buddy, and the cat she was going to name Tiger whenever Papa-Hank finally gave it to her. From Charlie, a braided horsehair wristlet Uncle Brady had shown him how to make.

From Dougal, a brooch he'd picked up during his soldiering days in India that was reputed to ward off bad dreams. And if that didn't work, Consuelo contributed a special sleeping tonic that she guaranteed would make Molly sleep like the dead—and when Molly learned the ingredients, she wasn't surprised—valerian, hops, and Jamaica dogwood. A potent combination.

From Iantha, a lovely bar of gardenia-scented soap to remind her of the home she had left behind. And from Brady and Jessica, a beautiful leather satchel like those that real doctors used, complete with a set of medical implements, including scalpels, tweezers, scissors, clamps, suturing needles, wire and horsehair ligatures, and jars, vials, and syringes of medicinal compounds, ointments, and restoratives.

She was so moved she almost burst into tears.

Then Hank gave her his gifts. The first were three notes written in bold script. One stated a set of medical books would arrive sometime in the next two months. The next said a saddle had been ordered, but she would have to go in for final measurements before it could be completed. In the third, he wrote that the horse the saddle was to go on should complete his training by spring. Once she'd exclaimed over his generosity, he presented her with a huge bundle wrapped in burlap and tied with double-knotted twine. Inside was a long shearling coat with a hood and a split closure up the back so she could wear it while riding, along with matching shearling boots with hard leather soles that were studded with nail heads for traction on icy surfaces. Apparently she would be spending a lot of time on horseback.

Delighted, Molly jumped up and tried on her wooly ensemble. "How do I look?" she asked, spreading her arms wide and turning in a circle.

"Like an inside-out sheep," Brady said. "Minus the guts, of course."

"Brady," Jessica chided. "Don't be vulgar."

"Vulgar?" He shot Dougal a smirk. "Hear that, codger? She's calling your favorite dish vulgar."

"Haggis is no' sheep guts. No' entirely. There's sommat else in there, though I'm no' sure what."

"I think she looks like a bear," Penny shouted. "Growl, Aunt Molly."

Molly growled. Ben hooted. Abigail ducked her head in her mother's lap.

Turning, Molly found Hank watching her with an odd expression. Raising her bandaged hands like claws, she snarled ferociously at him, but he just sat there watching with a bemused look. “Doesn’t my growl scare you?” she teased, trying to force out that lovely smile.

“Not at all. In fact, I’m hoping to hear it again before the day is over. Several times.” He grinned, and added for her ears only, “But without the coat.”

Did he mean what she thought he meant? Heat rushed into her face. Probably because of the coat. It was really quite warm. “Let me hang this in the entry,” she said, hoping he didn’t see her blush, knowing it would only encourage additional rascally remarks.

“Hurry back,” Hank called after her. “I still have one more thing to give you. For now anyway.”

Rascal, indeed.

After hanging up the coat and setting her new boots on a shelf, she returned to her place on the couch. The teasing look was gone from Hank’s eyes, and he looked quite serious. Perhaps even a bit nervous.

“Here.” He held out a small box.

As she took it, she noticed there was no wrapping other than a loop of red yarn tied in a double knot rather than a bow. “Do this yourself?” she teased, trying to work the knots free with her bandaged fingers. Pulling a folding knife from his pocket, he sliced through the yarn then put the knife away.

She lifted the lid. Inside was a simple gold band engraved with the letters "PHW to MMW." Molly stared at it in astonishment.

"Will you wear it?" he asked, his neck turning red.

And that was when she burst into tears.

It fit perfectly . . . once Hank adjusted the cast so she could fit the ring on her finger. She couldn't stop staring at it. Or crying. Which she realized made both brothers extremely uncomfortable.

"Women," Brady muttered.

"I know," Hank agreed.

"Hush, both of you," Jessica admonished, dabbing at her eyes.

But all three were smiling like cats in cream.

Her gifts seemed paltry in comparison, until she saw Hank's face when he tore open the wrapping paper on the keg of parts. His grin of delight brought fresh tears to her eyes, and when Brady asked him what it was and Hank laughed and said,

"The mother lode," Molly knew she had chosen well.

The only rough patch in that glorious morning came when Hank presented his gifts to the children. To Charlie, he gave a penknife and a block of soft wood for carving—which was an instant success with the eight-year-old but gave Molly serious reservations. To Penny, he gave a striped yellow kitty, which brought squeals of delight, then a violent fit of sneezes. Remembering that Nellie suffered a similar reaction to cats, Molly knew the only remedy was removal of the animal.

Penny wouldn't hear of it, shrieking and sneezing and coughing at the mere suggestion. Hank was nearly as distressed as the child and offered to get her a horse instead, or a dog, a bird, a bunny. But nothing would do for Penny but Tiger.

Jessica saved the day. Just after Abigail had been born, she had ordered a doll from a London doll maker. But since Abigail was so young and would have no interest in it for several more years, Jessica graciously offered it to Penny.

It was a treasure no little girl could resist. A beautiful doll with a hand-painted china face, real hair to comb, and a stuffed body with movable arms and legs onto which were sewn tiny china hands and feet. In addition, she came with her very own chair and several changes of clothing, including shoes, stockings, hats, and gloves, as well as a lacy parasol and a beaded purse.

Molly figured it would probably last a week in Penny's sticky hands.

"She'll take better care of it than you think," Jessica assured her. "There is something about a special doll that brings out the best in a girl. And I daresay a doll will inflict fewer scratches than a half-wild kitten."

After two hours of sneezing and watering eyes, Penny reluctantly traded in Tiger for the doll. Thereafter, the festivities proceeded without incident, through an elaborate feast, an afternoon of sledding, followed by hot chocolate and Christmas treats, then a light supper and finally utter exhaustion.

It was such a magical day that Molly was able to put from her mind the ticking clock and the scarred man and the threat he posed to these lovely people. For the first time in years, she felt a part of something most people took for granted. A family.

"So you like it?" Hank asked later that evening when he plopped down beside her on the couch. The children had staggered off to bed an hour earlier. Dougal and Consuelo had disappeared who-knew-where, and Brady had taken Jessica up for the night. It was just the two of them in the quiet, and it was lovely.

"I was hoping for a trick pony, but I guess this will do." Laughing at his expression, she leaned over and kissed his cheek. "Of course I love it. How could I not? And how about your parts?"

He blinked at her.

"I hope you'll be able to use them."

Confusion gave way to laughter. "Oh, you mean the parts in the *keg.*"

She loved to hear him laugh. She had a feeling he didn't do it often, and she took it as a sign that they were moving past the awkwardness that had lingered between them since the night of the cave-in. "What's the P for?" She twirled the ring on her finger. "I know the H is for Henry. What's the P stand for?"

"Patrick."

She looked up. "As in Patrick Henry Wilkins?"

He nodded.

It was difficult to keep her face straight. "You're named for the revolutionary orator? A man known throughout our history as an eloquent speaker? You?"

That wry smile.

"Are all of you named for American statesmen?"

All but Brady. "Sam for Samuel Adams, Jack for Andrew Jackson, and Brady for Grandpa Brady on my mother's side. As firstborn, he carries both family names."

She rolled her eyes. "Tell me you won't name our first son McFarlane Wilkins."

"You think we'll have a son?" The way he looked at her as he said it made her skin feel hot and tight.

She shrugged. "If your parts are as useful as you seem to think . . ."

Abruptly, he stood. "I've got to do my rounds."

Stepping onto the porch a moment later, Hank sucked cold air into his lungs and grinned up at the night sky. Tonight was the night, and a beautiful night it was. Overhead, countless stars glittered like tinsel in firelight, and the crescent moon rising over the peaks in the east looked like a glowing ornament hanging in the indigo sky.

He'd show her how useful his parts could be. He'd erase from her mind all memory of that other time, and show them both how perfect it could be.

Humming softly, he walked the perimeter of the house, checking windows and doors. Probably an unnecessary precaution, but he and Brady had agreed that until this thing with Fletcher and Scarface was over, they'd take no chances. After losing most of their family and the original homestead to one madman, neither was willing to risk those that were left to another.

He wished it would snow and cover over all the tracks they'd made that day so they would be able to tell if anyone else was checking the house. He wasn't worried about the French doors on the second story, since there were no staircases going up to the balconies. They'd placed ladders along the railing in case of fire, but unless someone from up there sent them down, or someone down below shimmied up a rope, there was no access from the ground.

Satisfied everything was secure, he crossed to the barn.

It was buttoned tight for the night, double slide bolts on the doors, front and back, as well as on the trap door into the loft. A guard was posted there now, the access ladder pulled up into the loft and the door bolted from inside.

"Enrique?" Hank called out. "It's me, Hank."

Footsteps overhead. The thud of the slide bolt, then the trapdoor lifted and Enrique Escobar peered down. "*Sí, jefe*?"

"Qué pasa?"

"*Nada.* Three, four coyotes. No *más*."

After exchanging a few more words, Hank said good night, waited to hear the slide of the bolt, then headed back to the house.

And Molly. His wife. Finally. The thought made him laugh out loud.

Nineteen

WHEN HANK DIDN'T FIND MOLLY IN THE GREAT room, he went up to her room. He didn't see her when he opened the bedroom door, but he knew she was there. He could smell her, that faint lemony scent she used on her hair, and he could feel her, as if by her presence the air had somehow changed and softened. He couldn't explain it and didn't even try.

Moving quietly, he went into the empty dressing room, then on to the water closet, where he found her sitting in the tub, arms crossed over her upraised knees, her head resting on her forearms. Her eyes were closed.

He stood watching her, memorizing all the details—the way water glistened on the gentle curve of her back. How the wispy curls that had escaped her pins clung wetly to her neck. The tiny strawberry birthmark on her right shoulder blade and the peach-tinted color of her skin.

He needed this woman, he realized. Needed her to ease the loneliness, to laugh with, to turn to when doubt plagued him. He needed her the way he needed his next breath. And he needed her to need him that way too.

Her eyes opened, found his in the doorway, and that connection arced between them, slamming like a hand against his chest. He stood frozen, his heart beating fast and hard. Then she smiled, and that familiar calmness washed over him as everything settled into place.

Taking a deep breath, he stepped into the room. "How'd you get undressed?" he asked, a bit disappointed that he hadn't been there to help her.

"Brady helped me."

Hank tensed, then realized she was teasing, although he didn't find her little quip particularly amusing. "Did he wash your back too?"

Her mouth quirked. "That wouldn't be proper. I decided to wait for you instead." Dropping her forehead onto her upraised knees, she lifted the damp curls from the back of her neck with her bandaged right hand. "Use the soap Iantha gave me."

Straddling the stool by the tub, he rolled up his sleeves, soaped a rag, and started scrubbing, focusing only on the small patch of skin he was washing.

He could do this. It might kill him, but he could do this.

Flower-scented steam rose from her back, then her shoulders, then her arms. It was so strong and sweet it almost made him dizzy. "Stand up," he said, his voice sounding gruffer than he intended.

In a sluice of water she rose. Facing away from him toward the wall, she stood while he drew the cloth across her butt and down her legs to where water lapped at her calves. He wondered if it was the heat that made her skin so red, or if she was blushing. He wondered what she would do if he slid his hand up and—

"I think you already washed that spot," she said, looking down at him over her shoulder.

Lifting an arm, he wiped steam—or maybe sweat—from his brow and motioned with the rag. "Then turn around."

She turned.

He stared at her round, bouncy bosoms. They seemed to stare back. This was the first time he'd seen her—really seen her—in full light, and she was a wonderment. Clearing his throat, he quickly scrubbed, distracting himself by reciting times tables in his mind, and when that stopped working, dismantling and reassembling clockworks by memory.

"You're mumbling," she said.

He looked up to find her smiling down at him.

"I'm sorry if this is difficult for you," she said.

"Difficult" wasn't the word for it. "Torturous." "Unhinging." He felt like a drooling adolescent at his first girlie show.

But she seemed to be taking it in stride, he noticed. Which bothered him a bit.

He had figured to be in control of this seduction, but it was clear he wasn't. And it was disconcerting that the wife he'd thought so shy and innocent was neither. Part of him was relieved that she wasn't a blushing bride he would have to coddle and tiptoe around. Another part was a little shocked by her worldly-wise attitude.

Shocked, maybe. But not truly disappointed. And admittedly, a bit intrigued by all the possibilities that opened up to him.

Avoiding her gaze, he dipped the rag into the water then squeezed it out over her shoulder, entranced by the way the soap bubbles slid slowly down to hang on the puckered tip of her breast.

"You don't seem bothered by it," he said, adding more soap to the rag then starting on her other shoulder.

She shrugged.

He felt the movement through the rag.

"I'm a nurse. The human body holds few surprises for me, and it would be ludicrous to pretend otherwise."

His head shot up. "I don't want you to pretend. Anything. Ever."

They stared at each other for a moment. Then she took a deep breath.

He felt that motion through the rag too.

"I think that's clean now," she said.

Realizing what he was doing, he jerked his hand from her breast and dropped the offending rag over the edge of the tub. "Step out."

"A good lesson for me, though," she said, using his shoulder for balance as she stepped over the high side of the tub.

Lesson in what? Hank wondered, staring hungrily at the bosom dangling inches from his face like a plump, downy peach.

"Now I know how my male patients must have felt when I bathed them."

That was certainly an image he didn't want in his head. Grabbing an oversized towel from one of the pegs by the sink, he threw it around her shoulders, thinking if he could relieve himself of the sight of her naked body, it might relieve the turmoil in his mind as well.

It didn't.

"Although, of course, this is different," she added, blotting at her face with one end of the towel.

"How?"

She chuckled. "Well, for one thing, they never look at me the way you do."

They better not.

"And for another . . ." Her gaze met his.

She was so close he could see little flecks of brown in her iris, the faintest dusting of freckles across her nose, every golden chestnut hair in her brows.

"I could never see them the way I see you."

You better not.

A sly smile spread across her beautiful face. She bent, skewered the dripping rag with her index finger, and pinned it against his shirtfront. "Your turn."

My turn? He looked down at his soaked shirt, then back at her. He took the wet rag from her hand. "But you can't get your bandages wet," he said in a voice that didn't sound like his.

"No I can't." Draping the towel around herself like a long shawl, she moved to the stool and sat, one leg crossed over the other, elbow on her knee. "But I can watch."

"OH MY," MOLLY BREATHED A WHILE LATER AS she stared up at the ceiling over the bed. "My heart rate must be sky high."

"It is." Hank nuzzled her breast. "Sounds like cows stampeding over a wooden bridge." Lifting his head, he grinned at her. "So maybe the human body holds some surprises for you after all."

She laughed softly. "Maybe a few."

Ha. He'd shown her surprises all right. And he'd shown himself a few as well. He wasn't even sure some of the things they did was allowed between husbands and wives, but he wasn't complaining. Mostly he'd learned that if bathing Molly had been stimulating, bathing himself with her watching had been unexpectedly gratifying.

Inspired anew, he worked his way up her neck, trailing kisses over her flower-scented skin, thinking of a few other surprises he wanted to spring.

"Although I knew most of it from my readings, of course."

He lifted his head. "Readings?"

"In Papa's medical books."

"They teach this in medical books?" He reminded himself to remember to check through Molly's when they arrived.

"Mostly the physical changes due to sexual excitation. Increased respiration and perspiration, elevated heart rate, and so forth. Did you know the pupils of the eyes dilate during intercourse and various nerves in special places react to a single touch—"

Hank held up a hand. "Didn't know and don't want to know." This was why people shouldn't discuss such things; it reduced a really fun activity to nuts and bolts.

"And then, I also talked to the camp prostitutes."

He blinked at her. Most proper women would never even speak to a whore, much less discuss such a thing with one. Then he remembered how chummy she had been with Martha Burnett. He frowned, wondering if they'd ever discussed him.

The idea didn't set well. In fact, it was so disturbing in so many ways, he didn't even want to think about it. "And what did you learn from them?" he asked in spite of himself.

She fluffed a curl from her brow. "Oh, the mechanics of the thing mostly. What goes where and so forth. Apparently most prostitutes find it all rather boring."

Even Martha?

"In fact, they have amusing nicknames for . . . well, never mind."

Again, more than he cared to know. Not that he intended to frequent whores anymore, but he hated having fond memories of previous trips tarnished.

Inspiration dwindling, he rolled onto his back and stared up at the rafters, wondering if any of the girls had a nickname for him and what it might be.

"But the best things I learned from you."

He turned his head and looked at her.

She lay curled on her side, her cheek resting on her bandaged hands, a smile tugging at her wide mouth. Her face was red from his whiskers, her lips slightly swollen, and her eyes full of joy and laughter.

She was beautiful.

And she was all his.

Emotion swamped him, bringing with it a sense of contentment and peace he had never known. It was as if he had finally come home to the place he was meant to be. "And what did you learn?"

Molly studied his beautiful face, wondering how to answer that. How could she put into words the indescribable pleasure he had brought to her—the wanting and needing and utter joy of connecting with another person on such an elemental level. It transcended time and thought and being. It was without reason or order.

It was bliss.

And there were no words for that.

So she told him what had taken root in her heart, and her mind, and her very soul. She told him the most important thing she had ever told anyone. "I learned that I love you."

She watched to see how her pronouncement affected him—if it was too soon or too intense for a man who armored himself so well—or if he would feel compelled to say it back—and if he did, what words would he use.

Silence stretched between them. Yet he didn't look away or try to dissemble, and she was encouraged by that.

His chest rose and fell on a deep breath. Then he smiled. "Me too."

Me too? That was all he gave her? The man was a blathering romantic. Fighting a smile, she poked his leg with her toe. "You make me giddy."

Laughing, Hank rolled over and kissed her soundly. "What special places?" he asked. "You said there were nerves in special places. What special places?"

She trailed her bandaged fingers up the back of his thigh. "Well, here for one."

"Holy Christ."

"I SENT WORD TO RIKKER," BRADY SAID WHEN Hank wandered into his office the morning after Christmas with two cups of coffee. Brady had been up for several hours already, too restless to sleep—his usual condition since he had learned Jessica was breeding again, but he was surprised Hank had slept in so late; his brother was usually up and out by the crack of dawn.

"Told him to play it close," he added, taking the cup Hank offered. "But to ask the federal marshal about Fletcher and keep an eye out for Scarface." As he sipped his coffee, Brady studied his brother over the rim of his cup. He seemed different. The frown was gone, and he was actually grinning. "What are you so happy about?"

"Am I happy?" Settling in his usual chair, Hank propped his boots on the corner of the desk and yawned.

He looked worn out. But pleasantly so.

"Rough night?" Brady asked.

"Long night."

"Didn't sleep?"

"Not much."

"Ah."

Hank looked at him.

Ignoring him, Brady stared past the grizzly's upraised paw to the sunny vista beyond the window. It was another crisp, bright day, the kind of day that reminded him how lucky he was to be here instead of trapped in some crowded city where the only view was of the building next door. He remembered how close he'd come to living out the rest of his life in rainy England, and shuddered at the thought of it.

Hank leaned forward, set his cup on the edge of the desk, and sat back.

Brady could feel his brother probing his mind, but held fast. He could be inscrutable too.

"Ah, what?" Hank finally asked.

Brady hid his grin behind his cup. "Seems you and Molly are getting on well."

"We are."

"Got over your mad, then?"

Hank looked at him.

"I'm only asking because of the annulment."

"What annulment?"

Brady studied the dregs in his cup. "The one I promised I'd get for Molly. If she still wants it, that is."

"She doesn't."

"Oh?" Tossing back the last swallow, Brady set the cup carefully onto his desk. It was part of a matched set Jessica had ordered from some English china company. Made from ground-up buffalo bones, or so the crate said. Sad use of a magnificent animal, he thought. "You're sure?"

"I'm sure."

"Ah."

They sat in silence for a time, then Brady said, "You know what today is, don't you? I mean, other than the day you finally dropped a rope on your wife."

Hank glared at him.

Brady grinned back. "Boxing Day."

"Aw, hell."

"I know." Boxing Day was another of Jessica's traditions that didn't necessarily translate well to the ranch. The English practice of giving Christmas bonuses to their employees was fine with Brady. Even spending the day in sporting contests between the workers and the owners was all right, especially since he and Hank ordinarily would have the advantage, due to size and general meanness.

But after the first year, the workers, being an inventive and vicious lot, devised their own events. Last year it had been a pepper-eating contest, which naturally the buckskin-bellied beaners won, but left him and Hank with a bad case of blisters in various places. The year before, wearing nothing but boots and bright red unions, they'd had to twist the tail of an angry bull then race it back to the corral fence and safety, which also favored the workers, since they were more agile and smaller targets. Brady's butt still ached if he sat in the saddle too long. This year the contest was to see who could stay in the creek longest . . . once the ice had been broken.

"I don't want to do it," Hank complained. "I'm a married man now. I got duties to perform."

"Stop whining. Be good for you."

"Us. Good for us."

Brady gave a long sigh of regret. "Sorry, little brother. You're on your own this year. With Scarface out there, somebody's got to stay and guard the house."

Hank's boots hit the floor with a thud. "It's my wife he's after. I should do it."

Brady scratched his chin in thought. "Then how about we flip for it? Leave it purely to chance." Pulling open the middle drawer, he retrieved his lucky silver dollar. "Call it." He tossed the coin into the air, caught it, and slapped it on his wrist. "But don't call 'tails' because that's what I want."

"Tails," Hank said promptly.

Brady hid a smirk. For all his brains, his little brother was pretty predictable. Lifting his hand, he showed the coin to Hank. "Sorry." Grinning, Brady slipped the two-headed dollar back into the desk drawer before Hank could see it. "I'll have Molly warm up a sock for you. One of Penny's to start."

HANK WAS THE UNCONTESTED WINNER OF THE ice-dunking event, mainly because when the other contestants saw his expression as he sank into the water, they quickly defaulted. Which had apparently been the plan all along, judging by their hoots of hilarity and the fact that he had been picked to go in first. Sometimes his own stupidity amazed him. Happily, Molly was able to warm him up pretty quickly, and it didn't involve any socks.

Eighteen seventy-one ended well for Hank—those last days spent enjoying his new family, his nights, his lusty wife. Thank God for second chances.

Eighteen seventy-two came in with an ice storm that turned the eaves of the house into hanging icicle forests and made going outside treacherous at best. Trees along the creek bowed under the weight of ice and snow, limbs snapping off with cracks as loud as gunshots. Then a warming trend turned the icy surface into four inches of mud until another storm covered it all over again with fresh snow.

Slowly the household returned to normal. Christmas decorations were packed away, the children went back to their primers, Hank and Brady spent more time in their offices, tending the endless chores that RosaRoja and the mining operations demanded. By the end of the first week of January, the mines resumed operations, and the first winter tally was completed, showing that, despite the stormy weather, cattle losses were down. It looked to be the start of a prosperous year.

And the days marched by.

Molly's nightmares increased, but instead of lost patients calling out to her, it was Scarface chasing her through the empty house. Often Hank would awaken to find her sitting by the fire or standing at the French doors, looking out at the night. Other times she would cry out in her sleep, then turn to him in shivering need, as if only through their joining could she find forgetfulness and peace.

Although he tried to put on a brave front for Molly and Jessica and the children, the waiting was getting to him, too, and his brother's added antics over his wife and her advancing pregnancy kept him on a frayed edge.

Jessica took it all in stride, having suffered through Brady's incessant worrying during her two previous pregnancies. The example of her equanimity in the face of Brady's histrionics kept everyone calm and the tension at a survivable level.

But Hank could see Jessica was worried too. Once he found her standing at the windows overlooking the hilltop cemetery behind the house, a wistful yearning in her eyes. Not knowing what else to do, he patted her shoulder and stood quietly at her side, offering silent support or a listening ear, whichever was needed. After a while, she hiked her chin, gave him a quick hug, then threw herself into such a flurry of activity Hank doubted she had energy left for worry or grief.

The other women in the household did what they could, quietly taking on Jessica's chores and keeping her distracted with less strenuous tasks. Molly encouraged her to take strengthening walks to help her sleep better, and taught Brady how to ease her backaches by massaging the muscles in her neck and shoulders and back. Meanwhile, Hank cautioned his brother repeatedly to find an outlet for his concerns other than terrorizing the household. To his credit, Brady tried, but he was so fearful of losing his wife he bordered on the irrational.

Jessica was wearing herself out, he complained. Jessica wasn't sleeping well. The babies were moving too much. The babies weren't moving enough. Doc O'Grady would never get through the pass in time. Molly better know what to do, and she better start doing it now.

It did little good to remind him that the babies weren't due for another month.

Hank tried to be patient. He was beginning to understand the depth of the bond between Brady and Jessica, because he felt the same about Molly. He'd never known caring about someone could be so worrisome. Life had been a lot easier when he'd held himself apart and kept his emotions under control. But not nearly as much fun.

Thinking to shield the children from the growing tension, and also hoping to curtail the imp's morning visits, Hank helped Molly move Penny and Charlie up to the children's nursery on the top floor. To ease the transition, Charlie was allowed to let Buddy sleep on the rug by his bed, and Penny was allowed to sleep with her new doll. Both took to their new quarters with great enthusiasm, which was a relief to Hank, although in weaker moments he missed waking up to Penny's sticky little face.

Everyone tried to stay busy. Everyone tried to remain cheerful. But it became harder as the days passed. Almost two weeks into the new year, Brady came into Hank's office with the frantic look of a man who sees disaster looming and his only defense against it is a hopeful smile.

"She bathed Buddy again today," he said, plopping into the chair across from Hank's desk. "Poor dog's scared to death of her."

Hank didn't look up from the clockwork toy he was making for Penny. A cat made out of rabbit fur, with a movable head and a tail that wagged. Not as good as the real thing, but hopefully it wouldn't make her sneeze. He held up the half-finished toy. "What do you think?"

Brady didn't even glance at it. "Damned dog's starting to smell like a flower garden. It's no wonder he rolls in manure every chance he gets."

Hank studied the cat from all angles. "I think she'll like it."

"And yesterday I caught her trying to throw out my lucky cutting shirt. Can you imagine?"

"You mean that stinking rag you wear when you're castrating?" Hank picked up a tiny screwdriver and tightened the set screw on the cat's neck. "Woman's out of control."

"Laugh if you will, but I haven't been kicked or cut since I started wearing it."

Hank didn't bother to respond to a statement so lacking in logic.

"Then this morning," Brady went on, "I found her throwing out half my socks. What am I going to do?"

"Buy more socks." Hank wound the key, then thumbed the spring release lever to test the motion of the cat's head. It tilted to the left, then to the right, then fell off. "Sonofabitch."

Leaning forward, Brady dropped his voice to a whisper. "What if she comes in here next? You know how she's always threatening to tidy up our offices."

Hank looked up in alarm. "Not mine?" His office might look a mess, especially as he sorted through the keg of parts Molly had given him, but in fact, it was a carefully thought-out arrangement of all the nuts and bolts and screws and springs and parts he would ever need. His own personal candy store. The thought of Jessica rooting around in it gave him the shivers.

Brady sat back with a sigh. "We're none

of us safe with a pregnant woman on the prowl."

Reminding himself to remember to put a lock on the door, Hank picked up the cat head and started unscrewing the springs. "She's nesting."

"I know that," Brady snapped impatiently. "I've been through this twice before, you know."

"Then talk to Molly." Hank was losing patience. He had other things to think about besides his brother's worries. Like Scar-face showing up any day, and getting this goddamn cat to work.

"I did. She said to quit worrying." Brady dismissed that foolish notion with a wave of his hand. "The point is it's too soon. She's still got three weeks to go."

The spring popped out of Hank's fingers and hit somewhere in the bookcases. "Damn."

Brady chewed on his thumbnail. "Maybe I should send for Doc."

"And keep him here for the next three weeks?" Hank dug through the parts strewn across the desktop until he found another spring. "We don't have enough whiskey. Be-sides you've got Molly."

"Two minds are better than one, they say."

"Not if one of them is pickled."

"To hell with you. I'm sending for Doc."

Twenty

IN LATE AFTERNOON SEVERAL DAYS LATER, Sheriff Rikker rode out from Val Rosa, bringing with him Angus Foley, the deputy United States marshal for the area, and another man he introduced as Mr. Jones, from Washington City in the District of Columbia.

"They've come about Fletcher, the man you were asking about," Rikker said, settling into one of the stuffed leather chairs beside the fireplace in the main room. "Seems you were right to be concerned." Reaching into his vest pocket, he pulled out the makings and began to roll a smoke.

"Not inside," Brady warned. "Makes my wife sick." He motioned to one of the French doors that led onto the porch. "Step out there if you want to smoke."

Mumbling under his breath, the sheriff went outside.

By the time Hank retrieved five tumblers and a bottle from Brady's office, the other two men were seated and the sheriff was back in his chair. After pouring an inch of whiskey into each glass, Hank passed them around, then took a seat on one of the couches.

Mr. Jones did the talking. A well-spoken man of middle years with the sound of education in his voice, he had sharp hazel eyes, a banker's smile, and a haircut that left most of his ears exposed. Hank noted that the one on the left had a chunk missing from the top edge that was the exact shape and size as a bullet hole.

The deputy marshal was more the watchful type, with quiet hands, sideburns that came around to join his bushy mustache, and dark unblinking eyes that took in everything but gave nothing back. Hank didn't know him but had heard of him—a hardline lawman with a stone for a heart.

Sheriff Rikker was an old acquaintance, having been the lawman in Val Rosa since the time of the feud between the Wilkins family and Sancho Ramirez. He was another loner who held his thoughts close. Brady called him a "quiet seeker," but right now the old man sat slumped in his chair, eyes closed, seeking nothing more than a nap.

"We've been watching Fletcher for some time now," Jones began. "He and his associates have been working with a man out of Baltimore who specializes in weaponry."

"What kind of weapons?" Hank had a keen interest in such things ever since reading about R. J. Gatling's Battery Gun. He'd even tried a few innovations of his own, but they hadn't ended well.

"Artillery."

"Why would that concern the government?" Brady asked, rolling his tumbler between his palms. "He's not breaking the law, is he?"

Like most Westerners, Brady had a natural distrust of government, preferring to handle legal matters in his own way. Most of the time he was honorable about it. Unless his family was involved.

"Not yet," Jones said. At Brady's questioning look, he explained. "You've heard of the pockets of unrest that have arisen throughout the South since the war. Despite the terrible toll the Rebellion took on this country, there are those who would see it begin again." Jones emptied his glass and set it on a side table, waving away Brady's offer of a refill.

His voice took on a sour note. "Confederates have always felt more aligned with England and France than they have with the North, and the economic pressures of the Reconstruction have only strengthened those sentiments."

Hank thought of the men in tattered gray uniforms he had occasionally seen wandering through Val Rosa, and Redemption, and El Paso. Some had looked broken and lost, others had stared back at him through a zealot's eyes, but most seemed true believers that, if given the money, the guns, or whatever, the South could rise again. "There's no real chance the war could resume, is there?"

"With the right motivation, it might." Jones propped his elbows on the arms of his chair and studied them over his steepled fingers. "Despite what you might have read, gentlemen, the outcome of the war was a near thing. The North was better fed, better clothed, better armed, and with Northern factories continuing to manufacture the equipage of war, it should have been an easy victory. Instead it took five long years. Why? Because of emotion. The Confederates believed in the fight. And they still do."

"And Fletcher is one of these believers?" Hank asked. He wondered if that was what Molly's sister had been trying to warn her about.

Jones nodded. "He and his associates are known Confederate sympathizers, led by a man named Edward Rustin, although they're driven more by profit than ideology. They have strong ties to foreign manufacturing, and if they can devise a weapon powerful enough to force a Southern secession and establish tariff-free trade with Europe, they stand to make huge profits."

Brady rose, added more wood to the fire, then stood with his back to the hearth, arms crossed over his chest, feet braced. Hank recognized the belligerent stance. "And how does this affect us?"

Jones nodded toward the deputy marshal. "I'll have Foley explain."

Other than murmured greetings when Rikker introduced them, Foley had remained silent throughout. Now as he spoke, Hank heard the gravelly voice of a tobacco user, even though there were no stains on the marshal's fingers and no telltale bulge in his cheek. Or maybe Foley was just unaccustomed to speaking, and that accounted for the rusty quality. Whatever the cause, the sound of it grated on Hank's nerves and made him want to clear his throat. "We know Fletcher's been looking for his sister-in-law, Molly McFarlane." Foley's dark gaze fastened on Hank. "The woman you recently married."

Hank returned the stare and tried to ignore the slow tightening in his gut.

"Apparently he's tracked her here."

"Here?" Brady glanced out the window then back at Hank. "At the ranch?"

"Val Rosa," Foley amended. "He's been at the hotel for the last week."

The clench in Hank's gut moved into his chest. Motion caught his eye, and he looked up to see Charlie standing at the railing that overlooked the great room. He was clutching the railing with both hands, his face pale. Concerned that the boy would overhear things he shouldn't, Hank made a shooing motion with his hand.

Charlie continued to stand there.

Rising, Hank excused himself and left the room. As he started up the stairs, Molly came out of the kitchen. He pulled her close and spoke in a low voice. "Charlie's upstairs at the railing listening to things he shouldn't. Would you take him to the nursery and keep him there?"

She glanced past him at the men gathered before the fireplace. "What's happening? Who are those men?"

"I'll explain it all to you later, Molly. I promise. But for now I need you to take Charlie out of here. Will you do that?"

She studied him for a moment, a worried crease between her brows. Then with a nod, she turned and climbed the stairs. By the time Hank returned to the couch, she was steering Charlie toward the third-floor staircase above the kitchen.

The men sat in silence until the footfalls overhead faded, then Foley turned to Hank and resumed speaking. "I was asking your brother why Fletcher would be seeking your wife, but he didn't know. Do you?"

Hank hesitated, not sure how much he wanted to reveal to this stranger.

Foley seemed to expect a quick response. When Hank didn't offer one, a look of impatience crossed his face. "She has no legal claim to his stepchildren, yet she took them from his care. Do you think that's why?"

"It doesn't matter. The children stay here."

Foley's impatience flared into irritation, but before he could vent it, Jones cut in. "We haven't come about the children, Mr. Wilkins. We think your wife has something of Fletcher's, maybe something she's not even aware that she has, and he wants it back badly enough to send trackers after her."

Hank thought of Scarface, and the bitter taste of rage rose in his throat. He glanced at Brady, wondering how much he should reveal.

Brady read his unspoken question and gave a half-shrug.

"There's a man," Hank said hesitantly, hoping he was doing the right thing. "A man with a burn scar on his face."

"Hennessey." Foley sat forward in his chair, his predator eyes taking on a feral gleam. "Gordon Hennessey. He's been known to work for Rustin. If he's after your wife, she's in grave danger."

Not sure if he'd grabbed the snake by the head rather than the tail, Hank reluctantly told Foley what he knew. "He staged a cave-in at our mine to lure us—and Molly—from the ranch. He cornered her in the livery and demanded she return a book she supposedly took from Fletcher. When she said she didn't have anything of Fletcher's, he dislocated her thumbs and told her she had a month to find it or he would start killing off everyone around her."

"Christ," Jones muttered.

Foley's gaze never wavered. "Has she found it?"

"No."

"And she has no idea what's in it?"

"No," a voice answered from the direction of the entry.

Hank looked back to see Molly walking toward them with Charlie by her side, a battered wooden box in his hands.

"But Charlie does."

* * *

It was one of those fleeting instants in time that solidified into a startling instant of clarity, like that moment when Hank realized all those lingering doubts about his marriage and his memory had substance, and he suddenly *knew* what had eluded him all along. This moment was the same.

Charlie was the key. And the answer lay in the box he gripped so tightly.

Everything pointed to it—his fears, the night terrors, the furtive way the boy had tried to hide the box when Hank had gone into his room. All this time Molly had been frantically searching for whatever it was Fletcher thought she had—and it had been right there in Charlie's wooden box the whole time.

Relief thundered in his ears. She was safe. They were all safe. They could end this.

He glanced at Molly, saw the same giddy release in her eyes, and realized how frightened they both had been, and how thoroughly they had kept it from each other.

"I'm s-sorry, Papa-Hank," Charlie said, cutting through Hank's thoughts. "I d-didn't know what to do. I was s-so scared and—"

"It's all right, son." Sliding to the edge of the seat, Hank beckoned Molly and Charlie closer. As Molly sank onto the couch beside him, Hank pulled the boy around and sat him on the footstool with his back to the strangers listening in.

Charlie held himself stiffly, his eyes round and wet, the box in his lap.

"No one's mad at you, Charlie. Everything will be fine. I promise. Take a deep breath." The room remained silent while the boy struggled to regain control. When he had stopped crying, Hank gave him an encouraging smile. "Now tell me what you know."

It was an ugly story, made uglier because it was told in a child's voice and seen through a child's eyes.

"I wasn't supposed to go into the office," Charlie began in a faltering voice. "Usually my stepfather kept it locked, but that day it wasn't. My real father used to keep hard candy in a jar on the bookcase, and I just wanted to see if it was still there." He lifted a hand from the box and dragged his sleeve over his runny nose.

"What did you see, Charlie?"

"Pictures. But not like those." He nodded

toward a small cameo painting of Jessica's sister on the side table. "Drawings mostly."

"Of what?"

"Airships, I think. And hot air balloons. And something that looked like a rocket. There was a whole book of them with lots of writing on the edges."

Across the room, Foley and Jones exchanged glances. Brady stood unmoving. Rikker made a snorting sound then settled back into his droning snore.

"Then what happened, Charlie?"

That panicky look came back into the boy's eyes. "I heard him coming and I got scared and ran out the side door into the garden. I didn't mean to take it, Papa-Hank. I didn't even know it was still in my hand. When I saw I still had it, I didn't know what to do. My stepfather is really scary when he's mad, and I was afraid to go back." The boy's voice ended in a wobble. Swallowing hard, he stared at his shoes.

Hank waited for his stepson to regain control.

Beside him, Molly's breathing sounded fast and shallow, which told Hank she was fighting tears too. The other men in the room sat without moving, as if fearing any motion or sound would frighten the boy into silence. Even Brady curbed his natural restlessness and remained planted before the hearth, a scowl drawing his dark brows into a ridge over his nose.

Once the boy had calmed, Hank said, "Do you still have the book?"

Charlie nodded and lifted the wooden box toward Hank. "In here."

As Hank took the box from him, Charlie's courage deserted him. "I wasn't going to keep it, Papa-Hank. I promise. I was going to take it back but—"

Fearing the boy would start crying again, Hank set the box on the footstool and pulled Charlie forward, tucking the small head between his neck and shoulder. "It's all right, son," he said, patting the small back. "You did nothing wrong. No one's mad at you." When the trembling stopped, Hank made a space for him on the couch between him and Molly. Once Charlie was settled, he nodded to the box resting on the footstool. "Can I look inside, Charlie?"

Charlie nodded and tucked himself tighter against Hank's back.

Hank lifted the lid.

Inside were a boy's treasures—arrowheads, a bullet casing, two buttons from a Confederate uniform, a glossy eagle feather, a ball of string, a tattered tintype of a woman who looked a lot like Molly. And at the bottom, a leather-bound journal the size of a primer. Hank lifted it out. After moving the box to the floor, he placed the book on the footstool and opened it.

Brady came away from the hearth. Foley and Jones shifted to the edges of their chairs, tilting their heads to look at the pages as Hank slowly flipped through them. Rikker continued to snore.

There was page after page of chemical notations in feathery script, as well as detailed drawings of odd canister-type things, hot air balloons, rockets, and airships. Some of the designs Hank recognized; others he didn't.

Halfway through the book, Molly reached out to stop him from turning to the next page. "I know that name." She pointed to a note in the margin. "McCullough. He's a chemist, I think. My father mentioned him."

"The Professor," Jones said. "One of the Lincoln Conspirators. He developed a very potent poison gas. Thankfully the war ended before it could be put into use. I understand he was also working on a way to accelerate Greek Fire into an inferno within seconds." He gave Molly a studied look. "How did your father know him?"

"I'm not sure." Resting her elbows on her knees, Molly pressed the palms of her bandaged hands together. "I do know Papa didn't like him, probably because of the Professor's association with Jeff Davis. Even though my father disagreed with his stand on slavery, he liked President Davis. I think it upset him that McCullough might be carrying out some highly questionable and unethical experiments under Davis's orders."

"What kind of experiments?" Jones asked.

"Things my father wouldn't talk about but that seemed to worry him a great deal. Dangerous things involving chlorine gas and cyanide gas and other poisons that could kill a lot of people very quickly."

Frowning, Hank rotated the book to study a drawing of an airship. The word AEREON was penciled beside it. He tried to remember where he'd seen it.

Brady looked up from the drawings. "I thought using poison was forbidden."

"It was," Jones said. "U.S. War Department General Order 100 banned the use of poison in any manner, gas or otherwise. But the South had no such strictures. A schoolteacher named John Doughty was even trying to devise a way to put chlorine gas into artillery shells. Other men, like Elmer Clements and Henry Kirkland and Fletcher, were looking for a way to deliver the gas to the battlefield or into the water or food supply, knowing it would cause widespread panic and open the door for a new rebellion."

"They may be planning to use airships." Hank thumped the drawing with his index finger. "I recognize this from a scientific paper I read. It's Dr. Solomon Andrews's design for his steerable airship, the *Aereon*."

"Well, there you have it then." Returning to his place at the hearth, Brady rested an elbow on the mantle. "Arrest them, hang them, and be done with it."

Jones settled back in his chair. "We can't."

"Why not?" Brady wasn't one to dally

with niceties. Or legalities. He was pretty much a "see it, do it, worry about it later" type of fellow. Hank preferred a more considered approach. Until now. But after seeing what Fletcher's man, Hennessey, had done to Molly, he was ready to tear all of them apart with his bare hands.

"They haven't done anything illegal," Jones argued. "You can't arrest a man for drawing pictures, or even for experimenting with poisons."

"So he gets away with hurting Molly and threatening all of us?"

"That was Hennessey," Foley said in his gravelly voice. "And we have no proof Hennessey was working on Fletcher's orders."

As they argued the point, Brady's voice got louder, Jones's got softer. Hank just got a headache. He glanced at Molly, wishing he could shield her from all of this. Her restless nights and frantic searches had taken their toll on her. She looked pared down, and there were dark circles under her eyes.

Charlie seemed no better, his fingers worrying the end flap of his belt, his face pale and watchful as he listened to Brady and Jones argue.

Wanting to offer reassurance, Hank

leaned over and said, "You did the right thing, Charlie, bringing this to us. Uncle Brady and I will see it through from here."

"Maybe I should take him upstairs," Molly offered, looking as if she'd like to escape upstairs herself. But before she could rise, Jones turned to her again.

"Did your father ever mention any of these other men?"

She shook her head. "Only Professor McCullough. He even went to Savannah to confront him. The Professor admitted he was experimenting with poison gas—not for the government, but for a group of private investors, one of whom was my brother-in-law, Fletcher."

Hank heard the stress beneath Molly's clipped tone and, reaching past Charlie, laid his hand over hers. She sent him a grateful smile.

"Did your father confront Fletcher?"

Molly shrugged. "I don't know. I doubt he would have told me if he had. My sister and I were close, and he probably wouldn't have wanted to worry me, or have me let slip to Nellie what her husband was up to." Something shifted in her expression, and her voice took on a bitter note. "But two days after he spoke to McCullough, Papa was found dead in Fletcher's office. The investigators said it was suicide, but I'll never believe my father killed himself. Never."

"He didn't," Charlie said.

All heads except Rikker's swung to the boy. Under so many watchful eyes, he seemed to shrink into himself.

Jones leaned forward again. "Why do you say that, son?" he asked gently.

"I saw."

"Saw what?"

"My stepfather kill my grandfather."

Molly inhaled sharply.

Hank felt something cold and deadly swell in his chest. No wonder the boy was frightened. And angry. And unable to trust anyone. He had seen the unimaginable and no doubt feared it would happen again if he told what he knew.

"It was my fault," Charlie blurted out, tears rising again. "They were yelling at each other. My stepfather thought my grandfather had taken the book, and he was really mad about it. I didn't want my grandfather to get into trouble, so I ran to get it, but when I came back, I saw him on the floor. He wasn't moving. My stepfather was shouting at someone on the other side of the room I couldn't see. I started to go in, but then—then . . ."

"Then what, Charlie?"

"T-Then I saw the monster."

Charlie's eyes were almost glazed now, focused inward on images in his mind rather than the people in the room. Sweat and tears streaked his face, and he was shaking so hard, Hank put an arm around him to give support.

"His face was all twisted and blotchy. He hissed like a snake when he talked, and he was really strong. He lifted my grandfather up and shoved him into a chair. Then h-he put a gun in my grandfather's mouth and pulled the trigger, and my grandfather's head jerked and blood—"

"Enough!" Weeping, Molly took the boy in her arms. "No more, Charlie. It's all right. You don't have to say anything more."

Hennessey. Hank looked at the other men in the room and saw that they had reached the same shocked conclusion. "Now do you have enough to arrest Fletcher?"

Foley glanced at Jones.

Jones nodded. "With the book and the boy's testimony, I think the circuit judge will issue a warrant. But he'll have to hear it directly from the boy."

As that sank in, all eyes swung back to the terrified eight-year-old boy sobbing in Molly's arms. The unasked questions hung in the air: Could Charlie do it? Should they even ask it of him?

Foley started to speak, but Hank held up his hand. "Not now," he said curtly. "He's had enough. Molly and I will talk to him later."

Brady pushed away from the mantle. "It's late. You'll have supper and stay the night." It was more of an order than a cordial invitation. "In the morning Hank and Molly will let you know what they've decided to do."

That impatient look crossed Foley's face. He aimed it at Brady, then at Hank.

Hank met it with a cold smile. "Or you can leave now. Your choice."

When no one spoke, Hank rose. Motioning for Molly to take Charlie upstairs, he turned to Jones and Foley. "We'll see this through, gentlemen. One way or the other. My word on it."

Once he was sure Molly and Charlie were all right, Hank promised to have a supper tray sent up, then went back down to their guests.

Supper was a quiet affair, the other children having eaten earlier in the nursery, and the visitors silently mulling over all they'd heard. As soon as the meal was over, they retired to the rooms that Jessica had readied for them in Jack's wing of the house. Jessica took a tray up to Molly and Charlie, and Hank followed Brady to his office. After pouring each of them a drink, Brady settled behind his desk and Hank took his usual chair in front, boots propped on the edge of the desk.

"Helluva thing," Brady muttered. "No wonder the kid's been so troubled."

Hank studied the whiskey in his glass and pondered how he might get to Fletcher before Jones and Foley did.

"You and the boy going with them tomorrow?" Brady asked.

Hank shrugged.

"Think Charlie will be up to it?"

"Maybe."

"If all he has to do is talk to the judge, he'll probably be all right."

"As long as he doesn't have to face Fletcher or Hennessey," Hank agreed.

They drank in silence for a while. As the whiskey spread like a slow fire through Hank's belly, he thought about all the recent changes in his life. It felt odd having a family of his own and people who depended on him. He normally left the worrying and family obligations to Brady. He was good at it, and Hank wasn't. Hank had always done his part, but he'd never felt essential to anyone. Necessary. But now he was responsible for three other lives. It weighed heavily on him, and he began to understand the burdens that Brady bore and had new respect for the way his brother managed to balance it all.

"You figure once Fletcher is in custody, Hennessey will have no more reason to come after Molly?" Brady asked after a time.

"Why would he? It was the book he was after, and that'll be in the marshal's hands from now on, not Molly's." He needed to have this over so he could get his life back on track. All this worrying had his mind going in circles. He couldn't be fretting over children and worrying about henchmen and thinking about bosoms all the time. He had mines to run.

Out in the valley a pack of coyotes yodeled and howled. "Bastards have been close lately," Brady said absently. "We'll have to keep an eye on the stock."

Hank swirled the last swallow of whiskey in his glass. "Maybe I should take Molly with me. Just in case." Penny would be fine at the house, but until this was over, Hank didn't want Charlie or Molly out of his sight.

Brady continued to stare out into the darkness beyond the window. "I wish you wouldn't," he said after a while.

Hank studied him, noting the weary slump of his brother's shoulders, the creases in his brow. He could see Brady was thinking about Jessica again, worried that if Molly left, there would be no one to tend his wife if the babies came early.

"We'd only be gone two or three days. Four at most."

Brady tossed back the last of his drink, then set the glass aside. Folding his hands atop the embossed leather desk pad Jessica had had shipped all the way from Spain, he looked directly into Hank's eyes. "I'd guard her with my life, Hank."

Hank didn't respond.

"She'd be safer here with two dozen men around her than out on the trail or in the middle of town."

Unsettled by the panic in his brother's eyes, Hank looked away. Was that what caring about someone reduced a man to?

"I wouldn't ask, Hank, if I didn't think there was a chance she'd be needed."

"There's still half a month before she's due."

Brady ran a hand through his hair, then gave a shaky laugh. "Hell, you're right. What am I thinking? Nothing's going to happen. Everything will be fine."

Hank finished his own drink and dropped his feet to the floor. He rose, then stood looking down at his brother's bent head. Brady wasn't one to ask for help, or even admit that he might need it. That he had done so now was an indication of how concerned he really was.

Pushing aside his own worries, Hank set his empty glass on the desktop. "I'll try to get her to stay. But if she insists on going, I won't talk her out of it."

Brady's relief was almost painful to see. "I appreciate that, Hank."

"Everything will be fine."

"Of course it will."

"Don't let anything happen to her."

"I won't. My word."

With a nod, Hank left and went upstairs.

They had moved Charlie back into his old room for the night in case the bad dreams came again. Hank stopped there first.

Buddy gave a low growl when the door opened, but when he saw it was Hank, he settled back into a tight curl against Charlie's side. The boy never moved. Closing the door, Hank crossed to Molly's room.

His room.

Their room.

Another change he had to get used to.

Twenty-one

MOLLY WAS DREAMING.

She knew it was a dream because it was warm and sunny, and even though she was in the surgery wing, there was no antiseptic smell and no patient moans. Papa was there, too, just ahead of her, coattails flaring as he moved quickly down the hall.

"I thought I lost you," she called, out of breath from trying to keep up.

"I'm not lost, daughter. I know exactly where I am."

"Wait." She reached out to slow him, but he kept rushing away from her, intent on some important task. Pressing a hand to the sharp stitch in her side, she walked faster, her footfalls echoing off the stone floor. “Papa, please wait.”

Without looking back, he waved a hand, slinging bright spatters of blood against the stark walls. “I haven’t the time, Molly. I’m already late.”

“Papa, please. Don’t leave me.”

Finally he stopped and whipped around to glare at her out of his ruined face. “Can’t you see I’m busy, daughter?” He held up his hands. Cradled in his palms was a beating heart.

She looked down, saw the gaping hole in her chest. “But, Papa, that’s mine. Why have you taken my heart?”

“You weren’t using it.” He spun on his heel and rushed away. “I can’t wait for you, Molly. I have to go.”

With a cry, she fell to her knees. She pressed her hands over the hole, but dark blood flowed through her fingers like hot sand.

WITH A GASP, MOLLY OPENED HER EYES.

The room was dark except for the glow

of the fire. Hank stood at the hearth, his hand braced on the mantle as he stared down into the flames.

Emotion swelled in her chest, filling that empty hole Papa's death had left. Hope, yearning, desire, joy . . . all the things she had guarded herself against for so long. Love. It filled her almost to the point of bursting. She didn't know if she could bear the weight of it. She didn't know if she could survive without it.

She must have made a sound, because his head swung toward her. And in the instant his gaze found hers, all the love she felt for this man came back to her through his eyes, and she knew in the deepest, most vulnerable part of her that he loved her as much as she loved him. He had never given her the words, and maybe never would, but it was there in his touch, in his smile, in that connection that flared between them like an arc of pure light.

He straightened and let his hand fall back to his side. "Did I wake you?"

Sitting up, she drew her legs to her chest and folded her arms on top of her knees. She studied him and saw how weary he looked. All this unrest had taken its toll on him as well. "No."

"I checked on Charlie. He seems to be sleeping soundly." As he spoke, he began unbuttoning his shirt. A simple act, but the intimacy of it made muscles deep inside her shift and soften. "Did you get a chance to talk to him?" he asked.

"I think he's relieved to finally get it off his chest." She watched him pull the shirt off his shoulders and down his arms. It was like unveiling a living statue.

Plopping into the chair, he tugged off his boots one at a time and tossed them into a corner. Then he rose, unbuckled his belt, and began unbuttoning his trousers. "Do you think he'll be up to meeting with the judge?"

Anticipation tingled along her nerves as his trousers slid down his long sturdy legs. "I think he needs to. It's important that he has a part in punishing Fletcher."

"Will you come with us?"

"Do you need me to? I'd rather not leave Jessica right now if I don't have to."

"Up to you." He began untying the tabs on his unions.

"Come here," she said.

He paused and looked up, then walked toward her, every muscle and tendon and bone and joint working in perfect synergetic harmony. It was the absolute ideal of the human form put into motion, and the beauty of it was like a song in her heart.

"What?" he said, stopping beside the bed.

She held up her bandaged hands. "Take these off."

"Are you sure they're healed? It's barely been a month. Doc said—"

"I want to touch you."

A slow smile spread across his face. "Well, in that case . . ."

Crossing to the bureau, he dug through her new medical satchel, found a pair of scissors, and came back to the bed. The mattress sagged as he sat beside her. While he carefully cut through the wrappings, she studied his bent head, wondering if his glossy hair was as soft as it looked, if his skin was as warm and smooth as she remembered. She leaned over to press her lips against his shoulder, drawing in the scent that was Hank's alone—the piney tang of the soap he used, old smoke, the musk of a healthy male.

When the casts finally came off, her hands felt weightless and strange. She closed and opened them several times then rotated her thumbs. Stiff from disuse, but not unduly sore. As long as she didn't reinjure them, she should be fine.

"How do they feel?" he asked, setting the scissors on the bedside table.

"Let's see." She trailed her hands over his chest, enjoying the way his pectoral muscles jumped beneath her palms. "They feel good. You feel good." She heard the change in his breathing when she skimmed her fingertips over his shoulders and up the corded muscles of his neck then around to his face, his perfect face, with his stern jaw, and bristly cheeks, and those soft lips parting on that perfect smile.

"Brown," she said. "Soft, sable brown. Like here." Leaning forward, she kissed his right brow, then his left. "And rich, dark chocolate brown like here." More kisses on his eyelids. "That's my favorite color." She pulled back and smiled.

"You know you're killing me, don't you?"

"I'm learning you. Lie back."

When he did, she hiked her nightgown and straddled his waist, with only the thin wool of his half-unions separating them. Planting her hands on either side of his head, she brought her face to within inches of his.

"Do you love me?" she asked, staring directly into his eyes.

He blinked up at her.

"You don't have to say the words," she added, trying not to smile. "Just nod 'yes' or 'no.'"

Instead, he grabbed her face in both hands and brought it down to his. It was a kiss she felt to her toes and left her squirming for more. "What do you think?" he asked when he finally released her and let his hands fall back to the mattress.

"I think you do."

"You'd be right." Watching her, he lifted his hands to stroke her breasts.

With a sigh, she dropped her cheek to his. "Don't leave me," she whispered before she could stop herself.

His hands stilled, then came up between them to lift her head. His eyes bored into hers. "Why would I leave you?"

She blinked hard against an unexpected sting in her eyes. She hated the show of weakness but was unable to stop the tears from cutting hot trails down her cheeks. "Everybody does." How needy she sounded. How pathetic.

"Not me."

She tried to drop her head from his probing gaze, but he held her fast.

"What's wrong, Molly?"

She felt like she was smothering, choking on words she didn't want to say. But they came out anyway, stripping her bare and leaving her defenseless before his probing gaze. "Today, hearing what Charlie said, it was like losing Papa all over again. I didn't want to believe he would take his own life. I didn't want to think he would leave me . . . that he didn't love me enough to stay."

"He didn't take his life. He was murdered."

"I know. But talking about it brought up all those thoughts, that pain. And I thought . . . I realized . . . I couldn't bear it if . . ."

"You're not losing me."

But once loosened, the flood wouldn't stop. "I treated you so badly. I lied—"

"You saved my life," he cut in gruffly. "You gave me a family." He kissed her fiercely, as if by the hard pressure of his lips against hers he could draw out all that fear and doubt. "You're not losing me."

The moment was too painful, too wrenching. She gave a shaky laugh and sat up, needing to pull back before she dissolved into some pitiful, blubbering, desperate person she didn't want to be. "How could I lose you?" she asked with a wobbly smile. "You're as big as a house. I'd find you anywhere."

He didn't smile back. "You're not losing me."

And before she knew it, she was on her back and he was sliding into her and words no longer mattered.

THEY LEFT AT DAWN, CHARLIE ON THEIR CALMEST gelding and flanked by Hank and two outriders. Jones and Foley took the lead. Sheriff Rikker and another ranch hand brought up the rear. They set a fast pace, needing to stay ahead of storm clouds building over the mountains, and wanting to arrive in Val Rosa in time to see the judge that afternoon.

Charlie's expression was grimly determined. Hank could see he was afraid, but not as panicky as he'd been. Maybe Molly was right, and the boy needed to do this so he could put it behind him. Hank just hoped there'd be no surprises.

Like Penny, the boy had wormed his way into Hank's heart. He was encouraged by the small strides Charlie had taken toward learning to trust again, and the thought of Fletcher undoing all that made Hank's hands clench. Despite the fact that he was sometimes called upon to defend himself against smaller men anxious to prove their manhood by forcing a fight, Hank wasn't a man who enjoyed violence. But the idea of getting his hands on Fletcher aroused the cruelty within him. For the first time in his life he understood the fire that burned in a father's breast.

They reached Val Rosa just past eleven o'clock and went straight to the Val Rosa Hotel. While Hank arranged for their usual rooms taking up the entire top floor, Jones went in search of the circuit judge to set up a meeting with Charlie. Rikker headed to the jail to alert his deputy that they could expect a new inmate before evening. After tossing his saddlebags in his assigned room, Foley went to check on the man he'd left to keep an eye on Fletcher.

Hank could tell Charlie was tired. Hoping to strengthen him for the ordeal ahead, he ordered food sent up, then joined him at the small table set up by the window. As they ate, Hank checked the street, watching for the return of Jones and Foley and hoping it wouldn't be long. He wanted Fletcher in jail as soon as possible, for Charlie's sake as well as his own. He wasn't sure what he would do if he came face-to-face with the bastard.

"I wish Buddy was here," Charlie said as he idly shoved peas around on his plate.

Hank noted he hadn't eaten much, but he didn't try to force the boy, fearing if the food didn't sit well, it might make a sudden appearance later.

"He seemed real sad that he couldn't come," Charlie added.

"He couldn't have kept up."

"He might have. He's really fast."

"He is that. And he'd have tried his best, but his paws would have frozen."

"Oh." Charlie went back to shoving peas. After a while, he looked up with a frown. "Do you think my stepfather will go to hell?"

Somewhat taken aback, Hank hesitated. Then he shrugged. "Probably." He forked up a bite of roast beef and studied his stepson while he chewed, trying to hear what hadn't been said. Kids, he found, spoke a special language that was sometimes as convoluted as a sidewinder's track.

"I hope so," Charlie said. "I don't want him anywhere near my mother and grandfather. But if he somehow gets to heaven, my real dad will kill him. He was big and strong, like you."

They ate in silence. Charlie finished off everything but his peas then sat back, idly kicking his foot against the leg of his chair. "Do you think Aunt Molly's mad?"

"About what?"

"About me not telling sooner."

"She knows you were trying to protect her and Penny."

"But the monster still got her, didn't he?"

Hank finally had an idea where this was going and he resolved not to let the boy add more burdens to the load he already carried. "That was my fault, not yours."

"It was?"

Hank saw a glimmer of hope in Charlie's eyes. He'd seen that same expression on Molly's face the night before when she'd asked him if he loved her. It bothered him that he hadn't been able to declare himself and tell her how he felt. He had never been a talker or a charmer, and he knew some people considered him cold or the big dumb one or, as Brady thought of him, just shy.

In truth, he was none of those. He just didn't feel comfortable saying the sweet things women seemed to want to hear. They sounded odd in his own head, and even odder when they came out of his mouth.

He needed Molly. He thought about her more than he probably should. And he was committed to protecting her and his stepchildren at any cost. Not very romantic, but it was the truth.

"She's under my protection now," he said to Charlie. "I saw the man you call 'monster' talking to her. I thought there was something strange about him, but I didn't go check. If I had, she wouldn't have been hurt."

Charlie seemed to digest that. Then he nodded. "We'll get him this time."

Hank nodded. "Because of you, we will."

Staring down at his bouncing foot, Charlie allowed a small smile. "Yeah."

* * *

THE HOUSE SEEMED EMPTY WITHOUT HIM.

To fill that void and to keep from worrying too much about the ordeal Charlie would be facing in Val Rosa, Molly threw herself into hectic activity, tending to chores Jessica had had to set aside owing to her increasing bulk.

While Molly had grown more frantic over the last weeks as the threat of the scarred man—Hennessey—loomed closer, Jessica had drifted into that serene phase that made the last weeks of her confinement tolerable, when worries seemed to melt into calm acceptance of whatever lay ahead. She was especially patient with Brady, but with a touch of poignancy that troubled Molly. It was as if she were preparing him for the possibility that this birthing wouldn't end as happily as they all hoped. She spent more and more time beside the great fireplace, gazing out at the tiny graveyard on the hill behind the house. But instead of the wistfulness that her face had shown several weeks ago, she now carried an expression of sad expectation.

The evening after Charlie and Hank left for Val Rosa, Molly saw Jessica standing again at the window. Determined to put an end to what she felt was an unhealthy obsession with that hilltop and all that it represented, Molly pasted on a cheerful smile and approached her. “Do you feel up to a walk?”

Jessica sent her a weary smile. “Actually, no. I’ve a bit of a backache today.”

“How did you sleep?”

“Brady would tell you I didn’t. And my restlessness kept him awake as well.”

Molly glanced over Jessica’s bulging midriff and realized something had changed. No wonder her back was bothering her; the babies had dropped lower in the pelvic cradle. Labor was imminent. “No other discomfort?” she asked, studying Jessica closely.

Jessica reached out and patted Molly’s arm. “I know what you’re asking, dear. I’ve been through this twice before. And yes, it’s getting close, but I feel we still have a bit of time left. I would like to stretch out for a while, though.”

“Then let’s get you to your room.”

“Shall I have Brady send for Dr. O’Grady?” Molly asked a few minutes later when she helped Jessica onto the chaise by the fire in hers and Brady’s bedroom.

"Oh, I don't think that's necessary. I feel we're still a bit premature and I think Hank was planning to bring him when he returns in a day or so."

"Is it still your intent to have the birthing in one of the spare bedrooms?"

Jessica settled back with a sigh, her gaze sweeping from the ornate mantle and stone fireplace to the oversized bed and heavily carved English antiques. This room was entirely different from any other room in the house, and a staid reflection of the most refined European tastes. "This is a room of happy memories," she said. "I wish it to remain so."

When Molly started to protest, Jessica held up a hand, adding, "Not that I foresee anything of a dire nature occurring, but the birthing process is, after all, not without its difficult and messy moments. And I would prefer not to have to rearrange the furniture or roll up the rugs. Besides," she added with a laugh, "a bed this size would be impossible to work around."

Molly conceded the point—the one spoken aloud, and the one that remained silent in their thoughts; if something went wrong, Jessica wanted this room to be a place for healing, not one tainted by bad memories.

"Shall I tell Brady we're nearing delivery? Or would you prefer to tell him?"

"I would prefer to have the whole thing over before he even knows we've begun. The man made a complete nuisance of himself last time. I dread his antics almost more than the actual delivery." Jessica said it with a tone of impatience, but Molly thought her eyes told a different story.

The love Jessica felt for her husband was more than a little surprising to Molly, especially considering they were so different in background and temperament and well . . . everything. It was like pairing a ball gown with hobnail boots. Molly wondered if she and Hank would ever reach that depth of devotion. They had so much yet to learn about each other, and so many tender spots around which they still had to tread lightly.

"Then we'll wait," Molly said with a cheerful smile, hoping that by the time the babies were on their way, Dr. O'Grady would have arrived. She was almost as nervous about this delivery as Brady was. Those old doubts rose within her, but she resolutely pushed them back down. This was not the time to weaken. This family depended on her, and she refused to fail them.

A SOUND BROUGHT HANK LURCHING UPRIGHT in the chair.

He looked groggily around, saw Charlie curled on the bed, and slumped back in relief. The room was dark except for the fading evening light that came through the hotel window. Heavy gray clouds pressed against the treetops, and a brisk wind made the signs hanging over the boardwalk across from the hotel wobble and swing.

He rubbed a hand over his face, wondering what woke him, then heard a knock on the door. Rising, he pulled his pistol from the gun belt hooked over the coat rack, cocked it, and opened the door.

It was Foley. He didn't look happy. Hank didn't know if that was his normal expression, or if he was bringing bad news, or if seeing a cocked revolver pointed at his chest put that irritable look on his face. Hank wasn't that fond of him either; the deputy marshal was so focused on his job he didn't see the people in his path. Hank suspected the man would run roughshod over anyone who got in his way, including an eight-year-old boy. Lowering the pistol, he stepped outside so they wouldn't wake Charlie. "Is the judge ready for us?"

Foley's dark eyes narrowed as he watched Hank ease the hammer down and slip the revolver into the waistband of his trousers. "There's a slight delay."

Hank waited.

"The trial in Raton took longer than anticipated. The judge won't arrive until tomorrow."

"Hell. What about Fletcher?"

"Still here. Holed up in the hotel at the other end of town. You and the boy will have to stay put so he doesn't see you."

After Foley left, Hank stepped down the hall to Langley's room. Carl Langley was one of their most reliable hands and a good man in a crisis, and Hank trusted him to cover their backs while he and Charlie were sequestered in the hotel room. After explaining the delay and posting the other two men at the head of the stairs and in the lobby, Hank sent Langley down for food and went back to the room.

Charlie was awake and looking scared. Hank realized he should have roused the boy rather than let him wake up to an empty room. After assuring him that even if Hank was out of the room, there would always be at least two other men standing guard outside, Charlie seemed to relax a little. A few minutes later, Langley returned with a tray heaped with food. Hank took it and set it on the small table by his chair at the window. He motioned Charlie over. "Take a seat."

"I have to wash my hands first."

"Says who?"

"Aunt Molly. You should wash yours too."

"We didn't wash before," Hank pointed out.

"I forgot."

Hank sighed. But not wanting to undermine his wife, he poured water into the bowl on the bureau, and he and Charlie washed.

"Now can we eat?" he asked as he took his seat at the table.

"After we say grace."

"Another rule of Aunt Molly's?" Hank reminded himself to remember to have a word with his wife. Too many rules could stifle a growing boy. Or anyone.

Charlie said grace.

"Anything else?" Hank asked, trying to ignore the rumbling in his stomach.

"No, sir."

They ate in silence. Hank was pleased the boy wasn't a chatterbox like his little sister. It wasn't that he minded talking, but sometimes all those words interfered with productive thinking. And right then he was thinking about how to fix Penny's cat so the damn head would stop falling off. That, and bosoms.

After they'd finished eating, Hank carried the tray to the hall then returned to his post by the window. Charlie remained slouched at the small table, bouncing his foot against the leg of his chair.

Hank tolerated it as long as he could. "You play poker?" he finally asked.

Charlie found the question amusing. "I'm not allowed."

"Says who? Wait, let me guess. Aunt Molly."

Charlie grinned.

"What does she have against poker?"

"She doesn't like gambling."

"Poker's not gambling," Hank argued.

"Not if you don't bet. And if you did bet, you'd be a fool to bet on a losing hand, wouldn't you?"

"I guess."

"And if you knew you had a winning hand, what would be the gamble?"

Charlie thought that over and, being a logical thinker, found the flaw. "What if the other guy thinks he has a winning hand too?"

"Then you have to outthink him. Fish the deck of cards out of my saddlebag over there, and I'll show you how."

Charlie retrieved the packet of cards and returned to his seat. "Aunt Molly won't like it," he said, watching Hank shuffle.

"Think of it as working on your numbers."

"She still won't like it."

"I'll make her see reason."

"How?"

Hank grinned, all kinds of ideas churning in his head. "Oh, I'll think of something."

MOLLY AWOKE BEFORE DAWN TO A LOUD BANGing on the door. Rising, she flung it open to find a white-faced Maria Garcia hovering in the hall. *"Señora, ven ahora! Los bebés—"*

"The babies?"

"Sí, sí. Ahora."

"I'll be there in a moment." Rushing into the dressing room, Molly pulled on the old work dress and apron she'd left hanging in readiness on a hook, tied a kerchief around her head, grabbed her medicine satchel, and headed to the birthing room that had been set up in the west wing.

Brady met her at the door. He looked ghastly. Setting her satchel in the hall, she pulled him outside and closed the door behind him. "You shouldn't be in there."

"She needs me." He tried to step back into the room, but she blocked his way.

"No, Brady. She needs calmness. She needs quiet. She needs to concentrate on bringing these babies into the world and not wasting her strength worrying about you." At his stricken expression, she softened her tone. "I know you're worried. But this is woman's work, and I'm here to see that everything goes smoothly. You must stay out of the way and not add to her burden with your fears. Do you understand?"

"But—"

She patted his arm. “I’ll call if I need you, or if there are any problems. I’ll keep you informed, I promise. But for now you can help by keeping the children occupied and seeing that nothing disturbs her. Can you do that?”

“But what if something goes wrong? I should be there in case—”

“Nothing is going to go wrong,” she cut in, trying to keep her voice from betraying her impatience. “You must trust me, Brady. You trusted me with your brother, and you know I’ll work just as hard for your wife. But I can’t do my best with you underfoot.”

He raked a hand through his hair and took a step back. “All right. Okay.”

“Good.” She picked up her satchel. “Now go take care of your family.”

Jessica was in the early stages of the birthing process, and everything seemed to be progressing normally. Knowing that a patient under stress did better in a quiet, softly lit room, Molly pulled the drapes and left only a few lamps burning, then sent everyone else from the room except Consuelo, who sat quietly in a corner, working her rosary and humming. Setting a chair beside the bed, Molly held Jessica’s hand

and spoke of mundane things to keep her distracted.

And herself as well. She was worried about what Charlie might be going through. Hopefully once Fletcher was behind bars, the boy would return to the happy child he had once been. Under Hank's guidance, he'd already made progress.

One hour led to two, then three. Jessica rested when she could, but by midmorning, the pains came more often and lasted longer.

Molly tied cotton straps with loops to the headboard for Jessica to grip when it came time to push. But that was a ways ahead yet, so meanwhile she concentrated on keeping her as calm and relaxed as possible while quietly monitoring the movements and heart rates of the fetuses with the stethoscope. Even though Jessica was tiring, all seemed to be progressing well.

At noon, Molly set Consuelo at Jessica's side and hurried to the kitchen to gather up the ligatures and assorted medical and obstetrical instruments she had put on to boil earlier. After directing Maria Garcia to carry up to the birthing room the toweling, fresh bedding, and infant items she'd set aside earlier, Molly went to report Jessica's progress to Brady, who sat with Dougal in the great room, reading to the children while he watched all the comings and goings from the west wing.

As soon as he saw Molly approach, he lurched to his feet, dumping children and books onto the floor. "How is she?"

"Doing very well," Molly assured him, setting Abigail upright. "It shouldn't be long now."

"Guess what?" Penny shouted. "Uncle Brady gave us candy, and I didn't even puke it up yet."

"Did he now?" Molly sent Brady a teasing look. "Then he has something to look forward to, doesn't he?"

"And guess what else? Dougal wears long pants *and* a dress!"

Ben rolled onto his back and laughed. Abigail crawled over his stomach.

"'Tis no' a dress. 'Tis a kilt!"

That Brady didn't enter into the fray told Molly he was in desperate need of distraction. "Dougal, could you keep an eye on the children for a few minutes? I need Brady to bring up more firewood."

"Aye, lass. But no puking, Miss Penny. I'll no' stand for it."

"Papa-Hank has a dress, but he doesn't wear it anymore. I don't think Aunt Molly likes him to."

Molly waited at the porch door while Brady gathered an armload of wood, then accompanied him up the stairs to the birthing room. "You can see for yourself she's doing well, but you may only stay for a minute."

He gave her an expression that was part gratitude, part terror.

"Smile," she whispered as she opened the door and motioned for Consuelo to step into the hall. "I'll knock when it's time to leave."

He didn't look quite so terrified a few minutes later when he left.

Molly returned to her post beside Jessica's bed. She looked more relaxed too. "Have you decided on names?" she asked, once again taking Jessica's hand in hers.

"For girls, I was thinking Heather, to remind me of home, and Adeline because that was my mother's name."

"And boys?"

Jessica's grip on Molly's hand tightened for a moment, then loosened. She let out a deep breath. "I've been threatening Nigel and Aubrey to goad Brady. His family has a tradition of naming children after American statesmen."

Molly smiled. "I heard."

Another contraction brought Jessica's shoulders off the pillows. "My, that was a strong one," she said with a shaky smile when it eased.

"What are Brady's preferences?" Molly prodded, mentally counting the seconds between contractions.

"He wants to name them Thomas Jefferson and Samuel Thornton. Samuel, for his brother, and Thornton for my family. Truth to tell, I don't care. I simply want them healthy. Oooouch!"

Molly reminded her to try to keep her body relaxed and take short, shallow breaths when the cramps came. "If you clench against the pain, you're fighting your body's efforts to expel the baby."

"Oh, really?" Jessica gave her a thin-lipped glare. "I have two melon-sized creatures trying to thrash their way out of my body and you tell me to relax? Honestly, Molly, don't be absurd—oh!"

"Sometimes it helps to keep your hands loose," Molly offered calmly as she extricated her mashed fingers from Jessica's grip. Papa said women in the latter stages of parturition often became combative. She could certainly see why.

"I really don't want to chat right now, Molly, truly I don't. Ah-oooh!" She half rose off the bed then after almost forty seconds fell back, panting.

"I think my waters have broken."

Twenty-two

THE JUDGE ARRIVED EARLIER THAN EXPECTED, and Foley came for Hank and Charlie just after they'd finished their noon meal.

Hank was greatly relieved. After spending nearly twenty-four hours cooped up in a small room with an eight-year-old, he was ready to get this over with. Not that Charlie wasn't good company. But Hank had already lost two thousand imaginary dollars to the kid, and he was tired of being humiliated by a boy who was barely out of short pants and who still had to count on his fingers before he made a bet. An imaginary bet. "Where are we meeting with him?"

Hank asked Foley as he reached for his gun belt.

"The jail. There's an office in back that'll be private. You won't need that."

Hank looked up, the gun belt hanging in his hand.

"We'll be with you. If there's a problem, we don't need civilians waving guns around."

Hank looked at him.

Foley looked back.

"I don't wave guns," Hank snapped. "I shoot them. And I don't trust anybody but me to watch out for Charlie."

Foley's dark eyes narrowed. His mutton-chop sideburns twitched over his clenched jaw. "Leave the gun or stay here. Your men too."

Realizing the only way to win this confrontation was to knock the mule-headed sonofabitch down, which might upset the judge or frighten Charlie, Hank tossed the gun belt and revolver on the bed.

Langley was waiting in the hall with Rikker's deputy, Eldon Whittaker, a man who possessed the intellect of a radish and was so lacking in gun skills that Rikker didn't even issue bullets to him. Unwilling to give up total control of a potentially dangerous situation, Hank pulled Langley out of earshot of Foley and explained the situation.

"You come with us, but unarmed. Have Curly and Bishop keep their guns, but hang back unless there's trouble."

Langley nodded. Removing his gun belt, he handed it to Curly, spoke to him and Bishop for a moment, then came to stand on the other side of Charlie.

They started down the stairs, Foley in the lead. With Charlie sandwiched between Hank and Langley and closely followed by the deputy, they left the hotel, crossed the muddy street, and moved quickly down the boardwalk to the sheriff's office. Rikker met them at the door and ushered them past the empty cells to his office in back. Except for a desk, a rack of rifles, two chairs, and a small coal stove, the room was empty. At Hank's questioning look, Rikker said, "Judge Utley is on his way. Got caught in a snow squall and had to stop off to change." He waved them to seats, then realized there were only two and offered coffee, instead.

Hank and Langley declined. Rikker didn't have any either. They'd all had Eldon's coffee. Foley took some, tasted it, then set it aside.

After sending Eldon to watch the front, Rikker settled in the chair behind his desk while Foley took the one in front of it. Hank stood looking out the window with Charlie close by his side.

It wasn't much of a view. A narrow back roadway that provided rear access to several of the shops fronting Main Street, and farther down, the livery. Almost at the end of town and in separate buildings because of their potential for fire, the smithy stood on one side of the street and the Chinese laundry on the other.

Business as usual, nothing out of the ordinary.

Yet something felt off to Hank.

Probably because he was unarmed. He wasn't a shootist. He rarely drew on anything other than snakes and varmints and hadn't shot at a human being since the feud with Sancho Ramirez ended four years ago. But the idea of being without protection should he need it made him uneasy.

Which was probably why Foley had insisted upon it. The man was worse than Brady for having to be in control. And by putting himself between Foley and Charlie, Hank had threatened the lawman's sense of authority. Stupid bastard. It wasn't a gun that gave a man authority, or even his willingness to use it. It was his willingness *not* to use it without just cause that made him someone to take note of.

"Papa-Hank?"

Hank looked down to see Charlie motioning him to bend closer.

"I got to pee," the boy whispered.

Hank straightened. "Where's the nearest outhouse?" he asked Rikker.

"By the smithy."

Hank steered Charlie toward the door.

"Let your man take him." Foley nodded toward Langley. "The judge will want to talk to you first anyway."

Hank hesitated, not liking the idea of only one man guarding Charlie.

"The deputy can go along, too, if you want." Foley gave a small smile. "Besides you've got two other armed men lurking out there, don't you?"

When Hank didn't respond, Rikker tipped his head back and yelled for Eldon.

Footsteps shuffled down the hall, then the deputy's blond head peered around the door. "More coffee?"

"Christ, no." Rikker set aside the smoke

he was rolling and fished two bullet cartridges out of his pocket. He handed them to Eldon with a warning look. "In your pocket unless it's necessary. You understand?"

Eldon gawked at the cartridges like they were made of gold instead of brass. "Yes, sir."

Hank and Langley shared a look of understanding, meaning if there was any trouble, Langley was to take charge of the pistol and bullets, and use them as he saw fit. Then Hank gave Charlie a reassuring smile and sent him on his way with his two bodyguards. He was watching their progress from the window when Jones and the judge finally arrived.

Judge Clement Utley. Hank had seen him a time or two when the judge made his stop in Val Rosa on his circuit of the area. A small, thin fellow with a bald dome and gunmetal blue eyes that reflected the weary, disillusioned look of a man who had seen more than he wanted to, Judge Utley had a reputation for quick judgments and harsh sentences, whether they be founded in fact, or not. He was also a strict abolitionist with a deep hatred for anything or anyone residing south of the Mason-Dixon Line. Hank foresaw no problems in convincing the judge to issue a warrant for the arrest of a Southern sympathizer.

"Where's this boy I'm supposed to talk to?" Utley said as he waved Rikker from his seat so he could take it. Foley vacated his for Jones.

"Taking a piss," Rikker said. "This here's his stepfather, Hank Wilkins. You might ought to hear what he has to say first."

"So talk then."

Hank recounted what Charlie had told them about finding the book, then later witnessing his grandfather's murder. At the judge's request, Foley handed over the book, then they all waited silently as the judge leafed through it, his expression growing more thunderous with every page he turned.

"Goddamn traitors. Should shoot them all."

Jones cleared his throat. "Although the contents of that book are extremely damning, they are not the primary reason for the warrant."

Utley looked up with an indignant glare. "You plan to do nothing about this filth?"

He threw the book onto the desk for emphasis.

"No, Your Honor," Jones said hastily. "But once we have Fletcher in custody for killing Matthew McFarlane, we hope to gather more information from him about his coconspirators and their activities."

Utley narrowed his eyes. "You intend to torture the bastard?"

Jones looked taken aback. "Not at all, sir."

"Too bad." Utley held out his hand, palm up. "Hand them over then. The papers. I don't need to talk to the boy if you'll vouch for him."

"I do," Jones said.

"Then hurry up, man. I've been in the saddle all day. My ass hurts, and I need a drink."

Quickly pulling the papers from his coat pocket, Jones rose and spread them open on the desk. "If you'll just sign here, sir."

Utley elbowed him aside. "I know where to sign, goddamnit. Give me something to write with."

Rikker rummaged in his desk drawer until he came up with a frayed quill and inkpot. Muttering under his breath, Utley dug from his vest pocket a stubby black lead pencil. After priming the tip with spit, he scrawled his name on each sheet of the warrant then shoved the papers back to Jones.

Jones took a copy, folded it, and handed it to Foley. "Arrest the bastard."

After Foley left and the judge headed to the nearest saloon, Rikker pulled a bottle of red rye whiskey from his bottom drawer and took a long swallow.

"Jesus, that man gives me the hives," he muttered once he quit coughing. He offered the bottle to Hank and Jones. Having seen the grimace and shudders that assailed the sheriff after a single sip, they both declined. Rikker took one more swallow, gagged and belched, then dropped the bottle back into his drawer.

Hank continued to stand at the window watching for Charlie and Langley. He had decided to wait for Foley to return with Fletcher so he could be certain Fletcher was locked up before Charlie got back. He wanted the boy to see that it was over. Hank frowned at the dark clouds building in the west. Too bad it was so late. They'd have to wait until morning to head back to the ranch, weather permitting.

A feeling of impatience nagged at him. They'd only been gone a night and two days, but he found himself anxious to get back, and that unfamiliar feeling of homesickness surprised him. And it wasn't really home that he was missing. It was Molly. And Penny. It was being away from where he was supposed to be . . . where he *wanted* to be.

Christ. He was as pathetic as his lovesick brother.

Footfalls pounded down the hall. Hank whirled as the door crashed open.

"He's gone! The bastard's gone!" Foley shouted just as gunshots sounded from the direction of the smithy.

THE FIRST BABY, A RED-FACED BOY WITH DARK hair and flailing fists, arrived without complication, although Jessica might have disagreed with that assessment. He was perfect in every way, and Molly almost wept with the joy of it. Leaving Consuelo to keep an eye on Jessica, and Maria Garcia to clean up the baby, she rushed to the balcony railing.

"You have a son," she called down to Brady.

He leaped to his feet, then his legs seemed to give way and he collapsed back down into the chair, a stunned look on his face. “A son.”

Dougal laughed and leaned over to cuff him on the side of his head. “A wee bairn, ye great lummox! Aboot time ye did sommat right!”

“The other one?” Brady called up in a shaky voice.

“Not yet. But soon.” With a backward wave, Molly hurried back into the birthing room.

“Okay, Jessica,” she said, all business once again. “You’re halfway there.”

“Oh, do be quiet, Molly,” Jessica panted. “Your wretched cheeriness is getting on my nerves—oooh!”

Positioning herself at the foot of the bed, Molly rested a hand on Jessica’s abdomen to judge how far the second fetus had descended. Oddly, it was still high in the womb and hadn’t yet begun to enter the birth canal. She glanced at Consuelo, who gave her a worried look and shook her head. Looking up at Jessica, Molly put on a smile. “Try not to push just yet, Jessica,” she said. "Rest for a moment while we see where we are."

"I can't help it," Jessica said through clenched teeth. "Oh, God, it hurts." Another contraction bowed her back.

Molly listened through the stethoscope to pinpoint the location of the baby's heartbeat. If it was below Jessica's navel, the fetus was presenting headfirst. If it was above the navel, it was buttocks or feet first.

It was just above Jessica's navel.

Starting to panic, Molly directed Consuelo to bring a lamp and hold it so the light would shine into the birth canal. When the next contraction came, she checked for the head of the baby. Instead, she saw a foot.

Oh, God. A breech birth.

"Jessica, don't push," she ordered. "Pant. You can't push while you breathe."

A look of terror crossed Jessica's face. "Is it breech?"

"Don't you dare give up," Molly ordered harshly. "You can do this. You can have this baby. But you must do what I tell you. Do you understand?"

Air hissed through Jessica's teeth.

"Do you hear me?" Molly was shouting now, desperate to make Jessica understand. "Just do what I tell you!"

"Y-Yes. All right."

"Breathe short and fast until I tell you to stop. I don't care how much you want to push, you mustn't."

Jessica nodded, tears and sweat streaking her face.

Working as quickly as she could, Molly ran her hands over Jessica's abdomen, trying to determine the position of the fetus. She found the buttocks then the head. "I'm going to try to get him to turn a somersault, Jessica. You absolutely must not push!" Molly waited until the next contraction ended, then pressed upward on the fetus's buttocks and down on the head. Nothing.

She did it again. Nothing.

A third and fourth time yielded no change in the position of the fetus.

Choking back her own terror, she realized the baby would have to come breech. But before it moved too far into the birth canal, she would have to make sure the head was tucked against its chest and the umbilical cord wasn't wrapped around its neck. "Open the jar of sheep tallow," she said to Consuelo.

Once she'd lubricated her hand and arm with the fat, she slid her fingers into Jessica's straining body. Protruding from the tip of the womb, she found one tiny foot, then another, tucked tight against the buttocks.

"Don't push," she ordered hoarsely as Jessica's uterine muscles clamped down on the fetus. It slid farther into the birth canal, then stopped.

Was its chin caught? Molly knew that was the most dangerous situation in a breech birth, especially with smaller babies like twins usually were. Another contraction sent the baby farther into the canal. Molly could feel the chest, the neck.

No cord was wrapped around it. Good.

"You're doing wonderfully, Jessica. It appears to be another boy."

The baby slipped farther.

She found the face, hooked her finger in the tiny mouth, and pulled down, tucking the chin of the fetus against its chest. Praying that it would hold that position, she pulled her hand back out. "Now push," she ordered.

Jessica pushed, her head thrown back, her body shuddering.

"Again." The feet, hips, and torso slipped free.

"Again. Last time, Jessica. Push as hard as you can."

Jessica rose off the sweat-soaked mattress, her hands twisting in the loops tied to the bedposts. With a scream, she pushed her son free in a gush of bright blood.

Molly caught him in trembling hands and wiped the mucus and blood from his mouth. Immediately, the baby sucked in a gulp of air then gave a tiny mewl of indignation. Another breath and the mewling became a healthy cry.

"You did it," Molly cried, holding up the baby for Jessica to see.

Jessica smiled shakily, tears of joy and triumph and exhaustion streaming down her ashen face. "Another . . . son." Then with a sigh, her body went limp.

"Jessica?" Molly called. "Jessica!"

Behind her, the door crashed opened. Still clutching the baby, Molly turned to see Brady standing in the threshold, staring in horror at his unconscious wife.

* * *

DEAD. JESUS, NO . . .

Brady staggered back, unable to tear his eyes away from his wife's still form. Then whirling, he stumbled down the stairs, shoving Dougal aside as he forced his numb legs to carry him past the great room into the east wing and through his office door. He slammed it shut, then stood gasping as a rage and grief so profound there were no words to name it filled his chest and pressed against his lungs.

Jessica.

Dead.

A smothered feeling came over him, and suddenly he was desperate to escape this moment, this place, this pain. But all he could do was stand there, shaking, his heart bleeding in his chest while tears ran unchecked down his face.

OUTPACING FOLEY, HANK CHARGED TOWARD the smithy, shouting for Curly and Bishop. When he ran past Gruber's Fix-it, they burst out of an alley, guns drawn, falling in behind Foley.

As they neared the end of the street, where the smithy and the laundry stood, Eldon rushed toward them, waving his revolver like a flag, his face so white it looked bloodless. "It's Fletcher! He's got the kid!" As Hank ran up, he pointed the pistol toward the laundry. "Took him in there! I tried to get him but I think I missed. Christamighty!"

Hank prayed the idiot hadn't shot Charlie instead. "Go around front," he yelled at Curly. "Bishop, cover the back." Without being told, Foley cut through the alley to block access to Front Street. Langley staggered around the corner of the laundry, blood pouring from a gash at his temple. "Ambush," he choked out then toppled face-first into the dirt.

"See to him," Hank shouted at Eldon and ran through the back gate.

Cutting through the laundry, he dodged black-robed workers, jumped steaming washtubs, and ducked through clothes hanging under a sagging canvas awning.

Gasping for air, he tore through the narrow halls, his heart pounding so hard blood roared past his ears. He crashed into a laundry cart, sent it toppling. Scrambling back to his feet, he rushed through the main room, frantically searching for Charlie.

A coolie he recognized waved him on

toward the side door. “He go there, he go there,” he shouted as Hank charged by. As he cleared the doorway, he saw a man dragging a child by the arm duck into a storage shed beside the smithy. Charlie.

Lungs burning, his boots slipping in mud, Hank raced across the street. He crashed through the door almost on top of them.

Fletcher whirled, a gun in his hand. He fired.

The doorframe exploded into splinters.

Before he could fire again, Hank lunged, knocking his gun hand up as their bodies collided. They went down, smashing over crates and boxes, Hank’s greater size and weight driving the smaller man hard into the dirt.

The gun fell from Fletcher’s grip. Hank kicked it away. He drove his fist twice into Fletcher’s face then lurched to his feet. Yanking the bleeding man up by his collar, he slammed him up against the wall and held him there with a hand around his throat.

Gulping in air, Hank ignored Fletcher’s thrashing and choking noises, and glanced over his shoulder at the boy trembling in the corner. “You all right, Charlie?”

"Y-Yes, sir."

"He didn't hurt you?"

"No, s-sir."

Hank turned back to Fletcher. "You bastard!" He tightened his grip. "I ought to kill you now!" His rage was so strong he shook with it. He wanted to pound Fletcher's face until his bones turned to mush. He wanted to break him into little pieces, then put him back together and do it again.

But Charlie was watching. And Charlie had seen enough.

Lowering his face to within inches of Fletcher's, he snarled, "It's over. They have the book. They know you killed McFarlane. It's over."

Fletcher gurgled something. Blood trickled from his bruised mouth. His eyes bulged like a rat choking on a peach pit.

Hank battled the urge to squeeze until he heard bones snap. "Call off Hennessey, or I'll kill you now."

"I c-can't," Fletcher gasped, his fingers digging at Hank's hand.

"What do you mean you can't?"

Fletcher made a gagging noise. Realizing the sonofabitch was trying to speak,

Hank forced his fingers to relax but still kept his hand on the bastard's throat.

Fletcher dragged in a wheezing breath. "Haven't seen him in a month. I don't know where he is." Then he rose on his toes as Hank tightened his hold. "Besides, I didn't hire him," he choked out.

"Then who sent him after Molly?"

"I don't know. Maybe one of the others. Rustin."

Hank hit him. Then because it felt good, hit him again. "I ought to kill you!"

"That won't stop them." Unbelievably, Fletcher's bleeding mouth split in a grisly smile. "You think this is just about me? I'm just a small part of it."

Hank shook him so hard, Fletcher's head banged against the wall. "What are you talking about?"

"It'll never be over." He laughed. "Not as long as there are Southern men who—"

Hank cut off his words with a fist to the jaw. Fletcher started to sag, but Hank pinned him tighter to the wall. "What about Hennessey?"

"Hennessey's an animal," Fletcher rasped. "He'll never stop. Hell, the bitch is probably already dead."

Dead? Molly?

Red mist exploded behind Hank's eyes.

Fletcher started laughing again, the sound of it growing louder and higher until it seemed to pierce Hank's skull. To stop it, he slammed Fletcher's head into the wall. Slammed it again. Then again and again until he felt bones snap in his hand.

Abruptly the laughter stopped and Fletcher went limp.

Chest heaving, Hank stepped back. He released his grip on Fletcher's throat and watched his body collapse into the dirt like a broken puppet.

Jesus, what have I done? His mind reeling, Hank stared at the body sprawled at his feet, then at the boy cowering in the corner.

Charlie stared back, his eyes round, his mouth slack.

A terrible feeling of dread swept through Hank. It wasn't that he regretted killing Fletcher. It was that he'd done it in front of a child. *Christ.* What new horrors had he brought the boy now?

"Is he dead?" Charlie asked in a quavering voice.

Hank nodded. He started to say more, but then Charlie rushed forward, a fierce look on his face. Before Hank could stop him, he kicked Fletcher's crumpled body, then spit on it and kicked it again. "I'm glad you're dead!" he shouted in a high, thin voice. "I hate you! I hate you!" Breathing hard, he looked up at Hank. "I'm glad he's dead!"

Hank stood frozen, chilled by the violence of Charlie's reaction. It didn't seem normal for an eight-year-old boy, but he didn't know what to do, what to say.

"I'm glad," Charlie said again. Then he burst into tears.

Relieved to have the child back, Hank scooped him up in his arms and held him tight as Charlie wept against his neck. "It's over, Charlie," he said, rubbing a hand over the boy's back. "He'll never hurt you again. It's over."

Voices outside, then a figure charged through the doorway.

Foley.

Straddling Fletcher's body, Hank met Foley's eyes over his stepson's head, watching to see what the deputy marshal would do and wondering if he would have to fight this man as well. No one was taking Charlie away from him.

Foley's dark gaze dropped to the body on the floor then back up to meet Hank's. "Christ, man, what have you done?"

Hank tightened his grip on the child in his arms. "I protected my son."

"You've complicated everything," Foley shot back. "This is why I didn't want you to have a gun. Goddamn civilians."

"I didn't use a gun."

"Christ." Foley stomped to the door of the shed, gave assurances to the men gathered outside and told them to stay put, then stomped back. "I ought to arrest you right now," he said in a furious voice.

Charlie lifted his tear-streaked face and glared at the deputy marshal. "You better not. It was him who shot at Papa-Hank."

Foley opened his mouth, then closed it. He knelt to examine Fletcher's body. "I wish you had used a gun," he muttered, watching Fletcher's head flop on his shattered neck when he tried to roll him over. "Be easier to explain than this." He let Fletcher flop back and rose.

"Hennessey's still out there," Hank said. "He's still after my wife."

Foley gave him a sneer of disgust. "And you're going after him, I suppose."

Hank looked at him.

"Can you at least wait for me to gather a posse?"

Hank continued to look at him.

"Christ, man, it's night. You can't ride out in the dark."

Foley was right, Hank realized in frustration. He might make it on his own, but not with Charlie. And he wouldn't leave the boy behind. "First light then. And I don't need a posse."

"Christ." Foley waved a hand in dismissal. "Go on then. Take your son and get the hell out of here before I shoot you myself."

Twenty-three

MOLLY WATCHED BRADY STUMBLE FROM THE doorway. “Brady, wait!” she called.

He didn’t answer.

She heard his footfalls pound down the staircase and wanted to go after him, but she couldn’t leave until she’d tended the baby and finished with Jessica. Tamping back her worry, she bent to the task at hand.

Before cutting the umbilical cord and handing the second infant to Consuelo to be cleaned up, Molly made certain the first baby had an identifying strip of ribbon tied around his ankle so they would know who was firstborn.

The afterbirth emerged intact, but still Jessica bled. Growing concerned, Molly did a pelvic examination and saw that the breech birth had caused damage to the cervical opening into the womb. It didn't appear serious, and Molly was able to quickly stitch it up while Jessica remained asleep or in a faint—she wasn't sure which—and that worried her too.

Sadly, there would be no more babies for Jessica. She might conceive, but she would never be able to carry a fetus past the third month, much less to full term. A blessing, really. Assuming Jessica made a full recovery after this delivery, and Molly could see no reason why she shouldn't even with the damage caused by the breech, the fact that she wouldn't be subjected to this ordeal year after year, as many women were, ensured she would lead a much longer, healthier life.

Working with brisk efficiency, Molly and Consuelo washed Jessica and changed her gown, put fresh linens on the bed, then tidied the room before Jessica awoke. When she did, Molly was relieved to see she was suffering nothing beyond the normal weariness one might expect after a difficult delivery.

She and Consuelo brought her sons to her. It was an emotional moment for Molly and a joyful departure from her previous sickroom experiences. All three women wept happy, exhausted tears over Jessica's perfect little babies and the miracle in which they had all taken part.

"Where's Brady?" Jessica asked after she had relinquished her sons to Consuelo to be returned to the cradle they shared for now. "I thought he would be here."

Molly did too. "I'll fetch him. But first there are some things I need to discuss with you." Sitting by Jessica's side, Molly quietly told her about the damage to her womb, and that there shouldn't, and probably wouldn't, be more babies. She suggested Jessica find a wet nurse to supplement the feedings and to help with their care, since twins could take an exhausting toll on a new mother. And finally, she said that because the birthing had been somewhat difficult, Jessica would be sore, and as long as she wasn't feeding the twins herself,

Molly would be able to give her laudanum to help with the pain if Jessica felt she needed it.

Jessica listened without interrupting. When Molly had finished, she thought for a moment, then said, "No more babies?"

"You shouldn't, Jessica. If you do conceive, you wouldn't be able to carry it full term." Realizing she was damning her friend to a future of conceiving babies only to lose them, Molly quickly added, "But there are ways to prevent conception. If you're interested and when you're ready, we can discuss them if you'd like."

"Yes." Blinking hard, Jessica looked over at the cradle in the corner.

Feeling the sting of sympathetic tears, Molly reached out and took Jessica's hand in her own. "I'm so sorry, Jessica. I wish I could have prevented it."

Jessica turned back with a tremulous smile. "No. You did everything you could." She gave Molly's hand a weak squeeze. "I thank God for you, Molly. And I thank you for what you've done here. I owe you my life, and my sons' lives."

"You owe me nothing, Jessica. You're my family now."

Jessica nodded. "Yes. Family. I'm so glad you see us that way. And how lucky we are that you're now a part of it." Releasing Molly's hand, she took a bracing breath, signaling a move to a less emotional subject. "You did a masterful job keeping Brady under control. However did you manage it?"

"I simply told him to stay out of my way. More or less."

"Ah. Well, he'll be beside himself. Twin sons. Every man's dream." She chuckled, then winced at the pull to her sore abdominal muscles. "No doubt he'll try to give you something. I'd guess a horse. Or perhaps two, since he has two sons."

Reminded of how stricken Brady had looked when he left the room earlier, Molly rose. "I'll get him now. I know he's anxious to see you." Hurrying from the room, she went to the hall overlooking the main room and looked over the railing. She didn't see him. He wasn't upstairs when she checked the nursery either. After giving the children the news of the two new additions to the family, she left them with the Garcias and went back downstairs.

Dougal awaited her at the bottom of the

stairs. "'Tis done, then?" he asked, tears brimming in his eyes. "My wee lass is gone?"

"Gone?" Molly stopped and stared at him. "Do you mean *dead*?"

Dougal flinched at the word.

"Of course she's not," Molly said indignantly. "Where would you get such an idea?" *Brady.* Molly sighed with impatience. The man was determined to believe the worst. "She is not dead," she told Dougal in a firm voice. "She is doing wonderfully, although understandably tired after giving birth to two healthy sons."

Dougal gave her an owly look. "A-Alive? My lass is alive?"

"Very much so. In fact, you can go up and see for yourself while I go hunt down her nitwit of a husband. Do you know where he is?"

"His office," Dougal called back, already halfway up the stairs.

She found Brady sitting in one of the chairs by the cold fireplace.

The room was a mess, as if a strong wind had blown through. Or an overwrought man. Even that nasty stuffed bear was tipped onto its side. Brady sat hunched over, hands gripping his head, his long fingers threaded through his dark hair. He didn't look up when she entered.

Closing the door behind her, she stood for a moment, waiting for him to notice her. When he finally lifted his head, she was shocked by the anguish on his face.

"She's dead, isn't she?" he asked in a ragged voice.

"No." She walked toward him. "No, Brady, she's not. She's fine."

He blinked at her.

"If you hadn't run off so quickly, you would have seen that." She stopped before him, overwhelmed with affection for this outrageous, foolish, distraught man. "You really are the big dolt she says you are, aren't you?"

He let his hands fall to his thighs and slowly sat back. "But—But I—you were crying—she was so still, and her eyes were closed and—"

"Resting. That's all." Seeing the sudden paleness of his face, she knelt beside his chair and put her hand on his arm to keep him from trying to stand. "She's fine, Brady. Tired, but fine."

She felt tremors move through his arm,

heard the rush of air as he took in great gulping breaths. "S-She's all right?"

"Yes. I swear it."

He seemed to deflate into the chair. "Jesus—I thought—" More tremors. He tipped his head back and blinked up at the ceiling. "Sweet Jesus."

Molly continued to hold his arm while she waited for him to pull himself together. It was both unsettling and touching to see him in such a distraught state. Men like Brady rarely showed such emotion. Or love.

After a moment, he lowered his gaze from the rafters and gave her the piercing stare that had once chilled the marrow in her bones. "Tell me again," he said in a shaky voice. "Tell me she's all right."

"She's all right."

She saw the words penetrate. It was like watching him reinflate until relief burst out of him in an eruption of emotion.

"Jesus Christ, Molly! Why the hell didn't you say so? I look in there and see her—Jesus—you were crying—all that blood—sonofabitch!" He took a deep breath, let it out, took another. "Why the hell were you crying if everything was all right?"

"I was happy for her. For you. For your sons."

"Women. Jesus." He dragged a shaking hand over his face, took another deep breath, and let it out in a huff. His face regained some of its color. "Don't ever do that to me again. No more crying without good reason."

"I had reason."

Bluster dissolved in a wobbly grin. "Sons? Two of them?"

"Two. Both beautiful and healthy."

His gaze settled on hers, and in that instant all his masks fell away, and Molly saw past the taunting sneers, the chilling glares, and the outraged ranting to the vulnerable man beneath. In all the years of her life she had never seen such a look of love and relief and humble joy. "You helped her. I owe you for that."

"You owe me nothing. She's my friend."

"A horse. Maybe one of High Roller's foals out of Her Ladyship. A filly."

Molly refrained from rolling her eyes. "Hank's already given me a horse." But a baby would be nice, she thought. Hank's, not Brady's, of course. With dark chocolate eyes and a smile to melt hearts and—

"I have to go." Brady stood so abruptly, he almost knocked her over. He took two steps toward the door, stopped, and whipped around. "It's okay? I can see her now?"

Pushing herself to her feet, Molly made a shooing motion. "Go. She's asking for you."

After he'd left, she sank into the chair he had vacated, feeling suddenly exhausted and empty and unaccountably alone.

She wanted Hank.

She wanted his arms around her.

She wanted him to love her the way Brady loved Jessica.

MOVING QUIETLY SO HE WOULDN'T DISTURB THE babies, Brady stepped into the dimly lit room.

Jessica was asleep and Consuelo sat in a rocker in the corner, holding one of his sons. When she heard Brady, she looked up with a wide, gap-toothed grin and held the infant out.

Brady gently took his child into his arms. He looked like a wizened old man who had cooked in the sun too long. "Which one?" he asked in a whisper.

Consuelo held up two fingers.

Brady smiled down at his youngest son. "Hello, Thomas Jefferson."

Thomas Jefferson stuck out his tongue and made a smacking noise.

"You think it's too big a name to carry around? Then how about we call you TJ for short? Is that better?"

TJ yawned.

"All right then." Returning the infant to Consuelo, Brady bent over the cradle where his oldest son slept. "And hello to you, too, Samuel Thornton."

Sam made no response.

Feeling an embarrassing surge of emotion, Brady straightened and glanced at Consuelo. He tipped his head toward his wife and raised his brows in question.

Consuelo smiled and nodded in understanding. She placed TJ in the cradle beside his older brother, then tiptoed quietly from the room. After the door closed behind her, Brady walked to the bed.

Jessica was asleep, curled on her side like a child. Despite the purple shadows beneath her eyes, she was as beautiful as he'd ever seen her. Love swelled inside him—too much for his chest to hold—too much for his mind to comprehend. He felt raw and ragged and diminished by the force of it. Easing quietly into the chair beside the bed, he studied his wife's face. A sense of peace and contentment washed over him, a gentle grace that he had never known until Jessica had blundered into his turbulent life. "Thank you," he whispered to God, to Jessica, to Molly.

Her eyes blinked open. "Brady?"

"I'm here."

Her lips trembled on a half-smile. "But I want you here." She reached behind her hip and patted the coverlet at her back. "I want you close."

Needing no further encouragement, he quickly pulled off his boots and moved around to slide in on the other side of the narrow bed. Slipping one arm beneath her neck, he looped the other around her waist and gently tucked her against his chest.

The feel of her heart beating beneath his hand brought tears to his eyes. "I love you, Jessica," he whispered into her hair.

"I love you too."

"But I'm never touching you again."

"You're touching me now."

"Don't be sassy. I'm never touching you, you know, that way."

She tipped her head back to study him over her shoulder. "Why not?"

He kissed the tip of her freckled nose. "I can't go through this again."

She turned back. "Poor dear."

He heard her smile. "I mean it, Jessica. I almost lost you with Abigail and then again today. I can't do it. The little ones depend on me. They need me. And if I lost you, I couldn't go on. I couldn't do what I have to for them."

"It would be rather inconvenient for you, I suppose."

"Don't mock me, Jessica. That's not what I meant and you know it."

She patted his arm. "I know. But I assure you I have no intention of dying anytime soon."

"You better not."

They lay quietly for a time. Jessica relaxed against him, comforted by his warmth, his heartbeat against her back, his breath against her hair. She wondered if now would be the time to tell him there would be no more babies. It was a private pain, one she needed to come to terms with on her own before she shared it with her husband. But he seemed to need peace, and if this would give it to him, she would speak now.

"I don't think it will be a problem, Brady," she finally said. "Molly told me there was some tearing, some damage to the womb."

She felt his body tense. "Are you all right?"

"Yes," she quickly assured him. "But she doesn't think there will be any more babies." She felt him go still, then the tension slowly eased from his arms. But he didn't speak, which was wise of him, for how could a man ever know the loss a woman felt when something as elemental as her ability to bear children was suddenly taken away. Not that she yearned to have more children—especially after today—but knowing she couldn't even if she wanted to . . . well, it changed her, diminished her in some subtle, indefinable way. "It's quite sad, really," she said after a while. Sad for her, for him, for the babies who would never be.

His arms tightened around her. She felt his lips move against her hair. "I'm sorry, Jessica."

She closed her eyes against a sudden sting of tears. "I'm sorry too."

Just hearing and saying those words, and acknowledging this change in their lives, somehow eased her feeling of loss. "I so love the babies you've given me," she murmured as her eyes fluttered closed.

"Not as much as I loved giving them to you."

Smiling, she drifted into sleep.

THAT EVENING, ONCE SHE HAD ASSURED HERself that the new mother was doing well and there would be no immediate complications—and hopefully none later either—Molly allowed Brady to move Jessica from the birthing room to the comfort of her own bedroom. Once she was settled in and had partaken of a light meal, Jessica left her in Brady's care while she supervised setting up the nursery in the adjoining bedroom.

Consuelo, bless her, had already arranged for another Garcia—Pilar, this one was named, and cousin to Lupe and Maria—to be available as a wet nurse. She also introduced Molly to Grandmother Oona, an ex-slave who had a gift with infants and who would be delighted to stay with the babies as long as she was needed.

Satisfied everything was in hand, Molly helped Lupe and Maria put the other children down for the night, then called Buddy and went down to her own room.

She was utterly exhausted. But in a wonderful way. As she relaxed in a steaming bath, she thought about what an exciting, hectic, rewarding day it had been. And surprisingly, not once had she felt queasy or panicky about what she was doing. She hadn't doubted herself or her skills, and was proud of what she had accomplished. Perhaps she was becoming a healer after all.

To stave off the loneliness of sleeping another night in her empty, oversized bed, Molly allowed Buddy to share it. Yawning, she closed her eyes, and with Buddy tucked tight against her back, and thoughts of Hank drifting through her mind, she sank into a deep, dreamless sleep.

Later—she didn't know how long—she awoke to an odd sound. She lay listening for a moment, then realized it was Buddy, whining and clawing at the French door onto the balcony porch. "You can't go out there," she muttered around a yawn as she rose and pulled on her robe. "You have to go downstairs."

As soon as she opened the bedroom door, the dog raced down the hall, his nails clicking on the wood floor. Molly went downstairs to let him out the entry door, but found him scratching frantically at the door by the fireplace instead.

"All right, all right," she told the whining dog as she crossed into the great room to let him out onto the back porch. The moment she opened the door, he was off like a shot. Almost immediately, she heard his frenzied barking along the back corner of the house. Realizing this wouldn't be a quick trip to relieve himself, and unwilling to stand at the door until he vanquished whatever mouse or stray cat had distracted him, she decided to go check on Jessica.

Brady answered the door in his unions. He looked disoriented and groggy, his dark hair poking out every which way, as if he'd been caught in a stiff wind.

"I came to check on Jessica."

He blinked at her.

"Your wife."

He dragged a hand over his face, then frowned. "What's all that racket?"

"Buddy. How's Jessica?"

"Asleep."

"Has she been restless? Feverish? Experiencing pain?"

"Ah . . ." That befuddled look again.

Molly wondered how long the man had gone without sleep before tonight. Pushing past him, she went to the bed and studied Jessica.

She seemed to be resting peacefully. There was no flush of fever and her brow felt cool to the touch. "Has she taken any water?" she asked quietly when Brady came to stand beside her.

"Twice."

"Has she used the chamber pot?"

"Once, I think. Maybe twice. Check with Consuelo."

"Have either of you noticed any excessive bleeding?"

His befuddled look became one of alarm. "Bleeding?"

Realizing he was near useless, she patted his arm. "Call me if you notice anything unusual."

"Why would she be bleeding?"

"It's normal. But if it's excessive, call me. Good night, Brady."

"Jesus."

After letting Buddy back in at the front door, she went up to her bedroom.

The dog still seemed agitated, and ran around the room several times as if trying to flush out his adversary. After checking the French door, the dressing room, the water closet, and the French door again, he finally came back to bed. But he didn't settle in as calmly as before, and when Molly drifted to sleep, he was still awake, sitting vigil at the foot of the bed.

HANK COULDN'T WAIT FOR FIRST LIGHT, AND A full hour before dawn, he and Charlie and the three RosaRoja ranch hands rode out of Val Rosa.

He hadn't slept at all, alternately berating himself for leaving Molly without knowing for sure Hennessey wouldn't show up, and pacing impatiently as he waited for enough light so they could leave.

Now that they were on their way, he worked hard to hold himself in check so he didn't wear out the horses before they were halfway there. Dawn came with low clouds looming behind them that hinted at a snow squall moving up fast. Hank exchanged a glance with Langley, and they both pushed the horses a little harder, hoping to outrun the storm.

Hank was proud of the way Charlie held up to the fast pace. After that grisly scene in the shed, he'd been worried about the boy. But Charlie seemed to have handled it well, and had slept through the night without any night terrors, so maybe he would be able to put this behind him as Molly hoped.

Molly.

Just the thought of Hennessey getting his hands on her made Hank's stomach roll. The idea of losing her so soon after he'd found her was intolerable to him. He couldn't—wouldn't—imagine a future without her smirky smile and healing touch and forgiving spirit there to bring sense to his life.

As soon as he saw her, he would give her the words she wanted. He didn't know why he'd held them back—held a part of himself back. He loved her. He was sure of it. This terrible, awful, worrisome feeling couldn't be anything but love.

But telling her that and admitting how deep his feelings for her were, well, that would change everything. She would own all of him then. Somehow he would have to find a way to live with that. He didn't think it would be too hard.

They were two hours out of Val Rosa and still over an hour from home when the storm caught up with them and the snow began to fall.

"AUNT MOLLY?"

Rousing from a deep sleep, Molly stared up into Penny's face. It took her a moment to realize the child was crying. Instantly awake, she sat up. "What's wrong?"

Penny held out her doll. "Her hands fell off."

Blinking in confusion, Molly looked at the doll, then around the room. It was full light. Buddy was gone and someone had set a fire in the hearth.

"I think maybe the monster did it," Penny said, wiping her nose with the sleeve of her flannel gown.

Molly pushed a tangle of hair out of her eyes and kicked the covers off. "There is no monster," she said as she rose. "What time is it?"

"I don't know. I can't tell time yet. Can

you find them for me? Miss Apple can't hold her parasol without her hands."

Molly pulled on her robe, then bent to pull her slippers from under the edge of the bed. Stepping into them, she yawned and pushed back a tangle of hair from her brow. "You named your doll Miss Apple?"

"Smell her." Penny lifted the doll up toward Molly's face. "Doesn't she smell like apples? At least, she used to."

Molly drew back as a sharp scent filled her nostrils. Not apples. Cloves.

Cloves?

Her heartbeat quickened. She took the doll from Penny's hands and sniffed it again. Definitely cloves. Panic skittered through her mind. She studied the doll's arms where the hands had been attached. Only tiny snippets of thread remained. The hands hadn't fallen off, they'd been cut off.

Panic became full-fledged terror.

Hennessey!

Turning to Penny, she tried to keep her voice even. "Where are the hands?"

"I don't know. I think the monster took them when I was sleeping."

"Did you see him take them?"

"No, but I saw him pick up Miss Apple.

Then I got scared and closed my eyes so he wouldn't see me, and when I opened them again, he was gone and so were Miss Apple's hands." Penny let out a huff of impatience. "You have to get them back, Aunt Molly. She can't wear her gloves without them."

"Y-Yes . . . we'll find them." Molly clutched at the foot rail, her knees so weak she feared they might buckle beneath her. She had to find Brady and tell him. They had to check the house—every room, every closet and cupboard. They had to—

Oh God . . .

She looked frantically around the room, remembering Buddy's odd behavior the night before. Had Hennessey been in here too? Was he still here? The thought was so horrifying, she almost grabbed Penny and fled, screaming, from the room.

Then she saw the two small bits of china sitting on her bureau. Miss Apple's hands. Too high for Penny to have put there. Too carefully arranged on top of the small slip of paper to be a random act. A message for her. Terrified that he might still be somewhere in the room watching, she gently nudged Penny toward the door, then almost shrieked when Maria Garcia suddenly appeared in the hallway. "Take Penny to Brady," she said, trying to keep her voice from betraying her fear.

"Why?" Penny asked.

"See if he has candy."

"Candy!" Penny shouted. Grabbing Maria's hand, she tugged her down the hall. "I know where he keeps peppermint!"

Molly closed the door, then heart pounding, her legs wobbling beneath her, she approached the bureau.

Under the severed doll hands was a note written in an elegantly feminine hand with all the pretentious flourishes one might expect from a man as demented and dramatic as Hennessey.

Time is up, Lovey. You know what I want.
Ride west.
I'll find you. Or that delicious little Penny.

Molly stared in disbelief at the note until her hands shook so badly she could no longer make out the words. He was still after them. He was out there somewhere waiting. And without the book to give him, there was no way she could stop him.

Oh God Oh God.

Her mind reeling, she thought frantically for a way out of this terrible quagmire she had dragged them all into. She couldn't go to Brady. He would ride out, and Hennessey would kill him. She couldn't wait for Hank—it might be too late. Even if every man on the ranch took out after him, Hennessey would see them long before they knew where he was. He would simply fade away, and they would never find him, and she would never know where he was, or when he would strike.

And one by one he would calmly and coldly kill off everyone she loved.

Dear heaven. What have I done?

Panic engulfed her. Her heart pounded so hard she thought she might faint. *No!* she chided herself. *Think! You have to think of a way to stop him!*

After a moment, the terror faded enough that she could think again. She paced back and forth, her mind racing with thoughts, plans, ideas. He was out there somewhere, waiting for her to bring the book . . . which meant he couldn't still be here in the house . . . which meant for a while, at least, everyone here was safe. But for how long?

What would he do if she didn't bring him the book as he'd demanded?

He would come back. He would start hurting people—the children—Hank.

She couldn't let that happen. There was only one way to stop him, she realized in despair. And only she could get close enough to him to do it.

Grimly determined, Molly went to her medicine satchel and gathered what she would need.

Twenty-four

WHEN HANK LED CHARLIE AND HIS MEN PAST the sheltering walls of Blue Mesa and down toward the home valley, the wind hit them with a vengeance. The storm was full upon them now, snow stinging their faces and piling up in deep, powdery drifts that churned around the horses' legs. Visibility dropped to less than ten feet, and landmarks began to disappear.

Hank had the men string a rope between riders so no one would wander from the trail and find themselves cut off from the others. Fearing Charlie might fall off and no one would notice, he took him up behind him, covering him with his duster and anchoring him with a rope around his waist. He could feel the small body shivering against his back and cursed himself for dragging the boy along.

But what else could he have done? He wouldn't have left him behind any more than he would have been willing to wait around on the hopes that the storm would end soon. Molly could be in trouble. He needed to get back and make sure she was safe. At least the snow might work in their favor and keep Hennessey holed up until they could get back to the ranch. Hank wouldn't even consider that he might already be too late.

They moved at a snail's pace as the snow grew deeper. Worried they might drift from the road and tumble into one of the dry arroyos that cut through the valley, Hank called a stop to confer with Langley, who knew this country almost as well as he did. "Stay low or go high?" Hank yelled.

Langley looked around, trying to gauge the direction and strength of the wind.

If they went high along the edge of the valley and next to the tree line, they might get some protection from the wind. They would also be better able to gauge their direction, since the trees ran in pretty much a straight line. But it would take longer, and the horses were already suffering. And if the visibility stayed poor, they could ride right past the ranch and never see it. Plus, there was always the danger of stumbling into a gully they couldn't see through the snow.

If they stayed low on the flats and rode parallel to the tree-lined creek that cut down the middle of the valley, it would be faster and lead straight to the house—as long as they didn't lose sight of the creek and didn't come across an arroyo hidden under the snow. It was some comfort that the flakes weren't coming as furiously as before and weren't as large. Maybe the worst of the storm had passed on ahead of them, and they would only have to suffer the tail end of it the rest of the way to the ranch.

"I say low," Langley yelled after a moment. "I trust Droop to keep us on trail. He'll get us home."

Droop was Langley's horse, a trail-wise old gelding with a reputation for levelheadedness. It was an indication of how desperate their situation was that they would depend on an old cow horse's sense of direction to get them home before they all froze to death.

Hank waved Langley forward. "Take the lead. I'll take drag." And falling in behind the last rider, Hank took up the trailing end of the guide rope as they rode down into the valley.

MOLLY THOUGHT THE HARDEST PART WOULD BE getting a horse. But the worker in the barn, another Garcia cousin, was young and inexperienced and no match for her determination. It also helped that the language differences precluded lengthy explanations. Apparently he was concerned about the weather, but once she'd assured him she only intended to take a short ride and would stay within sight of the house, he reluctantly saddled the horse she had ridden to Redemption after the cave-in.

After checking her right pocket to be sure the glass stopper in the medicine vial was secure, and checking her left for the syringe, she reined away from the morning sun and toward the bank of low clouds moving up the valley from the west. As she rode, she memorized landmarks, knowing if clouds obscured the sun, distant ridges might be her only guides. Luckily, since they hadn't had snow in over a week, the road was packed down and easy to follow. But it was hard riding into the wind, and before she had gone a mile, tiny ice pellets began hitting her in the face. Pulling the hood of the shearling coat Hank had given her tighter around her head, she rode steadily west, wondering how long before Hennessey found her, and when he did, would her plan work.

She might not have to execute it. If he'd been in Mexico for the last month, Hennessey might not be aware that Fletcher had been arrested and the book was now in the hands of the deputy U.S. marshal.

But if he did know, why was he still after her?

And if he didn't know, why would he believe anything she told him?

No matter how many ways she looked at it, it all came down to one thing: If Hennessey showed up, she would have to do what she must. There was no one else to stop him but her.

After a while, ice pellets turned into fluffy

snow that danced and swirled in the wind. The sun had disappeared, and the sky was such a uniform gray, landmarks were fast disappearing behind a veil of white. When the road curved to the south, she stayed right, hoping she was still headed west as she rode on into trackless snow.

An hour passed, and as the snow continued to fall, a new fear gripped her. What if she missed him and he thought she wasn't coming? What if he—

A clatter behind her, then suddenly a horse lunged up out of the ground. Not out of the ground, but out of a gully she hadn't even noticed in the thickening snow.

In her fright, she jerked her horse around so abruptly he almost lost his footing on the snow-covered rocks at the edge of the gully. By the time she got him settled, Hennessey was beside her, his horse headed in the opposite direction along her left side, his hand gripping the reins of her horse. He was so close she could smell his sickly sweet perfume, feel his knee digging into hers.

"Hello, lovey," he said, his reptilian voice barely audible through the muffler that covered the lower half of his face. "Miss me?"

"Fletcher's been arrested," she blurted out. "There's no need to pursue this."

"Fletcher's a fool." Tipping his head to the side, he studied her. "Where's the book, lovey? Will you hand it over, or must I come get it?"

She motioned to the scarf, needing him to lower it and expose as much of his face as possible. "I can't hear you. What did you say?"

In a quick, furious motion he struck out, catching her just below the eye.

With a cry of surprise, she rocked back, almost tumbling out of the saddle as her horse shied.

Hennessey gave a vicious yank on her gelding's reins, then held him fast until he settled back down. He glared at Molly. "Do. You. Have. It?"

She blinked at him, a hand on her cheek, her ears ringing from the blow. As she struggled to gather her thoughts, she noted the scarf had slipped down almost to his chin.

He drew back his arm.

"Yes! Yes, I have it." As she spoke, she reached into her right pocket and felt for the vial that held the solution of carbolic acid and chloroform.

"No tricks, lovey," he warned, his eyes narrow and crafty. "Or I'll do things to you that you could never even imagine in that empty little head of yours."

"N-No. I've got it. It's right here." Thumbing the stopper loose, she gripped the vial tight in her gloved hand.

"Then let's have it, lovey." He let go of her horse's bridle and held out his hand. "I'm out of patience."

She jerked the bottle from her pocket and swept her arm in an arc, slinging the caustic contents over her mount's head and his horse's rump and directly into Hennessey's face.

Hennessey screamed and clawed at his eyes. His horse reared. Cursing and reeling in the saddle, Hennessey grabbed for the reins as the animal's back hooves slipped on the icy rocks at the edge of the drop-off. For an instant the terrified horse hung in the air, front legs flailing, then it toppled backward. Molly heard a scream that could have been from the horse or the rider. Then a clattering cascade of falling rocks.

Frightened by the sudden commotion, Molly's gelding hopped and lunged. Fearing he would lose his footing, too, Molly fought desperately to bring him under control. When finally he stood shivering, his sides pumping, his breath steaming in the cold air, Molly was shaking so badly she could hardly hold on to the reins.

She gave him a moment more, then turned the gelding toward a cluster of low scrub. Dismounting onto wobbly legs, she tied his reins to a sage bush, then stood for a moment, listening. All she heard was her horse's labored breathing and her own pulse thudding in her ears. After checking to be sure she still had the syringe of laudanum in her left coat pocket, she moved cautiously to the edge of the drop-off and peered down.

The gully was bigger than she had expected. Maybe forty feet across and almost that many feet deep. The sides were steep and littered with boulders and loose snow-covered rocks. Both Hennessey and his horse lay motionless at the bottom.

The horse's neck was at an impossible angle. Several yards past it, Hennessey lay sprawled on his back, arms spread. Even through the drifting snow, she could see that he had several cuts on his head and face. One of the head wounds bled so profusely she knew his heart was still beating. She sat for a time, watching him, but saw no movement, and he never opened his eyes.

She should leave, get Brady and bring him back to dispose of this vermin.

But what if Hennessey regained consciousness while she was gone and was waiting in ambush when they returned?

Or she could leave and hope he never woke up and froze to death in the snow.

And if he lived?

No. It would be intolerable not knowing for sure that Hennessey was dead and no longer a threat. She couldn't live in endless fear, wondering if and when he would show up again.

This had to end now.

And she had to be the one to do it.

God help me.

On trembling legs, she started down into the gully.

THE WORST OF THE STORM HAD PASSED ON TO the east by the time Hank spotted the arched gate rising out of the snow ahead. Relieved, he spurred his tired horse toward the house. But relief quickly faded when he saw the horses and riders milling in the yard and his brother shouting orders from the porch.

As they rode up, Brady charged down the steps to meet them. "Molly's gone."

Hank rocked back in the saddle, the words striking him with the force of a blow. "Gone where?"

Before Brady could answer, Penny slammed out of the house, waving her doll. "Papa-Hank, Papa-Hank! Aunt Molly was supposed to find where the monster put Miss Apple's hands, but now she's gone and will you find them for me?"

Monster? "Hennessey?" Hank stared in growing horror at Penny, then Brady, then the empty expanse stretching in all directions. Had he come too late?

Brady frowned up at him. "Hennessey? I thought he was long gone. I thought Fletcher—"

"Fletcher's dead. And he wasn't the one who hired him." Hank's mind spun in circles. He couldn't think. Couldn't catch his breath.

Gone where? When? Christ!

Brady yelled at someone to bring a fresh horse, then helped Charlie dismount. "Take him and Penny to Consuelo," he told one of the men standing by the porch. "And have her send out coffee and food."

"We don't have time for that!" Hank swung stiffly from the saddle. How could his brother even think of food while Molly was out there lost? Or worse.

"You're frozen," Brady argued. "If you hope to stay in the saddle, you better get something warm in your belly."

"Where could she be?" Hank demanded. "Have you sent trackers?"

"Miley and Hench found a trail heading west. One rider, shod horse. They think it's one of ours. They'll follow it and we'll follow them, unless we find reason not to."

Hank knew they wouldn't be able to follow it far. The snow would have covered her tracks within minutes. "Was she alone?"

Brady nodded. "One of the Garcia boys saddled her horse. He says he told her not to go, that it would snow soon, but she said she was only going for a short ride and would stay close to the house. At least that's what he thinks she said. He's not that good with English, and she's got no Spanish."

"Christ." Hank studied the rolling valley,

scanning for something dark moving against all that white. Not even cows marred the starkness of the new snow, no doubt waiting out the squall in the shelter of the trees spilling out of the canyons.

He had just ridden in from the northwest. He must have cut across her trail without even knowing it. The thought of being so close made him want to shout in frustration. "Damnit! Why would she ride off like that?"

"Maybe she just wanted some fresh air. She's had a rough couple of days."

Hank looked at his brother.

A reluctant smile creased Brady's face. "The babies came. Twin boys."

"Already? Is everybody all right?"

Brady nodded. "But it was another breech. Without Molly, I don't think Jessica or the second baby would have made it. Thank God she was here." He made a show of looking around. "Especially since it appears you forgot to bring Doc."

"I didn't wait for him, but he's on his way."

Hank scanned the valley again. He remembered how Molly told him that after a bad day in surgery she would find a high place to scream the tension away. Maybe that's what she'd done. Maybe she'd just gone out for some fresh air and had lost her bearings when the squall came through. Maybe she was on her way home right now.

Or maybe Hennessey already had her.

The thought sent such fear through Hank for a moment he felt light-headed.

"Here," Brady said, holding out the food and hot coffee Consuelo had sent.

Hank choked down what he could until the Garcia kid brought his fresh horse. A leggy bay with a hard mouth and cantankerous attitude, but a stride that could cover ground fast.

He was still chewing when he swung up into the saddle and headed west.

SLIPPING AND SLIDING OVER THE SNOW-COVERED rocks, Molly carefully worked her way to the bottom of the gully. The wind wasn't as strong below the rim, and although the snow continued to fall, it had changed from fluffy to small, denser flakes almost like sleet. It was so cold it didn't immediately melt when it landed on Hennessey or the horse.

Hennessey still hadn't moved.

Standing at a distance, Molly studied him, trying to assess his condition. He was breathing, and she could see he was still bleeding, but it had slowed somewhat in the cold. His eyes remained closed and showed little movement even when the snow landed on his closed lids. She moved cautiously forward. Just out of arm's reach, she stopped and scanned for weapons.

She saw a scabbard tied to the saddle on the horse, but she wasn't that familiar with rifles. Two belt buckles showed beneath the flap of Hennessey's coat. She assumed one was a gun belt. Watching him for the slightest movement, she flipped back the coat, yanked the pistol from the holster, then jumped back.

He didn't move.

She studied the gun. A revolver like Papa's. Pulling the hammer to the half-cocked position, she checked the open back of the cylinder and saw that five of the six chambers were capped, with one empty chamber beneath the firing pin. She eased the hammer back down, then slipped the gun into the pocket of her coat.

Hennessey still hadn't moved.

Bending, she checked his other hip. No

second holster. She opened his coat to see if he wore any other guns or knives, but found none. Letting the coat fall closed, she rose and studied his body for other injuries.

From the angle of his right foot, she thought his lower leg or ankle might be broken. She nudged it.

No reaction.

Moving back out of reach, she sat on her heels, her shoulders hunched against the stinging snow, and tried to decide what to do. She couldn't leave him. Not alive anyway. But she didn't know if she could kill him either. If he threatened her, yes. But an unarmed, unconscious man? She didn't know. She was a healer. Not a killer. And even though she hadn't been allowed to take the Hippocratic Oath like a real doctor, Papa had drilled every word into her memory and had made her promise to abide by its principles to the best of her ability.

First, do no harm.

But neither of them had anticipated Hennessey.

Molly shivered as the cold wind seeped through the wool interfacing of her shearling coat. Even in heavy gloves, her hands were starting to go numb, and her toes ached with a vengeance despite the fleece lining of her boots. She had to make a decision soon, or they would both freeze to death. She had read that freezing wasn't an unpleasant way to die, but she had no intention of finding out firsthand.

How long before Hennessey stopped breathing? How long could she wait?

Somewhere out on the flats a coyote howled. Then another, and another. The sound was eerie in the silence and made the nerves prickle under her skin. They would smell the blood. Or a cougar would. Or wolves. They would come as soon as it grew dark. Maybe sooner.

She couldn't wait. She had to do something now.

She rose, then almost fell backward in fright when she saw Hennessey's eyes were open. Fumbling in her pocket, she pulled out the gun, thumbed back the hammer so that a live round rested beneath the firing pin, and pointed the barrel at him.

He groaned. His lids fluttered closed.

She waited, the gun bobbing in her hands, her breath fogging the air.

His eyes opened again. Blinking against the tiny snowflakes peppering his face, he scanned an erratic arc without moving his head until his gaze found hers.

"Lovey."

She watched, the pistol aimed at his face, waiting to see what he would do.

He just lay there, blinking groggily at her. Other than his eyes, he still hadn't moved.

"Are you hurt?" she finally asked.

"My . . . head."

"Anywhere else?"

"My face. Eyes. What did you do to me, bitch?"

Stepping closer, she nudged the leg she thought might be broken.

He didn't react.

"Can you move?"

A frown crossed his face. Then a grimace. With obvious effort he lifted his head an inch off the ground, then groaned and let it fall back. "What . . . happened?"

She lowered the pistol but kept it cocked. "Your horse fell on you. I think your back is broken."

She watched that sink in. She sensed his efforts to move and his growing fear when he couldn't. He started breathing hard and fast and a look of sheer terror crossed his scarred face. “Do something. You’re a healer. Do something!”

She uncocked the pistol and slipped it back into her pocket. “No.”

His eyes widened until white showed all around his dark irises. Air hissed through his bared yellow teeth. “You have to! You have to help me!”

“No, I don’t.” Dropping onto her heels, Molly folded her arms across her knees and looked at him. “You killed my father,” she said in a voice that sounded distant and flat even in her own ear. “You hurt me. You threatened my family. You don’t deserve to live.”

“Damn you, bitch! Do something!”

“No.” Molly rose.

On the flats, the coyotes howled again. More this time. Closer. She looked down at the monster sprawled at her feet. “Do you hear that, *lovey*? They’re coming for you. I’d start praying if I were you.” She turned and started up the slope.

“No! You can’t leave me!” Hennessey tried to scream, but his damaged voice made it sound like a dying gasp.

She kept climbing.

He kept screaming.

She tried not to listen.

"Shoot me, at least! Don't let them eat me alive!"

She stopped and looked back, hating him, wanting him to suffer, relishing the vengeful satisfaction that coursed through her. "You won't feel it. Your nerves are damaged. Except for the tugging and the sounds, you won't even know. But while it's happening, think about all the people you've hurt and the lives you've taken. Think about my father." She started walking again.

"They'll tear me apart!"

She climbed on, her breathing harsh and loud.

"Please . . . oh, God . . . help me."

Unable to stop herself, she looked back.

He was weeping now. Staring blindly up at the snowy sky, a broken wreck of a man who was already half-dead.

She felt herself weaken and fought against it. *This is what he deserves. This is what Papa deserves.*

"Kill me," he begged in his raspy voice. "It's what you want. Just do it."

She didn't realize she was crying until she felt the cold wetness on her cheeks. Papa's face loomed in her mind.

First, do no harm.

Then what? she wanted to shout. *I can't fix him and I can't kill him, so what am I supposed to do?*

The wind soughed.

Beyond the rim, a coyote howled.

Below her, splayed like a supplicant before God, Hennessey sobbed.

"Damn you!" she shouted at Hennessey, at Papa, at herself. Then swiping a hand across her face, she turned and started back down into the gully.

TWO MILES PAST THE GATE, HANK SAW MILEY and Hench riding to meet them. Without Molly. Cursing under his breath, he pulled up to wait.

"Lost her tracks in the snow a mile up," Hench, the older of the two ranch hands, said when they stopped in front of Hank and Brady and the dozen riders crowding behind them. "Still headed west, far as we could tell."

"Found a second set of tracks along the

ridge line," Miley added. "Running parallel to the first."

"Like someone was following her?" Brady asked.

Hank's stomach knotted even tighter.

Miley shrugged. "Maybe. The tracks weren't from one of ours. Except for the one, all our horses are accounted for."

Hennessey.

Pushing aside his fear, Hank tried to guess what Molly was thinking. What was her destination? She wasn't familiar with this country. How would she know where to go? There was nothing in the direction she was headed for fifty miles or more. So what was she looking for?

The answer hit him. Not a destination—a direction. Her tracks had pointed steadily west until Hench and Miley lost them under the snow. Maybe she would continue on that heading until she found whatever she was looking for.

Or until whatever—or whoever—she was looking for found her.

"I'm riding west," he told Brady. "She started off that way and I'm guessing she's still on track."

"Then I'll follow the ridge, see if I can spot anything." Turning in the saddle, Brady told the riders behind him to split into pairs and spread out across the valley. "Stay in sight of each other," he cautioned. "Fire two rounds if you find her. Three if you need help."

Hank rode on, following the tracks Hench and Miley had laid until they stopped and turned back. Then he continued west through unmarked snow.

Even though more clouds were building in the west, the afternoon sun shone through misty breaks, reflecting off the snow in a blinding glare. If there was trouble waiting ahead, he wouldn't see it until he was on top of it. But he didn't slow.

Molly was out there somewhere. Maybe lost. Maybe hurt. She had no idea how quickly things could go bad in this country, whether it was Hennessey, a sudden storm, a drop-off hidden beneath the snow, or a hungry cougar on the prowl. She could be in trouble and not even know it. And with the sun dropping toward the mountains and more snow on the way, she was fast running out of time.

Memories assaulted him—her fierce

determination to save him when his arm got infected. Her blushes and reluctant smiles. The way her skin quivered under his questing hand and the little sounds she made when he moved inside her.

He quickened his pace, constantly scanning, stopping every now and then to listen. Sound carried a long way over unbroken ground, but he heard nothing, not even birdcalls or the distant bawling of cattle up in the canyons. Once he thought he heard coyotes up ahead, but it was so far away he couldn't be sure. He tried to use his vision and color deficiencies to help him see patterns in the snow or shadows where tracks had been before they'd been covered. But there was nothing.

As the sun dropped, fear began to erode his resolve. Molly filled his thoughts, her laughter echoing in his mind, her gentle spirit wrapping around his heart. He would find her. He would give her hell for causing him so much worry, then he would bring her back home where she belonged.

Maybe then he could breathe again.

The miles inched by, and the sun dropped lower. He bounced between anger that she had wandered off like this, and terror that he would never find her—or that Hennessey already had. But he doggedly kept riding because it was all he knew to do, and stopping would mean giving up, which would kill him.

Twenty-five

MOLLY STAYED AS LONG AS SHE COULD, NOT OUT of concern for Hennessey, but because she needed to know for certain that it was over.

She'd given him the full syringe, the largest dose of laudanum she'd ever administered. She didn't know if it was enough to kill, but it should put him out for a long time. Hopefully, until he froze to death. Or died of his injuries. Or the scavengers had done their work. She didn't care which. She just wanted him dead and the threat of him gone forever.

Pacing back and forth to stay warm and

keep blood flowing in her legs and feet, she waited for the drug to take effect. When his pulse finally slowed and his breathing grew shallow and his skin took on a grayish pallor, she turned and climbed back up the steep side of the gully.

It was hard going. She kept tripping on the long coat, and the rocks were unstable and slippery, and she was so chilled her muscles felt stiff and sluggish. By the time she reached the top, her throat burned from the cold air and she was so winded she bent over, panting. When she caught her breath, she straightened and looked around for her horse.

And didn't find it.

She was so shocked she simply stood there, staring in disbelief at the broken branch of the bush where she had left him tied. For one hopeful moment she thought maybe it was the wrong bush, but the churned-up snow at its base told her otherwise.

Her heart almost stopped in her chest. She searched frantically, then saw his hoof prints heading back the way they had come, and knew she was truly abandoned.

You fool! Now what are you going to do?

Forcing herself to breathe calmly and evenly, she tried to assess the situation.

How far was she from the ranch house? Six miles? Eight? If she covered two miles in an hour, it would take her almost five hours to get back. Glancing at the sky, she saw that the sun was already poised on the peaks of the mountains. In an hour it would be dark. She didn't remember if there was a full moon or if there would be enough starlight to see where she was stepping. What if it started snowing again?

She could fall into a gully.

Or lose her bearings and walk in circles.

Or freeze to death.

Unless the scavengers found her first.

If her teeth hadn't been chattering so hard, she would have shrieked in frustration. She wanted to weep. And curse. And scream at the injustice of it—at Hennessey for forcing her out here—at herself for not tying her horse more securely—at Hank for leaving her behind—at God for allowing this to happen.

Damn—damn—damn! Realizing she was

edging toward hysteria, she struggled to bring her shattered emotions in check. Closing her eyes, she breathed deep and slow while she silently chanted the phrase that had sustained her countless times in the surgery room.

I can do this. I can do this. I can do this.

Her heartbeat evened out, her mind cleared. Reason returned.

"I can do this," she said aloud, and almost believed it.

After securing the hood more tightly around her face and neck, she checked her pocket for the pistol then started walking east, away from the lowering sun.

Hopefully, by now they would be looking for her. If she followed her runaway horse's tracks, they should lead her back to the ranch, or the searchers would follow the tracks back to her. Unless her stupid horse had as poor a sense of direction as she did, and led her away from her rescuers rather than toward them.

At least it had stopped snowing. Maybe the sky would clear. Which meant moonlight or starlight. But it also meant a deadly drop in temperature.

Fighting panic and the urge to run, she forced herself to keep a steady, manageable pace, comforting herself with the knowledge that the scavengers would be busy with the horse for a while. Then Hennessey.

And then, well, she still had the pistol and five rounds.

AT FIRST, HANK THOUGHT IT WAS A COW THAT had wandered from the herd during the snowstorm, but as he drew closer, he saw it was a horse. A riderless horse with an empty saddle and dragging reins.

Teeth clenched in frustration, he pulled up and waited for the animal to approach, afraid if he charged toward it like he wanted to, it would spook and run off. As it neared, he recognized it as the sorrel gelding Molly had ridden to Redemption and the one the Garcia boy said she'd taken today.

With a feeling of dread, he scanned the saddle for blood. He saw none, but what he did notice was the broken sage branch tied at the end of the dangling reins. He took some comfort in knowing she hadn't fallen or been thrown. But he felt like putting a bullet in the horse's head for running off and leaving her. Then he wanted to kiss his hairy lips in gratitude because he realized that, in running off, the horse had left a trail that would lead straight back to Molly.

Grabbing the sorrel's loose reins, he kicked his bay into a gallop.

He was close now. He could feel it. Feel her. That connection he always sensed whenever she was near was almost humming now.

He wanted to shake her. Hug her. Yell at her until he rid himself of this helpless terror.

He'd find her, and then . . . bigod . . .

MOLLY SAW HIM COMING AND ALMOST FELL TO her knees in relief. She knew it was Hank. Who else would ride so furiously to her rescue? Who else had always come to her whenever she needed him?

Her Hank. Her beautiful dark knight.

Pressing both hands to her face, she wept into her gloves, then laughed, then wept some more. By the time he pulled the horse into a snow-churning slide in front of her, she had regained control of her tears, even though the shaking continued.

He loomed over her, his face livid, his mouth set in a tight, grim line.

Blinking up at him through the steamy breath from his winded horse, she tried to smile. "What took you so long?"

"Goddamnit, Molly!" He yanked the pistol from the holster at his hip, pointed it into the air, and fired off two rounds.

Both she and the horse flinched. Ears ringing, the smell of spent gunpowder sharp in her nose, she watched him reholster the pistol, realizing he'd been signaling other searchers.

"Are you all right?" he demanded, still glaring down at her.

She nodded.

"Do you know how many people are out looking for you? How worried we all were? Christ, Molly, what were you thinking?"

She would have been offended if she hadn't seen the tremor in his hands and the worry and exhaustion in his face. She had seen this kind of frantic reaction to fear before, and knew not to be hurt by it. He had come for her. Others searched for her. She shouldn't have been surprised by that, but she'd been alone for so much of her life she was both shocked and humbled that so many people cared enough to put themselves at risk on her behalf.

Not that she regretted what she had done, despite the worry she might have caused. She was the only one who could have stopped Hennessey. And she had.

She had.

She didn't know whether to laugh in triumph or weep in despair. "I'm sorry, Hank, I—I—"

Then suddenly he was on the ground beside her, wrapping her in his arms, his grip so tight she could scarcely draw in a breath. The muffled thundering of his heart against her cheek was the most welcome sound she had ever heard.

"Don't you ever do that to me again," he said in a ragged voice against her hood. "I thought he had you."

Pressing her face against his jacket, she drew in her husband's clean masculine scent and tried to rid herself of the stench of Hennessey.

He drew back and studied her face. She could see the confusion in his eyes. And doubt. "What happened, Molly? Why did you get off your horse? Why didn't you come back when it started snowing? What's going on?"

She began shivering so hard her teeth chattered. "H-Hank, I—"

Immediately his confusion gave way to worry. "Christ, you're freezing." He rubbed his gloved hands up and down her arms. "Can you ride?"

When she nodded, he swept her up into his arms. "Then let's go home."

"WHY AREN'T YOU UPSTAIRS WITH YOUR WIFE?"

Turning from his perusal of the moonlit stretches beyond his office window, Hank saw his brother leaning against the door-frame, a pair of cut-glass tumblers in one hand, a crystal decanter in the other. "Why aren't you with yours?" he countered.

"Consuelo's tending her." Crossing to Hank's desk, Brady used the bottle to clear a spot amid the parts strewn across the top, then set down the glasses. "Women things," he added, pouring an inch of Scotch whiskey into each glass. "Things I'd just as soon not know about." He held out a glass to Hank. "What's your excuse?"

Hank didn't answer. What could he say?

That his wife was keeping secrets from him again and he didn't know why, and he was afraid to bring it up for fear of damaging the trust they'd worked so hard to rebuild between them?

"She's talking to the children," he said instead. "I told her about Fletcher, and she wanted to make sure Charlie was all right."

Brady dropped into one of the chairs by the desk. "She tell you why she ran off?"

Hank looked at him over the rim of his glass.

"That'd be a 'no,' I'm guessing." Brady took a swallow then sucked air against his teeth. "Give it time. Silence and time are intolerable to women. She'll come around."

Hank settled in his chair behind the desk. He considered Brady's words, then discounted them. Molly wasn't like other women. Bold one minute, blushing the next. Eyes crackling fire, then dancing with laughter. She was smarter, more headstrong, more complicated than any other woman he knew. And far too self-reliant.

He blamed her father for that. In forcing her to be so independent, he'd taught her not to ask for help. And in keeping her so isolated by her work—his work, really—he'd taught her that her wants and worries weren't as important as those of the people she served. She didn't seem to understand that she was part of something bigger than herself now—a family—and her actions impacted them all.

So how was he to counter that? How was he to convince her that he was there to support her and that she was no longer alone? Didn't she realize that keeping secrets from him and the rest of the family was just a subtle way of saying she still didn't trust them to take care of her? That she didn't really need them? Or need him?

Hank sighed and studied the pistol and medicine vial sitting in the center of his desk. He could guess what she'd done. He even had an idea why she'd done it. Probably thought in going after Hennessey she was protecting her family, not realizing that by putting herself in harm's way rather than turning to them for help, she'd insulted them—insulted him. It was an insane, courageous, foolish thing she'd done, and the thought of her facing Hennessey alone was so terrifying to Hank it made his head pound and his hands shake.

He didn't like what she'd done. But he understood why she'd done it.

What he didn't understand was why she hadn't turned to him for help. He needed her to explain that to him, to look him in the eye and tell him why, at the most frightening and dangerous moment of her life, she hadn't wanted or felt she'd needed him by her side. Hard words for her to say, harder for him to hear.

Which was his excuse for why he wasn't upstairs with his wife, instead of sitting here drinking with his brother.

"Where'd you get that?' Brady asked, nodding toward the pistol on the desk. "That's not one of yours, is it?"

Hank shook his head. "Hennessey's, I think."

"Hennessey's? How'd you get it?"

"Molly had it. Fell out of her coat when I hung it up."

Hank watched that sink in, wondering if his brother's reaction would be similar to his.

"She went out there to meet him?"

"I think so."

"On her own?"

Hank nodded.

"Why didn't she tell me?"

Confusion to shock to outrage. A predictable sequence of emotions. Hank wasn't surprised, although he was a little disturbed, that he and his brother thought so much alike.

"Hell, Hank. She could have gotten herself killed."

"I know."

"You better talk to her."

"I intend to."

Outside, the coyotes started up again, heading west by the sound of it.

"Let's see if I have this right," Brady said after a while. "She rides out all by herself, into unfamiliar country, during a snowstorm, armed with what?—a bottle of medicine?—to confront a murderous sonofabitch."

Put that way, it did sound pretty unbelievable. And stupid.

"At which time she takes his gun," his brother went on, "presumably kills him, loses her horse, then comes strolling home like a virgin after a church social."

Hank looked down at his glass, surprised to see it was empty. "She wasn't exactly strolling." In fact, she'd been in near hysteria when he'd found her. "And she's damn sure not a virgin. And it was definitely not a church social. But otherwise, yeah, that's what she did. I think."

"Damn."

"I know." Despite his irritation with his wife right then, Hank couldn't help feeling proud. Who would have guessed that beneath his sweet Molly's round, bouncy bosom beat a warrior's heart. He reminded himself to remember to watch himself. This was not a woman to cross.

"She should have come to me," Brady said.

Or me, Hank thought. *She should have trusted me to take care of her.*

"Jessica did the same thing, you know, when she went after Sancho."

"She didn't go after Sancho," Hank reminded him. "He dragged her off."

"There I go," Brady expounded as if Hank hadn't spoken, "riding to the rescue only to find the deed was already done. After twenty years of fighting the bastard, she ups and does him in with a damn kerosene lamp. Kind of makes a man feel . . ."

"Superfluous?"

"Yeah. Useless. Makes a man feel damned useless."

Hank liked superfluous better. Useless was so . . . deflating.

"You have to talk to her. Explain to her that women don't go around doing things like that." Brady grinned. "And hope she doesn't come after you with a roll of gauze or maybe one of those tongue sticks."

"Depressors."

"Yeah, it is. Damned depressing."

Hank never knew if his brother was really as stupid as he sometimes pretended to be. Probably not. It was a ploy both his brothers used from time to time, although with Jack it had risen to the level of art. And for some unfathomable reason, women seemed to eat it up. Molly wouldn't, of course. Molly was too smart to fall for Jack's foolishness . . . if Jack ever got himself home. At least he hoped she was.

Knowing he had put it off as long as he could, Hank gathered up the pistol and medicine bottle, and rose.

"You tell her I'm disappointed she didn't come to me first," Brady said.

"I'm sure she'll be upset to hear it."

Brady laughed. "Better hope that gun's

not loaded," he warned as Hank stepped into the hall.

"It isn't."

MOLLY WAS STANDING AT THE OPEN DOOR ONTO the balcony when he came into the bedroom. Even though she wore one of his spare jackets over her robe and a fire was roaring in the hearth, he could see she was shivering.

"What are you doing?" he asked from the doorway.

She whirled, fear showing on her face. When she saw him, she gave a shaky smile, which quickly faded when she saw the pistol and medicine bottle in his hands. "Where did you get those?"

"Fell out of your coat when I hung it up." He didn't want her to think he'd been going through her things. Although what would it matter if she had nothing to hide? "Were you ever going to tell me what happened?" he asked, moving toward the bureau. "Or were you going to let me worry that he was still out there?"

"I—I was going to tell you."

He set the bottle and pistol on the bureau, then turned to face her. "When?"

Her face reddened. She gripped the collar of his jacket tight at her throat.

Shielding herself. Shutting him out.

"When I felt strong enough to think about it," she said. "To talk about it."

He waited.

"It's so ugly, Hank. I—"

She flinched as a coyote yodeled somewhere on the hill behind the house. From the west came an answering bark, then a chorus. He could see it worried her that they were so close.

"They're just coyotes. They won't bother you." Crossing past her to pull the French door closed, he added, "If it'll make you feel better, I'll go out tomorrow and see what they've been up to."

"No! No, it's all right." She gripped the coat tighter—a gesture that spoke of turmoil within.

"We don't like them bothering the stock," he said, watching her.

She opened her mouth, closed it, then shook her head. "Oh, Hank." She seemed to shrink into herself. Sinking into one of the chairs before the fire, she dropped her head into her hands. "It's not the stock they're after."

Hank blinked at her, the words slow to make sense. When they finally did, he couldn't hide his shock. "Hennessey?"

Palms still pressed at her temples, she nodded.

"He's still alive?"

"I don't know."

He stared at her bent head in mingled horror and disbelief. She'd left a wounded man to scavengers?

People thought the West was a lawless, violent place. In many ways it was. But there were still codes that men lived by. You don't take a man's horse or his food. If you come across a deserted cabin, use what you need, leave behind what you don't, and replace what you can. Share your campfire or your roof with any pilgrim who comes by, unless he gives you reason not to. And never leave an injured man with no way to defend himself against predators or hostiles, or a way to end his life, if that's his choice.

"Molly, what did you do?"

"What I had to. What you told me to do."

He frowned in confusion. "I don't understand."

Dropping her hands, she sat back. He

could see tear tracks on her cheeks. Wearily, she motioned to the chair across from hers. "Come sit down and I'll try to explain."

Once he'd settled into the other chair, she said, "Remember the day the children and I first came to RosaRoja? We were in the coach, riding out of Redemption. The children were asleep, and you were telling me about Sancho Ramirez and your brother, Sam, and Jessica."

"I remember."

Leaning forward again, she rested her elbows on her thighs and clasped her hands tightly at her knees. "You said Jessica was prepared. She was willing to do what she had to do, and that's why she survived. Harsh times call for hard choices. That's what you said."

The room was so still he could hear the soft scrape of her palms brushing against each other as she clasped and unclasped her hands. "So that's what I did." She lifted her head. In her eyes he saw both defiance and a haunting sadness. "I made a terrible, awful choice. Because that's what I had to do to protect myself, and the children, and you, and—" Her voice cracked.

She swallowed hard. "And I don't regret any of it."

In the fireplace, a log collapsed, sending up a burst of sparks like startled fireflies. In the flare of light, Hank saw the glitter of tears and the beginnings of a bruise under her eye. "What happened, Molly?"

She sank back in the chair as if she no longer had the strength to sit upright. "I didn't go there to kill him. I hoped once he knew Fletcher had been arrested, he would let it go. But he wouldn't."

In a halting voice she told him how she threw the caustic solution in the medicine bottle into his face, and how his horse reared and fell backward, killing itself and breaking Hennessey's back.

"He wasn't in pain, but he couldn't move. And he was fully conscious. I knew the predators would come for him. I thought what a perfect punishment for the butcher to be awake for his own butchering."

Hank was repelled by the images her words evoked. To be eaten alive—without pain, but with the full awareness of it happening. But as horrible as it was, there was an element of poetic justice to it. "You had his gun. Why didn't you shoot him?"

"I should have, I guess. But after my father . . . well, I couldn't. I just couldn't. Besides, I took an oath. *Do no harm*." She gave a bitter laugh. "But there's the dilemma, you see. Which was the greater 'harm'? Killing him by my own hand, or walking away and leaving him to God and the coyotes?"

Hank had no answers, and the idea of his gentle wife being forced to make such a choice sickened him. Why hadn't she gone to Brady? Or waited for him? Why did she think she always had to face everything all on her own?

Because that was what her father had taught her. That was what he'd expected of her.

Desperate to relieve the tension building inside him, Hank rose and stirred the coals with the poker, then tossed more wood onto the fire. Standing with one hand braced on the mantle, he stared into the flames. "So you left him?"

"I wanted to. Lord, how I wanted to. I wanted him to be aware when the coyotes and other predators came to do what I couldn't. I wanted him to suffer for all the suffering he had caused."

He turned his head and looked at her.

"But I couldn't." She seemed upset by that.

Hank was relieved. "So what did you do?"

"I gave him a syringe full of laudanum and stayed with him until the drug took effect. After he lost consciousness, I left. I don't know if it killed him or not."

Hank thought about all that she'd told him. He understood why she did what she did. But there was still one question he needed answered. "Why didn't you tell Brady? Or wait for me?"

Instead of answering, she rose and went to the table by the bed. Retrieving a piece of paper from the drawer, she came back and handed it to him. "I found that on the bureau this morning," she said, sinking into the chair again as if she feared her legs wouldn't support her.

Hank read the note. Then read it again, not wanting to believe what his eyes were seeing. "He was in the house? In our room?"

"And in Penny's. He cut off the hands of her new doll and brought them here for me to find. A reminder, I think, of what he would do if I didn't bring what he wanted."

"He was in the goddamn house?" That same choking rage that had gripped him when he was in the shed with Fletcher burned through Hank's chest. His hand shook as he thrust the note toward her. "Did you show this to Brady?"

"Why? So he would ride out and get himself killed? Hennessey was obviously watching the house. He would have seen him or anyone else coming and would have disappeared or even doubled back to harm the children. The only one who could get close enough to stop him was me."

Hank stared down at her, seeing the logic in her assessment, but wanting to believe there was a better way. "Brady isn't stupid. He would have thought of something."

"He would have tried. But I couldn't risk his being killed. I brought this upon all of you, and I—"

"All of *you*? Have you forgotten you're a part of this family too? And it wasn't your risk to take. It was Brady's. Or mine. That's our job—to look out for the people in our care—to protect you from butchers like Hennessey." Hank was so furious he could hardly get the words out. When would she understand that, as part of the family now, a threat to her was a threat to all of them? "Don't do to me what your father did to you, Molly. Don't take away my choices and try to run my life by your design. I get enough of that from Brady. I won't tolerate it from you."

"B-But I wouldn't—"

"You already have! From the very beginning. The marriage. Covering it up. Not telling me about Hennessey. Now this. I'm not an idiot!"

He could see his words had hurt her, but they needed to be said. He just hoped she understood what he was trying to say. He loved this woman. He needed her. But he didn't know if he would ever understand her.

He could almost see his words circling in her head and knew the instant they all fell into place. "Oh my God. You're right." She looked up with brimming eyes. "How could I have not seen that? From the moment I found you in Murray's infirmary, I've run roughshod over you, taken all of your choices away. How could I have done that to you?" She laughed, a broken, bitter sound of disgust. "All these years I've worked so hard to fix everybody else, I never realized I was the one broken."

"Not broken," Hank said, his own anger fading. "Confused. I blame your father for that. He might have taught you how to save a life, but he damn sure never showed you how to live one."

"I was just trying to protect you."

"And who protects you, Molly?"

She was crying in earnest now, hands pressed to her face. "I was so afraid. If I lost you, I don't think I could go on."

Hunkering beside her chair, he pulled her hands from her face. "And you don't think I feel the same way? That it wouldn't hurt me just as bad if I lost you?"

She looked at him, eyes swimming. "I'm sorry, I'm sorry . . ." Then suddenly she threw herself against him, her arms wrapping around his neck so tightly he almost choked. "Don't send me away. I'll do better. I promise I will."

Send her away? Pulling her arms loose, he trapped her head so he could look into her face. "Why would I send you away?"

She cried harder, her body shaking with tremors.

And suddenly he understood. "Look at me," he said, giving her a gentle shake. When she did, he lowered his head until their faces were inches apart. He looked hard into her eyes. "You have nothing to prove to me, Molly. I'm not your father. I'll never send you away."

Her breath came in tiny little gasps. Her tears burned hot against his hands.

But he saw the wobbly beginnings of a smile. "You won't?"

"I love you, Molly. I'd never send you away. I need you too much."

"You need me. You." She made a pitiful attempt at a laugh, as if the notion was too ridiculous to be believed.

"Like I need the next breath." He set her back into the chair then leaned over her, his hands braced on the armrests so she couldn't escape. Tilting his head, he kissed her bruised cheek. "Like the moon needs the stars." He kissed her other cheek. "And the oceans need sand." He pressed his lips to hers then drew back to see how he was doing.

Her eyes glittered wetly. Her lips trembled.

Entranced already, and he was just getting started. Pushing his jacket off her shoulder, he slipped a hand inside her robe. "I need you like the desert needs sun," he said as he stroked her breast. "And birds need sky."

"And horses need oats?" she asked in a tremulous voice.

He stopped stroking.

"And toads need stagnant ponds and flies?"

Not entranced. Laughing. He drew back to scowl at her. "You're mocking me." He tried to sound severe, but it was difficult with her hands busily unbuckling his belt and her round, bouncy bosom nestled in his palm.

"Oh, Hank. I love you, too, and I'm sorry I treated you so badly." Reaching up, she looped an arm around his neck and pulled his head down to sweep his face with feathery kisses. After a moment, she released him and began loosening the buttons down the front of his trousers. "Did you make up all those lovely thoughts yourself?" When he didn't answer, she looked up with a grin. "Or did you read them somewhere?"

"I read some," he admitted, trying to stay focused.

Laughter danced in her eyes. "Some?"

"Most. All." Realizing he'd lost ground, he redoubled his efforts on her breast, hoping to encourage her to hurry up with his trousers. "I thought that was what women wanted to hear."

"Some women perhaps."

"But not you."

She smiled.

"Stand up," he said.

When she did, he shoved his jacket the rest of the way off her shoulders, then tried to push the robe aside, too, but it was tied. *Christ.* "Then what would you like to hear, sweet Molly?" he murmured against her neck as he worked at the knot. "What do you want me to say?"

"That you love me—"

"I just did." *Goddamn knot.*

"And that you want to marry me."

He lifted his head and grinned down at her, thinking she was joking.

Her expression said she wasn't.

"But we're already married," he reminded her, fumbling with the knot again. He hated knots.

"*I* am. But you're not." At his look of confusion, she gently stroked his cheek. "I married *you*, but you never got a chance to marry me. I took that choice away from you."

"And now you're giving it back?"

"And now I'm giving it back."

"Hmmm." He finally got the belt of her robe loose. "When do you need an answer?" he asked, pushing it aside.

Laughing that sexy, throaty laugh that made him forget everything but getting her on her back, she leaned forward and pressed her body against his. "Soon."

Enough talk. "Okay. I want to marry you. Now strip."

"Truly? You'll marry me?"

"Sure. Here, let me help you get that robe off."

A smile of delight split her face. "When?"

"Tomorrow. Whenever." Tossing the robe aside, he started on the ribbon tabs of her gown.

"Oh, Hank." She laughed and clapped her hands like a child.

Which interfered with his removal of her gown, but he managed. He paused to admire her fine body, then started tugging loose the buttons on his shirt.

"We'll have a real wedding this time," she expounded as he quickly divested himself of his garments, then swept her up and carried her to the bed.

"With bunches and bunches of flowers." She wiggled down under the covers. "And everybody will be there, and Penny bombarding us with flower petals, and Charlie the proud ring bearer. Oh, I know! We'll invite Reverend and Effie Beckworth . . . let him do the ceremony. Legally, this time. What do you think?"

"Fine. Whatever." Sliding in beside her, he set about reacquainting himself with her fine, soft body.

"But if we're going to have flowers, we'll have to wait until spring."

"Spring's nice," he said, slipping his head beneath the covers.

"If we do wait until spring, we could have it outside and . . ." She lifted the quilt. "What are you doing under there?"

"Practicing."

"For what?"

"Our honeymoon."

"A honeymoon too? Oh, Hank! Where? California. No, New Orleans. I've always wanted to go to—Oh my . . ."

And finally she shut up.

Epilogue

ANGUS FOLEY, EX-DEPUTY UNITED STATES marshal and now interim sheriff of Val Rosa since Sheriff Rikker died in his sleep two months ago, watched a group of buzzards dipping and soaring in the crisp April sky. He'd been watching them ever since he'd started down into the RosaRoja Valley and was pondering what might have brought in so many.

Maybe a cow or an elk. Even a griz. Something big. He reined his horse over to find out.

Knowing he was on Wilkins land and wanting to maintain some level of friendly concourse with the most powerful and influential family in the area—despite their hardheaded, high-handed ways—he figured reporting the carcass to the landowners would be the neighborly thing to do.

Besides, he was already headed out to the house.

He hadn't been to the ranch since that meeting after Christmas, almost four months ago. And he hadn't come face-to-face with either brother since the day he found Hank Wilkins standing over Daniel Fletcher's crumpled body with his stepson in his arms. The older brother was a hard, ruthless sonofabitch. But Hank was downright frightening. Definitely not a man to cross.

Angus drew close enough to smell whatever the buzzards were after. It was pretty rank. Probably something in the gully he'd been following. It had been a slow melt this year, and there hadn't been the normal rush of water coming down out of the canyons to wash these dry creeks clean. Might even be something that had lain frozen all winter and was just now thawing out.

As he neared, buzzards burst out of the ravine like black feathers thrown into the wind, making his horse sidestep and snort. Once he had calmed him, Angus reined him over to the rim of the gully and looked down.

A man, by damn. And a horse wearing a saddle with a rifle still in the scabbard. From this distance, Angus couldn't tell what had killed the rider, but it was apparent the horse had a broken neck. Probably fell. As far as he could see, no obvious bullet wounds on either. Odd.

After securing his horse's reins to a sturdy sapling, Angus tied his kerchief over his mouth and nose against the stench, then worked his way down into the gully.

The buzzards had been busy, as had various other scavengers. Most of the damage was recent, and from the look of it, the man had died some time ago before being covered over with snow until spring. Probably that three-day blizzard that had come through a day or so after Fletcher was killed. But there was enough of his scarred face left to give Angus an idea of the man's identity.

Gordon Hennessey.

Other than a twisted leg, he had no noticeable wounds except for the damage done by predators after his death. Angus found several gold pieces in his pocket, so if Hennessey had died by foul means, it hadn't been motivated by robbery. Then what?

Sitting back on his heels, Angus scanned the area, trying to piece together what had happened. At first glance, it looked as if both Hennessey and his horse had died when they'd fallen down into the gully. But two things struck Angus as odd.

There was no gun in Hennessey's holster, or anywhere around his body.

And there was a glass medical syringe by his neck.

He knew of only two people in the area who would have medical paraphernalia—Doc O'Grady, who, along with him and Mr. Jones, had been stranded in Val Rosa during the same storm that had probably covered over Hennessey's carcass—and Molly Wilkins, the woman Hennessey had been tracking.

Why had she been out here with Hennessey? And if she had killed him in self-defense—although the syringe hinted at a planned attack, rather than a defensive move—why hadn't Wilkins reported it?

And finally, what was Angus going to do about it?

He thought for a while, trying to satisfy both his sense of duty and his need for justice. In the end, he decided to do the only thing he could do.

Wait and see.

After detaching the needle, he slipped it point first into the empty syringe, wrapped the syringe in his kerchief, and slipped it into his pocket. For now he wouldn't do anything. Maybe he never would. But the syringe would be there, just in case.

The sun was starting its downward slide as he climbed out of the gully and mounted his horse. Realizing he'd dallied long enough, he kicked his gelding into a mile-eating lope, leaving the buzzards to do what they do.

He had a wedding to attend, and a letter to deliver from a long-lost brother. No need ruining a pretty day with ugly news.